BLOODLINE

GERRY BOYLE

BERKLEY PRIME CRIME, NEW YORK

"Anthem for Doomed Youth" by Wilfred Owen, from *The Collected Poems of Wilfred Owen*. Copyright 1963 Chatto and Windus, Ltd. Reprinted by permission of New Directions Publishing Corp.

BLOODLINE

A Berkley Prime Crime Book / published by arrangement with the author

PRINTING HISTORY
G. P. Putnam's Sons edition / April 1995
Berkley Prime Crime edition / March 1996

The Putnam Berkley World Wide Web site address is
http://www.berkley.com

ISBN: 0-425-15182-4

Berkley Prime Crime Books are published
by The Berkley Publishing Group,
200 Madison Avenue, New York, NY 10016.
The name BERKLEY PRIME CRIME and the BERKLEY PRIME CRIME
design are trademarks belonging to Berkley Publishing Corporation.

PRINTED IN THE UNITED STATES OF AMERICA

10 9 8 7 6 5 4 3 2 1

For Emily, Carolyn, and Charlie

BLOODLINE

One

The bats had kept me up all night, swooping around the bed, making that tissue-paper flutter in the dark just inches from my face. I'd tried to sleep but even when I'd been able to drift off, the bats had moved in and out of my dreams like little furry spirits. Finally, when it was morning and the sun had lit the room like a shopping mall parking lot, I'd dreamed that the loft was full of flying bugs, so many bugs that the bats were outnumbered and overwhelmed. I woke up with a start, exhausted and mildly hung over and generally ornery.

When the phone rang . . .

"Jack," a man's voice said, cheery and energetic and soothing as a chainsaw. "You old dog, you. You are one tough hombre to track down."

Not tough enough, I thought.

"Who's this?" I asked.

"Jack, it's Dave. Dave Slocum."

Slocum. From the *Times*. Wore expensive suspenders

and chased the summer interns. Went to Harvard. All talk. Well, maybe eighty percent.

"What, did I get you up, fella? Hey, I thought you Mainers were up at the crack of dawn. Out splitting wood or cleaning the outhouse or whatever it is you can find to do at that ungodly hour. Am I right? Jack, are you there? Come in, Jack."

I took a deep breath.

"No, Dave, been up for hours," I said. "Just got done milking the chickens. Where are you?"

"Beautiful downtown Amherst, Mass. The heart of the Berkshires. *New England Look* magazine."

Amherst, Massachusetts, I thought. That's far away. I felt better.

"You left the *Times*?"

"By mutual agreement," Slocum said. "We both needed to grow, you know? And they got this idea that the magazine could run without me. Poor deluded bastards."

"I saw it last week," I said. "A shell of its former self."

"You noticed, too, huh? Yeah, it lacks that certain style and grace and insight that is the hallmark of a magazine at the top of its game."

"I don't know about that. I just look at the ads for the fancy houses."

"Hey, that's all right," Slocum said. "Fantasy's okay. I'll give you the number of my therapist."

"Don't tell me. It begins 1–900 . . ."

"Hell, yes. Ask for Brandy. She does the groups. You do have phones up there, don't you?"

"There's one at the general store. I'm sitting on a cracker barrel."

"Well, say hi to Jethro for me, Jack. Your former drinking buddies on Seventh Avenue will be glad to hear you've found your niche."

"Fits like a glove."

"I'm glad for you. I'll come up sometime and chew tobacco with you and your friends."

"After that, we'll go out to the dump and shoot rats," I said.

"Ha, ha. The same old Jack McMorrow. I gotta tell you, buddy. When you left the *Times* it created a terrible void."

"A vacuum, you mean."

"Right. A black hole right over the metro desk. They still talk about you. Leaving for a weekly in some hick town in Maine? I mean, that was like going from the Yankees to Little League. I mean, Babe Ruth going to play Babe Ruth."

I felt myself bristle.

"It wasn't that much different," I said. "Just smaller."

"But now you're free-lancing, right? I saw your story on the flowers in *Downeast*. Zen and the art of the bearded Siberian whoseywhatsis."

"Irises," I said.

"Yeah. But I didn't know they were like dog owners. You know, after a while they look like their dogs. The guys with the beards looked like their flowers. What a riot."

"They were nice people."

"I'm sure," Slocum said. "Which brings me to my reason for calling. What do you know about birthin' babies?"

"Not much."

"Then you're our man. This is the story. Kids having kids in the boonies. You know. Six generations in a trailer and all that. The antithesis of the first-baby-at-forty syndrome that is so rife among urban professionals. What's it like to be a grandmother at thirty? What's it like to be stuck out in the woods with some screaming brat and some guy who spends all his time under his pickup truck. You know, the rural hopelessness thing."

"I take it this wasn't your idea."

"Not exactly," Slocum said. "It's Maddy's. She's the editor. One of those sensitive liberal types."

"She must hate your guts."

"Give her time. Right now she likes me because I told

her I knew a first-class writer who would be perfect for this piece."

"How much?"

"Three thousand plus expenses. Seventy-five hundred words. We hire the photographer."

"When?"

"Sixty days. Let's say December 1."

"Payment on acceptance?"

"Oh, yeah. Hey, Jack. This is a class operation."

"Then how'd you get in?"

"Slipped in the back door," Slocum said.

"Okay."

"Okay what?"

"Okay, I'll do it," I said.

"Jack, my man. Going to be fun working with you again. Now tell me. What's this I heard about people getting killed at this little paper you were with?"

"It's a long story."

"I've got time," Slocum said. "I'm working for a magazine now. I mean, in this place, their idea of deadline pressure is taking an hour for espresso instead of two."

"It's a longer story than that," I said.

TWO ▮

I sat at the big oak table and had tea and toast. Outside the window, goldfinches were swinging like ornaments on the pods of the milkweed that had grown up among the rubble of timbers and angle-iron and tractor parts. Most were unidentifiable hunks of rust but there were old chrome car bumpers that still glinted from the thick weave of saw grass and burdocks and daisies and asters.

When I'd first moved in, in early spring, I'd had the idea that I would clean up all the junk. The stuff had been gathered by the woman who had built the place and still owned it, but now lived in Santa Fe. Her name was Millie Tint and she was a sculptor and painter who'd come to Prosperity from Brooklyn back in the sixties. We'd connected through a friend in New York but we'd never met. When I'd sent the April rent to her post office box I'd enclosed a note asking if she'd mind if I cleaned up some of the debris out back. Millie sent me a one-word response, written in charcoal pencil on a torn piece of paper: "Why?"

I had the note stuck to the wall by the stove. Over the summer, it had become my credo.

Why clean up the junk that had been out back for twenty years? Why pore through *Editor & Publisher* to find another newspaper job? Why worry about my career when there was beer in the refrigerator and, as of this week, $9,308, give or take a couple of hundred, left from my *Times* retirement money? Why worry about the path that had taken me, at the age of thirty-eight, from a job as a reporter at the best newspaper in the country—kiss my ass, *Washington Post*—to a home-built bat-trap of a house on a dirt road in the backwoods of Maine? Why try to plug the cracks in the house when I could pretend I liked having bats swarm around my head all night? Why put pressure on myself when I could sit out back with a six-pack of Bud and look at stars that were so bright that when I'd first come to Maine, it was like a cataract had been scraped from the sky?

And why get involved in a free-lance deal with Dave Slocum?

"Because he called," I said aloud, shrugging to myself. "And three thousand bucks is a lot of beer."

* * *

I made another cup of tea and considered what I'd gotten myself into.

This wasn't going to be like Zen and the art of iris-growing, hanging out in beautiful gardens with people who were like the most gentle of scientists. It wasn't going to be writing about a school board meeting in Androscoggin, knocking out fifteen inches on whether elementary-school kids really need sissy stuff like art and music. Or writing a series about some big paper company throwing its weight around a small town. Or even explaining in print that a member of your own newspaper staff had been murdered.

Like a eulogy, that story had written itself. Shortly after that, I'd packed up and left, not because I'd chickened out but because the owner had decided he'd had enough of me and my "stirring things up," digging into the black pool of muck that was life in that little town. He told me to hit the road and the surface of the black pool congealed behind me, like chocolate pudding. I'd gone into hiding but Slocum had reached out from my old world and found me in my new one.

From the Yankees to Little League to an occasional pickup game. Irises. It was hard to explain.

I hadn't bothered to try with Slocum. He was glib and slick and very big-city, fun in a bar at night but nobody you wanted to see the next morning. He wouldn't understand what I'd accomplished in the last six months, that I'd been accepted by people who didn't tolerate phonies, who didn't know the East Side from the West Side but would have tagged Slocum with a scarlet "P."

But they talked to me, and that was something. Wasn't it?

I sipped the last of my tea, which was now lukewarm. The goldfinches had moved on, bounding across the field in their undulating way like a school of bright yellow porpoises. It was sunny and breezy and the field was full of butterflies, getting in a few last days of flight before September turned cool. Six months since I'd worked. Six months of drinking and reading and walking in the woods. Six months and practically the only people I'd seen were the people on the road. I got up from the table and put the dishes in the sink. Probably, I should have washed them but I decided to go down the road instead. As I walked across the yard to the truck, I felt this funny little tremble of regret, like I was going to say good-bye to somebody, like I was leaving something cherished behind.

Three ∎

"Hey, it's Bones," Claire Varney said, looking up from the bench in his barn. "Jesus, what you doin' up? Ain't dinnertime yet, is it?"

Bones was short for Lazy Bones, which Varney said I was. But lazy was one thing he wasn't. If it was ten o'clock, he'd been up for five or six hours. His two-acre vegetable garden was tilled. The last of the tomatoes and cukes were picked. Mary, his wife, probably had fifty quarts of sauce canned, just that morning. Varney, tanned and fit with silver hair and forearms that still did justice to their Semper Fi tattoos, was scraping at a big chunk of steel that had come off of the top of the motor in his truck.

"Started steamin' like a bastard yesterday," he said, staring down at his work. "I knew she was close but not that close. Goddamn lucky she didn't blow halfway to East Cornpatch. Gasket was junk. Goddamn things they call a gasket today, I wouldn't blow my nose on."

He looked up at me.

"So, Bones. When we goin' huntin', anyway? We got to get you a deer. Nice big eight-point buck."

"I'd have to wrestle it down," I said.

"Well, Jesus man. We'll get you a rifle. Maybe even a bullet or two. You think you'll need more than one?"

"Only if you want me to get your deer, too."

"Oh, listen to him," Varney said, picking up a putty knife and whittling at the motor head on the bench. "Gonna get me my deer, too. Bones, we're gonna make a hunter out of you, yet. Get you one of those guns that the flag pops out of, says bang. The deer'll die laughing."

I grinned and picked up a greasy bolt from the bench and put it down, then looked for something to wipe my fingers on.

"Seen any?" I asked.

"Oh, hell yes," Varney said.

He whittled at pieces of old gasket. Sort of like a sculptor, I thought.

"Me and the old lady went out back to the old orchard last night. Musta been, I don't know, six-thirty. Quarter to seven. I says, 'Just sit there and hush your mouth.' "

"You said that, did you?"

"Well, maybe I did put it a little bit nicer. So we're sitting there on a couple of grease cans. Marmon left 'em up there when he was cutting that oak and beech up on the ridge. Goddamn son of a bitch. Stove the place all to hell and shorted me to boot. But anyway. What goes around come around, right? So we're sitting there and we're real quiet and it ain't five minutes before they come. There were two does, one good-sized one, and then a third one comes out of the woods, sniffing and slow like and, I says to Mary, 'You just wait. These girls are gonna have an old man with 'em.' It's getting a little darker and there he comes, big old boy, eight points, over two hundred pounds and he's out there under those apple trees, eating the drops, tame as a goddamn sheep. From here to that shed. Could've hit any one of them with a rock."

"But they won't be there November first," I said.

"Won't be there. Won't be anywhere where you'll find 'em easy. They'll go back in those cedar swamps way up on, well it used to be part of the old Tracy place. Old man Tracy, he's dead now. What a tight son of a bitch he was. Used to hay with him when I was a kid, me and my brothers. Penny a bale. Had to beg to get that out of him. Old man owned something like six hundred acres. So friggin' crooked, they didn't bury him, they screwed him into the ground."

I smiled. Varney put the putty knife down and dipped his fingers in a can of hand soap. He was meticulous that way. Always clean shaven. Hair short and neat. Tools all lined up like the barn was a BMW garage in Westchester.

What twenty years in the Marines will do for you.

"We gotta get you shootin', Bones," he said, smiling but more with his eyes than his mouth. "'Cause you know what's gonna happen. I could look for that buck for years and not even see a track. You'll walk out there the first morning and he'll tap you on the shoulder."

"He does that, I'm gonna tap him back," I said.

Varney pulled a clump of paper towels from the dispenser above the bench.

"Ain't that the truth," he said. "Hardest thing to shoot is something that's lookin' you right in the eyes."

For a moment, Varney was quiet and you could hear the flies buzzing in the warmth of the windows. He did this every once in a while. He'd go off somewhere else, disappearing into the wells of his eyes. I waited, as I usually did and then he was back, the lines on his temple crinkling as he smiled.

"Come on, Bones. Come on in and have something real to eat, instead of that tuna fish or whatever it is you live on."

Dinner was pot roast, potatoes, carrots and cabbage. Mary Varney piled it on a plate and put it in front of me at the table, then swooped back with another plate that was stacked with warm corn bread. I sat there feeling sheepish, as I always did when she waited on me, and she came back with a tall glass of milk.

Claire Varney had the same.

"He's been eating tuna fish again, mum," he said.

"Jack McMorrow," Mary said. "I've told you. You don't know where that stuff has been."

"Only place to eat out of a can is a foxhole," her husband said, buttering his corn bread. "And then only when you can't find something better."

"I was reading in the paper this morning," Mary said, sitting down across from me to a miniature version of my meal. "The obituaries. Cancer, cancer, cancer, cancer. You know it's got to be because of the air we breathe. The water we drink. The food we eat. Our bodies get filled with chemicals. The other day I was at the checkout at Bud's over in Unity and this man in front of me has all this stuff. Ugh. This blue cereal. Diet soda, which is all chemicals. Artificial this and artificial that. It took everything I had not to say something."

"There's a first," Claire said.

"Oh, hush," she said.

"You're right," I said. "Look at the label on just about anything and it looks like they took all the cans out from under the kitchen sink and just dumped it in."

"And people gobble it all up," Mary said.

"I swear that's what's wrong with this country," Claire said. "Productivity. GNP and all that. Most of the people in this country are working at half energy. Drones, you know?"

Mary Varney ate a couple of bites and went back to the stove, where she was boiling canning jars in a big kettle. She bent over to pull another pan out of the cupboard and her shirt rode up above her jeans, exposing five or six inches of smooth muscular back. For Claire's sake, I tried not to look, but still I could picture her. More of her than her back, I mean.

She was a handsome woman, small and strong with blonde-silver hair pulled straight back, and, I thought, a perfect match for Claire. They could have been in ads for vitamins or self-help books: the good-looking fiftyish couple who give the rest of us hope. Fit. Capable. Productive. Content with their lot in life.

We were an odd threesome.

I'd thought this before and I thought it again as I sat there eating the beef from their steer, the vegetables from their garden. Mary was pulling the jars out of the steaming water with a pair of tongs. Claire got up to put an orange cat out the back door. There was a calendar on the wall to my right, one from the auto parts store in Unity. Somebody had torn off the picture of the girl and Mary had made notes for each day. "Can paste tomatoes" . . . "Henry to vets" . . . "Pick last cukes . . ."

If I had a calendar, and I didn't, it would show the day and the date.

Period.

We were so different and yet they'd befriended me almost from the time I'd moved in, just down the road. It had been February, cold and wet, and I'd been tinkering with my old Volvo, which had conked out at the end of the driveway, when Claire had come by in his majestic red four-wheel-drive Ford pickup. Looking up at him in the driver's seat, I felt my testosterone level plummet.

Claire had asked what the problem was, as if I had a clue. I had told him what I knew, which was that it wouldn't start. He had looked down at me benevolently, then, without another word, had pulled his truck up a few feet and then back to the Volvo. Climbing down from the cab, Varney had pulled a tow chain out from behind the seat, hooked it to the car's front axle. Without saying more than a half-dozen words, he had towed it and me down the road and into his barn.

"You a mechanic?" I remember asking, as I had stood beside the woodstove and watched as Varney had poked at the Volvo's innards.

"Nope," he'd said. "It's your regulator. It's junk. You know you really shouldn't even have this thing on the road."

Varney wasn't a mechanic. He wasn't a woodsman. He wasn't a farmer or a hunter or a retired soldier. He was all of these things and none of them. And whenever you thought you had him pegged, he did something that threw you off again. Like telling you, over a couple of Budweisers, that he really could have stayed in Thailand because the Buddhists were in harmony with their world. Like the American Indians. Or saying, as he worked on his tractor or his truck, that he'd been rereading Thoreau's *The Maine Woods* the night before and decided that he, Varney, had been born a hundred and fifty years too late. Or the time he'd told me, in uncharacteristic seriousness, that I should get married and have children because it was the most joyous thing a man could do on this earth.

"Bones, there's nothing lonelier than a lonely old man," he'd said.

So what did Bones contribute to this relationship? It had taken me a while to figure that out. I was from New York, and other places like it. I was a newsman, which meant I didn't know how to actually do anything. I'd never fired a gun. I'd never been in Vietnam. Until I'd come to Prosperity, I'd never even run a chainsaw. I lived in a run-down house owned by a New York artist.

But I could talk about Thoreau, which Varney couldn't do at the auto parts store. I knew the basics about Buddhism, and even a couple of Buddhists. I was respectful of Mary and asked about their two married daughters, Susan and Jen, who lived in North Carolina and Maryland and were married to an Air Force pilot and a State Department something or other. When the college girls jogged by, I didn't leer at their backsides.

Much.

And I was a good listener. A listener by trade.

So dessert was a small dish of homemade coffee ice cream. As we finished up, Mary Varney said she was going into Unity to get some more jar lids. Claire said he was going to start hauling in some firewood he'd bucked up on the edge of the woods last winter and left to dry. I offered to help and Claire said, no, he was just going to putter around. I said I had work to do too, that I was going to be doing another magazine story.

"More gardening, I hope," Mary said, her back to me as she put the dishes in the dishwasher. "I really enjoyed that one on the irises."

"No. No more gardening. This time it's something I know even less about. Kids."

Claire looked incredulous.

"Yeah. Kids," I said, getting up from the table. "Kids who have kids. Fifteen-year-old mothers. What it's like to be fourteen and have two children."

"Where do you go to do that?" Mary asked.

"It's supposed to be about kids out in the country," I said. I sorted my words carefully so that they wouldn't offend two people who had grown up in the town of Prosperity, and after seeing the world for twenty years, had come right back.

"Kids who live in rural Maine but face a lot of the same problems that poor kids see in the city," I said.

Both Varneys looked skeptical.

"I have to talk to the magazine people again," I said. "I'm still not exactly clear on what they want."

Or whether I still had the nerve.

Because this was going to take some. Getting these kids to talk to me. Their mothers. Their fathers. Their boyfriends. Sitting in their trailers, drinking black coffee and breathing cigarette smoke. People rattling through the door and looking at you like you'd just landed from another planet and they'd be glad to get you back on the ship and headed home.

Which after coffee, is exactly what I did.

As I rattled back down the dirt road, maneuvering the old rust-bucket Chevy around the worst of the ruts, I could feel the doubts seeping in. I could call Slocum and tell him I didn't want to take the story, after all. I could tell him I had too many other things going. He wouldn't know that the only thing I had going was on the shelf in the fridge and came in sets of six. He wouldn't know that I had an urge to have one right now, at twelve-thirty on a sunny early-September day. That I was deathly afraid that I'd lost my nerve for stories like the one he was talking about. That it had taken everything I'd had in me just to put the iris piece together. And the day after it had been done, express-mailed from the Prosperity Post Office, I'd sat out in back of the house listening to the birds, feeling the sun on my face and watching the pile of empty beer cans grow at my feet.

All day and well into the night. Numb with nature. No different from the roughneck guys who got arrested for drunk driving and got their names in the Belfast paper. I bought the paper, the *Waldo Independent*, at the store in Knox every week and I'd found myself turning to the police blotter to see the ages of the drunks. Thirteen. Twenty-six. Thirty-eight. I'd read that one again, inserting my name instead: Jack McMorrow, thirty-eight, Prosperity. Charged with operating under the influence.

I physically shook the thought from my mind as I pulled in the driveway. Three grand, I thought. A byline in *New England Look*. A magazine that had big circulation in New York, too. All those people who had country houses in Vermont and Connecticut read it. Rhode Island, too, and all my old buddies from the *Providence Journal*. God, I'd been around.

Up the ladder, story by story, rung by rung. Hartford.

Providence. New York. Then the little milltown in Maine, where the slide had begun. I wasn't sure it had ended.

Four

Waldo Regional High School was a low, sprawling brick complex that filled most of what had at one time been somebody's cow pasture, off Route 137 on the western outskirts of Belfast. Like most of the county, the former cow pasture was close by rolling dark hills, the quiet beauty of which had only lately begun to appeal to moneyed tourists from the south. For nearly a century and a half, those hills had been a beautiful but unrelenting enemy to anyone who tried to farm or log the steep terrain. While a few merchants and lumber barons made the fortunes that threw up the stately mansions in the towns by the sea, most people gouged a hard living out of woods and pastures and gardens. Instead of mansions, their legacy was tiny back-road cemeteries where many of the graves belonged to children.

The place hadn't changed much.

I turned at the school driveway, which was long and black against the still-green grass, and lined with some strange skinny trees that, in a state filled with pine and spruce and maple and oak, looked distinctly foreign. I drove between the trees and passed what must have been the teachers' parking lot. It was filled with mostly nice cars. Most of the nice cars had bumper stickers that said something complimentary about education. I continued on, past the big gym building and parked in a lot filled with pickup trucks, most of which were old and beat-up but none as old and beat-up as mine.

So much for upward mobility.

I walked back toward the front of the school where, presumably, I would find the main entrance. I passed a kid with a cigarette who gave me a slow assessing nod from under a baseball cap that had the name of an auto parts store written on the front. The kid was small and thin and had what in a few years would be a mustache. His construction boots were untied and looked too big for the rest of his body. On the back of the hand that held the cigarette to his mouth was a homemade tattoo that said "Dave" and "Raise Hell!" in crude block letters. I thought of asking him how Latin was going but I held my tongue.

It turned out that the main entrance was halfway around the complex, toward the front. I figured there probably was a shuttle bus from the student parking lot to the door but I didn't see one. I walked until I came to the biggest set of glass-and-metal double doors, heaved one open and stepped into Penn Station. North.

The doors opened into a lobby that was filled with kids, all of whom seemed to be shouting something to someone. At first, nothing from the din was intelligible, as if they were all speaking some unrecognizable language. I felt like a foreigner seeing the Port Authority bus terminal for the first time.

Alone.

And these kids even had luggage: backpacks slung over their shoulders so that everybody walked slumped to one side. Maybe they all were enrolled in a masonry course and the packs were filled with their homework: bricks.

Which could have been true, for all I knew. Standing there in the lobby, with the kids bumping past me, I felt like I hadn't been in a high school since, well, high school. I stood and watched for a minute, like Scrooge brought back to his childhood by the Ghost of Christmas Past, then stepped into the maelstrom.

The tide seemed to be running to the left so I went with it, shuffling along with our nation's future. There were guys wearing bandannas and long dangling earrings. Bigger guys wearing sweatshirts that said "Waldo Football" and had numbers and names on the back, like game uniforms. Most of the football guys were accompanied by at least one attractive girl, sometimes two or three. The girls wore lots of black eye makeup and had masses of wild wavy unkempt hair. They probably got up at 4 A.M. to make it look like they'd just rolled out of bed.

I continued along with the flow, walking behind a couple of tightly buttoned, 100-pound boys who were carrying 50-pound backpacks and were probably on their way to calculus. They walked close together like wary tourists in Times Square and I followed behind them until I saw a sign that said, "All visitors *must* report to the office." It was hanging from the ceiling outside a door with a big window in it. I opened the door and went in, realizing as I shut the door behind me, that I had no idea what I was going to say.

"May I help you?" a voice said.

I looked over a wooden counter to where several women were sitting at desks. They were all staring at me and from their expressions it was impossible to tell which one had spoken. I picked one at random, an older woman with big red glasses and hands poised on a computer keyboard. As I started to say something, the "May I help you?" came again, from a much younger woman to Red Glasses' right. She was perhaps twenty-five, hair in a braid, wearing slacks and a white blouse with a button that said something I couldn't make out from that distance.

I smiled. She didn't. Everyone else stared.

"Hi, I'm Jack McMorrow," I said, moving to the counter. Her eyes didn't even flicker.

"I'm a writer, for magazines, and I live in Prosperity."

She still stared. Maybe I should have brought my piece on irises.

"And I know it might sound sort of vague," I said, "but I was hoping to talk to somebody who works with kids."

"We do a lot of that here," the woman said.

Not only vague, but stupid.

"I don't mean classroom work, really," I said. "I mean counseling sort of things. Their lives outside of school."

She was still sitting at her desk, with only her head turned toward me. I tried to read her button but couldn't. I smiled again. She didn't, again.

"We have guidance counselors. Career counselors. Crisis counselors. Substance abuse counselors," the woman said.

"And counselors for the counselors?" I asked.

She gave me a hard stare and reached for her phone. Five minutes in school and already I was being expelled.

"Is Mr. Leonard in?" the woman said. "Oh, there's someone here with a question I think he should answer. No, it's not that important."

Maybe not to you, I thought. But I've got a houseful of bats to feed.

"You have to talk to Mr. Leonard," the woman said. "He's the principal but he's in a meeting and he won't be out for an hour and then he's got to leave for a meeting in Augusta."

She said this in a tone that put Mr. Leonard's meetings on a par with emergency sessions of the U.N. Security Council.

"I'll come back," I said.

Don't bother, her look said.

"Thanks for your help," I said.

She sort of nodded and turned back to her desk, which was piled with some sort of forms. I started to turn to leave, then stopped.

"One question you might be able to help me with," I said. "What's your button say, there on your shirt?"

She looked at me as if I'd asked the brand of her underwear. First things first, I figured.

"Cooperation," the woman said, slowly and with evident distaste. "Makes it happen."

"Ain't that the truth," I said, giving her a long look and

my most disarming grin. She looked away and said nothing.

Jack, I thought as I walked to the door, you haven't lost the old touch.

Back in the hallway, the commuter rush had thinned. I took a right and continued deeper into the school. There was a display case with computer printout signs proclaiming "The students of the week." Beside the signs were blurry black-and-white photographs. The students of the week were two girls and two boys, all of whom looked relatively wholesome. My buddy from the parking lot was noticeably absent.

I shuffled along and, for a second, realized that I was probably old enough to be a visiting parent, which made me feel older still. How long we cling to the fallacy of eternal youth.

The corridor was going past classrooms now and, through the doors, I could see teachers standing in front of classes. A heavyset guy was saying, "Now, people," in a way that told me the people weren't listening. At the next door was another guy, young and blond and probably a coach. On the board behind him were the words "Jacksonian democracy." If the coach could make that relevant to these kids of the 21st century, he was earning his pay.

At the next crossroads, I decided to break down and ask directions. Four girls were huddling near a bank of gunmetal-gray lockers and I stopped behind them and waited for them to notice me. This offered the opportunity to listen to a few seconds of academic debate.

"So I'm like, 'Jimmy. I'm goin' out with Ronnie,'" a dark-haired girl was saying. "He starts, like, punching the side of his truck. I'm like, 'Oh, my God. I gotta get outta here.'"

"Did you tell Ronnie?" another girl, taller, in black stretchy pants, said.

"Oh, yeah, right," the first girl said. "I'm gonna go, like, 'I was down at the pit with Jimmy and he was hittin' on

me.' I mean, he'd kill me and then he'd really kill Jimmy.
His probation officer told him he was, like, this friggin'
close from being revoked."

She held up two fingers with long red-painted nails.

"He frigs up once and he's gone," the girl said.

On that note, they looked up and saw me.

"Excuse me, ladies," I said. "I seem to have lost my
way."

I took "like a right" and "like a left" and eventually ended
up back near where I started, up the yellow-brick corridor,
past the trophy case, to a door over which hung a small sign
that said "Guidance." Maybe if I kept going down the hall
there'd be signs for help, and consolation, and constructive
criticism. Sort of an open-air bazaar for your emotional and
spiritual needs.

But I turned in at "Guidance" because it was guidance I
needed. There was nobody in the outer room. Just a cup of
coffee on the desk. A computer terminal which was hum-
ming quietly to itself. On the wall behind the desk was a
poster picture of a black fuzzy bear cub. Underneath the
bear it said, "Have a beary nice day."

No psycho-babble here.

I waited for a minute and listened. A couple of kids went
by in the corridor, their heels tapping against the tile floor. I
waited another minute and was turning to leave when a
woman came through the door fast and low and caught me
in the shoulder.

"Oh, I'm sorry," she said.

"An emergency?" I asked.

"They're all emergencies," the woman answered. "Are
you a parent?"

"No," I said, "but someday I hope to be one."

She was small and dark, maybe twenty-eight, twenty-
nine. Sort of pretty, with dark hair and large intense brown
eyes set in deep shadowed hollows. Her sweater was thick
and coarse and hand-knit, probably in the Andes or some-

place. Her earrings were long and silver and no doubt made by some local artisan whose sweater came from the Andes, too.

"Jack McMorrow," I said. "Are you the guidance counselor?"

"The one and only," she said, as if all the king's horses and all the king's men would have a tough time putting these kids back together. She turned and walked into the office to the left of the bear poster. I assumed the invitation to accompany her was implied.

Her name was Janice Genest, but she pronounced her first name "Janeece." She shook my hand over her desk. Her hand was tanned and strong. She was attractive in a handsome sort of way. High cheekbones and dark brown eyes. A lot of unruly hair pulled back and clipped. Very little makeup and very slim. A woman too busy to preen. And too busy to clean her desk, which was a mess. The poster directly behind her—a boy and a girl in sunglasses and leather jackets, models masquerading as tough kids—was an ad for condoms.

"What can I do for you, Mr. McMorrow?" Genest said.

I pointed at the poster.

"It has to do with that," I said. "Sort of."

She didn't flinch.

I told her about *New England Look*. The story, I said, was about teenage pregnancy and how it shapes the world of rural Maine. She listened with no-nonsense directness and I tried to make every word count. It was as if I had gotten in the door with the head of a very large company and I had one chance to make my pitch.

"So here you have this vicious circle," I said, both of us still standing. "They have kids at sixteen because their mothers had kids at sixteen. And I would guess—you would know more about this than me—that when you have kids at sixteen, it's tough to do a heck of a lot more. You must see this. Grandmothers who are thirty-five. All these generations packed into a few years."

"The record is thirty, I think," Genest said. "That was the grandmother. The great-grandmother was under fifty. But looked sixty-five."

"Hard life?"

"Harder than yours or mine. You know, it's a matriarchal thing. The woman, or girl, has the babies. Mommy's boyfriends come and go. Stay long enough to make more kids. In jail as much as not. Alcohol is part of it ninety-nine percent of the time. He's a drunk. She tries to keep things going but it's pretty hopeless, so she ends up a drunk, too. Between drinking and cigarettes and general abuse, nobody lives very long."

"It does sound kind of hopeless," I said.

"Close to it," Genest said, shuffling through phone messages on her desk. "Unless you get 'em early."

"Which is what you do here?"

"Try. Like fishing with a net full of holes. Too many of them slip through. Sexually active at thirteen. Hanging around with guys who are twenty. Lambs among the wolves, you know? Little girls looking for a man to love them. Men looking for something else. I mean, it's a minefield. Try to teach them about contraception and some fundamentalist parent goes to the school board. Contraception? I've got fourteen-year-olds who need prenatal courses. Fetal alcohol syndrome. What smoking does to a fetus. Nutrition. You can't grow a healthy baby on warm Pepsi and potato chips."

She shook her head.

"But that's what they pay you the big bucks for," I said.

Genest almost smiled. Almost.

I told her I'd like to talk to her more. She shrugged her shoulders.

"Hey, I can talk, but what good is it going to do?" she asked. "I mean, my kids don't read *New England Look*. So it's sort of like a freak show, isn't it? Parade the poor dumb

bumpkins up and down for the people who went to
Williams and Wesleyan. So when the summer people come
up to Owl's Head or Hancock or any of those places,
they'll think twice about crossing over to the west side of
Route 1. I mean, face it. They don't really care about any of
this. Not really. Come on, Mr. McMorrow."

"Jack."

"OK, Jack. But I'm right, am I not? I mean, what's the
point? So these people in rich suburbs around Boston and
Hartford and Greenwich will maybe have a pang of pity before they put the magazine down and jump in the Volvo to
take the kids to soccer practice? Or drop little Erica at bal-
let?"

"If you think like that, the *New York Times* would only
report on Scarsdale. Pretend the Bronx doesn't exist," I
said.

"Maybe they should, for all the good it does the kids in
the Bronx. I did my student teaching in Roxbury, in
Boston. This woman from the *Globe* came and did a story
about violence in the schools. You know. Kids bringing
guns to class. Shooting at each other at locker break. That
place was like the Wild West, it really was. And this was
back when that was news. So the story was fine. I mean,
she did a good job. Talked to a lot of people. But in the
end, what did it change? Kids are still killing each other.
Drugs and drug money are just eating them up. And some
guy in Newton skimmed the story before he turned to the
important stuff. Like the Red Sox."

"But people should know," I said. "The chances of it
doing your kids any good may be, I don't know, slim to
none. But if nobody knows, they're just none. Forget the
slim."

"I know what you mean," she said, conceding maybe a
millimeter. "But I only have so much time, and spending it
talking to you may be wasting it."

"Thanks a lot," I said.

"Nothing personal," Genest said.

A buzzer went off in the hall, followed by a growing roar, like a subway train approaching. There were footsteps and then the shuffle of somebody behind me. I turned to see a girl. She was small and slight with thick black eye-shadow and bright red lipstick that made her look like a female impersonator.

"Miss Genest," she said urgently. "I gotta talk to you."

I smiled at Miss Genest and excused myself. I said I'd still like to talk to her.

"Whatever," she said.

As I stepped out the door, the girl slipped in, giving me a practiced glance that was supposed to be provocative. She smelled of cigarettes and bubble gum.

Five

The smaller maples on the fringes of the swamps were always the first to go. They flared crimson and red-orange and orange-red, Crayola colors that were shocking against the still-deep greens of the bigger maples and alders around them. These were the first brushfires, fuses that sizzled around the low, wet edges of the woods and ignited the blazes that would, in two or three weeks, engulf the hardwood ridges around Prosperity with the beautiful flames of autumn.

It was mid-September and the first color was beginning to creep in. It appeared suddenly along the roadways as if sprayed by some graffiti artist during the night. Each day, the colors would spread, so gorgeous that I would stop the car and get out and just stare, trying to absorb this thing that was wondrous but passed as quickly as a sunset.

It was Saturday, midmorning, and I had stopped on the Albion Road, on my way back from the Albion General Store, where I had picked up a coffee and a *Boston Globe*. I sat by the side of Route 137, at a spot where flickers of red were showing in a line of swamp maples that grew along the margin of a bog. Four-wheel-drive pickups rumbled by, their big rippled tires whirring on the pavement. I picked up the *Globe* and read a page-one story about a teenage girl who, sure enough, had been shot and killed in Roxbury. A very pretty girl, she smiled sweetly in the photo in the paper. She had been caught in the crossfire of a gunfight between two feuding gangs.

Somebody ought to take these gang kids out and teach them how to shoot straight.

That was life for kids in Boston, three hours and several light-years away from Albion, Prosperity, and Belfast, Maine. On the streets of Roxbury and Dorchester, kids ran the risk of dying from a stray bullet. But what were the risks here? I wasn't sure. Maybe driving drunk on twisting country roads. Latching on to the wrong guy or girl and a life of domestic hell. Or the welfare rut. Or the habit of petty crime that saw whole lives spent moving from county jail to state prison to county jail. Or even more subtle than that, maybe it was just the risk of growing old too fast, and living a life full of regret.

Maybe.

I didn't really know, when it came down to it, and the plan for the day was to see if I could at least begin to find out.

But how?

There was a funny thing about small-town reporting. It was hard.

In the city, you had hundreds and thousands of people to pick from. They stood in bunches on street corners, in subway lines, gathered by the fountains in shopping malls. City people were accustomed to strangers, so they didn't spook easily. They might tell you to drop dead, or some raunchier equivalent, but at least that was the beginning of a dialogue.

In the closed world of small-town Maine, a stranger was an event, an aberration from the routine, something inherently suspect. A stranger asking questions was more suspicious still.

And there was the logistical problem. Where were these kids I needed to get to know? Behind which trailer door? In which house, set back at the end of a long driveway carved out of the woods? And when I knocked, who would answer? Daddy? Gramma? Some guy with a handgun on his hip?

Well, Jack, I said, starting the truck and heading back toward Prosperity. That's why they pay you the big money.

My first stop was home. Bumping down the road, I waved to the girls who were living in the cabin near the corner, where the road turned from pavement to gravel. The girls were from New York and Massachusetts and went to Unity College, five miles away in the town of Unity. They were athletic and wholesome and their cars, a Jeep and a Subaru station wagon, had racks for skis and mountain bikes and kayaks and sailboards. The college girls were nice kids but they kept somewhat to themselves, as if Maine were one giant national park and their neighbors were just the people at the next campsite: strangers who would be gone in the morning.

When I went by the Varneys', Claire was on his tractor, an old but immaculate John Deere. He was tilling under a section of his vegetable garden and he waved and I waved but I didn't stop to talk. For the first time in many months, I had built up some momentum and I didn't want to lose it.

I grabbed a couple of notebooks from the desk, three pens from the jar by the phone on the kitchen counter. At the door, I stopped and pondered the jackets hanging on the hooks. I was wearing a brown canvas hunting jacket from L.L. Bean. It was comfortable and durable but I wondered if it didn't have too much of an air of gentry. I took it off and put on a faded denim. Then I grabbed a Red Sox hat, a real one without the plastic adjustable band.

Outside, I viewed my ensemble in the window of the truck. Would you talk to this man? I smiled my most winning grin. Hey, I talked to myself all the time.

A whole schoolful of kids and on Saturday they slipped away into the landscape like guerrilla fighters.

It was late afternoon, getting chilly, and the sun was dropping lazily toward the low ridges to the west. I was at the counter at the Western View Restaurant in Knox, a few miles east of Prosperity. There were four stools and two were occupied: one by me and the other by a dishwasher, a boy about sixteen who was passing his break by eating half an apple pie. A few employees like him and this place could kiss its profits good-bye.

But nobody seemed to mind. The cook was standing by one of the tables, talking to three guys who were having coffee and eggs, hash browns and bacon, the hell with cholesterol. The three guys had gotten out of a big dump truck, which was idling noisily in the parking lot. They were all in their forties, all big, with muscular upper bodies and no buttocks, the kind of physiques you saw in men who lifted a lot but spent a lot of time behind the wheel. I figured they'd be over to see me any minute, having noticed from across the room my superior metabolic conditioning. I would generously suggest they join their wives' aerobic dance programs. They could begin by chasing me around the parking lot.

At the moment, my metabolic rate was elevated by coffee, which the waitress kept pouring and I kept drinking. She was high school age, slim and pretty, and friendly in that breezy way that comes from deep-seated self-confidence. Her parents had done something right. She was also one of the few teen-age kids I'd seen in my travels that day and I was trying to figure out how to broach the subject of

teen pregnancy without seeming too, how shall we say, forward.

I smiled at her as she breezed by with the coffeepot.

"You ready for a refill, Dad?" she said to the biggest guy
from the dump truck.

This was not going to be easy.

I sat at the counter through another cup, and waited as
my self-confident friend served a fiftyish couple who had
pulled into the parking lot in a dressy new Ford pickup with
Connecticut plates and the big metal racks that are the
trademark of antique dealers. They ordered decaf and
seafood baskets and the woman, who was dressed in jeans
and running shoes and expensive jewelry, got out some sort
of catalogue. The guy, ruddy-faced and catalogue handsome under an Irish tweed cap, gave the waitress that lingering look that is the mark of a lecher.

I didn't want to be there when she introduced him to her
daddy.

When I paid the bill, I left a dollar tip by my cup, on top
of the paper placemat with the venison recipes on it. I gave
the waitress another smile that I hoped she'd remember
when I came in again, then went out to the parking lot,
where the antiquers' Ford was laughing at my Chevy. As I
sat there consoling the rusty old steed, an old four-wheel-
drive pickup drove in and parked. A girl got out and tossed
her mane of hair as she climbed down from the raised-up
cab and walked to the restaurant door. She came back in a
minute with a pack of cigarettes in her hand.

It was the girl from the hallway at the high school. I
wondered if they would, like, remember me. I got out of the
truck and walked over.

"Hello, ladies," I said.

"You're the lost guy," one of the girls said.

"And still lost," I said.

"Still looking for guidance?" she asked.

"Oh, yeah," I said.

She was sitting in the middle of the seat, smoking a cigarette under her hood of big hair. The girl to her right was smaller and blonder. The driver looked more like the one in the middle except heavier. They were all wearing jeans and denim jackets, all smoking. And they all looked at me, wary but curious, too.

"I'm Jack," I said. "I was at the school to see Janice Genest. Thanks for your directions. I'd still be there, wandering around the halls."

The driver and the one in the middle smiled. The smaller one kicked the middle one and giggled.

"I'm a writer. For magazines," I explained. "I'm doing a story, and this is gonna sound kind of weird, but it isn't. Really. The story is about girls in high school who have babies."

The smaller one snorted. The driver's expression hardened. She took a drag on her cigarette.

"Yeah, I know it sounds like I'm some kind of pervert," I said. "But I'm not. The story is supposed to be about what it's like to have a baby in school. Somebody your age."

I watched their eyes peering out from under black eyeliner. It was right here that I'd either lose them or hook them. I looked at them, lined up in the truck cab like birds in a nest. The small one had her work boots on the dash. She whispered something to the middle one and giggled. The middle one nudged the small one with an elbow. I smiled.

Paternally, I hoped.

"So?" the middle one said suddenly. "Lots of kids have babies. What's the big deal?"

"Well, it's just about whether they stay in school. If they don't, what do they do. Do they live at home? Do they get married?"

"Yeah, right," the driver, the bigger girl, said.

"Here comes the bride," the smaller one sung. "All fat and wide."

"Sharon!" the middle one said.

"Some do, but it's a joke," the driver said. "Guys usually ain't worth marrying."

I looked at her and grinned.

"What's your name?" I asked.

"Belinda," she said.

Belinda was the hard-boiled one of the three but seemed to have the most going on upstairs.

"So the guys are scum, huh?" I asked her.

"They got what they wanted," Belinda said. "You get your kid. Got nothing to do with them. Mostly it doesn't."

"So girls usually keep the kid?"

"Hey, it's your kid and nobody else's. Why should you have an abortion just because the guy's a dink?"

A new slogan for the pro-life movement.

"Oh, my God," the smallest one said.

"Sharon," the middle one said. "Come on."

"I just can't believe she's talking to this guy about this," the smallest one said.

"Do some kids give the kids up?" I asked. "For adoption I mean?"

"Missy Hewett," Sharon blurted.

"Sharon!" the middle one said.

"Well, she did," Sharon said. "And so did that girl who used to go out with Jason. I think that sucks."

"What do you know about it?" Belinda said. "You never had a baby. You don't know what you'd do if you were them."

"I wouldn't give my baby away like it was a kitten or something," Sharon said.

"Sharon, you're so weird," Belinda said, shaking her head. "Isn't she, Dulcy?"

Sharon leaned over and whispered something to Dulcy, the one in the middle.

"Sharon!" Dulcy said.

"What'd she say?" Belinda demanded.

"Don't tell her," Sharon said, giggling.

Dulcy was giggling, too.

"She said, if it was Jason, it wouldn't be a kitten. It'd be a puppy," she said.

"Oh, Jesus, you guys," Belinda said. "This guy is gonna think you're totally stupid."

She turned to me.

"You gonna put that in your story?" Belinda asked.

"Sure," I said. "Girl has puppy. I could sell it to the *Inquirer*."

I smiled. Sharon was still laughing as she tried to light a cigarette. Belinda was reaching for the key in the ignition. Dulcy gave me a quick direct glance that, if I hadn't known better, I'd have thought to be an indication of something other than passing interest.

"Well, thanks, guys," I said. "I'll see you around, I'm sure. But one more thing."

Three heads of unruly hair turned in unison. Three pairs of black-lined eyes.

"Where do kids hang out around here? When they get together, I mean?"

"The pit," Dulcy said.

"Yeah, the pit," Belinda agreed.

"Where's that?"

"Right past her house," Belinda said. "Knox Ridge Road."

"Yeah," Sharon said. "And her phone number is 568—"

"Sharon!" Dulcy protested and punched her friend in the shoulder.

Belinda started the truck and gave it a blatting rev.

"Thanks, ladies," I said.

They pulled out, spinning the tires on the gravel. Dulcy was shaking Sharon by the shoulder. Belinda was holding her cigarette out the window.

I walked back to the truck and picked up a notebook.

"You don't have to have an abortion," I wrote, "just because the guy's a dink."

Under that I wrote four names. Belinda. Dulcy. Sharon. And Missy Hewett.

Six

"I really see this as a piece about women's attitudes in rural New England in the nineties," Maddy was saying. "And if their attitudes haven't changed in a century, I think that would be very interesting."

I was sitting at the big oak table, on the phone to *New England Look*. As I listened, I sipped from a can of Budweiser. Next to that can was an empty one. It was Monday, a few minutes before five in the afternoon. I was easing into the work week. Slowly.

Saturday night I'd had supper with Claire and Mary, then a few beers with Claire, listening to the crickets on their back porch. We had talked about the integrity of a tractor versus the integrity of an automobile. Claire had told me about a Buddhist monk he'd met in Vietnam. On the road outside Pleiku, Claire and the monk had talked about all kinds of lofty things: the world-view of Americans, Christianity and the inherent evangelism of Western culture, the way the conventional Christian notion of afterlife had shaped the world in the 20th century. Claire said he'd been waiting for a Marine unit to catch up and when it did, he went on toward Dak To. A couple of days later, coming back through the same way, he'd walked by the monk's body: riddled by bullets, open eyes covered with flies.

"So I buried him," Claire had said. "This brilliant guy turned into a rotting piece of meat. That's what war does, Jack. Like all those poets who got killed in World War One.

"What passing-bells for these who die as cattle?
Only the monstrous anger of the guns.
Only the stuttering rifles' rapid rattle
Can patter out their hasty orisons.
No mockeries for them from prayers or bells,

*Nor any voice of mourning save the choirs of wailing
        shells;
And bugles calling for them from sad shires."*

"What's that?" I'd asked.

"Wilfred Owen. 'Anthem for Doomed Youth,'" he'd
said. "Got killed in the trenches in 1918. He was twenty-
five. When I was in high school, Miss Frost, my English
teacher, made us memorize ten poems to graduate. That's
the only one I remember now."

"Kind of a funny poem for a Marine," I'd said.

"Not really," Claire had replied. "Not at all."

I found myself thinking about that as Maddy talked. She
had called to confirm that I existed. With Dave Slocum involved, this probably was a prudent move. But I found that
I'd rather be talking to Claire, that I had less patience for
people like Maddy. Maybe I'd been in Maine, my Maine,
too long, but she seemed cold and affected. Bright enough
but presumptuous. She seemed to see the kids in this story
as pieces in some sort of sociological study. I didn't get the
feeling that she would be truly moved by their lives. Or fascinated by them. Or surprised by them.

"So it sounds like you have everything under control,"
Maddy was saying. "Oh, I understand from Dave that you
worked at the *Times*. Did you know Marla Manstein? She
worked on the international desk?"

"Doesn't ring a bell but it's a big place," I said. "And I
only got as international as Queens."

"Marla and I went to Smith together," Maddy said. "Her
husband and my husband, now ex-husband, but that's a
long story, knew each other from Harvard. The business
school."

"Small world," I said.

"Yes, it is," she said brightly. "Even in Manhattan. I
lived in New York for a couple of years after Columbia j-
school. I must have read some of your stories in the *Times*."

"Could be."

"I was working for *Ad Age* and then I met my husband and then I divorced my husband and now here I am. In politically correct Amherst."

"A long way from the Upper East Side," I said.

"How'd you know I lived on the East Side," Maddy said.

"I guessed," I said.

Would have put a hundred bucks on it, I thought.

Maddy paused.

"So what brought you to northern Maine?" she said carefully. "I mean, Amherst is a long way from Manhattan. But northern Maine's a real jump."

"Well, it's not really north. It's more South Central. Like L.A. And that's being generous."

"What does your wife think?"

"I don't have one," I said. "I live alone on a dirt road in a house full of bats."

"Yuck," Maddy said.

Ah, a nature lover.

"Actually, they're quite fascinating," I said. "Tremendous powers of flight. And carefree. You just empty the guano box once in a while."

"No wonder you don't have a wife," she said.

"No wonder at all," I said.

I sat there at the table, finished my beer, and got another from the refrigerator. I drank half of that one.

"No wonder at all."

I felt like I'd just sat through an hour of therapy. Confront your feelings. Face the fact that you just didn't fit in on the so-called fast track. Wonder if you fit in on any track. Consider what it is about women like Maddy that make you withdraw. She was pleasant, doing her best to make conversation. But she reminded me of other women, from other times, who had made me feel that ultimately I was just one more prop. The right career. The right clothes. The right restaurants. The right guy.

"This is Jack. He's a reporter at the *Times*."

"Oh, really. How exciting."

So women had come and gone, through no fault of their own, with a regularity that I had long ago decided was a sign of some sort of problem with me, not them. I was closer to some than others but I always felt that the relationships were built on some sort of shifting sand, a shoal that would be eroded with each passing storm until a rift would appear in the barrier beach and the ocean would pour through and dissolve the bond that, just weeks or even days before, had seemed as permanent as bedrock.

I looked at Claire and Mary, cemented together, and I wondered what it was about me that kept me apart. It had happened in New York, and then when I came to Maine, it had happened again. Her name was Roxanne and she had been more giving than any other woman I'd known. But when it had come time for me to give something back, something big, I'd said no.

She had been a social worker, working with battered kids. Her job had required her to go out every day and stick her head into the maw of families whose only bonds were fear and anger and cruelty. But even that she approached with a cool conviction and when she left it, it was with her psyche still smooth and intact.

And the rest of her didn't look bad either.

We'd been drawn together by something that felt very powerful and, once together, we'd rested easily in each other's presence, even the morning after, which was always the test. Roxanne was beautiful, full of energy and motion, a skier who took life surely, moving surely through the days like she was carving turns on a mountain someplace. But even that faded, probably because of my darker side, and now that's where she was.

Carving turns on a mountain someplace.

Roxanne had left for Colorado and friends who were more like her. They lived in places like Vail and hung out with the U.S. Olympic Team. They wore the latest, brightly colored parkas and traveled widely on the income from their trusts. Alaska. New Zealand. The Italian Alps. They had their kayaks airlifted to the headwaters of remote mountain rivers. They skied off of helicopters. They drank only the best European beers and didn't get hangovers. They were all tanned and good looking and had perfect teeth.

After months with me, for Roxanne they probably were a relief.

Because things had gotten pretty dark. A petty little scheme led to murder. Roxanne wanted to go and to take me with her. But the worse things got the more I felt a need to stay. She couldn't understand that but she'd hung in there with me until the danger had passed. And then she had packed her bags and left. Where I'd once awakened to the feel of her bare back against my chest, now I got an occasional phone call, a postcard from some place where she'd skied or snorkeled or sailed.

I was home alone, in Prosperity, Maine, wondering when the bats would be ready to hibernate.

They weren't ready that night. It had been warm for September and they had begun circling at dusk, like props from a Dracula movie. I slept part of the night in the big chair in the living room, then crawled into bed after the bats had gone on their rounds. When they came home, just before dawn, they let themselves in.

The dears.

So I was almost refreshed when I got up. Over tea and a bagel with peanut butter, I finished reading the day-old *Globe*, then watched the birds from the deck for an hour. There was a wood thrush in the brambles at the edge of the yard and when it finally flitted deeper into the brush, I made my move to the shower. By ten-thirty, I was poised at the edge of the maelstrom of the high school corridors.

Looking for Missy Hewett.

Janice Genest was out, gone to one of those myriad seminars that keep seminar people employed but accomplish little else. I was surprised she had time to waste on such nonsense but I didn't say this to the guidance office secretary, who looked at me suspiciously through her school-issue red-framed glasses, and, despite the poster over her head, did not seem inclined to wish me a "beary nice day."

She didn't introduce herself. She didn't smile. She said she didn't know when Genest would be back. When I said I was looking for Missy Hewett, she cooperated only to move me on my way.

To Portland.

"Oh, she's no longer with us," Beary said.

"Something happen to her?" I asked.

"Yes," she said. "She graduated."

Hallelujah, I thought. A success story.

"Oh, yes," Beary said. "She's in college, at the University of Southern Maine."

"In Portland?" I asked.

"Is there another one?" she said.

Pleased with her razor-sharp repartee, Beary finally smiled.

Seven

Of course, there was no Missy Hewett in the Portland phone directory. For lack of any other obvious way to make progress on the story, I drove down that afternoon, rumbling along in the truck at a tortoise-like sixty miles an hour in what turned out to be, as usual, a two-hour exercise in humility. As shiny new cars whizzed by me on Route 95, I

smiled calmly and congratulated myself for my rejection of
the material world.

And kept one eye on the temperature gauge.

There was only one University of Southern Maine and it
was, indeed, in Portland, just off I-95, a few blocks west of
downtown. I got off the highway at Forest Avenue, which
was conspicuously short on trees, not to mention forests,
but did have fast-food places sprouting like sumac on va-
cant lots. I was hungry, but not that hungry, so I took a
quick left off of Forest and drove head-on into academe.

Though it is hard to say exactly where a university starts,
the first sign that I had crossed the perimeter was the fact
that every available parking space along the drab residential
street was filled. Most of the cars were small and had USM
parking stickers on the side windows. The houses, mostly
square, plain post-Victorian, were chopped into apartments
and there were bicycles sprawled on the porches.

This was the right place.

I drove past a couple of big brick buildings, including a
long low one that looked like a student union, and a big one
that I assumed contained classrooms. Outside the classroom
building, a small security van was parked and a campus cop
was fitting cars with wheel boots for illegal parking. If you
flunked chemistry, they tied cement blocks to your legs.

There were people walking everywhere and I could see
why. I drove past the classroom building, past a big open
lawn that fronted more big brick buildings. There were people on the lawn, stretched out in the September sun, no
doubt exhausted from having hiked in from the nearest
available parking space, somewhere in the adjoining city of
South Portland.

And for this truck, one space wouldn't do.

I drove past the big lawns, past a round modern building
that looked like an oil-storage tank with windows but, ac-
cording to the sign, was the university law school. Beyond
the law school, the streets were neat and the houses all had
university signs on the lawns, as if the whole neighborhood

were for sale. It probably had been at one time, and the university had been buying.

Finally, I found a space in front of a square white house for which the sign read, "Department of Classics." My old truck was certainly a classic, but even so, it stood out in the long row of little cars like a high school kid trying to hide in a kindergarten class.

"At least try to look academic," I told the truck, and began the hike back to the center of campus.

I already knew that Missy Hewett wasn't in the Portland phone book. This was probably because she didn't have a phone, but she had to have an address and somewhere on campus they would have to have it. That meant exploring a few of these brick buildings and hoping that if I stumbled into a calculus quiz, they wouldn't make me take it. Or at least they'd let me use my notes.

Education is a very big business, and as I crossed the big lawn at the center of the campus, the employees and customers were all around me. Kids with backpacks. Professors with canvas briefcases from L.L. Bean. A lot of older students, women in their forties, men older than that, who wore determined expressions, as if they knew what was waiting out there and it wasn't pretty.

I walked along the lawn, past the big classroom building that turned out to be something to do with nursing. The long low building was next, across a parking lot, and there were lots of people going in and out. It occurred to me that I should have brought a backpack full of bricks just to look the part, but it was too late.

Feeling conspicuously empty-handed, I went in.

The entrance led to a long hallway that was like some sort of indoor bazaar. There were tables set up on both sides. At the tables, people were selling sweaters and posters and handwoven blankets that the sign said were from Guatemala. The blonde-haired, rosy-cheeked girl behind the table was not Guatemalan.

I walked along slowly with the crowd. There was a gay-

rights table, with a couple of guys sorting out literature.
They were laughing. One guy had many earrings in his left
ear.

There was a nuclear-waste table. A table set up by people trying to save at least a postage stamp of the rain forest.
I took a crumpled five-dollar bill from my pocket and
stuffed it into the slot in their donation can. A small young
woman looked up at me, startled.

Some guys were selling music tapes of a band called
Scum. Snappy name, that. Another guy selling sunglasses
was doing more business than the woman at the next table,
where the sign said something about AIDS awareness. We
will be cool to the death. Sad commentary.

Finally I came to the end. There was some sort of cafete-
ria ahead, and though it was almost noon, I wasn't that hungry. I turned around and walked back down the hallway
and outside, where I stood for a minute until two guys came
and stood next to me. They were college age, wearing bandannas over their hair in a way that made them look like pi-
rate extras in a high-school production of *Peter Pan*. Ever
the diplomat, I didn't tell them that. Instead, I asked where
I could find a student directory.

One of the guys—blond, tall, gold-rimmed glasses, with
the big-boned glow of health that comes from family
money—started to tell me. The other guy, who was smaller,
with dark hair in a short ponytail, asked me why I wanted
to know.

"Because I need to find a student here," I said.

"You a cop?" he asked.

"No, but I can get one if you need one," I said.

"No, like, who are you, I mean," the small guy said.
"Like her father?"

"No," I said. "I'm like her uncle. A lot like him. A spitting image."

He looked at me silently. The blond guy looked embar-
rassed.

"What's her name?" the small guy persisted.

"Missy Hewett," I said. "Who are you? Head of campus security?"

"Hey, you should thank me," he said. "There are a lot of weirdos around here, you know? People aren't always what they seem."

"They're never what they seem," I said.

"Down there on the left," the blond guy interrupted, shaking his head at his buddy and pointing the way. "The big white building."

"Thanks," I said.

I turned to the small guy and took a step closer.

"And her Uncle Jack thanks you," I said. "Like, really."

"No problem," the small guy said.

That remained to be seen. I backtracked across the parking lot and up the street to the big white building, picked a likely door, and went in. There were offices and bulletin boards covered with brochures about grad schools and internships. A couple of hours in this place and I could find a new direction for my life. In the meantime, I stopped at the information desk and asked a heavyset woman wearing headphones for directions to Missy Hewett. The woman pulled the headphones down around her neck long enough to thumb through a worn directory.

"Thirteen Fessenden," she said, the music blaring tinnily around her neck.

"That a dorm?" I asked.

"A street," she said. "Fessenden Street."

And she gave me a look that said, what kind of uncle are you?

Fessenden ran from Forest Avenue, the main fast-food drag, up to Brighton Avenue, which cut through the middle of campus. Number thirteen was at the Forest Avenue end, around the corner from a radiator repair shop. It had been a nice old house, once upon a time, but now it was dilapidated and rotting. My truck fit in just fine here.

I parked in front and looked the place over. There was a

tipsy picket fence running across the front and someone had replaced a few of the rails with raw new wood. The new rails stood out like bad false teeth.

The same treatment had been given to the porch, which had once been ornate, but had been repaired crudely with pressure-treated wood. Around the porch, sumac was growing up as nature took back its own. Some blind optimist had placed a house-for-sale sign on the strip of dead sod that constituted a front lawn.

I waited for a minute and watched. There was no sign of life. The first-floor windows were covered with shades, pulled all the way down. A beat-up red Subaru station wagon was parked at the side of the driveway, its front right tire flat. If there were any trick-or-treaters left in the neighborhood, this would be the kind of place they'd skip.

I didn't have that choice.

But before I went up, I took a moment to consider what I knew about Missy Hewett. It didn't take much longer than that.

She was from Prosperity, or at least from that part of Waldo County. She'd gotten pregnant in high school and had a baby but had given it up for adoption. That behind her, she had gone on to college in this relatively big city. She was not living in the lap of luxury, and she was not expecting me.

I walked to the front door but it didn't look like the entrance. That was to the left of the house where there was another door, this one with four mailboxes nailed to the wall beside it. The names were taped on the boxes, one on top of the other, in chronological order of occupancy. On two of the boxes, the tape was weathered, the names washed out. On the other two, the names were legible. The name "M. Hewett" was neatly printed in what appeared to be a feminine hand.

I pushed the door open and a black and white cat slipped out. The hallway was dark and there was a 10-speed bicycle chained to a pipe at the bottom of the stairs. Bicycle bondage. I went in and closed the door behind me.

There was a door to my right and a pair of men's muddy work boots on the floor. I knocked on that door and waited. Then knocked again. There was no sound from inside.

I walked up the stairs, two flights. The stairs dead-ended at another door, outside of which was a pile of newspapers. The paper on top was a *Casco Bay Weekly*. I nudged it with my boot and exposed a *Portland Press Herald*, a week old. I stood for a moment and listened. A dish clattered. There was a beep, like from a microwave oven. I knocked and the door cracked open.

"Missy Hewett?" I said.

"Yeah?" she said, peering out from behind the door chain.

"My name's Jack McMorrow. I'm a writer and I met some of your friends at Waldo Regional. I would have called first but I didn't have your number."

"About what?" Missy Hewett said.

"Well, it's kind of hard to explain," I said, smiling. "But it has to do with high school. And babies."

Her face went gray.

Eight

It took me five minutes to get her to take the chain off the door. I passed my driver's license through the crack. My old *New York Times* I.D. If I'd known, I would have brought a portfolio. Maybe Missy would have been convinced by my compelling piece on irises.

"Why should I talk to you?" she said when I had finally

made my way into the very small, very neat kitchen. "I don't know you. Why should I talk to you about this?"

"You don't have to," I said.

"I know that," she said.

She was leaning against the counter with her arms folded across her chest. Her arms were thin, and in her plain white T-shirt and jeans, so was the rest of her. Her dark hair was stylishly cut, for a hip college kid, and it had been tinted a very faint shade of red, a tint so faint that you almost thought you imagined it. Even with the hair she was very pretty, with pale skin and large dark eyes. She was wearing purple socks without shoes and she didn't look old enough to be in college.

"I know this sounds strange," I said, "but it really isn't."

"I don't think I'm interested," Missy said. "It's nobody's business. And I don't think you have any right to come here and ask me to talk about something like this, something personal."

I waited for her to ask me to leave but she didn't.

"Yes, it's personal," I said, moving into the opening she had left me. "But in another way, it's not. It's like I was telling Janice Genest, the guidance counselor at the school. You know her?"

"Oh, yeah."

"Well, it's something lots of women have gone through. Lots more will go through it in the future. This kind of story—not just this one but other stories like it—helps people understand what's going on. They might help kids avoid, I don't know, the decision that you had to make."

"I didn't have to make it," Missy said. "I chose to make it."

"Why?"

"Because I was seventeen and I didn't want my baby to have a shitty life."

"Why would it have been shitty?" I asked.

"Because I would have been sitting home collecting welfare," Missy said. "Because I don't have family that gives a shit about me. So it would have been just me and the kid. And the kid deserves better than that. That's what she got."

"It was a girl?"

"Yup," she said.

And stopped.

Missy looked away. I looked around the apartment. There was another room with an old sofa and a small television on a cable-spool table. A bedroom after that. The bed was made.

The kitchen we were in was dreary but spotless. There were books and notes spread on the table. It looked like chemistry and biology.

"What are you studying?" I asked.

"I'm in the R.N. program," Missy said.

"Pretty tough?"

"Not yet," she said, "but I've only been here three weeks."

"Any other kids here from Waldo Regional?"

"Yeah, a couple. But it's a big place. I don't see 'em."

"What do you do most of the time?" I asked.

"I study. I work in the library. Part of my scholarship deal, you know? I got a big scholarship because I'm poor and from the boonies. But I study mostly. I study a lot."

"Were you like that in high school?"

"Like what?" Missy said, her arms still folded.

"A serious student," I said.

"I had to be serious," she said.

"Why?"

"Because nobody else was gonna do it for me," she said, her voice hard as stone. "If I blew it, I blew it."

"Where did the baby fit into that?" I asked.

"She didn't," Missy said. "She deserved better."

"It must have been hard."

She shrugged.

"A lot of things are hard," she said.

"Do you think talking about it would make it easier for somebody else?"

"Might teach them," Missy said.

"Teach them what?"

"That you can't trust anybody but yourself. And guys suck."

"That's kind of a hard attitude," I said. "How old are you? Nineteen?"

"Eighteen," she said.

"That isn't always true, you know."

"It has been for me," Missy said.

"The baby's father was no good?" I asked.

"He wasn't a father. He was a sperm cell. One sperm cell."

"But she has a father now?"

"A real one," Missy said. "And a mommy, too. She's on her way. She's all set."

"I think we would have something to talk about, if you wanted to."

"Maybe," Missy said. "I'll think about it."

"I'll leave you my number," I said.

She nodded and I took out a notebook, scribbled my name and number, and tore out the page. When she took it, I noticed there were no rings on her fingers. None.

I turned toward the door.

"One thing," Missy said.

"Yeah?" I said.

"Those girls. Dulcy. And Belinda."

"And Sharon," I said.

"Yeah," Missy said, a trace of high school creeping into her voice. "What did they say about me?"

The plan had been to inquire of Missy Hewett, then grab lunch and a good beer or two at one of the Old Port pubs. When it had been conceived, about two minutes into the trip, a mile out of Prosperity village, the thought of an outing in the city, paid for by Dave Slocum, had made me almost grin. But as I sat at a long bench in an ale house called "Three Dollar Dewey's," I could barely muster a smile for the waitress.

She was about Missy Hewett's age, another child hiding under makeup and dyed hair. But if these children had to make decisions like Missy's, what would they have to face as adults? What kind of scars did these decisions leave behind?

Life was hard, as Missy said. Forget the moralizing about kids having kids, about lost opportunities, kids who would never get to Wellesley. Life was hard. Period. In Prosperity, Maine. In most places. If your life wasn't hard, you were one of the fortunate few.

No wonder these kids liked to wear black.

I thought about it over a bowl of chili and a Samuel Smith's Nut Brown Ale. Normally, a Sam Smith's would lead me to thoughts of England and pubs in old stone buildings, thick black stout poured into heavy pint glasses. One nut brown ale would leave me at peace. Two would be a religious experience. There is a God and he is benevolent, for he—or she—invented hops and yeast.

Today there was ale but no peace.

I sat at the bench and played with the chili, which, like the ale, was good. But as I picked at the bowl, sipped from the glass halfheartedly, my mind was on Missy Hewett. There was Missy in her apartment, a little kid with a brittle hard shell. Missy, who barely had breasts and already hated men, who had reduced them not to a body or an organ but to a single cell. The father of her child was a sperm cell, she had said. The next step was a single strand of DNA.

It was chilling. And sad.

I pictured Missy in a hospital room, one where the only flowers were from the nurses. I pictured her in labor, grunting and crying and letting out teeth-clenched screams that should not come from a child's mouth. The nurses probably gave her chunks of ice to suck on, cool cloths for her head. Perhaps they had been even more gentle and kind than they were for other mothers, the ones who had men to hold their hands, to awkwardly lead them through the huff and puff learned in childbirth classes. Men to share the joy of a brand-new life.

Missy had given her new life away.

She probably had been right, even noble. Certainly, she had put her child's life ahead of hers, its future before her pleasure. But I wondered for how long she'd relive that moment. Did she hold the baby and say good-bye? Did she give the baby a name in her mind? Did she decide that it had her eyes? Was there a last moment when she gave its tiny hand a squeeze, said a prayer for it to be happy and healthy and content forever and ever?

"Can I get you another ale?" the waitress said.

I looked up, startled.

"No," I said. "It's just no use."

Nine▮

Mary Varney was canning pickles. The kitchen was like a spicy steam bath and the big canning pot was rattling explosively on the stove. Mary worked at the counter, dropping small pickling cukes from her garden into quart jars of brine, screwing on the lids and whirling to drop them into the boiling water.

"You know any Hewetts in town?" I asked.

"Used to be Hewetts on Knox Ridge," she said. "Could you go in the pantry there and get me another bunch of dill? It's the long feathery stuff."

It was Wednesday, late morning, overcast and cool. I was drinking tea with Mary until Claire got back. He had gone into Belfast to get a belt for the mower for his small tractor. Actually, I didn't really need to see him but it was a gloomy day and the Varney kitchen was a clean well-lighted place.

"What are these little black things?" I said, putting the dill on the counter.

"Peppercorns," Mary said. "Why do you think they call them that? They should call them pepper kernels."

"Too late now," I said. "So did you know these Hewetts?"

"By sight and reputation, which may or may not have been deserved."

"Why? Were they outlaws?" I asked.

"No more than a lot of people," Mary said, wincing as she splashed boiling water on her fingers. "The father never really worked. Took a lot of deer out of season. Did odd jobs. Drank up most of what he made. I think he went to prison for stealing. They had seven or eight kids, something like that. I remember seeing the mother at the store. Poor woman. Her life was one cross after another, stacked up on her back like cordwood. Of course, this is a generation back. Those kids were my age so they'd have kids by now. You don't hear the name much anymore. Of course, there were a lot of Hewett girls and they'd be remarried so the name would be lost but the family would be around."

"I met one," I said. "She's in college in Portland."

"Well, good for her. That's a first for that family."

"I don't think she has much to do with any of them."

"Probably good that she doesn't," Mary said, filling more jars.

"She seemed like a nice kid but very sad," I said. "She had a baby but she gave it up for adoption."

"In that family, that's got to be a first, too. Babies mean checks from the state every month. A steady income."

"She said she wanted hers to have a future. A real mom and dad. Not an easy decision to make, I would think."

"Not easy to do. Not easy to live with after," Mary said.

She shook her head.

"This girl must be one tough kid," she said. "It isn't many young women who are able to put their babies first like that."

"She was in high school," I said, refilling my cup from the porcelain tea pot.

Mary shook her head.

"Somewhere she got some good advice," she said. "Probably a good thing for both of them."

I sipped my tea.

"But not easy," I said.

"No," Mary said. "It couldn't ever be easy. Even harder in a small town like this. Everybody knows your business."

"And everybody has an opinion."

"Oh my, yes," Mary said.

By noon, Claire hadn't come home so I left Mary with her pickles and walked back up the road to home. On the way, one of the college girls stopped her car as she passed me and asked if she could borrow my truck sometime. The car had Maryland plates. Her name was Kippy or Skippy and she was attractive in an athletic sort of way, like a woman you'd see in the Olympics.

"I found this humongous bureau that I can have if I can get it home," Kippy said. "I'd just need it for an hour or so."

"Hey, anytime," I said. "But if the truck breaks down just be sure to take the plates with you when you leave it by the side of the road."

She laughed and gave me what seemed to be a lingering, and even inviting, smile. It seemed like I was seeing that a lot lately. Either I was getting better looking in my old age or just plain lecherous. After lunch I would take a walk in the woods and pray to St. Francis to give me strength.

Which I did. Take a walk, I mean. Grabbing my binoculars, I cut through the poplars and brambles for a couple of hundred yards toward the Varneys' until I hit the old log-

ging road that went up the hill to the beech ridge. The road
dated back to when they last cut these woods, which probably was thirty years before. In ten more years, it would disappear completely. I found this very encouraging, that
nature had this unrelenting side to it, a tortoise in a race
with the hare of paving and cutting. Leave a hayfield uncut
for five years and it's well on its way to wildness. Thirty
years and it's woods once again.

That's what had happened with these woods, many years
ago. Claire Varney said his grandfather had told him how
you could come up to this ridge back then and look out in
every direction and see nothing but pasture and fields. It
had been heartbreaking labor to clear that forest, cutting the
trees and pulling the stumps, one by one, year after year,
with horses and oxen. The rocks, which grew like a crop
unto themselves, were piled in long walls that now snaked
through the trees like the vestiges of some long-lost Mayan
city.

And in many ways, it was lost, their civilization. The
woods had reclaimed the land. The families had left the
hardscrabble farms for jobs in mills and factories to the
south. It all seemed so futile, but then again, those farmers
hadn't cleared that land to build a civilization. They had cut
those woods to feed their children. It had been a matter of
survival, nothing more, and where disease hadn't sliced
through families like a broadsword, the mission, through
the mercy of their stern taskmaster of a God, had been accomplished.

But even now, as the trees grew taller in the farmers'
fields, the exodus continued. Missy Hewett would not come
home. There was nothing in these hills for her. No job. No
husband. Not even a baby.

As I walked down the damp trail, I stopped every once in
a while to train the binoculars on the flitting shape of a
bird. I was in the deeper woods now, out of the tangle of
second growth, and the birds were mostly chickadees and
nuthatches, bobbing through the trees like bands of tiny

Gypsies. I spotted a couple of warblers but they were high in the beech trees, camouflaged in the yellow-green leaves, and I couldn't come close to an identification. I watched them until my arms grew tired and then I walked on.

The path led to the top of the ridge, maybe a mile above the road. My routine had been to follow it until it crested the ridge and then to look for the hulk of an old car on my left. The car was little more than a rusted shell of metal, sprinkled with bullet holes, courtesy of several generations of hunters. It looked like it dated to the nineteen-thirties, when it probably was driven or dragged into the back of a field and left like a sunken ship on some ocean floor.

I spotted the car and turned off the path and into the woods. There was no real trail here but I had walked this way so many times that each tree and deadfall was a landmark. After ten minutes, I turned back to my right, up the ridge and then down, following the contour of the land toward home. I stepped over limbs and around trees, my boots silent on the wet leaves and mosses. At one deadfall, I stepped on a branch and it cracked loudly. I winced and then, some distance behind me, heard another crack and a rustle. A deer? I turned slowly and watched but there was no movement in the trees. I waited, breath held back.

Nothing. If it had been a deer, I'd missed it.

It surprised me that deer would be up this high at midday. There were deer yards in the cedars down below, groves of Druid trees where the ground was covered with deer droppings, and there were feathers of deer fur on the branches. I had made it a habit of stopping there until Claire had told me that doing so would chase the deer away. Ever since, I had skirted it by several hundred yards, leaving the deer to their refuge.

I was heading downhill now, bushwhacking in the direction of the road and the house. The mist had turned to light rain and the woods were silent except for the dripping in the trees. And then there was another crack, behind and above. I turned expecting to see a buck bounding through the trees but saw nothing.

For the rest of the walk, the woods were dark and deep but not quite so lovely. I fought back the urge to break into a trot and walked, pretending, as do so many people, to have everything under control.

Ten

I drove back up to the store in Knox that afternoon, waited a half-hour for Dulcy and the girls to show up in their big truck, and then took them up on their invitation to follow them to see "the pit" where they hung out.

The pit was three miles out Route 137. The entrance was a dirt path cut through the wall of birch and spruce that ran along both sides of the road. We slowed and pulled in and I followed the girls' truck, branches raking my windows on both sides. After about fifty yards, we emerged from the woods into a sandy clearing, rimmed by raw, eroded bluffs which were ringed by a fringe of blood-red sumac.

The place had been a gravel pit and later some kind of dump where people had left refrigerators, a couple of stoves, and old cars and trucks that now were flipped over, their rusting undercarriages exposed like the bellies of dead beetles. When we passed close to one truck, an old red Chevy, I could see that its sides were perforated with bullet holes and the bigger, peach-size tears made by shotgun slugs. The place had the desolate feel of a wasteland, which probably was why, in a part of Maine where there were mountain trails, hillside pastures and majestic ocean views just down the road, the kids had picked it as their refuge.

Bring teenagers to the Louvre and they instinctively will gather in the restroom.

Here, they'd gathered at the far end of the pit, in a small dogleg section that could not be seen from the point where the road first came out of the woods. The girls swung their truck in beside two others, both older models, both lifted high on big tires. One was painted with black primer but had a blue tailgate and blue doors. One was white with gray primer spots and a Confederate flag across the back window.

"Ah," I said to myself, as I pulled up and shut off the motor. "A Civil War buff."

Three guys stood between the trucks and all three stared at me, ignoring the girls, who slid down from the cab of their truck one by one. I got out of the truck and walked toward them slowly, but with what I hoped was an easy confidence, the kind you try to exude as you're approaching a mean dog. What was the old saying? He's okay as long as he doesn't know you're afraid.

Which I wasn't. It was just that I was getting the feeling that these guys would no more want to talk about teenage moms than about Lee's blunders at Bull Run.

One was bigger than me. One my size. One smaller. They had long hair tucked under baseball caps, which topped a uniform of dungaree jackets and jeans. The jeans were tucked into work boots, which were unlaced. How would they put it in fashion pages of the *Times*? A loose, casual look for those weekends in the country.

The girls broke the already-long silence.

"Hey," Dulcy said.

"This is Jack," Belinda began. "He went to Portland to talk to Missy Hewett about her kid. Except she doesn't have it now. She gave it away so she could go to college."

I detected disapproval of Miss Hewett's maternal instincts.

Dulcy again.

"Jack's a writer. He does articles for magazines."

The boys did their best not to gush.

They stared some more. I stared back.

"How ya doin'?" I said, finally.

The biggest guy nodded first, then the one who was my size. The little guy, who was standing with his feet planted wide apart as if he were ready for my charge, just stared some more.

Perhaps we'll pass on the Civil War, I thought, and move right on to Napoleon and his neuroses.

I looked at them and they looked at me. Their hats advertised Ford trucks, a brand of shock absorbers, and Winchester firearms, respectively. I had a hunch they didn't want to talk about American history. But they probably wanted to talk about that far more than they wanted to talk about babies.

"Kenny," Dulcy said to the smallest guy. "I forgot your cigarettes."

She smiled teasingly from under her mane of hair.

"Sorry."

Hey, Dulcy, I said to myself. Way to soften him up.

"So you know Missy Hewett?" I said.

"Know who she is," the big guy said, and almost smiled.

"She's a bitch," Kenny said. "She a friend of yours?"

"No," I said. "I met her once. That's all. Through kids at the high school."

"Well, she's a bitch," he said again.

Ever the diplomat.

Probably he hoped I would try to defend her honor and we could have it out right there. I didn't take the bait.

"Why do you say that?" I said.

"Because I want to," Kenny said.

"No, I mean why do you think that?"

" 'Cause that's what she is. Put that in your article."

He pronounced "article" as if it were a woman's undergarment, something small and dainty.

"Yeah, a lot of kids thought she was stuck-up," Belinda said.

"How come?" I asked.

"I don't know," she said, uneasy for a moment and then plunging on. "I mean, like she was too smart for everybody else or something? Didn't party or nothin'. But my step-mother knew her mother and she used to be wild."

"Who was that?" the big guy said, suddenly interested.

"Joyce Hewett. Too old for you, little boy."

He shrugged, then turned to me.

"That old truck got a three-fifty or a three-twenty-seven?" the big guy said.

"Three-twenty-seven," I said.

"Them's good motors," he said. "Guys put 'em in stock cars."

"Runs great," I said.

We were en rapport.

There was a moment of silence and we stood between the trucks like people on a blind date. The pit was deadly quiet. The girls looked on as if the whole thing were some sort of reunion gone awry. The medium-sized guy and Kenny seemed tense and poised. I noticed Kenny had a large clasp knife in a leather case on his belt.

"So what do you want?" Kenny asked abruptly.

"Nothing really," I said. "I'm gonna be talking to kids around here for this story and I thought I should meet some people."

"Where do you live?" he asked.

"Right here in Prosperity," I said. "Dump Road. You know the artist's house?"

If he knew it, he didn't acknowledge it.

"How long you lived there?" Kenny continued.

"Six months or so," I said. "I came here from Androscoggin. I worked for the newspaper over there."

Kenny looked at me, turned his head slightly, and spat, then turned back.

"I think you smell like a cop," he said.

"Kenny!" one of the girls gasped. Nobody else moved. The big guy smiled. I didn't turn to see the girls.

"Hey," I said. "Think what you want but you're wrong."

"That's what you say," Kenny said.

"Yup."

"But I say you're a narc," he said.

"You can think I'm a Martian," I said. "I don't give a shit."

The words hung there. Somewhere in the brush, a chickadee gave that long dee-dee-dee call. A second chickadee answered. Then a blue jay, farther away and the titter of a warbler. A yellow warbler, it sounded like. Too bad I hadn't brought my binoculars. Perhaps one of the boys would have a Peterson Guide in his truck.

I shifted on my feet and grinned.

"What you smilin' about?" Kenny said.

"What're you all pissed off about?" I answered.

"None of your friggin' business," he said.

"But you don't even know me," I said.

"I know you're here and I didn't invite you," Kenny said.

His mouth moved but his eyes were fastened to mine, unblinking, like a knife fighter's.

"They invited me," I said, nodding toward the three girls.

"That's not what we're talking about," Kenny said.

"What are we talking about?" I asked him.

"Some guy from away who walked in here like he owned the place. Why don't you go back to New Jersey, cop? Where you belong."

"I never liked New Jersey," I said. "Except maybe for the Jersey Shore. And the Pine Barrens. Ever heard of the Pine Barrens? They're a lot like Maine except they have ticks. And deer. Lots of—"

"I don't like cops," Kenny interrupted.

"Oh, but they speak very highly of you," I said. "Exemplary social skills. For a sociopath."

"I oughta kick your ass," he said.

"I rest my case," I said.

"Let's do it right now," Kenny said. "Come on."

He took a step forward so he was about eight feet away. I had four inches on him, maybe fifteen pounds. But I didn't lift truck motors for fun.

"You sure, Ken?" I said, smiling. "I've got to remind you that an assault charge isn't gonna increase your chances of getting into law school."

"Come on, pussy," he said, beckoning me forward.

I shook my head and grinned, then looked away, first to the two guys and then to the girls. I figured Kenny would either sucker punch me or be left hanging, like a dancer without a partner.

The punch didn't come.

"Well, boys and girls," I said. "It's been real. If you're ever on the dump road, stop in."

All three girls decided to light cigarettes, despite the surgeon general's warnings. The big guy leaned back on the truck fender and, pushing his hat back, gave me a good-old-boy grin. The other guy looked to Kenny to see what to do. I'd guess that in the pecking order of the pit, Kenny was number two. I wasn't sure what this little exchange had done for his standing.

"Ken," I said, walking over to my truck and stopping by the door. "I don't know what to tell you. I'm not a cop. I'm just a newspaper reporter. Come over some time and I'll show you my clippings. In New York City, I wrote about people who would chew you up and spit you out. Either that or they'd just kill you. Kill you and never give it another thought."

"Colombians, right?" the big guy said. "My cousin was in prison in Connecticut with 'em. Said they were mean mothers. He's rugged, too. You know Lyle, right?"

The medium-sized guy started to answer.

"I'm not through with you, narc," Kenny said to me suddenly.

"Whatever," I said.

I climbed into the truck, shut the door, and started the motor. There was a puff of blue smoke.

"Motor job," the big guy said.

The third guy stood poker-faced.

"Take it easy, boys and girls," I said. "And, oh yeah. If I were Missy Hewett, I would have been a bitch, too."

I backed the truck up, put it in gear, and lurched back through the pit and out the path onto the road, leaving them to their dreary Hole in the Wall hideout. The route back was due west, right into the sun, and I pushed the visor down. Squinting into the glare, I made a mental note to call *New England Look* in the morning.

The price for this one had just gone up.

Eleven

Of course, by morning I'd reconsidered. The bats had been relatively quiet, allowing me a good night's sleep and the passage of time—and three or four beers before bed— had made my little chat in the gravel pit seem innocuous, or at least not so threatening. I snuggled under the covers, lis- tened to the birds outside the window, and thought to my- self that Kenny probably wasn't such a bad guy, once you got to know him. Hey, and that big guy, he was quite thoughtful, really. Mr. Medium-sized would just have to get over that painful shyness. And the girls, they were nice kids. Make somebody a nice ex-wife some day.

With this feeling of grand benevolence—and denial—I went about my Sunday.

The morning was a trip to Waterville for the *Times*, then a long leisurely brunch on the back deck. With my feet up on one of Millie's sculptures—a large piece of melted metal with one end that looked like a face and the whole thing skewered on a pipe like something that would have graced Frankenstein's waiting room—I ate fried potatoes from Claire Varney's garden and English muffins with Mary Varney's raspberry jam. In Prosperity, Maine, I became entirely engrossed in the travel section story on what to do in Milan.

All in all, it was a pleasant morning. And afternoon. And right into cocktail hour. I read every word in the *Times*, even the classified ads for apartments. At about that point, I remembered a rather jaded colleague, a guy named William, who worked the national copy desk and, in his blackest hours, maintained that the newspaper's function was not to inform but to distract.

"Millions of words," he would say, "and it matters not which ones, or that they appear in any particular order but only that they are available every morning to give the readers something to take with them to the john. And, of course, to create the illusion that each day brings us something other than one step closer to death."

The power of positive thinking.

But I put William out of my mind by reading the mansions-for-sale section at the back of the magazine. For the price of one of these palaces in the Hamptons you could buy most of Prosperity and maybe the adjoining town of Liberty, too. Of course, anyone who would want a palace in the Hamptons wouldn't know what to do with Prosperity, wouldn't know what to say or how to dress or where to go to dinner. They would look out on the supple tree-covered hills and see desolation. They would drive past the trailers, dug into the woods like battle emplacements, the home-built houses, and the old farmhouses and see something more foreign than the South Bronx. Where they would be repulsed, I was fascinated. Where they would be uneasy, I was at home. Where they would see a bleak landscape of dark woods, I saw the richness of nature.

And Claire Varney wouldn't hand them a bottle of Bud and talk about Vietnam.

Yup, I was feeling pretty good about myself. And then the phone rang.

"It's Kenny," I said, walking to the kitchen. "He's calling to apologize. He doesn't know what came over him but he thinks he's got to cut back on caffeine."

I grabbed the phone.

"Hello," I said.

"Hi, Jack," a woman's voice said.

"Hey, Roxanne," I said. "How are you?"

She was good, she said. She was still in Colorado Springs and hadn't started skiing yet.

"Another six weeks," Roxanne said. "But I've been mountain biking a lot. I'm getting into that, it's really big out here. How are things there?"

"Good," I said. "I've been out on the deck. Read the whole *Times*. Gonna take it easy. I decided I've been pushing myself too hard."

"Whatcha been doing?"

"Oh, this and that. Hanging out with the Varneys. Drove down to Portland the other day and had a Sam Smith's at Three Dollar Dewey's."

"The place is still going, huh?" Roxanne said, as if she'd been away for ten years instead of six months. In some ways, ten years seemed more like it.

"Oh, yeah," I said. "Same old place. Same old Portland."

"What took you down there?"

"Oh, a story. Maybe a story. A guy I knew at the *Times* called. He's working at *New England Look* now. Wants a freelance piece."

"You never sent me the one on the irises," she said.

"Oh, yes," I said. "My horticultural debut. The phone's been ringing off the hook."

"I'm sure you did a nice job."

"And it's gonna lead to all kinds of opportunities," I said. "The *Inquirer* called. They want a piece on botanic cults."

Roxanne laughed. She had a nice laugh, sort of low and throaty. When I heard it, I almost winced.

"So what's this new story about?" she asked.

I was at the counter opening a beer.

"Babies," I said. "Kids who have babies. Right up your alley, Miss Social Worker."

"The vicious circle, you mean?" Roxanne said.

"Yeah, I guess," I said. "What it's like. Where it leads. Are kids in rural New England any different from the four generations before them?"

"Sounds like a big project."

"Nah," I said. "I went out yesterday afternoon and did the research. I'm gonna have a few beers tonight and write it. At that rate, I'll be making about five hundred dollars an hour."

"Finally somebody recognizes your true worth," she said.

"Finally," I said.

The irony, unintended, made us both pause.

We had a nice talk. Roxanne said she was working for the local school system and taking some courses to get certified as a counselor. She was thinking of getting her master's in psychology. I almost made a joke about her getting me on the couch but decided not to engage in double entendre. Those days were over, or at least on long-term hold. I wondered if somebody else was holding her now.

Roxanne didn't say so and I didn't ask. We talked for fifteen minutes and when we hung up, with no plans to do anything but talk again sometime, I wondered what I had done in tossing her away.

The feeling was still there, I thought, as I wandered into the living room and stretched out on the couch. Not the lust, though that was lurking about a millimeter below the surface. No, make that half a millimeter. But what was still there was this feeling of comfort, that I could open all the doors for Roxanne and not worry about what would happen when she came in.

The guard I raised for everyone else all came down with Roxanne. There was no filter for my thoughts, my impressions, my bad jokes. And talking to her, I realized what hard work it was to be with anyone else.

Oh, Jack, I thought. You blew it.

But maybe not. There was something still there, a fondness at the very least. At the most, she still was in love with me. When she had her fill of tall, good-looking, wealthy adventurers, she'd be back. I wondered if I should wait up.

The thought of her made me smile to myself. And I had lots of thoughts of her.

I sipped my beer and crossed my feet on the end of the couch. The sun had dropped below the hills out back and the house was still and dim. In the quiet, I remembered snippets of our six months together, subliminal flashes of making love, walking down a street in Portland, having dinner, Roxanne leaning over me to kiss me good-bye as I slept. I remembered the smell of her, the feel of her, her shoes on the floor in the living room, the way they'd be strewn where she kicked them off as I uncorked the wine and she started to tell me about the day's social morass. I remembered all of it and then remembered it again and again until finally I dozed off.

And woke up in a shower of glass.

The first boom sent me off the couch, onto the floor on my knees. The second dropped me to my belly with my hands over my head and the room disintegrating all around me. I waited for another but there was nothing. Silence. A clink of glass as shards dropped somewhere. A cool breeze on my hands, clasped behind my head. Something warm running down my temple. I touched it with the back of my right hand. In the dark, the blood looked black.

I listened. Heard a motor start somewhere in the distance, in the direction of the dump. It revved once and then it was in gear. First. Second, then third, then a hush. They must be going around the corner. Now a roar again, fading into the night.

Still, I didn't get up. I got myself to my knees, waited to feel if there was any pain. The blood from my temple had dripped onto the floor but it was a slow drip that already was stopping. I touched my hands to each other and felt a sting on my left palm. Paused. There was no other pain. No other blood, that I could tell. I turned toward the couch and could see the stars where the window had been.

The bats were going to like this.

I waited and listened. Heard a night bird and nothing else. Crouching, I made my way across the room and into the kitchen, glass grating under my socks. In the kitchen, still in the dark, I found the phone. My hand went to the dial. I didn't know the number.

The phone book was on the counter, I thought. I patted my way along the counter and found it under some papers. Should I turn on the lights? Probably not. I opened a drawer and felt around for matches. Miraculously found some. Struck one and opened the front cover of the phone book. There were little symbols for cops and fire and poison. The cop number was the Waldo County Sheriff's Department. An 800 number. I dialed it as the match went out. A woman answered as I shook my singed fingers.

"Hi," I said. "This is Jack McMorrow on the dump road in Prosperity. I think somebody just shot a window out of my house."

It was a shotgun, Claire Varney said. He held up a pellet he'd found on the floor.

"Buckshot."

"Teach me for wearing those antlers around the house," I said, dabbing a wet hand towel at the cut on my forehead.

"Not even in season," Claire said.

He'd gotten there as I hung up the phone. First he'd

called to me from the yard and when I said I was OK, he'd walked in the kitchen door slowly and silently, holding a deer rifle with the barrel pointed at the floor.

"Somebody didn't like what you wrote about those flowers," Claire said.

"But they seemed like such gentle people."

"Those are the one's who'll backshoot you every time," he said.

Claire said he'd had a good idea what the first shot was, and knew for sure with the second. Unless I'd taken up night skeet shooting, he figured I was in some sort of trouble. And I would have been, if I'd happened to sit up.

"How far from the house do you figure they were?" I asked him.

We went into the living room and looked at the window. Actually, it was two windows, side by side, with twelve panes in each. Both windows were shot out, the panes mostly shattered, the wooden mullions splintered at the center.

"Thirty feet, maybe," Claire said. "Sure as hell not much more than that. You can tell by the spread. Buckshot doesn't spread like lighter shot."

"Would have taken my head off," I said.

"Or at least a good chunk of it."

"Would have been the end of my modeling career."

"Have to find some honest work," Claire said.

The question hung there in the air even before anyone said it. Finally it was Claire who broke the silence.

"So what's the deal, my friend? Those flower guys play rough or what?"

I told Claire about the kids at the pit. We talked as we walked out to his truck, which was parked in the road about fifty yards from the house. Claire had said he wanted to put his rifle away before the sheriff's deputies got there. Save time by avoiding a lot of questions.

As we stood out front, I told him about the high school kids. Kenny, who didn't seem to like me. The other boys, who didn't seem to care one way or the other. The girls, who seemed nice enough but probably had this way of stirring things up.

"If it was them, it didn't take 'em long," Claire said.

"They're not procrastinators."

"If this is their idea of a joke, they're not too sane, either."

"What's the old saying?" I said. "Boys will be homicidal maniacs?"

As we walked back toward the house, one of the college girls came out and walked up to us. She was wearing gym shorts and a sweatshirt that said YALE.

"What was that big boom?" she asked.

"Oh, somebody who forgets that people have to get up in the morning," I said, smiling.

She looked at me quizzically. I supposed I had an obligation to tell her.

"Somebody took a shot at the house," I said.

"With a gun?" she said.

"Either that or a cannon."

"Oh, my god. Was anybody hurt?"

"Not really," I said. "A couple scratches. And of course my belief in the innate goodness of people was tragically shattered."

She got the quizzical look again.

"No, nobody was hurt. Just somebody's idea of a joke, I guess."

"Jeez," she said. "What do they do when they get serious?"

"Good question," I said.

It was fifteen minutes before we heard the rush of tires on pavement and then saw the flashing blue strobe lights of the police cruiser. A quarter-mile down the road, the blues went out and the car slowed. It rolled up to where we stood and stopped. The radio rasped once and the deputy got out warily. He was very big and very young, with a Marine haircut and shoulders that seemed nine feet wide.

"Mr. McMorrow?" he said, approaching us.

"That's me," I said.

"Deputy Franckel. Waldo S.O. You reported a shooting?"

"Right."

"And who are you, sir?" he said to Claire.

"Varney. A neighbor."

"Well, Mr. Varney. I'm going to ask you to—"

"That's OK," I said. "He can show you the buckshot."

Which Claire did. After we showed the deputy the window, the couch covered with glass and splinters. Told him there were just two shots, then the sound of a car or a truck taking off. I briefly told him about the kids at the pit. He said he'd been there many times.

"I'm gonna go see if I can come across them, sir, in case they've been drinking or something and are still out there cruising around," Franckel said. "Also, I'm the only one on patrol in the northern half of the county. What we'll do is notify an investigator from our department. I'd say he'll probably be out in the morning to talk to you and take the report. I could do it but we'd be better off with a cruiser on the road. But I'll try to stay somewhere in this area in case they come by again. You have a place to stay?"

"Right here," I said. "Don't want 'em burning the place down while I'm gone."

"Don't want 'em burning the place down while you're here, either," the deputy said.

I spent the night tossing and turning and listening to the night sounds through the broken window. Claire suggested I put plastic over it to keep the bugs out but I figured any bugs that might stray in would be eaten by the bats. This wasn't a house. It was an ecosystem.

Franckel seemed like he was on top of things, and sure enough, at about quarter to nine the next morning, a brown

Chevy sedan pulled up out front. I wiped the last of the dishes and went to the door. After a minute, I heard the car door slam and steps and then he was there.

"Mr. McMorrow," he said. "I'm Mark Poole. Waldo County Sheriff's Department. I understand you had a little excitement here last night."

"Good thing, too," I said. "There wasn't anything on TV at all."

He was sort of small and maybe even slight, though it was hard to tell because his sport jacket, a bland brownish tweed, was a size too big. He was about my age, with thick straight hair parted on the side, a small sheepish smile, and the general air of a Scout leader or someone who might have come to the door handing out religious tracts. I asked him if he would like a cup of coffee and he said no, why didn't we just go and view the damage.

Poole looked the window over for what seemed like a very long time. He picked at the glass with a pen and another shard fell on to the couch.

"Sorry about that," Poole said.

He took a small black coil-bound notebook out of his jacket pocket and wrote something in it.

"Find a clue?" I asked.

Poole just smiled. Jotted and then put the notebook away.

"I found some buckshot," I said.

"I was gonna say buckshot. Somebody standing maybe twenty or thirty feet away. You said it was two shots?"

"Both barrels."

"You're probably right," Poole said and gave me that small crooked smile again.

"Mr. McMorrow," he said. "Are you employed?"

"I'm a writer," I said. "Used to work for newspapers but now I'm doing freelance writing for magazines."

"There much work in that?"

"Some. You have to look to find it."

"What paper did you work for?"

"Different ones," I said. "*New York Times*, mostly."

"Huh. What magazine do you work for?"

"Right now *New England Look*. I did a story for *Downeast*."

"About what?"

"People who grow flowers," I said.

After each question he smiled and looked at me with mild curiosity. Then he turned and looked around the room. His gaze ran over the shelves of books, the Nikon binoculars. He seemed to pause at the stereo. A very nice digital receiver that cost eight hundred bucks. State-of-the-art speakers. A double-dubbing tape deck. High-end CD player.

Hey, I found myself thinking. So I don't watch TV. Gimme a break.

"You like music," Poole said.

"Jazz," I said. "And lately more and more classical. You?"

"My wife likes country. Kenny Rogers. I don't really know much about it. Whatever station comes in clear in the car is fine with me. When I have some time at home, I take my boys fishing. You fly-fish?"

"No. Never tried it."

He smiled again. Took a couple of steps toward the bookshelf and read some titles.

"OK, Mr. McMorrow. Now tell me about these kids you said you had this problem with. And tell me, how exactly did you come to meet them?"

So I did. I talked and he smiled his Boy Scout smile. He reminded me of a nurse who says, "We're going to have a shot." And as I told the story, from the call from the magazine to my stop at the high school, to Missy Hewett, Kenny and the boys, I had this growing feeling that I wasn't the victim.

I was the suspect.

"This was the first time you met these guys?" Poole asked.

"First time."

"You had no contact with them at all before yesterday?"

"Nope. Had no idea they existed."

"But this one, Kenny, took some sort of dislike to you?"

"It appeared that way."

Poole paused for a moment. Smiled. Walked back toward the window and looked out. My truck was parked out there and he considered it.

"Mr. McMorrow," he said, still looking out. "Did you get any indication that these kids were involved in drugs?"

"Just that the kid said I was a narc. Maybe it was acute paranoia from chronic cocaine use."

Poole turned to me.

"And you don't use drugs?"

"Not since Jimi Hendrix died," I said. "Took all the fun out of it."

"And that was in the seventies, right?" he said, straight-faced.

"It was 1970. But I was only kidding."

"Oh, I see. So you don't use drugs or anything?"

"Me? No. I mean, of course not."

He looked at me and smiled.

I gave Poole two pieces of buckshot, which he stuck in his pants pocket but said there was no way to trace shotgun pellets, not like you can trace a bullet or a cartridge casing. He walked slowly through the house, his eyes running over everything like he was casing the place. At the back window to the deck, he stopped and stared at Millie's sculptures and junk.

"What's all that stuff?" he said.

"Art," I said.

"Oh."

To his credit, he didn't even raise an eyebrow.

"Not mine," I said. "The woman who owns the place is an artist."

"Where is she?"

"Santa Fe, New Mexico. And sometimes New York City."

"What's her name?"

"Millie Tint," I said.

Poole looked at me.

"That's what she goes by," I said. "I don't know her real name."

"Cute," he said.

We shook hands and he said he'd be in touch and to give him a call if I thought of anything that might be useful. Poole left and I watched him from the doorway as he paused by my truck, took out his notebook, and wrote down my license plate number.

"You forgot to take my fingerprints," I said to myself.

Poole backed his cruiser into the driveway and headed out the way he came. As he went by he nodded. And smiled.

Twelve

It got warm that afternoon and the bugs were out for an Indian summer fling, having such a good time that I decided I'd get new windows.

To hell with the ecosystem.

I measured the old ones and drove to the building supply store on Route 1 in Belfast where a very earnest kid on commission tried to sell me some sort of double-paned, super-insulated window, the glass for which was probably developed by the space program.

"I don't think so," I said. "I just need windows. You know, to keep the rain out."

"That's the Dark Ages," the kid said.

"I have deep Celtic roots," I said.

He looked at me blankly.

But I got my windows, unpainted frames and all. They were packed in wooden crates which the kid helped me place carefully in the back of the truck. I got them home in one piece, carried them in, and considered calling Claire for help but decided to tough it out. I almost reconsidered when, trying to get the old windows out, I found Millie had nailed them in with what appeared to be railroad spikes. It took a hammer and a crowbar and more than an hour to pry them loose, which left a gaping hole in the wall just as the light was fading to dusk. As gnats and moths streamed in like refugees seeking political asylum, I lifted one of the new windows into the hole, holding it up with one hand while I reached for the wooden strips that would keep it in place. It was a stretch and I had just about reached one . . .

When the phone rang.

"Damn," I said.

I grabbed a nail and drove it into the frame to keep the new window from falling, then sprinted to the kitchen.

"Yes," I said.

There was a moment of silence, then a hesitant "hello."

A girl's voice.

"Hello," I said.

"Um," she said. "Is this Jack?"

"Yeah," I said. "Who's this?"

"Oh, well, this is Belinda? From the school. You know. And the pit?"

"Right. How are you?"

"Oh, I'm good. I mean, I was just calling to say, like, I don't know, that the guys at the pit didn't mean nothin'."

"Oh?"

"Yeah, like Kenny. He's just like that. He gives everybody a hard time. I felt, I mean, we all felt bad."

"Don't worry about it," I said.

"Yeah, well, we felt bad, we really did. I mean, Kenny was being a real dink but he can be that way. But sometimes he's this really good guy."

"I'm sure."

"I mean, I think maybe he thought, like, you were hitting on us. And he's, like, goin' out with Dulcy. Well, not really goin' out. They used to but then she found out he was with other girls and they had, like, this big fight and stuff. Now they don't fight or anything but he still really likes her."

"Deep down," I said.

"Yeah. So I think when he saw you, he, like, freaked. And we felt bad. We really did. We were talking about it after and we were like, 'Jeez, Kenny, What is your problem? The guy's just trying to do this, like, article and you're all over him.' We gave him a real hard time."

"What did he say?"

"Oh, he was all pissed off. Saying you was a cop and he could tell and all this. You were undercover and all this and we're like, 'Kenny. Where do you get these ideas?' Even Scott, he was the really big guy, he was, like, 'Kenny. Calm yourself down.'"

"So did he calm down?"

"Well, sort of but not really. I think when Dulcy started saying this stuff, like you were a nice guy and all that, it just got him more pissed off, because it was Dulcy and he still has this, like, thing for her but she doesn't have anything for him."

"So what's with this narc stuff? Is he some kind of big drug dealer or something?"

"Oh, no, but Kenny . . . You gotta know Kenny. He hangs around with these kids in Belfast and they're, like, druggies but he isn't. But he talks that way 'cause he's with them and they're, like, 'Everybody's a narc, man.' But some of them got busted for selling all this coke and acid last summer and a couple of 'em are eighteen so they're gonna go to the Correctional Center. They got their pictures in the paper and everything."

"And everything, huh?" I said. "Listen, Belinda, do these guys use guns? You know, to scare people?"

"Maybe, I guess. But they're not gonna, like, shoot somebody or anything."

"No, of course not. I don't know what made me think that."

"Yeah, well those guys are pretty crazy but mostly it's drugs. Now everybody's scared, you know? I mean, who wants to go to jail for, like, months and months?"

"Not me," I said.

"Me neither," Belinda said.

She paused. I didn't say anything.

"Hey, well, I don't know if you care about this, but you were asking about babies and Missy Hewett and all that?"

"Uh-huh."

"I know this other girl."

"Yeah."

"She had a baby and gave it up, too. I don't know if she'd talk to you."

"She still around here?"

"Oh, yeah. She's living with her folks. She quit school."

"How long ago did she do this? The baby I mean."

"I don't know," Belinda said. "Maybe a year. Maybe a little more."

"What's her name?"

"Tracy. Tracy Crown."

"She a friend of yours, Belinda?"

"Well, I know her pretty good. We didn't, like, hang out, but I used to talk to her in school. When she was pregnant, she used to bum cigarettes from me. I even told her it wasn't good for the baby, 'cause the smoke goes right to the baby, too, but she said, 'Come on, it's only one.'"

"One baby?"

"One cigarette. So I'd give her one but I never really liked it."

I thought for a second.

"Listen, Belinda. You think you could do me a favor? You think you could call Tracy and tell her I'm OK and all that and see if she'd talk to me? It might be better than if I just go knock on her door out of the blue."

"Oh, yeah. I mean, I guess so. Like, what would I say?"

"Just tell her I'm doing this story and you thought of her and I'm just talking to some people and if she didn't mind, you'd mention her to me."

"Okay. I mean, I guess."

"It would be a big help."

"Okay. I'll call her right now."

"Call me back?" I asked.

"Yeah, okay. Sure."

And she did. Ten minutes later, when the window was again leaning precariously. I propped it up and prayed.

"She'll talk to you," Belinda said. "I mean, she wasn't, like, thrilled about the idea. I think she thought she owed me one 'cause I was really nice to her when she was pregnant and some kids weren't. They like talked behind her back and stuff."

"About her having a baby?"

"Well, yeah. And then about giving it away."

"That's her business."

"Yeah, well, not around here. Sometimes everything is everybody's business, you know what I mean? It gets to you."

"I'm sure."

We talked a little longer. Belinda gave me directions which were somewhat vague. I thanked her and was ready to hang up but she hung on, as if there was something else she wanted to say.

"So I'll stop and see her," I said.

"Okay," Belinda said. "So I guess I'll see you around."

"I'll be around."

She hesitated.

"That would be good, 'cause I'd like to see you again," she blurted.

"Oh," I said. "Sure."

"Would you like to see me?"

Oh, no, I thought.

"Uh-huh," I said. "You've been a lot of help and I appreciate it. I do."

"I can be more help than that."

Whoah, I thought.

"Yeah, well, thanks," I fumbled. "I'm sure I'll see you around."

"We'll make a point of it, Jack," Belinda said. "Bye bye."

I hung up and let out a long exhale of relief.

"Where do they get these kids?" I said. "And where were they when I was eighteen?"

The next morning the window was finished and I was back in the saddle early. Can't let a couple of shotgun blasts slow you down, I thought, pulling out of the driveway and bumping my way up the road. Of course, one or two more might give me pause.

Tracy Crown's house was on Knox Ridge, where I sometimes drove just to take in the view that rolled away far to the east. The hills undulated all the way to the coast, like a vast rumpled blanket that changed color with the seasons. In the summer, it was a thousand shades of green but now the green was tinged with pale yellows of birches and poplars and, in the coming weeks, the blanket would change into a patchwork quilt of red and orange and yellow on a background of dark spruce green. I suspected it was vistas like this that had kept these ridges and hollows populated over the years. How many farmers and homesteaders of the last century, on the verge of giving up their dream of independence and retreating to a town or city, had pulled their wagons over to the side of the trail, looked out over the rippling ridges and hills, and been filled with the strength that comes from being in proximity of anything of great beauty?

When I had climbed to the high point on the ridge, I pulled the truck over myself and watched balls of big puffy cumulus clouds far to the east. I imagined them far out over Belfast Bay, where seabirds rocked on the swells and bell buoys gonged but there was no one to hear them. I thought about that for a few minutes, and then, my spirit recharged, I pulled myself away and went to work.

Belinda had said the Crowns' house was blue, on the left as you drove out from Prosperity. It turned out to be green, a small single-story ranch house tucked into a stand of oaks, but finding it was no problem because the name was on the mailbox by the road in those black and gold letters you buy at the hardware store. I parked out front and looked the place over as I crammed a notebook in the pocket of my hunting jacket. In the gravel driveway, there was a gold Toyota and an old red one-ton Ford truck with a stake body. In the back of the truck were gas cans and two chainsaws.

Oh, great, I thought. Her daddy works in the woods.

I took a deep breath and tried to get pumped up. In New York, the equivalent to this had been a ten-story building in a project, unlit stairwells littered with broken crack vials, the smell of urine everywhere. A different world but the jitters I felt then and now were the same.

It looked like they used the side door, so that's where I headed. As I approached the steps, I noticed a loop of dog chain that snaked its way toward the backyard. I stopped. Took another couple of steps. Heard the chain rattle and then a low woof and the chain whipped around the corner of the house and disappeared. I took another step and the dog end of the chain came around the corner, pulled up short and then, to my relief, started barking in place, loud and belligerent and harmless.

The dog was an old barrel-chested beagle with a white

snout and rheumy eyes. As he bounced up and down on his arthritic legs there were footsteps from in the house and then a gray-haired woman pushed the aluminum storm door open and screamed even louder than the dog, "Shaddup!"

He did. Instantly. In the silent vacuum that followed, the woman and I eyed each other for a moment.

"Hi," I said. "I'm Jack McMorrow. Is Tracy home?"

The woman, short and solid and maybe fifty-five, looked at me warily. From inside the house, I could hear the applause from a television game show.

"Yup," the woman said, and slowly turned away. As I waited, the dog and I stared at each other. He probably was wondering how long that "shaddup" was in effect and so was I. The dog risked a low growl but then Tracy came to the door and he gave up and went back around the corner.

We both said hello but I smiled and she didn't. She was chunky and somewhat plain, with a wide face and big eyes and a placid expression. As I gave my pitch, she stood on the landing by the door with her hands in the front pocket of her sweatshirt and I stood two steps down.

I told her about the magazine and tried to give the best public-service slant to the story. As I talked, I tried to read her expression but it was blank. I wasn't sure I'd reached her when she interrupted.

"So what do you need from me?"

"I just wondered if you could tell me what you went through."

Tracy shrugged. Inside the house, the game-show audience still was laughing. I took it we were not going in for coffee and Danish.

"What did I go through?" Tracy repeated. "What does anybody go through? You have a baby, you know? It's not a day at the beach. What can I tell you?"

"And you gave the baby up?"

She stared away for a moment and her expression hardened.

"Yup."

"Was that hard?"

"It wasn't a friggin' picnic."

"I'm sure," I said. "A tough decision to arrive at?"

"Yup."

"What were the biggest reasons for going that route? If you don't mind my asking."

Tracy thought for a minute. Her lips were pressed and thin. Something clattered inside the house.

"The baby's future. My future. It was best for both of us."

"How was that?"

"I could keep her and stay here and she could grow up and get pregnant and have a baby and that baby could stay here and have a baby and on and on. It's like a cycle, you know? A dead end."

"So this way you both get a chance to break it?"

"She's out. The baby. She broke it right off. Clean."

"What about you?"

"I want to go to school to be a physical therapist. Miss Genest says I could make fifteen bucks an hour. Get a job anywhere in the country. My aunt lives in Florida. Right near Orlando. She said I could come live with her. There's jobs all over the place down there."

"You don't want to stay here?"

"There's nothing here," Tracy said. "Nothing. I mean, what am I gonna do? Hang out with these kids for the rest of my life?"

"So your baby didn't stay here?"

She looked away again.

"Oh, she's fine. She's got a great situation. She'll get to go to college. Be a lawyer or something."

"You know where she is?"

She looked uncomfortable for a second.

"Pretty much. But I don't need to know, really. She's got a mom and dad, a big house."

"Did you meet the parents?"

"Didn't want to. Better that way. You'd have to go through it to understand."

"No, I think I understand," I said.

"I doubt it," Tracy said.

I paused as a feed truck rumbled by.

"So how did you arrange the adoption? Did you go through an agency or something?"

"It was all taken care of."

"Well, what do you have to do? I mean if somebody else wanted to do the same thing?"

Tracy looked away from me, her hands still stuffed in her pockets.

"It's just taken care of," she said woodenly. "You just have the baby and that's it. Hey, I gotta go."

She turned to the door.

"Can I call you if I have more questions?" I asked.

"Nothing more to tell," Tracy said, and disappeared inside, the door clattering shut behind her.

"I guess not," I said.

The dog came around the corner again as I turned and walked toward the truck. I'd gone a few steps when I heard the front door of the house open and a man came out. He was in his fifties, dressed in green work clothes. We walked parallel for a few yards and met at the truck.

"Jack McMorrow," I said.

I held out my hand. He shook it with a big hard hand with skin like bark. He didn't tell me his name.

"I'm the girl's father," he said. "This was awful hard on her, this whole thing with the baby. I can tell you we wanted her to keep it. Her mother could have looked after it when she was in school. We told her that. Our grandchild, you understand."

"I understand."

"The boy, he would've kept it, too. Just a kid but what the heck. That's something, right? Well, she was bound and determined, come hell or high water, she was gonna give this baby up. I don't know where she was getting this idea but she was getting it someplace."

"What'd she say to the father?"

"First she tells him it's none of his business. Then she says she doesn't think he's the father. There's this older man. The mystery man, I called him. Hell, there wasn't nobody else. There was just him. Ought never to have happened but it did."

"Who was the kid?"

"Well, you didn't hear it from me but his name is James Cowett. Jimmy Cowett. He even said, well, he wasn't gonna let this baby go and he was gonna find it and take it back. Nice enough kid. I felt bad for him. He was over here one day and they had one rip-roaring fight over the whole thing and we ain't seen him since. The girl says he left town."

"How old a kid is he?"

"Nineteen, I think. A year out of school. Was working at this mobile home place on Route 1. Setting them up for people. Nice kid. They coulda worked things out. But she got this idea someplace. The baby's future and all. She was talkin' like somebody got to her."

"You don't know who?"

"Not a clue," he said, standing there at the end of the driveway. "We don't know nothin' about nothin' is what it comes to. And I don't think that's right. That's our grandchild and we didn't give it up. We should have some rights."

I nodded.

"So you can look into this stuff, can't you? The old lady said you were some kind of writer. Well, I'd like to know what our rights are, if you could find that out."

"I can try."

"Good enough," he said.

He turned to the house then turned back to me.

"Listen, we weren't included in any of this adoption

crap. Ask the girl about it, she just walks away. Something ain't right."

"You don't think so?"

"The girl never went to court, that I know of. She just went to the hospital with her belly out to here and came home empty-handed. I saw on television this show, and most of it's made up, I know, but it was about adoption and the new parents and how they wait for friggin' five years and pay umpteen thousand dollars to get a white baby with nothin' wrong with it. They got these books with pictures of the parents and these girls go through and pick them out, meet with them and stuff. The girl never did any of that. She just left one day and came home a couple days later."

"Does seem a little funny," I said.

"Well, you find out what you can. And do it quiet like. I'll make it worth your while."

"That's okay. You don't have to—"

"No, I'll take care of it. This has been real hard on the girl, I'll tell you. It's been six months and she won't talk about it. I mean, she'll talk about the baby, that it's gonna be all right and all that, but she won't say how it came about. I mean, nothing. Not a word."

He turned to the house then back to me. Looked me in the eyes with the equivalent of a gentleman's handshake. I looked back and he nodded and walked back across the scrubby grass to the door. He was already inside as I got in the truck. I drove a mile down the road, pulled over, and took the notebook from my pocket and wrote down everything I could remember of the conversations with Tracy and her father.

"You have a baby, you know?" I started. "It's not a day at the beach."

Thirteen█

When I got back home, the phone was ringing as I came through the door. It stopped just as I grabbed the receiver, which was about what I expected. I put water on for tea and went out on the deck and waited for it to heat. As soon as I sat down, a huge billowy cloud eased in front of the sun and a chill went through me. I got up and went back inside.

One of those days.

I went over my notes at the kitchen table, then just sat and thought. It was Tracy Crown that bothered me, even more than Kenny or any of those people. There was something about her that was unnatural. Repressed. Maybe she just wasn't going to expose her feelings to me, but there was something about her that was brainwashed. Be a physical therapist. Work near Disneyworld or wherever the hell it was she wanted to go. I supposed she had more options than if she was sitting home with a baby, but it wasn't a small price to pay. Shouldn't she be feeling something? If she was, maybe she needed some kind of counseling to help her get it out in the open.

Thank you, Dr. McMorrow.

The kettle whistled and I got up from the table. As I reached for the kettle the phone rang again. I grabbed it.

"Jack, you old dog you," the voice said.

"Dave," I said. "I was thinking of calling you."

"Why, you need bail money?"

"What?" I said.

"Jack, I don't know what you're up to, but I thought I'd let you know that we got this call from some deputy sheriff up there."

Oh, great, I thought.

"Was the guy's name Poole?"

"Yeah, that was it. He called this morning. It was kinda funny. I'm sitting at my desk, trying to decide whether to go out for a bagel or go out for a muffin, and the phone rings on Tina's desk. Tina works here, too."

"Uh-huh."

"So I hear Tina, she does design for us, she's saying, 'No, we don't have anyone by that name. No, I've never heard of him. No, I think I would have remembered. Jack McMorrow. No, I don't think so.' "

"Helpful," I said.

"Always," Dave Slocum said. "So I tap her on the shoulder and she covers the phone and I say, 'I know Jack McMorrow. He's from Maine and he's doing a piece for us. Who's asking?' So she puts the phone in my hand, just like that, just hands it over and says, 'Some cop. You talk to him.' "

"So you did and gave me a glowing recommendation?"

"Well, I said you were abiding by the terms of your parole and we all had high hopes that you'd turned your life around."

"Thanks."

"Don't mention it."

"So what'd Poole want?"

"You know him?" Slocum asked.

"Met him last night. I thought I was the crime victim but I could have been mistaken."

"What happened? Somebody poach your pet moose?"

"Sort of. No, it wasn't that big a deal. Just that the people you've got me talking to don't take kindly to the press."

"Even about babies?"

"Doesn't much matter. Some of these guys, you ask them the time and they come out swinging."

"You got beat up?"

"No, nothing like that. I got shot at."

"Jesus," Slocum gasped.

"Had a window blown out of my house. The first drive-by shooting in the history of Waldo County. I was wondering how to write that on my expenses."

"The hell with that. I'd be asking for life insurance."

"Do me a lot of good."

"But think of the security of the people you'll be leaving behind."

"Would be leaving, you mean," I said. "Please, let us not write my obituary too far in advance. So what did Poole ask?"

Slocum paused. I thought I heard him slurp his coffee.

"Well, let's see. He asked if you worked here. I explained about freelancing. He asked how long I'd known you. I said too long. I told him about the *Times*, how you threw your future away to go to some podunk town in upper Saskatchewan. How am I doing so far?"

"Great. He won't arrest me but he'll have me committed."

"We'll all come visit."

"How much do I have to pay you to stay away?" I said.

"Not much. But you know what was funny? This Poole guy, he asks me if you do drugs. If you were into cocaine or that scene."

"You said no."

"I said you were an Eagle Scout."

"Liar."

"With a weakness for English ale."

"No scout's perfect."

I thought for a moment.

"So it was drugs that he wanted to know about?" I asked.

"I'd say so. That seemed to be the direction he was heading. I got the feeling he wanted to know what kind of connections you would have. So what's it all about? If you don't mind my asking."

"I'm not sure. But I think Poole finds it hard to believe that my interest in these high-school-age kids is confined to a magazine story. He probably thought I made the whole thing up. That I'm dealing cocaine. When he was here, I got the feeling he was trying to figure out what I did for a living."

"Reasonable question. And when you told him you were a journalist, he slapped the cuffs on."

"No, he didn't even blink. The guy's kind of inscrutable, actually."

"Seemed like a nice enough chap," Slocum said. "Not enough to crack this hardened witness, but I must admit that he was polite and pleasant, in a quiet sort of way."

"But thorough."

"Yeah," Slocum said. "Quiet and unrelenting."

"Great," I said.

That afternoon I heard from a personnel person at the *Times*, Regina something, whom I'd known a little bit. Regina had read about the irises, called the magazine for my whereabouts, and rung me up to let me know she'd heard in the halls that some cop from New Hampshire or someplace had called about Jack McMorrow. The water-cooler speculation was that I was in some sort of serious trouble. Either that or I'd been in a bad accident. I didn't tell her it was a little of both. In fact, I didn't tell her anything. I was sure that when she hung up the phone she would immediately convey to my former colleagues at that giant news mill that I hadn't been in an accident.

So it had to be serious trouble.

And what had I done?

The more I thought about it, the more annoyed I became. Some idiot blows the windows out of my house with a shotgun and a detective calls all over hell-and-gone asking questions about my character. If I'd been killed, would they have asked the same questions? Probably more. After all, you can't slander a dead man.

I'd never been in this position before. Even in Androscoggin, when one of the guys on my staff actually had been murdered, I never felt like I was at all a suspect. In fact, I'd had to push the cops over there to get off their duffs. But then, Investigator Poole didn't work in Androscoggin County.

So what should I do? Call the guy up and proclaim my innocence? Leave the guy to pull out his high school Hamlet: "He doth protest too much, methinks."

Well, I doth think I was getting smeared, that was for sure. No matter how discreet this guy tried to be, every inquiry raised suspicion. Some detective calling from out of state? Asking if I had connections to the drug trade? Come on. What were they going to think? That it was a routine background check for the Rotary Club?

The more I thought about it, the more outrageous it seemed. Was the guy going after Kenny and his buddies or was he spending all his time sifting through my résumé? Was it the BMW in my driveway that raised his suspicions? Or my cellular phone, Rottweiler, and machine guns? Good thing Poole didn't see the bats. He'd be calling around to see how long I'd been practicing black magic.

I picked up the phone and put it back down. Picked it up again. Put it down and stood there with my hand on the receiver. Threaten to sue him? Tell him to worry less about me and more about the guys who took target practice in my front yard? Tell him I wasn't any more a drug dealer than I was Al Capone? Or was I losing perspective on the whole thing?

Grabbing a six-pack of Budweiser bottles from the fridge, I went off to find some.

Perspective, that is.

A walk was always good for the head, so I hoofed it up the road to Claire's. A white cat trotted out from the college girls' yard and entangled itself in my legs. I shooed it back toward their house and told it to stay but it didn't. There was no other sign of life at the girls' house. They'd probably gotten a call from Poole and now they didn't want to be left alone next door to a drug-crazed coke dealer who was always getting into shootouts.

Either that, or they'd be over to make a buy.

Claire's pickup was parked in front of his barn door and the lights were on in the shop. I walked up the drive and saw Mary out in the perennial gardens behind the house. She was cutting off some tall plants and putting them in a garden cart in sheaves. When she saw me, she waved and smiled.

Poole hadn't gotten to her yet.

There was music on in the barn, country western. I stepped past the pickup and in the door and looked for Claire. There was no one in sight and I waited, then heard a clatter in the loft. In a moment, Claire appeared at the top of the loft ladder, some long boards balanced on his shoulder. I put the beer on the workbench and went to the base of the ladder and he handed the boards down to me.

"Got 'em?" Claire said. "Now turn 'em into a jelly cupboard."

"What are you gonna do?"

"I'm gonna supervise. Otherwise you'll cut corners."

"Cut fingers is more like it," I said.

It was woodworking that day, another of Claire's many skills. He had more power tools than a catalogue. A table saw. A band saw. A chop saw and a router. The blades for the table saw were hung on the wall over the bench, round disks with teeth of all shapes and sizes, arranged like big metallic flowers.

Claire had explained to me the differences between them. Plywood blades with fine teeth. A dado blade for cutting grooves. Cross-cut blades for just lopping stuff off. It was all interesting and I'd even helped him out on a couple of occasions when the crudeness of the project suited my modest abilities. But even then, my cuts were always off a sixteenth of an inch. My angles were off by a couple of degrees. If I ever had to give up drug dealing, woodworking probably wouldn't be my next career.

"You just getting started on this one?" I asked as we set the boards on the floor next to the bench.

"Old lady's been after me for months. I figured I better at least scope it out."

"So you don't want a beer, then?"

"Well, Jack," Claire said. "I figure you lugged those things up here for a reason. And I hate to see a man drink alone. Mary can get along without this jelly cupboard for one more day, I suppose."

So I popped open a couple of beers and we leaned against the workbench and sipped. Neither of us said anything for a minute or two.

"You hear about the woman who went down to the corner store?" Claire said.

"Nope," I said.

"She's up by the counter and she sees this barrel of nice red apples. She says to the lady behind the counter, 'Those look good. My husband loves those apples. But do they have any sort of poison sprayed on them?' "

" 'No, they don't,' the lady behind the counter says. 'You'll have to go up to the hardware store and get that yourself.' "

I smiled.

"Yessir," Claire said. "You're gonna do the old boy in, you gotta poison your own apples."

He paused.

"So your buddies with the shotgun getting to you or what?"

"I don't know," I said. "I didn't think so. Even though it isn't my idea of a good time. Getting shot at, I mean."

"Beats getting shot."

"By a long shot," I said.

"You got that right."

Claire sipped his beer. He wasn't a heavy drinker. When he had a beer, he savored it, like a man who knew what it was like to go without.

"No, what's bugging me is this cop."

"The guy who was there when I was?"

"No. The next morning. A detective. Poole. He's jumped right on the case, all right. He's spent the last day calling my former employers to find out if I'm a drug dealer or a cokehead."

"Mustn't have liked your looks," Claire said.

"Either that or the postcards from Colombia on the refrigerator door."

"I think it was that truck you drive."

"Oh, yeah?"

"He probably figures a junk like that has to be some kind of front."

We both sipped.

"I don't know," I said. "It's just pissing me off. Really pissing me off. I came up here because it was either that or drive down to this guy's office and let him have it. I get shot at and he starts investigating me to find out if I'm a criminal. Maybe I'm wrong, but I thought cops were supposed to catch the bad guys."

"He's trying to figure out who that is."

"I'm not riding around with a shotgun across my lap."

"Not yet."

"Maybe I should, but the nuns didn't raise me that way."

"That's your problem. The New Testament. In the good old Old Testament, you would have marched over to this kid's house and blown him away."

"Or his family."

"Right. None of this namby pamby turn-the-other-cheek stuff," Claire said.

"Right," I said. "That's for sissies. What we need to do is turn this town into a war zone."

"Half the world can't be wrong."

Claire leaned back on the bench.

"You know what I think?" he said.

"Nope, but I'm gonna find out."

"I think you should put yourself in this cop's place. You figure he doesn't know you from Adam but he knows this kid is a wise guy. Here you are, this guy who just got here. From New York City, mind you. An evil goddamn place. You're from away, you listen to Beethoven, and you go bird-watching. And who are you having a run-in with? The local bad-ass."

"Not by choice."

"But look at it like this guy Poole would look at it. And remember. This writing stuff to him is just a lot of mumbo jumbo, I would think. The bottom line to this fella is that you don't have a job."

"I'm a struggling writer."

"Well, this ain't Paris, Jack. To him, you're living here with, how do they put it, no source of income. He can't tell where you get your money so he's gonna ask questions."

"How 'bout if I show him the story about the flowers?"

"Then he'll decide you're something else altogether."

"If he hasn't already."

I finished my beer and pulled out two more. Claire still had half of his left. A man of discipline.

"No, I had this sergeant. Dooley his name was. Guy was into war like nobody you ever met before. Not killing people. I mean the thinking part of it. The gray matter. And he used to tell me, before you meet a man in battle, you've got to understand how he thinks. What motivates him. Why does he do what he does? What will he do next?"

"Kind of outdated in the age of laser-guided missiles, isn't it?"

"Well, this was a long time ago," Claire conceded. "But you aren't fighting with laser-guided missiles."

"Not yet."

"And this Poole's job is ninety-nine-percent psychology. Goddamn detective, that's all they do. Try to figure people out. I like that. If I hadn't gone into the military, I would have liked to be a homicide cop. Oh, couldn't I get into that."

"And you'd be calling all over hell to check me out, too, I suppose."

"Hell, yes. I'd know what brand your underwear was, Bones. What you put under your picture in your high school yearbook. How much money you make, how you spend it, and who you spend it with."

Claire spoke like a starving man describing a steak.

"So you'd be worse than Poole," I said.

"You'd better believe it."

"But I didn't do anything wrong."

"So? That don't matter. What matters is you're the unknown quantity, you know what I mean? You're the x in the equation, the missing variable or whatever you want to call it."

"So you're saying the guy's just doing his job."

"Yessir. And you're getting all wound up about it is going to send him the wrong message."

"That I've got something to hide."

"Which you might. I won't know for sure until I complete my investigation."

Claire drained his beer, put the empty bottle on the bench, and reached for another one.

He grinned at me.

"I'd just call this Poole fella up today and say you're ready to sign a confession," he said. "No use prolonging the agony."

"It is a first offense," I said.

"That's what you say. You could've been shot all kinds of times."

"But that was under an alias."

Fourteen

This was getting awfully complicated and I hadn't even started.

I was sitting at the table with my notes and my morning coffee. Outside it was overcast and gray. The same inside, where the beer of the night before was ringing in my head, which already had been buzzing. I scratched my unshaven chin and went down the list.

I had Genest at the high school, who didn't think I should do the story. Missy Hewett in Portland, who had opened her door for me but hardly her soul. Tracy Crown, who was about as helpful as Missy Hewett, only closer. Her dad who wanted a grandchild and whose contribution to my cause was an offer to foot the bill.

But I couldn't leave out Belinda and the Bimbettes, who might steer me to people but couldn't make them talk. Kenny probably could but somehow I didn't think he was itching to do me a favor. Unless the itch was on his trigger finger.

Last but not least, there was Inspector Poole of Scotland Yard, sifting through my background like a raccoon pawing through garbage. And wait until he got to the good stuff.

The fact was I had been shot at before. More than once.

It had been sixty miles west of Prosperity, in Androscoggin, my previous home and place of employment. An old woman in Androscoggin had thought I was trying to destroy her husband and had blown a hole in my bedroom wall. From the inside.

Then one of my friends and colleagues on the little paper there had turned out to be someone else entirely. That "someone else" had tried to shoot me but had missed. And in my spare time, I'd been beaten, threatened, harassed and hounded.

Lots for me and Poole to talk about.

I figured if he'd called the *Times*, he would have called Androscoggin. And the next step would be to call me.

At that moment, as if on cue, the phone rang.

I got up and went to the counter and brought my coffee with me, ready to talk until Poole's little notebook was full and he was scribbling on his pants leg.

"Yeah," I said, a little blustery for his benefit.

"Hello."

It was a woman's voice, young and hesitant.

"I'd like to speak to Mr. Jack McMorrow."

"This is Jack."

"Mr. McMorrow, this is Missy Hewett. Melissa Hewett. You came to Portland to see me?"

"I remember, Missy. How are you?"

"Well . . . Been better, I guess. I was wondering if we could talk. I mean, not over the phone."

"Yeah, sure. I can come down there. Meet for coffee or something."

"Yeah," Missy said. She hesitated for a moment. "Yeah, okay. I hate to have you come all this way but it is kind of important. It's about your story."

"All right. Is there something wrong? You don't sound quite right."

"Oh, no," she said. "I mean, yes, I'm okay. Just a lot of things going on in my head. So, like, when do you think you could come?"

"I'm flexible. When do you want me to come?"

"Well, I've got classes this afternoon. A big lecture tonight. Physiology. How 'bout tomorrow afternoon. My last class is at three, gets out at four-twenty. How 'bout around four-thirty?"

"Okay. Where?"

"Well, you remember where I live?"

"Yup."

"Well, at the corner of the street, Forest Avenue, I mean, if you take a left, there's a doughnut shop just up the street, toward downtown. How 'bout there?"

"Fine. But listen, Missy, could you give me any idea what this is about?"

She didn't answer for a moment.

"Well, I don't—I'm not sure how to say it, but, you should know this hasn't been easy."

"What hasn't?"

"Giving up the baby. Ya know? It's pretty hard when it comes down to it. And I just thought, I don't know, if I was talking to you, they'd maybe listen to me. 'Cause it wouldn't just be me by myself."

"Who?"

"About my baby, I mean," Missy said, her voice tiny and weak. "When I ask if I can have her back."

"You've changed your mind?"

"Yeah. I mean, I don't know. I think so. I think I want her with me. I could do it. I know this girl, she's in one of my classes, she's got a kid. Why can't I have mine?"

"So who's—"

"Hey, I gotta go. There's some guy who's waiting for the phone and he's practically climbing in here with me."

"Tomorrow?"

"Yup."

"Take care of yourself."

"Oh, yeah."

There was a click, then the dial tone.

"Whoah," I said out loud.

So Missy wanted her daughter back. Her hard resolve had melted for some reason. Was it talking to this other girl who seemed to be able to swing both having a baby and a future? And what were the terms of the adoption? Was it one of those open agreements where the natural mother had months to change her mind? Did she have a lawyer? Who was the "they" she had to convince? Did she go through an agency? Which one?

I put the water on for another cup of coffee, and while I waited for the water to boil, I made notes of the conversation. Tried to get every word, hers and mine. When I'd done that I went and stood at the window. Paced a little. Went back to my notes. Over to the stove. Back to the window. This story had just come alive and my whole body was tense, tingling. I felt like I'd just come alive, too.

The water boiled. As I turned off the burner, there was the sound of tires on the gravel out front. I went to the new window and looked out. Came back to the stove and took out another cup. When the knock came at the door, I answered it.

"Hey, come on in," I said. "Can I get you a cup of coffee?"

"Sure," Poole said. "Black's fine."

He was wearing a short khaki jacket instead of the sport coat, but he'd still put on a tie. It made him look like a chemistry teacher or somebody who sold mobile homes. No matter what he did, Poole wouldn't look like a cop.

I leaned against the kitchen table, while he took his coffee and stood by the window to the deck, ten feet away. He remarked again on Millie's sculpture and asked me if people bought it. When I said I assumed so, he just shook his head.

Fools and their money.

"So I've been looking into your incident," Poole said.

"I heard," I said.

"I figured you would. The press sticks together, right?"

"I don't know. I think maybe they were hoping to find out I was in some kind of serious trouble."

"So they could write a story about it," Poole said.

"Something to break up the day."

He sipped his coffee and looked out the window. I looked, too, and saw purple finches and goldfinches in the milkweed at the edge of the yard. If I'd been outside, I would have been able to hear their ticks and warbles. Inside, the silence was getting heavy.

Poole cleared his throat.

"Yeah, well, I hope you know it's nothing personal," he said, still looking away. "Just routine investigation. In my business, and yours, I guess, things often aren't what they seem."

"Never, you mean."

Poole looked at me.

"Never what they seem, I mean," I said.

"Yeah, you're probably right. So you understand. I know all about Kenny and that crowd. I don't know much about you."

"A little more than you did a couple of days ago."

"A little more."

"What else do you want to know?"

Poole walked toward me and put his coffee cup down on the table. It was empty. Did I detect a caffeine problem?

Two could play this game.

"More coffee?" I said.

"Sure," he said.

Refilled, he moved back to the window.

"I did some checking on your background, as you know. Talked to some people who think you fell off the edge of the world or something."

"Their worlds are kind of small."

"Yeah, well, I also talked to a couple of people in Androscoggin, where you worked."

"Uh-huh."

"And I've gotta tell you, Mr. McMorrow. For a newsman, you sure lead an exciting life."

"Those people in New York wouldn't think so."

"I don't know. How many people died in Androscoggin while you were there?"

"Two, if you mean in an untimely way."

"Well, that was quite a case," Poole said. "I read about it but I didn't remember your name from the stories."

"Celebrity is fleeting."

"And you don't mind that."

"I'm not looking for speaking engagements, if that's what you mean."

I poured him another cup.

"So what exactly brought you over to Waldo County, Mr. McMorrow?" Poole asked.

"What brought me here? Oh, I don't know. Let me think for a sec. Get my story right. I don't want you tripping me up."

He looked at me blankly.

"Just kidding. Let's see. Well, first of all, things went to hell in Androscoggin. The scum-sucking bottom-feeder who bought the paper wanted a shopper kind of thing. You know. All ads. Some canned feature crap. It wasn't for me, and besides, working there was pretty tough after everything that happened."

"I can see how it would be."

"Hard to report the news when you are the news. So I had a friend in New York who knew the woman who owns this place. The artist whose work you so admire. She was looking for somebody to live here and I needed a place to live. And some peace and quiet."

"Where's the artist lady?"

"Santa Fe. New Mexico."

"But she doesn't come here?"

"Just in the summers and not for the last two. She's sort of an old hippie, I guess you'd say. I guess there was sort of a hippie community here twenty years ago. That's when she came here."

"Yeah, there used to be a whole bunch of 'em," Poole said. "When we were kids, we used to sneak through the woods and watch the girls skinny-dipping in Unity Pond."

I smiled.

"And they're all gone?"

"Not all," he said. "But now they're older. Kids of their own. It isn't like it was back then."

"No fun to sneak through the woods to watch somebody's grandmother."

"Don't suppose," Poole said.

He put his cup down, empty again. The guy was a caffeine freak in sheep's clothing.

"So if you don't mind, tell me again how you met up with Kenny and those guys," he said, smiling. "And start right at the beginning."

So I did. Dave at the magazine leads to Janice at the high school. Janice at the high school leads to the girls in the parking lot. The girls lead to Missy Hewett and Tracy Crown. The girls in the parking lot also lead to Kenny and the boys. Kenny and the boys lead to Investigator Poole of the Waldo County Sheriff's Department. The hipbone's connected to the thighbone . . .

"And here we are," I said. "One big happy family."

Poole allowed a flicker of a grin.

"So you drove all the way to Portland to talk to this girl at the college?"

"Oh, yeah. It's either that or stay home and make the whole thing up."

"Which you don't do?"

"Not if I can help it."

"She talked to you?"

"Some. She took a little while to get used to the idea. Kind of a personal thing, you know? But there's a knack to getting people to talk, don't you think? Some people have it and some people don't. You must have to have it to do your job."

"You too," Poole said.

"You know, we have a lot in common."

"Except you don't fly-fish."

"And you're fishing right now."

"Maybe," he said, flickering the smile again. "Maybe not."

I put my cup in the sink and leaned back against the counter.

"I know you think I'm some sort of drug dealer or something," I said.

Poole shrugged.

"I don't think things. I rule things out."

"So how do I get you to rule that out? I am what I seem. Really, I am. A newspaper guy who took a detour. The only drugs I do come in sixteen-ounce cans. And I don't sell them to minors. The fact that I was shot at says more about the maniacs around here than about me. I mean, I don't know why they shot at me. You know this kid. Does he do that to everybody who rubs him the wrong way?"

"Kenny's an outlaw," Poole said. "From a long line of outlaws. He's got two older brothers, one in the correctional center in Windham. He broke into something like seventeen camps a couple of winters ago. Got three or four years out of it. Because of his priors."

"What'd the other brother do?"

"He killed a guy. A disagreement over a drug deal. They were selling coke. Pretty big time."

"How'd he kill him?"

"Drove by his trailer and shot him with a shotgun. Through a window."

It was my turn to smile.

"Looking up to your big brother," I said. "That's nice. And they say the family is a dying institution."

Fifteen

I didn't think Poole was convinced.

During the conversation, he'd remained alert, watching for anything that might help fill in the jigsaw puzzle of Jack McMorrow the drug dealer. Even when outwardly he seemed to relax, there still was this underlying and unstated relationship: he was the cop and I was the suspect. Or at least I could be.

After he left, I made breakfast. Cutting a cinnamon-raisin bagel, I wondered what his conclusion had been. Maybe that I'd seemed like a nice enough guy but a big piece of the picture was missing. Here's this guy who was a big-time reporter, for *The New York Times*, mind you. Went to a little paper and found nothing but trouble. Now he's living in a hippie house on a back road in a town where he knows no one, has no family, no woman, no job to speak of, no real connection to anything. He arrives in town and in no time at all he's hanging around with the local outlaws, pissing them—or somebody else—off enough to get a hole blown in the side of his house.

I crammed the bagel in the toaster.

Poole was right. It didn't add up. I could see Poole thinking I had to have a screw loose. A skeleton in the closet or under the bed. Was I running from somebody in New York? Had I been dealing drugs down there? Was I a stashed federal witness? Who was this guy?

If Poole could figure that out, he was a better man than I.

I pried the bagel loose from the toaster, spread it with cream cheese, and brought it over to the table. It looked so good I went back and put another one in to toast. Looked for orange juice but there wasn't any so I had milk instead. I sat down at the table and took a bite, chewing the bagel and mulling the questions that Poole didn't so much ask as imply.

The self-assured, well-adjusted, small-town, fly-fishing son of a bitch.

I sat and ate. Drank my milk. Thought to myself that I really wasn't any different. It was just that I didn't have the *Times* and all of its assumptions to fall back on. When you were there, or anyplace like it, you were part of a bigger picture, a massive machine. You didn't doubt yourself because, after all, you worked for the best newspaper in the world. It was like being on stage in a long-running musical extravaganza. You just sang and danced and got off the stage to make room for the next guy. The play was the thing, as the Bard used to say, and the *Times* was the longest-running show in the world. I left it to go to the weekly, thinking it would be the summer stock of newspapers. A break from the grind. It turned out it was just a different kind of grind. Some nice people, really. A close relationship with a small closed community. Life reduced to this miniature scale that made everything intimate and intense, like a weekend retreat. And in the end, it had gotten so intense that it had blown up. The paper. The people. Roxanne.

Roxanne.

I knew as soon as I thought of her, my mouth full of bagel, that I was going to call her. I would tell myself I wouldn't, I would think of all the reasons I shouldn't, I would try to distract myself with something, everything else, and then I would get her number from the top drawer of the desk in the living room and call her.

So I went through the motions. I told myself she didn't need me, that it was over, that she'd given me my chance to stay with her and I had turned her down. Flat. And even if I did call her, it shouldn't be in angst-ridden doldrums that would just remind her that I could be a real drag and the underwear models she hung out with now could not. That they were sophisticated world travelers who went skiing with royalty and had documentaries done about their outdoor adventures, while my present associates were people whose adventures were documented in the police blotter of small-town papers, if at all.

Ah, but that was part of my charm, n'est-ce pas?

I walked to the desk and rummaged for the piece of paper that had Roxanne's number on it. I found it and remembered it was earlier in Colorado, but on a workday Roxanne should be up, even if she'd been out the night before with Prince Andrew. Assuming she hadn't joined the prince's entourage.

I dialed with a twinge of nervousness, like a junior-high boy calling for his first date. The phone was an old black rotary that torturously prolonged each number. I dialed the last one and waited for the endless clicks and ticks to end. Then the rings began. One, two, three, four—

"Hello," Roxanne said.

"Hi," I said. "How was Prince Andrew?"

*   *   *

It was quarter past eight there and Roxanne said she was getting ready for work.

"I'll let you go," I said.

"No. I've got time. Just close your eyes because I'm getting dressed."

"Thank God for portable phones."

"Makes it a lot easier to get a dress on over your head while you talk," she said.

"Or to take it off."

We both paused.

"Jack, I was just thinking about you. Really. I swear we're telepathically connected."

"Even in our estrangement. Kind of like still getting cable TV after you've stopped paying for it."

"You were the one who pulled the plug."

"I know," I said. "A day that will live in infamy. Has somebody already said that?"

"Yes."

"Story of my life. My best lines come via reincarnation. So what were you thinking about me?"

"That I'd like to see you."

"In the next line at the checkout or up close and personal?"

"I don't know," Roxanne said. "Maybe in the same line at the checkout."

"I'd have difficulty counting my items in your immediate proximity."

"Your items or mine?"

I stopped the patter for a moment and took a long deep breath. I got the feeling she did the same.

"It doesn't take long to go right back to it, does it?" I said.

"No. Not long at all."

"I wonder what that means?"

"I don't know," Roxanne said. "That something's still there, maybe."

"That maybe it never left."

"I left," she said.

"Because I wouldn't go with you."

"Nope. Turned me down flat."

"Must've been the medication. I wasn't thinking straight."

"How are you thinking now?"

"I think maybe my head's starting to clear."

"How would you like a visitor?"

"Don't tell me," I said. "Your grandmother's signed up for one of those foliage tours."

And just like that, Roxanne was back, if not in my bed, then in my head. The truth probably was that she'd never really left, my head that is, and no amount of Budweiser could evict her. Maybe it was just the situation that had separated us. The small world where we'd lived gave her claustrophobia. She had to break loose. I felt it was my duty to stay.

But now she was coming back. Maybe.

Roxanne said she had a social-worker conference to go to in Boston. Three days of name tags and hospitality suites. She left Colorado the next day. She could tack on a few days' vacation time if that seemed like a good idea.

"Maybe we could have some quiet time together," Roxanne said. "Without cops all over the place and people shooting each other and all that craziness. I really think that was the problem. No relationship can flourish in the midst of all that."

"Maybe you're right," I said.

"You know I still love you."

"I do now."

"Do you love me?"

"I haven't strayed far from it."

"Is that a yes, Jack?"

"I think it might be," I said.

"Do you remember how easy it was for us? I was thinking that. Things started out so naturally. We just fell—"

"Into bed."

"Jack. I was going to say into step. But bed, too. Oh, baby, did we ever."

"We didn't fall. We dove. Or is it dived?"

"Dived, I think," she said. "And I haven't forgotten. Not at all. You know, maybe we could make it work if everything around us wasn't turned upside down. Maybe if we were where you are now. I don't know. On a quiet back road, with nobody to bother us."

"Right," I said. "A quiet back road would be nice."

Maybe I could find one.

So Roxanne asked how things were going. I said, "Good," a white lie. Then I told her about the baby story and the mothers old enough to be her little sister. Roxanne said they needed counseling before and after making a decision like that and why didn't the agency help them with that. I said I didn't know, that I hadn't been able to come up with an agency yet. She said it was standard practice because agencies want successful, smooth adoptions, not "birth mothers" who drag the adoptive parents into court, or worse than that, haunt them for months or even years.

"I've got one who seems to be having second thoughts already," I said.

"After how long?"

"A few months, I think. Less than six."

"That's typical. Unless they're adequately prepared for the feelings that follow something like that, and even if they are, they go through a tremendous emotional upheaval. There can be overwhelming feelings of guilt and loss and grieving. In the long run, it can be the right decision for everybody involved, but the girl needs a lot of people propping her up."

"Strange," I said. "This one doesn't seem to have any."

"Maybe she hasn't availed herself of it. Sometimes that's a problem. The birth mother tries to pretend none of it ever happened. Leave it all behind. Of course, it all comes crashing down on her later."

"How do you know so much about this?"

"There's lots of stuff in the literature. There are tons of counselors who specialize in just this sort of postpartem trauma."

"Maybe we should collaborate on this one," I said.

"Maybe we should collaborate on a lot of things."

"Oh, you say that to all the guys."

"No, Jack," Roxanne said. "I don't."

There was more, but probably the conversation could have ended right there. Roxanne talked about how her clients now were mostly well-to-do, even wealthy. In a lot of ways, their kids were more screwed up than the abused kids she'd worked with in the Portland projects. The rich kids were harder to reach, but at the same time didn't have the tough kids' hard outer shell.

And then she talked about her new mountain bike and how I really had to get one, that I'd love it, riding through the woods. I said I wouldn't be able to hear the birds with all that clatter and she said the good bikes were very quiet.

But the whole time, I wasn't listening to her story or even to her words but to her voice. I was thinking how nice it was to be talking to her, easily and quietly, how I'd missed these conversations, how there wasn't anyone else I could just mesh with so easily.

And boy did I want to mesh with her.

Standing there with the phone to my ear, I took a mental cold shower and contemplated an actual one. Into my monastic world, images of Roxanne rushed one after another. Our making love. Roxanne getting undressed. Walking from the shower to the bedroom with a towel around her, complaining that I didn't vacuum and sand stuck to her feet. Roxanne in a dress, crossing her legs on the couch. Kicking off her pumps after getting in from work. Her legs in running shoes and shorts. Her legs wrapped around me. Her eyes looking into mine. Her eyes, mostly worried.

That's the way they'd been most of the time, especially

toward the end. Worried that something was going to happen to me, to us. Worried and then angry, when I wouldn't come with her. When I wouldn't walk away from the situation that surrounded us, a situation a lot like the one I was facing now.

Roxanne still was talking.

"So when will I see you?" I said.

"How's Friday sound?"

"Thursday night."

"I'll be at the Hyatt Regency. In Cambridge. You ought to be able to find that."

"Like a bear finds honey."

"Oh, Lord," Roxanne said. "That place has you talking like Grizzly Adams."

"Drives you crazy, doesn't it?"

Sixteen

Roxanne had asked how things were. I'd said they were good. Now I had three days to make it come true.

I started out by doing the dishes. Sometimes it was the little touches that made all the difference. Or so I hoped. I wiped the counter and the table and swept the floors, preparing for the pitter patter of Roxanne's feet. Then I picked up the piles of newspapers—the *Globe*, the *Times*, the *Waterville Sentinel*, the *Waldo County Independent*—and carried them out to the shed. I did the same with the beer cans, filling a grocery sack. Coming back in, I surveyed the room. I made a neat pile of my books, put my binoculars back in their case, then vacuumed the floor in front of the window that had been shot out.

If I was going to be terrorized, I could at least be neat about it.

I hadn't gotten into that with Roxanne, but I figured I would wait until the right moment. A candlelight dinner. A bottle of Moët-Chandon. Soft music. Roxanne would leave the room to slip into something more comfortable and when she came back and settled into my arms, I'd whisper into her lovely ear: "Do you know that window behind your head was shot out by a shotgun just two days ago?"

"Please," she would say. "Can't it wait until tomorrow?"

Yes, this was going to be difficult to explain, and my fear was it would put us right back where we'd been when Roxanne last left. Things had spun out of control in my life and Roxanne's had been swept into the whirlpool of threats and violence. Her reaction then had been to leave. I wondered if she'd want to get out of Prosperity, too.

Of course, the situation here still was manageable. Kenny, if it was Kenny, was a loose cannon, so to speak, but maybe Poole would do something about that. And the story was moving in all directions but at least it was moving. Things were okay. Just a couple of rough edges, that's all. Roxanne and I would have some time to sort things out. To see if we could start out, not where we left off, but where we were before that. Close and on the verge of getting closer. Of course, if we did, I wouldn't be getting much work done.

Speaking of which, it was time for me to earn my daily beer.

I puttered around the house for a while longer. Stared at my notes. Missy Hewett and Tracy Crown. I thought about the kid, Jimmy Cowett, the father of Crown's baby who didn't want to give the baby up. Did he sign the paternity forms? Was paternity established? Where was he now and how could I find him? And what about Kenny and his brothers in the can? Maybe I should just find Kenny and talk it out.

But I couldn't do any of that milling around the house.

I made lunch: tuna salad on whole wheat with olives, celery, lettuce and tomato from the Varneys' and English hot mustard. I stuck the sandwich in a bag with a banana and, feeling like a kid again, went out the door.

To school.

It was still overcast and gray and a gentle rain had started to fall. There was something tranquil about rain in autumn and I drove slowly up the road. One of the college girls was getting out of her car and she waved and smiled and I waved back. She looked happy and healthy and without a care. She was Missy Hewett's age and she was everything Missy Hewett was not.

It struck me that to be terribly unhappy at eighteen was unnatural and unfortunate, a real tragedy. There was more than enough time for that later.

The truck lurched down the rutted road and I turned on the windshield wipers. They smeared the raindrops across the windshield and turned everything into an Impressionist blur. "La Rue de Dump," by Claude Monet. I lurched to where the pavement began, but still I didn't speed up. I was thinking and the faster one drove, the less clearly one thought. It was one of the things that was wrong with our society. Smoother roads, faster cars, dumber people.

I was thinking about Missy Hewett and her change of heart. Where were the counselors and shrinks that Roxanne had talked about? Had she refused their help? Had it been offered? And what kind of adoption agency did she go through? Was it through the hospital? Who was the "they" she spoke of? Why did she seem so alone?

Something about the situation didn't seem right. Missy seemed so much on her own, this hardened little girl with the weight of the world on her shoulders. Or at least the weight of a baby girl. I wondered if she thought of that at all, that piece of information about a baby to which people seemed to attach so much significance. "She was born at 8:33 A.M. Seven pounds, six ounces." It was pronounced as if it were a mark of character, a clue to the child's future. In

Missy Hewett's case, that future had been placed in some-one else's hands.

It was a noble thing to do, a tremendous sacrifice, but I wondered if it wasn't so unselfish as to be unnatural. It would take a very strong person to give a baby up and then just go on. Either very strong or very cold and I didn't get the impression that Missy Hewett, underneath her emotion-less exterior, was either.

Before we met I wanted to get a better feel for her, to know more about the circumstances that had led her to col-lege and Portland. She had enough drive to push herself that far. Where did it come from? Family? School? If it were friends, where were they now that she needed them? Why would she call me?

I drove through the village mulling it all over. There were a couple of cars and a truck parked in front of the post office. An old man who looked familiar was standing by the door of the truck. When I drove by, he waved, a reflex action that probably dated back decades, to the days when to live in this town was to be a part of a fraternity of farm-ers and woodsmen. If they wanted to invite me, I'd be glad to join.

From there, I drove out of town to the east. The roads were empty and black and glistened in the rain. I drove out to the big brick school and pulled in the drive. The rain had picked up and the parking lot was deserted. With Kenny and friends in the back of my mind, I parked the truck close to the building and walked down the wide sidewalk to a side entrance. There was someone standing just outside the brown metal doors, hunched in the rain, hurrying through a cigarette. At first I thought it was a student, but when I got closer I saw that it was a woman, maybe a teacher. When I got within thirty feet or so, she dropped the cigarette and hurried inside.

She didn't hold the door for me.

I followed the woman inside. Like the roads, the corridor was empty, too. I walked along, glancing through the classroom doors that passed like frames on film. A teacher, a man in bow tie and suspenders, speaking French loudly and slowly. "Je m'appelle Monsieur Elliott. Et vous?" An unseen woman calling out sharply: "Mr. Smith. Do you mind?" A big, sloppy boy in gigantic sneakers writing something on a blackboard: "Plato. The cave. Reality . . ."

That corridor ended and I turned a corner and came into the atrium near the office and the main entrance. There were three or four kids huddled forlornly near the front doors, like homeless people in an office-building lobby. They stared out at the rain as I hurried by the office, not wanting to risk another encounter with the principal's phalanx of secretarial security police. They were busy, probably interrogating some unfortunate student about a suspect sick note. I couldn't hear the screams but I suspected they were using the soundproof room.

Down the hall and around the corner to the right was the guidance office. I went in and stopped in front of the secretary's desk. Her red glasses were unfolded on a folder and there was a new poster on the wall: "Happiness is a habit. Practice happy attitudes, become a happy person." This credo was accompanied by a photograph of a kitten.

Funny. I'd never thought of cats as happy.

I waited five seconds and then went to Janice Genest's office door and looked in. She wasn't there. I stood for a moment. They were lucky I was an honest person. I could have pilfered the place of paper clips. Instead, I stood a little longer, then went into Genest's office and sat down in a chair. There was a brochure on the corner of her desk and I picked it up. It was about the dangers of deliberately inhaling fumes from aerosol cans. No kidding. Did these kids need to be told not to walk blindfolded on I-95 at night, too?

A buzzer sounded in the corridor and the express-train roar started to build in the distance. Doors opened and slammed shut like it was a school possessed. The secretary came in and just as quickly left. There were footsteps and then Genest came in, saw me, and pulled up short.

"The door was open," I said. "I was just reading about why I shouldn't spray air freshener into my mouth."

"Causes brain damage," she said, walking around the desk and standing by her chair. "I've got three guys right now who used the stuff. While it's scrambling your brains, it causes hallucinations and some sort of euphoria. For that, they've significantly reduced their chances of being Rhodes Scholars."

"Which weren't great to begin with?"

"It wasn't a sure thing, if that's what you mean."

"What ever happened to beer?" I said.

"Shows up on your urine test when you're on probation. There's no test for air freshener."

"Who would have thought there'd have to be?"

Genest shrugged.

"You'd be amazed," she said. "Kids have an endless capacity for self-destruction."

"They come by it honestly."

Genest looked up and sniffed.

"True," she said.

She was opening what appeared to be her mail. I watched her for a moment and decided she was more attractive than I remembered, with that thick hair and high cheekbones, and maybe not as prickly. Maybe she was warming up to me.

"So how's your story coming?" she said. "Saved the world yet?"

"It's coming. And no, I guess I haven't. How 'bout you?"

"Nope. But some days we can take it off life support."

"About all you can ask, right?"

"I guess."

She tossed a stack of envelopes and papers into the trash. I was pleased to see we used the same filing system.

"I wanted to ask you about a student. An ex-student, actually. Missy Hewett."

Genest looked at me.

"I know Missy," she said.

"She had a baby," I said.

Genest looked up.

"I know that, too," she said.

"And she gave it up for adoption."

Genest didn't respond.

"You don't have to worry about confidentiality or anything," I said. "This is off the record. Background. Because I already talked to her and she told me about most of it. The baby. The adoption. The missing daddy."

"He did her a favor."

"Sounds like it. But she seems like such a levelheaded kid. Nice kid. How do they end up with these guys who turn out to be so worthless?"

"They're seventeen," Genest said. "Everything's young in them but their hormones."

"But she doesn't seem young."

Genest came around the desk and walked over and shut the door. I waited for her to come back and sit down. Instead she came over and faced me.

"Missy Hewett is one of the strongest kids I've known," she said vehemently. "She has this inner strength. She's had to have it, the way she's grown up."

"How has she grown up?"

"With everything going against her. She's—and this is off the record, right?"

I nodded.

"She's the youngest. Has two older sisters. Both of them got pregnant and dropped out of high school. Pammy, I think that's the oldest one, I don't think she finished ninth grade. They had their babies, got their state checks, and that's been their life ever since."

"What about her parents?"

"Lived with her mother. Father, I think she told me he

left them when she was seven or eight. He drove a truck and ran off with some woman from Connecticut. A waitress or something. He moved down there and left Missy's mom with the three girls. The mother did the logical thing, which was to start drinking, go on the state, and take her unhappiness out on her kids. Missy did not have a happy childhood."

I remembered her. How she said the father of her child was a chromosome or something like that.

"I got that impression," I said. "She has this hard shell. I don't know. This grimness to her."

"What do you expect, McMorrow? I don't think there was much to laugh about in her life."

"Was she like that here?"

"Pretty much. Kind of quiet. Didn't act silly like the rest of the kids. It was like the silly had been beaten out of her somehow."

"Literally?"

"I don't know. If not literally, then figuratively. You don't have to hit a kid to wound him."

"Or her."

"Or her," Genest said.

"But Missy Hewett came through it somehow. How'd she end up in college? I mean, it doesn't seem like that would have been—"

"A likely destination? No, I guess not."

"But you got her there?"

Genest paused for a moment. Looked away. When she looked back, her eyes were brighter, almost glowing.

"We got her there," she said, that same resolve creeping back into her voice. "Well, she got herself there, really. I just gave her a push here, a pull there. When she needed it. It wasn't all that much. She's a very tough kid. Very determined."

"Where does that determination come from, do you think? She wasn't getting it at home, was she?"

Genest snorted.

"Are you kidding? All she had at home was her mother, who was drunk most of the time, and the succession of drunks her mother brought home. I guess the mom was kind of a barfly. Made the bottle club circuit. Kind of sad, really. From what Missy said, she didn't stop trying to find somebody. Of course, the guys she ended up with were the worst thing for her."

"So what about Missy?"

Genest got up from her chair. If she'd smoked, she would have lighted a cigarette.

"Missy is one of those kids that make me think who we are is something genetic. Or just something you're born with. Something that comes out of nowhere."

"The piano prodigy with the tone deaf parents?"

"Who hate music," she said. "Some kids are just born different from their families. Some, not all, of those kids manage to pull it off. Missy is one of them."

"Is she smart?"

"Fairly. No genius. But she has this determination. A lot of guts. She got A's because she had decided she was going to get A's. I remember she started to have some trouble in math and I got her some tutoring here at school. She asked me for it. Most kids, it's the parents who want the tutoring. You know, so they don't flunk and get kicked off the basketball team. Missy asked for the tutoring because she was afraid she was going to get a B."

I thought for a second.

"And then she got pregnant?"

"Hmmm."

"Not on the program?"

"Nope. I don't know how it happened. I guess everybody needs somebody to be close to and Missy didn't have anybody else. So she started dating this guy."

"Not a good kid?"

Genest looked right at me before answering.

"Off the record, right? All of this?"

"Yup."

"I don't know who the dad was," she said. "She never told me his name."

"A mystery man."

"A coward." Genest sniffed.

"What did he think of her giving up the baby?"

"I don't know. She never told me. We talked about her options, about what she wanted to do with her life. Which was basically to make one for herself. She'd worked so hard for so long, it would've been a shame to just throw it all away."

"And end up like her sisters, you mean?"

"Like her sisters. Except for Missy, it would have been worse. Because she isn't like her sisters. Sitting at home with a baby at seventeen would be like a jail for Missy. She is just driven to make something of herself."

"To be a nurse," I said.

"Four years of college, have a career. And then if she meets somebody, you know, ten years from now, then that would be the right thing. For her to just throw it all away would have been a terrible tragedy, for her and her baby. It was a tough decision but I think Missy showed a lot of courage. Tremendous courage, really. And in the end, she made the right decision."

"Then I'm not sure how this fits in," I said. "But she called me this morning. She wants her baby back."

Seventeen

Genest had looked stunned for a moment. Then deeply disappointed. I'd told her I thought it was because Missy was in school with these older students with children.

Maybe that had given her the idea that she could have her career cake and baby food, too.

"Oh, the poor kid," Genest had said. "She's going to go through it all over again."

"Through what?" I'd said.

And then the bell had rung, the hordes had been unleashed and I'd never gotten an answer.

I thought about it as I drove back toward Prosperity village on my way to Missy Hewett's mom's house, at least in the direction of the road listed under her name in the Waldo High yearbook in the school library. Nobody had asked who the old guy was poking around the shelves. At thirty-five, I could have been mistaken for some kid's grandfather.

When I reached the village, I pulled over in front of the Prosperity General Store, left the truck running, and went in. It was a little after one o'clock and the place was deserted, the chairs out back by the coffeepot empty. I stood by the counter for a minute, tapped it with a stick of homemade beef jerky from the big glass jar. Nobody ever bought any of it but the stuff never went bad.

The perfect product.

Finally, I heard the sound of a toilet flushing and water running. The bathroom door opened and Mary the cashier came back to the counter. I popped the jerky back in the jar.

"What can I do you for, Mr. McMorrow?" Mary asked, adjusting her store jacket.

She smiled. I smiled back. She was friendly and motherly and steady as a rock. I liked her.

"I need directions, Mary," I said. "You know where the Hewetts live?"

"Joyce Hewett?" she said.

"That Missy's mother?"

"Yup, if you can call her that," Mary said, her voice dropping. "She never lifted a finger for those kids. Once Bobby left, she just crawled in a bottle. Kids had it tough. Oh, yeah. I went to school with her oldest sister. Marlene.

They were Rollinses back then. Very pretty girls, too. Shows what drinking can do to you. What're you going up there for?"

I thought for a second.

"I met Missy," I said. "I just wanted to talk to the mother."

"That the one in Portland or someplace?"

"Yeah. She's in school."

"Best thing she ever did, getting away from that bunch. If she's smart, she'll stay away. Those kids had to raise themselves. You'll figure it out when you meet old Joyce."

"And how do I get there?"

Mary's directions were simple. Out to the South Pond Road, fifth place in on the left. An old trailer up a little way from the road. If I came to a big new log house, set up on a hill, some college professor's place, I'd gone too far.

I did go too far, turned around in the professor's driveway, and stirred up the two white Samoyeds in the chain-link kennel by his garage. Somebody had to be the highlight of their day.

The Hewett trailer sat perpendicular to the road at the end of a long rutted gravel driveway. At the road end of the driveway, the Hewett mailbox had been tied upside down to its wooden post with twine. I drove past it and rolled the truck slowly up the drive.

I parked beside a Chevy sedan, an old one. Stuck in the brush next to it was another old Chevy, identical to the first except the first one was maroon and the second one was a faded, rusting red. The two tires I could see were flat. The hood had been removed and was leaning against the trunk of a spruce. Someone had spread a blue plastic tarp over the engine compartment, but the tarp had come loose and you could see the open carburetor on top of the motor.

Unless Joyce Hewett was a mechanic, she'd had some help. And it looked like the help had taken an extended vacation. Probably the story of her life.

I got out of the truck and walked to the steps. They were

under a green plastic canopy which was blanketed with pine needles. I went up the steps and stopped. There was an empty vodka bottle in the corner of the entry. A crushed plastic milk jug. A black plastic bag ripped open by an animal that had pulled out some of the trash inside.

An empty cigarette pack. An empty can of tomato sauce. One of those white foam trays that meat comes on. The tray was stained dark brown with blood and it had been chewed.

From inside came the sound of television. Voices from a talk show. A clink of dishes. I hesitated, then knocked on the metal storm door three times. There was no knock, just a loose jangling rattle.

After a minute, there was a flash of movement behind the door, which then swung open.

A woman peered out, squinting at the light. She was forty-five, maybe a year or two older, with dyed blonde hair pulled back from her face. She was wearing jeans and a tight sort of sweater thing with flowers on the front. The jeans were tight, too. Her face was sort of pretty but her skin was mottled. She pushed the storm door open and stared.

"Mrs. Hewett?"

"What do you want?" she said.

I smiled into her expressionless face.

"I'm Jack McMorrow. I live in town and I met your daughter. Missy."

She still stared.

"Could I talk to you for a minute?"

"About Missy?"

"Yeah."

"She in trouble or something?"

I thought for a second.

"No, not really. I just had a couple of questions about her. I'm a reporter."

Joyce Hewett looked at me for a moment without answering.

"Come on in," she said suddenly. "It's cold out there. At least I'm cold. Always cold."

I followed her inside, into the living room of the trailer, where the talk show was playing on a big console television. On the screen, a very made-up blonde woman was leaning toward another woman, who was also blonde but not as made up.

"It was different the second time we got married," the other woman was saying. "I felt like I'd won his respect."

"What a crock," Joyce Hewett said, walking past the television and into another room. And then, from the other room, "The only time they respect you, honey, is when you're on your back."

She came back into the room. I stood in the middle of the floor in front of the TV, but then, everything was in front of the TV.

"No offense," Joyce Hewett said as she walked by me.

"None taken," I said.

She walked to the counter of the kitchen, which was at the end of the living room, in the same space. When she passed, I smelled perfume and a faint odor of alcohol. She picked up a mug and sipped from it and something told me it wasn't hot cocoa.

"Coffee? A drink?"

"No, thanks," I said.

"Then have a seat," Joyce Hewett said, and she did.

She sat on a couch beside a pile of folded laundry. I sat in the matching chair. I looked at her more closely and saw that she'd put on makeup: black eyeliner and wet-looking red lipstick. The talk-show lady was still talking. Something about sex on a second honeymoon.

"A little old for my daughter, aren't you?" Joyce Hewett said.

"A lot old," I said. "But I'm not seeing her. I talked to her. To do with a story."

She took a long sip of her drink.

"Missy's a college girl now," Joyce Hewett said. "I don't know what I can tell you because I never see her."

"She's busy at school, I'm sure."

"I didn't see her before that."

"She didn't live here?" I asked.

"She slept here up until this past summer. Then she moved to Portland. My youngest and I barely know her anymore. Life's hard sometimes, don't you think?"

"Sometimes."

"Most of the time," Joyce Hewett said.

She crossed her legs. Looked at me across the top of her mug.

"What'd you say your name was?"

"Jack. Jack McMorrow."

"And you're doing an article?"

"Yeah."

"About Missy?"

"About kids like her," I said.

"And what kind of kids are they, Jack?" Joyce Hewett asked.

I felt uneasy. How much did she know about her daughter?

"Kids who grow up fast, I guess," I said.

She didn't say anything. Sipped again. Looked at me. The talk-show woman was talking about sex.

"You sure I can't get you a drink?"

"Yeah, I'm sure. Thank you."

Joyce Hewett got up from the couch.

"I'll make you one, in case you change your mind," she said.

She went to the refrigerator, opened the top door to the freezer, and took out a bottle of vodka. Smirnoff. I watched her as she went back to the counter and poured the vodka in a black mug and splashed some orange juice on top. She was on the small side, slim, with narrow hips and a big chest. A girlish-looking woman who still would have attracted a lot of attention in a bar full of truckers. Maybe that was her problem, I thought. And mine.

She turned and brought me the drink. I took it and put it on the glass-topped table next to the chair, on top of a *TV Guide*.

"Vodka," Joyce Hewett said. "I hate brown liquor. Won't drink it. Reminds me of my father."

She picked up her mug and brought it back for a refill, then went back to the couch and sat down.

I smiled. Paternally, I hoped.

"So," Joyce Hewett said, with a faint leer. "What are you gonna write about my daughter?"

I took the plunge.

"The story's about girls who have babies."

"And give 'em away?" she said.

"Sometimes."

"You know that's what she did."

"She told me."

"Missy must like you to tell you about that. You sure you two didn't have a little . . ."

"I've only met her once. Kids at the high school gave me her name."

"What? She famous over there now?"

"She was a good student, wasn't she?"

"Oh, yeah. Head always in a book. Couldn't even get her to look at me. I guess you could say we didn't see eye to eye."

"Was she here when she was pregnant?"

"Part of the time. Didn't want Mama's help, though. I guess she learned about that from books, too."

I didn't say anything. She took another sip. The talk show was over and the credits were rolling.

"And then she gave it away," Joyce Hewett said. "My fourth grandchild. Can they do that? Maybe you could find that out. They'll tell you. Ask 'em if they can just do that, without the grandmother's even having anything to do with it. I mean, it's my grandchild and it's just gone. I never even saw it. Never even laid eyes on that baby. That can't be right, can it?"

"I don't know."

"What kind of law is that? Take somebody's grandchild away. What is this? Nazi Germany? I said that to Missy, I said, 'What is this? Nazi Germany? Don't I have a right to see my grandchild?' She said all they need is her permission and the permission of the father. If they can find him, I mean. She never even told me who it was. I mean, it's like the whole thing never happened."

"Where did she have the baby?"

"Portland, I think. She'd left by then. After she finished school she was here but we wasn't getting along. Something new and different, you know? She must've been due in the middle of June."

"She didn't leave school?"

"Hell no. My daughter in school, walking around like a bred heifer. I said to her, 'Don't you have any pride?' She didn't say anything. That was her way, you know? Look right at you and not say a word. My other girls, you have it out, 'You this, you that,' and then it's over. Missy just looks at you and walks out of the room. So it's never over, you know what I mean?"

I did and I said so. Joyce Hewett took a drink. It was beginning to show.

"She just looks right through you," she said, a vague sloppiness creeping into her voice. "She was just different. Sometimes I wonder if they got the babies switched at the hospital with Missy. From a different mold, you know?"

"I noticed."

"Always like that. Quiet. Off in her room with a book. There could be World War Three going on around here, and there was, most of the time, and that kid would have her nose in some book."

Her only escape, I thought.

"Talked to her teachers more than her mother. Ever since she was a little thing. Miss So and So says this. Mrs. So and

So says that. And then this one at the high school. Janice
something or other. I blame her for a lot of this, that bitch.
She planted this idea in the girl's head about giving the
baby away. Helped her get into college. Got her thinking
she was too good for the rest of us."

"You and your daughters?"

"We were nothin' to Missy. Just getting in the way of her
plans. That's the way she'd put it. 'But I have plans, Ma. I
gotta study. I have plans.' And nothin' was gonna get in the
way of her plans. Not me. Not the rest of the family. Not
even a baby."

I looked at her, this paragon of maternal instinct. The lipstick. The black-lined eyes staring through a boozy film,
the frosted glass of alcohol. The tight jeans, an awkward
and desperate attempt to remain twenty.

"So you didn't approve of the adoption?"

"What would you think?" Joyce Hewett demanded.
"Give away your flesh and blood? To some stranger? My
God almighty. I still can't believe it. That I'm never gonna
see my granddaughter. Not ever. I mean, she's just gone
like she never existed."

"Where did she go?"

"Nobody knows. Maybe Missy knows but I'm not sure
of that, even. One time she told me, you know, during one
of our fights about it, that the baby was safe, that it was in
New Jersey or Rhode Island or some place like that. I don't
remember."

She sipped again. The fog must have been lifting.

"So I said, 'New Jersey? Oh, yeah. That's real safe for a
little kid. Drugs and these gangs and people getting killed
all the time.' I said, 'Don't you watch the news? You call
that safe?' She says the baby's new parents teach in a college or something. Like I'm supposed to be impressed. Excuse me for living but I thought I did pretty well for my
girls, all by myself. They had clothes. They had food on the
table. They had a roof over their heads. Sorry if that wasn't
good enough. She takes my grandchild and gives her to

some college professor someplace. I said, 'That's my flesh and blood and you're giving it away like it was a friggin' kitten.' I told her that."

"What did she say?"

"She said, 'Drop dead, Ma.' Nice, huh? I'm only her mother."

With that, Joyce Hewett got up and headed for the freezer. I was beginning to think it was time to leave the two of them alone but when she slid back on to the couch with her mug, she smiled and started right in.

"Where'd you say you live, Jack?" Joyce Hewett said.

"Right here in town," I said.

"You got people here?"

"Nope."

"Kids?"

"Nope."

"Married?"

"Nope. Just me."

She looked at me with a new glint in her eye. With one hand, she held her mug on her lap. The other hand moved to the buttons on her sweater. She began buttoning and unbuttoning the top button, then left it undone and moved down to the next one.

Oh, no, I thought.

"Must get awful lonely up here all by yourself," Joyce Hewett said, a new softness in her voice. I pictured her using the same line on some trucker, an eligible bachelor with his house all paid for.

"You get used to it," I said.

Her cleavage was showing now. Her finger ran up and down it, anything but absently.

"I could make you a fresh drink?" she said.

"No, thanks. I haven't even touched this one."

"How 'bout a beer? I didn't even ask you if you wanted a beer. That was dumb, huh. I'll bet you drink beer."

"No, I really have to go. Thanks, though."

I sat up in the chair. Joyce Hewett looked at me languidly, her finger still running up and down her chest. I found myself thinking her attractive but fought it off.

"You seem like a nice guy," she said. "And you're cute."

"Thanks."

"If I'd been Missy, I would've been all over you. Older guys treat you right, if you know what I mean."

I thought I did but I hoped I didn't.

"I gotta go," I said. "Thanks for your help."

I got up. She got up, too. Moved toward me with her mug in her hand, her hips rolling as she walked. She stopped inches in front of me and unbuttoned another button. If I'd dared to look, I would have seen the curve of her breasts.

"Why don't you stay?" Joyce Hewett said. "I like you."

I could smell the vodka on her breath, see the lines of her lips.

"No, I really have to go. Really."

"We could have a nice afternoon. A nice long afternoon. We could . . . talk."

The word hung in the air. It still was hanging as I tried to ease my way by Joyce Hewett. She moved against me.

"You going back to that empty house?" she breathed. "Don't you know there's nothing worse than being alone?"

I looked at her. Her eyes dull under the makeup. Her lips open. Her breasts half bared to a stranger.

"You're right about that," I said. "Nothing worse than being alone."

Eighteen

But I felt alone that night, more than usual.

"You got family?"

"Nope."

"You got kids?"

"Nope."

"You got a wife?"

"Nope."

Joyce Hewett had touched a nerve and it wasn't in my pants. It was in the back of my mind, always. The loneliness, the feeling that I was missing what others took for granted.

Family. Kids. A wife.

I didn't have family. I was an only child of parents who married late and died early. The fact that they loved me completely and wonderfully in between sometimes just made it worse.

My father had worked for the Museum of Natural History in New York. A big gentle man, he'd commuted by train from Long Island to spend his days in rooms full of dead bugs. My mother had stayed home and taken care of me. When they'd gone, a couple of years apart, I'd been left with a feeling of being marooned. For some reason, it had become my natural state.

With occasional exceptions, I'd been alone most of my adult life. Women came but eventually went. They never stayed long enough to bring kids into the situation. There was never any big fight; they usually said they just felt more for me than I felt for them. And they were usually right. So I'd be left to stand in the doorway while they packed their bags, plucked their makeup from the bathroom shelves. Sometimes I'd even called them a cab.

Nobody ever said I wasn't a nice guy.

But nice guys don't just finish last. They finish alone.

And seeing Joyce Hewett as she reached out to me, to anyone, made it hard to keep saying that alone was what I wanted to be.

So I went home a little somber. I made notes of my conversation with Missy's mom, omitting the part where she unbuttoned her sweater. I really did feel for her, though, as a mother, she may have been a good barfly. But losing a grandchild to a stranger? Perhaps never to be seen again? It didn't seem right and I made a note to talk to somebody about the process. Did she have any rights? How did the whole thing work? Maybe I could talk to somebody at probate court, or at an agency. I wondered if they'd tell me what seemed to be increasingly apparent in this case: that adoption may have been the best move but nobody said it was easy or natural, or that it didn't give a great, wrenching yank to everyone concerned. Missy, her mother, the father and the baby, for whom I had no name. Curious.

As I sat at the dining-room table, I found myself staring out the window. I thought of Missy and her mother and the fact that we had more in common than they would have thought. We were alone and were trying, with varying degrees of success, to convince ourselves we liked it that way. That night, I wasn't very convincing.

I thought of Roxanne and wished she were within arm's reach. We wouldn't have to talk or make love. We could just be in the same house and, instead of the shadow that had moved into the house with me, I'd have a companion. I'd hear her clatter the pans in the kitchen. Hear the toilet flush. Wake up in the night and listen to the reassuring rhythm of her breathing, in and out, like waves breaking on a shore and running back out to sea.

That night, I woke often. I heard a bat flutter in the dark above my head before he, or she, slipped out a crack into the night. I listened to the hum of the refrigerator, separating it into two or three distinct sounds. I heard the house creak, a phenomenon I would never understand. I heard a screech owl, recognizable because it didn't hoot as much as whinny. And then I heard the distant roar of a car or truck, which became louder and more familiar as it came closer. It was practically out front before I realized what and whose it was.

A truck. Kenny's.

As I rolled out of bed, I heard a shout. I got to the bottom of the loft stairs and heard the muffled crunch of glass breaking and a loud metallic bang. My truck. There was a whoop as I got to the back door. I slid the bolt back, yanked the door open and heard the truck rev and tires spinning on the gravel road. Barefoot, in my shorts, I ran out into the yard in time to see the dark shape of a pickup disappearing up the road with its lights off. The brake lights flashed red once and then the truck was out of sight, its motor roaring in the distance.

I stood for a moment and waited as the sound of the truck receded. It was dark, with no stars showing, and cold. My feet were wet from the dew on the grass and as I padded over toward the truck, I stepped on a stone or something hard and sharp and flinched. More gingerly, I walked to the rear of the truck and saw that the back window of the cab was buckled and splintered. In the bed of the truck, below the window, was a rock the size of a baseball. I stood and stared.

"These boys," I said aloud, "should find something better to do."

In my underwear, I tiptoed back inside and called the cops.

It was a couple minutes after three by the clock on the shelf in the kitchen. I dialed the sheriff's department number and a woman answered in that nasal tone you hear in people who answer phones for a living. To her credit, she sounded wide awake.

I told her my name and where I lived. I said somebody had just thrown a boulder through the back window of my truck. She asked if I'd been operating the vehicle at the time. I said no, I'd been in bed. She asked if the perpetrators were still there. I said I didn't think so. She said the nearest patrol unit was tied up on a domestic complaint in China, a half-hour away. I said there was no real rush, the damage was done. She said to call if they came back and she would either dispatch a sheriff's department unit or contact a state police unit in the area. I told her that was fine but asked that she let Poole know about what had happened because he was already involved in the situation.

"Officer Poole doesn't come on duty for another four hours," the dispatcher said.

"I'll be here," I said.

Picking pebbles out of my feet.

That's what I was doing when there was a knock on the door, not two minutes later. I got up from the dining room table and walked toward the door, slowly.

There was another knock. I stopped.

"Hey, Bones," a voice said. "It's me and all your friends."

It was Claire and he grinned when I opened the door. Hanging by his right side was a shotgun, with the muzzle pointed down.

"Bird season?" I said.

"Beginning to think it's open season on you," he said.

Claire followed me in and closed the door. He was wearing dark green pants, a dark red plaid jacket, and a black baseball hat that said "Remington" on the front.

"Aren't you supposed to be wearing hunter orange?" I said.

"So call a game warden."

"Probably get here faster than the cops. I called the sheriff's department and the nearest guy was in New Brunswick doing marriage counseling. They said to call back if somebody was chopping through the front door with an ax."

"You could always write a letter," Claire said.

He stood by the kitchen counter, the shotgun slung easily in the crook of his arm.

"Three-thirteen in the morning," I said. "Is that beer or coffee?"

"Right in the middle. Got any tea?"

"Coming right up. One crumpet or two?"

"None for me. I'm watching my figure."

"So what's this?" I said, nodding toward the shotgun. "The NRA twenty-minute workout?"

"After a week, I tote a shotgun and a rifle," Claire said.

"The way things are going around here, that wouldn't be a bad idea."

I put the water on the stove and got out two mugs. There was herb tea in the jar on the shelf but I got the real thing from the box. I just wasn't in an herbal sort of mood.

We stood and waited for the watched pot to boil. It did and I poured the water in the mugs. We dabbed the tea bags up and down, and Claire's looked incongruously dainty hanging from his gnarled-oak fingers. With the shotgun behind him, he looked like some British army officer taking a break from the battlefield. Colonel Varney. I passed him the milk.

"Supposed to rain hard later in the morning," Claire said, putting the mug back on the counter after his first sip.

"Oh," I said.

"Gonna be a little soggy in that truck of yours, don't you think?"

"Probably."

I walked over and took a chamois shirt off the hook by the door and put it on. Claire leaned against the counter and drank his tea.

"Bring her over later and we'll drop a new one in," he said. "Chevy pickup windows are dime a dozen. We can pick one up at a junkyard."

"Sounds good."

We drank the tea. Stood for a minute and said nothing. Finally, it was Claire who broke the silence.

"You and this kid musta really hit it off," he said.

"Just clicked. Sometimes it happens."

"And sometimes it doesn't."

"Look at the bright side," I said. "At least he left his gun at home. From shotguns to rocks. Next time it'll be water balloons. What you call deescalation."

"That's a Vietnam word," Claire said. "I always hated it."

"Sorry."

"No problem. But I think you're wrong. About the deescalation."

"Why's that?"

"I don't think this kid, or kids, is gonna just go away. He's got a thing for you."

"It's my rugged good looks."

"Whatever it is, he wants to get a rise out of you. You don't do anything, he's gonna just turn up the heat more to make you react."

"So what would you suggest?"

"If the cops can't scare him, you mean?"

"I don't know if they've even found him," I said.

"But he can find you. I think before he does something serious, you ought to have a chat with the boy. Face to face. Man to man. It's what they do in the Army. Sometimes it's to your advantage to demystify yourself in the eyes of the enemy. Harder to kill somebody when you know 'em."

"But we did that. He said I was a narc and he was gonna kick my ass. Or something like that."

"Which he's doing," Claire said.

"Does this mean I have a glass jaw?"

"It means he's gonna keep it up until something happens."

"And you're sick of getting up at three in the morning."

"Yeah, but mostly I'm sick of seeing you in your friggin' underwear."

"I've known a woman or two who came to feel that way," I said.

Claire put his mug down on the counter.

"Speaking of women," he said, "I've got one at home

who might even notice I'm gone, if I stay away long enough."

"So go home. Just leave your friend."

"You want me to?"

"Yeah it's okay," I said. "I couldn't sleep with a loaded gun in the house."

"A lot of people can't sleep without one."

"Yeah, well, I guess things haven't gotten to that point. Yet."

Claire walked to the door and picked up the shotgun. He put it in the crook of his arm, nodded to me, and left. When he closed the door behind him, I felt very much alone.

Alone in the house. Alone in the town. Alone in the state. Alone.

So all by my lonesome, I finished my tea and considered what to do next. What had been simple—a story about children having children—was turning into something very tangled, very complex. I could write a story about just Missy Hewett and the events that led up to her having a baby, the ramifications of her decision to give it up. Her mother. Her sisters. What did they think of Missy and her desire to break out of the family track? And where was the baby now? What would Missy have to do to get it back? What had she done to give it up? What had made her change her mind?

It wasn't going to be an easy story to do. And having to dodge a psychopath with a shotgun and a truckful of rocks wasn't going to help things.

I sat at the kitchen table and pondered it all. The house was still except for an occasional flutter from upstairs. I sat there in the dark and then in the half-light and then in the gray gloom of dawn. Finally, as the birds were tuning up their orchestra, I picked myself up out of the chair and climbed the stairs to bed. My last thought before dropping off to sleep was that maybe Claire was right. Maybe I should talk to Kenny, find out what made his time bomb tick.

*   *   *

I slept soundly, strangely enough. When I stirred, the first thing I heard was the sound of rain drumming on the roof. For a moment it was almost cozy there in the warm cocoon of bed but then it all came rushing back—Kenny, the truck, Claire and his gun. I kicked the covers back and sat there on the edge of the bed, wondering if I had any plastic.

The plastic was for the back window of the truck. I found a roll of clear poly sheeting in the clutter of Millie's old studio, and after pulling on jeans and a sweatshirt, went out to the truck. I cut the plastic to size with a utility knife and taped it to the inside of the cab with duct tape. Not only would the plastic keep the rain out, but if I had to make a sudden stop and the window fell in, I wouldn't get glass down the back of my shirt.

Just call me Handy Andy.

It was a diligent rain, falling steadily from a dark cheerless sky. I got out of the truck and felt the damp spot on the back of my sweatshirt from the wet seat back. Maybe I could wear a raincoat whenever I was behind the wheel. That little son of a bitch.

The rock was still in the truck bed, big and wet and probably of no use for evidence, unless, of course, the D.A. called in a forensic geologist. ("Yes, your honor. From my examination, I would say that this particular boulder is from the Pleistocene Period, most likely dropped by the receding glacier roughly 10,000 years ago in the mid-coast region, whereupon it sat until being picked up and thrown into Mr. McMorrow's truck window.")

I left the rock where it was, even if it was for nothing more than dramatic effect.

Like me, the house was cold and damp. I crumpled up some newspaper and shoved it in the firebox of the woodstove. A handful of broken cedar shingles went in next and then some small split sticks of maple. I lit the newspaper with a lighter and then closed the door and opened the damper. As I rummaged for something for breakfast, the cedar snapped and crackled.

It was a little after eleven-thirty. I was supposed to meet Missy in Portland at four-thirty, which meant I should leave before three. That gave me a couple of hours to accomplish something or at least make an attempt. As the fire warmed the kitchen, I sat down to an English muffin with peanut butter and considered where to make my next stab at this story.

I considered looking for Kenny and his friends but, as a pacifist and a procrastinator, decided to leave that for another day. It seemed to me that it would be more constructive, and much safer, to try to learn something about the adoption process, of which I was woefully ignorant. If I was going to write about this stuff, I'd better know at least the basics. That meant it was time for a crash course.

My first stop might be probate court, where I assumed the legal end of adoptions were handled. The nearest one was in Belfast and I could stop there and get some information and then continue on to Portland. There were also adoption agencies, the places that matched kids with adoptive parents. For that, I'd need an appointment. I could make some calls before I left, see if I could set something up for this week.

And then there were those advertisements in the newspapers, the ones placed by couples desperate to have a child. I went to the stack of papers by the stove and found a section of classified ads from the Waterville newspaper. There they were, just under the number for Overeaters Anonymous:

> *"Bob and Nadine seek precious baby. We have city home, vacation home on lake with boat. A wonderful life to share with your baby. Confidentiality and support for you. All expenses paid. Call collect . . ."*

I looked down the column. Bob and Nadine. Roger and Linda. Tom and Carmella. The ads were so plaintive. The prospective parents so willing to do anything to have what most people took entirely for granted: a child.

Please let us have your baby. Please pick us. Please.

I read down the column. One poignant plea after another. Offers of boats and cats and big backyards. How could someone like Missy decide? It was one thing to be born to parents. It was another to choose your child's life so deliberately. Do I go with Bob and Nadine or Roger and Linda? But then Tom and Carmella sound nice . . .

God, I thought. What an absolutely mind-boggling responsibility.

I took scissors and clipped the column from the paper. As I looked for more in the stack, the phone rang. I picked it up and a woman answered, looking for Jack McMorrow.

"Right here," I said.

"Jack. Maddie at *New England Look.* Just checking to see how the story's coming."

I had to think for a second.

"Good," I said. "It's going pretty well. It's really quite fascinating."

"Great. Have you connected with the right people?"

Connected with the right people. I thought again.

"Well, I think so. I've met one girl, woman, I guess, who I think will be a good person to focus on. I think that might be the way to go. Let this woman be the example."

"Rather than a broader focus?" Maddie said.

"Well, yeah. I don't know. These situations are really kind of fascinating. I think doing one in-depth treatment is the only way to do justice to it."

"I know what you mean. And like it. Now what about art? When can we send up the photographer? I'm going to tell you that we're considering this for the cover story for the book. But we can't make that decision finally until the art is in hand. We have a guy in New Hampshire we'll probably use. I can get him up there in a day or two."

A day or two, I thought.

"Too soon," I said. "This story is, I don't know, kind of sticky. I need more time. I don't want to scare the girl off."

"Okay," Maddie said. A trace of unease crept into her voice.

"Are we going to have a problem with that deadline?"

"No. I don't think so. It just takes time to get these people to open up. Have you ever been up here?"

"Oh, yeah," Maddie said. "My husband's family has a summer place in Camden."

Oh, Lord, I thought. And she thinks she knows Maine.

"Well, these people aren't exactly the same as the people in Camden. They're not like people in New York. They're more private, I guess you'd say. They don't just open up to you right away."

"Are things not going well, Jack?"

The unease was more than a trace now.

"No, they're fine," I said.

As I said it, I heard the sound of a car in the driveway. I moved to the window and saw Poole's unmarked car.

"Because if there's a problem, I need to know very soon," Maddie was saying. "We've got these stories all lined up and if one stalls, the whole process is shot. I think you know that."

Poole was looking at the broken window in my truck.

"No, it's going fine," I said.

"Because we've got to communicate on this," she was saying. "I don't like surprises—"

Poole was knocking on the door.

"No, I don't either. No surprises. Right. Hey, listen, Maddie. There's somebody at the door. Could I call you right back?"

Poole knocked again. Impatient little bugger.

"Coming," I called.

"No need, Jack," Maddie said. "Just keep me posted. Remember. I have to know if things get screwed up."

"You'll be the first," I said, and hung up and went and

opened the door. Poole was there and he had somebody with him."

"Mr. McMorrow. This is Detective Parker of the Maine State Police. Could we come in?"

Parker was big and a little thick but strong, like an ex–football player who still worked out. His face was broad and tanned with deep-set brown eyes and he was good-looking like a television cowboy. Like Poole, he was wearing jeans and a short-waisted light jacket, the kind cops wear to cover the guns tucked in their waistband holsters. They walked as far as the kitchen and stopped. Neither of them wanted coffee. Neither of them offered to shake my hand.

"I understand you had some sort of problem here last night, Mr. McMorrow," Poole said. "I was telling Detective Parker here you seem to have made some enemies here in Prosperity."

"At least one. But I didn't make him, he made me."

"Right. Guy's name is Kenny White."

He turned toward Parker, to his left, my right.

"Kenny's a regular customer around here."

Turned back to me.

"Detective Parker doesn't usually work this area. But listen, I heard you called and reported somebody tossed a rock at your truck or something. Tell us what happened."

I did, starting with hearing the sound of Kenny's truck, which sounded a bit farfetched as I said it. Then the sound of the rock hitting my truck. Running outside. Seeing a truck, one that I believed to be Kenny's four-wheel-drive, driving off.

"The rock's still in the truck bed," I said.

"We saw it," Parker said.

It was the first time he'd spoken.

"So what time was all this?" Poole said.

"A little after three."

"And you called right away?"

"Still in my shorts. I thought maybe you guys might be

nearby and you could catch him going up to some quarry to reload."

Poole smiled. Parker didn't. I got an uneasy feeling.

"The patrol guys had a bad accident to cover in Montville a little before that," Poole said. "Nobody would have been available. But listen, what makes you think it was Kenny's truck?"

"The sound of the exhaust, I guess. They all have a different rumble. You know these big four-wheel-drives."

"Could it have been some other truck?" Poole asked.

"Sure. I guess. But, you know—because of the problem we'd already had, I thought it was pretty likely that it was Kenny. Not some random rock-thrower."

"So you couldn't say in court that it was him," Parker said.

His voice was flat and noncommittal.

"Nope. Couldn't say it here, for certain."

Parker looked unimpressed. He shifted on his feet and looked at Poole, who glanced back, almost knowingly.

"Let's go out and look at your truck, Mr. McMorrow," Poole said, and the two of them turned and started for the door, leaving me to follow.

They looked at the truck, the rock all shiny wet in the bed. If they were impressed with my repair job, they didn't say so.

Probably jealous.

We stood there in the rain for a few minutes and then Poole suggested we go back inside. We did and they went back to their places at the counter again, leaving wet footprints between the kitchen and the door. This time, Parker did most of the talking, asking me to tell him again about hearing the truck outside. I did and he asked me to tell him about my run-in with Kenny. Parker said to take my time, so I did.

But I was beginning to wonder why I was getting this special treatment.

I went over the story a couple of times. I talked about the

girls and the story and Kenny saying I was a narc. Poole had heard it before but he seemed to listen closely. Parker took a small notebook out of the inside of his jacket and took notes as I spoke.

The pit. The shotgun blast through the window. And back to the rock.

Parker wanted to hear again about the rock.

I told him, and this time I told them about Claire coming down, though I didn't mention his shotgun. They perked up for that part and Parker wanted to know more about Claire, his last name and how I knew him. I was beginning to think that these were the most thorough cops west of Scotland Yard.

They seemed to be in no hurry to leave, so I offered them a cup of coffee again. Poole said no but Parker said yes, please. I put the water on the stove and glanced at the clock on the wall above it.

"Is there something we're keeping you from, Mr. McMorrow?" Parker said.

"No, not really. I have to meet somebody in Portland at four. But I've got a little time before I have to get ready. No problem."

"What, you got an interview?" Parker asked.

He seemed to expect an answer. Poole was waiting, too.

"Yeah," I said, a little uneasily. "A woman for the same story that got me hooked up with the three girls and Kenny and the rest of this."

"What woman is that?" Parker asked.

I looked at him and wondered what that had to do with a broken window in my truck.

"What's her name, you mean?"

"Yeah."

He seemed to have taken over from Poole, who seemed to be watching me with freshened interest.

"Her name?" I said.

I felt like saying it was none of their business but I didn't.

"Yeah," Parker said.

"Her name's Hewett," I said, as the kettle on the stove began to hiss. "Missy Hewett."

"And you're supposed to talk to her?"

"Yeah. At four. Four-thirty actually."

"You've met her before?" Parker asked.

"Once. In Portland. She goes to USM. She's from here. Still has family—"

Parker broke in.

"Mr. McMorrow. We should tell you something."

He looked serious. Poole's face had hardened.

"Missy Hewett's dead, Mr. McMorrow," Parker said. "They found her this morning."

Nineteen

They said they found her at dawn alongside the road on Forest Avenue, not far from the doughnut shop where we were to meet. She was wearing a running suit and running shoes and it was thought that she could have been hit by a car while jogging at night. They hauled her away to do a postmortem but before that they found my name and phone number on a piece of paper in her pocket.

Poole and Parker wanted to hear the story again from the beginning. We sat at the kitchen table and they had coffee and I had tea. I told them about the three girls in the truck, that one of them had blurted out Missy Hewett's name when I'd asked about babies.

I thought it was Belinda but I wasn't absolutely sure.

They listened as I talked about tracking Missy down through the college. I told them about my conversation with

Missy at her apartment, my impression of her then. At some point, Parker started taking notes. I told them about talking to Missy's mother, that I didn't think they were close. I told them I didn't know the name of the father of the baby but I didn't think Missy was close to him, either.

"So would you say she was something of a loner type?" Parker asked.

"Yeah," I said. "Kind of quiet. Not real happy. But tough enough to be on her own."

I told them about Missy's phone call. That she wanted to meet me, that she was going to tell "them" she wanted her baby back. I said I didn't know if "them" meant the parents who had adopted the child or an agency or what. They wanted to know what Missy's mental state seemed like on the phone, where we were supposed to meet. I told them about her saying somebody was waiting to use the phone, that Missy had said the guy was practically climbing in the phone booth with her.

And then I told it all again.

This time Parker had questions. Poole got up and watched from the counter.

"Did she seem frightened when she called you?" Parker asked.

"Not frightened of anybody, like somebody was out to get her," I said. "Maybe frightened like she was setting out on something she knew wasn't going to be easy."

"Getting this baby back, you mean."

"Yeah. It was like she knew it was going to be a battle."

"But she didn't say with who?"

"No. The conversation was just a minute or two. I presume that's what we were going to talk about when we met. No, she never told me where her baby went or how. She just said the baby was better off where she was."

"It was a girl?"

"Yeah. I think her mother referred to the kid as a girl, too, but I'm not as sure."

"The mother's some kind of lush, right?" Parker asked.

"Appeared that way."

"Did Missy drink that you know of?"

"No," I said. "She wasn't the type. I don't know. She just seemed driven to reach her goal, which was to go to college and be a nurse and not end up like her mother."

"Good plan," Parker said.

"I thought so. The people at the high school here seemed to think so, too. Her mother blamed the guidance counselor. Janice Genest is her name. I got the impression she gave Missy a lot of advice."

"About the baby stuff?"

"I don't know that for sure but that would be my guess."

Parker scribbled some more in his notebook, then shut it and put it back inside his jacket. He shoved the chair back with a scraping sound and heaved his big bulk into a standing position. I got up, too. The three of us moved toward the door.

"So you think it might not have been an accident?" I asked.

"The autopsy will tell us that," Parker said. "Probably."

"Wouldn't tell you if somebody ran her over on purpose, would it?"

"Not necessarily," Parker said.

The three of us stood by the door and didn't say anything for a moment. Poole reached for the door and opened it and outside it still was raining. Parker paused and turned back to me.

"Mr. McMorrow," he said slowly. "I don't mean to pry, but what exactly is it that you do?"

I looked at Poole.

"Why don't you ask him?" I said.

So she was dead. Erased, just like that. The Waldo High success story. The little dour girl with the grim determination. The thorn in her drunken mother's side. The kid who didn't quite fit in. The kid who had a kid.

She wouldn't be asking for her baby back now.

I almost didn't want to think it, but the coincidence kept shoving itself back in my face.

Missy Hewett tells me she wants to get her baby back and less than twenty-four hours later, she's dead. Who else did she tell? Who else did she call from the pay phone? And where was her baby now?

Of course, the coincidence could be just that. She could have been hit by a car. Her untimely death could be the adoptive parents' gain. But would they know? Was the baby somehow included when they notified the next of kin? When they listed Missy Hewett's survivors, would they include a baby girl, name unknown?

Sitting there at the table, I fielded the questions as they came. Really. Where was the baby? Would the adoptive parents even know? Who would tell them? Who was the "they" Missy was going to talk to? What had made her change her mind, which had been set in such relentless resolve? And what was I going to write about now?

I couldn't write the same story now, not unless I ignored Missy Hewett completely, excised her from my notes and my mind and went on as if she'd never happened. But I couldn't do that. I wouldn't.

Even at that moment, with the news of Missy's death still unreal, I knew I couldn't just abandon her. There was something about her. Her face peering out from behind the security chain on her apartment door. Her gritty bid to make something of herself. Her fighting the good fight alone, like some little Joan of Arc marching off to do battle, armed with nothing but a pile of books.

She was a brave kid. Whatever had happened, she didn't deserve it. There was no fairness in her death, maybe not in her life, either. Missy didn't deserve to die but she did deserve justice. Funny. Sometimes the dead are the most deserving.

It's strange how life goes on after death, relentless as the tides. We pause for the dead only momentarily and then get on with our business. An entire industry, one of funeral homes and big black cars, has been invented to make us think this isn't so, but it is. The big black cars are gone the next day. We get on with it. Missy or no Missy.

In my case, the business was a rear window for my truck. The guy at the junkyard in Waterville made me wait while he tapped in enough numbers on a computer keyboard to program navigation for the space shuttle. The mainframe at junkyard central told him he had one and it was thirty-five bucks. I called the second place, in Searsmont, and a woman answered the phone. I told her what I needed and she said, "We got any back windows for Chevy pickups? Older ones?"

A man's voice said, "Hell yes," and she asked him how much.

"I don't know," he said. "Twenty-dollar bill."

Searsmont was about ten miles to the south, across Route 3, the pipeline for out-of-staters headed for Belfast and points downeast. When I pulled up to Route 3 on the Thompson Ridge Road, the cars were hustling up and down the highway, but mostly headed west toward home in Massachusetts, New York, Connecticut, Pennsylvania. They were summer people, up for the foliage. After one last gulp of Maine coast, it was back to the offices where they would earn enough money to come back.

I sat there at the intersection in my beatup truck an extra minute or two and watched them rush past. It reminded me of just how much on the sideline I now was. And I was glad. For the most part.

When a car pulled up behind me, I turned right and drove along Route 3 until the next crossroad. I pulled off and drove at a leisurely lazy pace down into the little forgotten village of Searsmont, invisible to the legions that marched up and down the highway just a couple of miles away. Past the village, I followed the woman's directions, which were to stay to the right up on to Appleton Ridge. I did and soon was loafing along the ridge under the white-gray afternoon sky, on a road right out of West Virginia. I passed old sagging farmsteads, with apple trees bravely bearing fruit in grown-up pastures. Trailers with toys scattered in their yards like brightly colored birdseed. Trucks like mine, sitting alongside barns, their dismantled motors slung on tripods of tree trunks, monuments to the blind optimism it takes to get by poor in the woods.

The junkyard was off the Appleton Ridge at Pitmans Corner, a dirt road to the right. I pulled in and parked in front of a trailer surrounded by old cars and trucks. It was hard to tell whether this was customer parking or an overflow of stock.

I got out and walked past the trailer to the tipsy wooden fence that surrounded the yard itself. There was a truck-sized gap and I went through and saw a hand-built shack sort of building. It had a couple of windows and a door and the door was open. I stepped in and a cat slipped by my legs and out. Country western music was playing and a woman said, "You must be the guy for the window," before I could even say hello.

She was small and trim, sitting at a desk piled with repair manuals and order forms and scattered greasy parts. Her ashtray was from a car and she had a cigarette going in it. A cat jumped up on the desk and she didn't shoo it off or even show she'd noticed.

"He's popping it out right now," the woman said. "I'd tell you to have a seat but you'll get your pants all dirty."

So I stood and waited and watched. She was fiftyish, sort of mannish but handsome. Her hands and arms were tanned where her sweatshirt was pushed up. The sweatshirt said "USS Saratoga" in big letters, blue on gray. The woman whistled along with the music as she shuffled through the piles of papers.

"You know somebody on the *Saratoga*?" I asked.

"Not just somebody," she said. "My son."

I was thinking that there was something great and very

American about that, the kid from this backwoods hollow in Maine sailing the world on an aircraft carrier, when the cat jumped down and came over and rubbed my legs. The woman picked up the phone and said, "Danny, you still there?" and Danny was because she started talking about having a complete front-end for a Dodge four-wheel-drive and she'd let it go for three.

"Where's the man needs the Chevy window?"

I turned and a guy turned to me. He was her age, tanned, too, with big greasy hands and an easy grin.

"That's me," I said.

"Well, my friend, you're in luck," he said.

He walked out the door and I followed. Outside, a long window was leaning against the fence, and he stood it on end and brushed it off with the hand.

"I knew I had a couple of the plain-Jane ones," the guy said, reaching with his other hand to get a cigarette from his shirt pocket. "One was cracked and I busted the other one trying to get it out. That leaves this one. This one's got the sliding window and it's perfect and I'll let you have it for the twenty, since we got you all the way out here. Cost you a hundred new and this one's all good."

He moved the sliding part in the center.

"Only slid on Sunday," he said.

Claire put the window in. He was sawing wood when I pulled up, with the window between two pieces of cardboard in the back of the truck. Claire turned his chainsaw off and pulled his ear protectors down. I called over that I'd gotten a window and he pointed toward the barn. I pulled the truck up the ramp and into the dim raftered cavern and parked beside his tractor.

"Have to hunt all over?" he said.

"Nope. Some little place in Searsmont."

"Hurd's place."

"Yeah," I said. "Nice people."

"Hell, yes. Jimmy Hurd's an awful nice guy. Wife's a peach."

"Son in the Navy, huh?"

"Didn't know that. Guess I haven't been down there in a while."

"On the *Saratoga*, the carrier, she said. Seemed kind of proud."

"Has a goddamn right to be," Claire said, putting his saw on a workbench. "A goddamn right to be. There's a kid who's gonna make something of himself, if he plays it right. The service has saved a lot of kids, I'm telling you."

Maybe Missy should have signed on, I thought. Then I realized Claire didn't know.

"I got some bad news this morning," I said.

Claire was climbing into the bed of the truck. We lifted the window out and put it on the bench by the saw.

"Whoah, a slider," Claire said. "What's the news? You gotta get a real job?"

I smiled.

"No. Not yet. But you know that girl with the baby? I guess I told you about it. Maybe it was Mary. This girl who goes to college in Portland. She gave up her baby for adoption. It was part of this story I'm doing."

"Yup."

"The cops came this morning and said she was dead. They found her by the side of the road down there in Portland."

Claire stopped rummaging in his toolbox and looked up and listened.

"I was supposed to go see her. Today."

"What, she get hit by a car or something?"

"They didn't know yet. If she was, it was hit and run."

"What'd she want to see you about?"

"She was having second thoughts about the adoption. She said she was going to ask for her baby back."

Claire looked at me.

"And the next day she's dead?"

"Yup."

"These baby people play rough, don't they?"

"Oh, I don't know about that."

Claire took a thin-bladed chisel from his toolbox.

"Let me tell you something, Jack. I don't believe in coincidences."

"No?"

"Nope. When things seem to be connected, nine times out of ten, they are."

I didn't say anything. Claire climbed into the bed of the truck and started prying the rubber gasket out from around the smashed window.

"You know what I think?" he said. "I think we better teach you how to shoot."

The old window came out in pieces. Claire handed them to me and I tossed them into the 55-gallon drum that was his trash can. He took a piece of clothesline and stuck it in the slot in the gasket and then we picked the window up and held it in position. As Claire eased the edge of the glass into the slot, I pulled the clothesline out just ahead of him. We went around and the window slipped into place.

"Hey, look at that," Claire said.

I grinned.

"One for the good guys," I said.

"Yessir," Claire said. "Come on up to the house and we'll celebrate."

I backed the truck out of the barn and parked it, sliding the window open and closed a couple of times. It worked fine. Let Kenny just try to break this one. I'd . . . I didn't know what I'd do.

Claire was washing his hands at the kitchen sink when I went in. He finished and tossed me the towel and I did the same. Mary came in from out back, her arms full of clothes from the line.

"Hi, Jack," she said, and dumped the clothes in a pile on top of an antique blanket chest. She started folding and stacking the laundry. I leaned against the counter and Claire handed me a cold bottle of Budweiser and opened one for himself.

"Mare?" he said.

"Chablis," she said. "There's a bottle open in the fridge."

Claire poured her Chablis into a rose-tinted wineglass and put the glass on the kitchen table.

"You're a dear," Mary said.

"I know it," Claire said. "Jack, pull up a chair. Take a load off."

I sat and he sat and Mary kept folding. One pile was for her and one was for him and a third was for things like towels. Claire raised his glass, first to his wife and then to me.

"Cheers," he said.

"To your health," I said.

"And a new window," Claire said. "May it have a long life."

"So what's this kid's problem, Jack?" Mary asked. "He just doesn't like you?"

"I'm beginning to get that feeling."

"No, he just didn't get enough attention growing up," Claire said, his big hand wrapped around the brown bottle. "I think we ought to get him some counseling."

"We could all chip in," I said.

"Right. Poor kid just never learned to express his feelings. I think you owe him an apology, calling the cops on him the way you did. Should have had him in for Oreos and a glass of milk."

"Right. Shooting at me was really just a cry for help."

"Absolutely," Claire said.

Mary looked up from her folding and rolled her eyes.

"What was his name?" she asked.

"Kenny," I said.

"And how did you cross paths with this fellow?"

"Just lucky, I guess. No, I was trying to find some high school kids for this story on kids having babies. I met these girls and they took me to a gravel pit that's some sort of hangout for kids around here. Kenny was there and he decided he didn't like me. Said I was a narc and all this nonsense."

"If you were, wouldn't he be in big trouble, shooting at a policeman?"

"I'm sure. But he knows I'm not a cop. He just didn't like my looks. Or he didn't like me being with the girls."

"Moving in on his women," Claire said.

"Who are old enough to be my daughters."

"Wouldn't be the first time."

"Yeah, I know," I said. "Seventeen going on twenty-five."

"Kids are in such a rush to grow up," Mary said, leaning over to take her first sip of wine. "They don't know how good they have it as children."

"Children having children," I said.

"So how is your adoption article coming?" she asked.

Claire looked at me, suddenly somber.

"Jack's running into some heavy weather."

Mary looked at him, then at me, and waited for an explanation.

"Yeah, you remember when I was talking about this Missy Hewett girl?"

She nodded.

"Well, she gave up a baby for adoption. Would have been about four months ago, I guess. She's, I mean, was in college. So I went to talk to her about it, this was in Portland, and she went on about doing it for the good of the little girl, how she didn't want her baby or her to be locked into the kind of life she had with her mother. Her mother's a serious alcoholic, has had ninety-three different guys over the years. Nice enough person, though."

"You met her, too?" Mary said.

"Yeah, but she might not remember it. She was drinking vodka like it was water."

"She must be very sick. Very troubled," Mary said.

I hesitated, as if not saying it would make it go away.

"Well, she's got more troubles now. They found Missy dead. On the side of the road in Portland."

Mary looked more saddened than shocked.

"What happened to her?" she said softly.

"When I talked to the police this morning—God, that seems like years ago—they didn't know. They had to wait for the results of the autopsy. So maybe she was hit by a car, I don't know. They said she was dressed to go running."

"But she couldn't run fast enough," Claire said.

And after that, there was a moment of silence.

Yes, I sure knew how to bring down the party. Mary's wine sat on the table, minus one small sip. Claire was holding his beer, lost in thought. I picked at my Budweiser label, digging at the warning about pregnant women drinking.

I wondered what kind of warning Missy Hewett had gotten. If any.

"Well, you know, that's very sad," Mary said. "It's very sad because this girl was working so hard to do the right thing."

"Got herself down to that college," Claire murmured.

"And the baby," Mary said. "That must've been very difficult."

"I'm not a mother, or a parent, but I think that would be hard as hell," I said.

"Very, very hard," Mary said, her voice almost wistful, her hands playing absently over the laundry. "The very same instincts that were telling you to do it for the baby's own good would be telling you not to."

"Your head would say one thing and your heart another?" I asked.

"No, I think it's more that your heart would say two different things. You carry a child for nine months and there's this bond there, believe me. When I was carrying our girls, I felt like I knew them long before they were born. We talked. They kicked me, did their little flips and flops. When they were born it was like, I don't know, like meeting a pen pal you've had for a long time or something."

"And then you'd say good-bye," I said.

"And it might really be in the baby's best interest," Mary said. "You know, it's funny. These girls who give their babies up are probably the ones who would do anything for that child. I mean, if they can go through that, the separation and everything, they probably could go through anything."

There was a pause and we all stared.

"And you know what's funny, too?" I said. "Missy Hewett, this kid, went through all this. Having the baby. Giving it up because she didn't think she could offer it a life any better than her own. Went through this whole thing, put herself through this unbelievable wringer, all for nothing."

"Just to get hit by some drunk and left by the side of the road," Claire said.

"Just a kid," I said.

Mary looked thoughtful.

"Well, if you're looking for some kind of justice, maybe that's it," she said. "At least the poor thing had some say in where her child ended up."

It was a gloomy gathering. Mary finished her folding and brought the piles of clothes upstairs, leaving her Chablis untouched and growing tepid. Claire took a couple of pulls on his beer but his heart wasn't in it. Mine wasn't either and we both knew it. After five minutes, I put the bottle on the counter, gave Claire a smile and a wave, and went out the door to the truck. I drove back home and, this time, backed the truck into the driveway so the windshield was facing the road. I could get another windshield but I probably wouldn't find another window, "only slid on Sunday."

Inside, I sat in the chair by the back window and watched it grow dark. I listened to the birds chirping and trilling in the dwindling light of dusk and I thought about Missy and her baby, on whom I couldn't put a face. I wondered where that baby was, whether she had felt some twinge when her mother died. I thought about this for a long time, about the push and pull that Missy must have felt, the need to be alone, to get ahead versus the need to nurture her own child. It made me feel alone, too, and I felt some of that push and pull myself until finally, I hoisted myself out of the chair and up the loft stairs to bed, where a single bat scratched at the rafters and then, as I drifted off, disappeared.

Twenty

Probate Court in Belfast was in a big room at the end of a long dark corridor in a gray sandstone building that, as I stood on the granite steps, seemed bleak and forbidding and cold.

This was in the morning, Thursday, and the town was bustling, with people and cars moving under a chill drizzle. As I stood there on the steps, lawyers stepped past me in their suits and trench coats, their little black shoes tapping on the stone officiously. I let several of them pass, then followed, with the boom of the closing of the big oak door echoing through the hallway around me.

The building probably dated to the 1870s or 1880s, a time when institutions like the courts were respected and even feared. This was less true today and our courts were built with all the formal dignity of a dentist's waiting room. This flaccid excuse for architecture probably contributed to the increase in crime and general mayhem as nobody was intimidated by cheap carpeting and a judge's bench built out of plywood.

But the court building in Belfast was imposing and I felt like a schoolkid on a field trip to an old and venerable museum. I walked down the corridor reading the hand-painted signs over the glass transoms. There was the clerk of courts, the district attorney, the county commissioners. At the end of the corridor, I turned right and passed several unmarked doors. A white-haired security guard came out of one and I could hear water running from within. He nodded and I asked him where probate court was and he pointed straight ahead.

It was a big room with a tall wooden counter that fenced the public off from the clerks. There were four of them and they sat at big desks positioned here and there around the room among the shelves and cabinets. The clerks were all women and when I stepped to the counter, they all looked up.

"Hi," I said, and waited.

They looked at me and then at each other and finally one of them, a dark-haired woman in her late thirties, got up and approached the counter.

"Can I help you?" she said, businesslike but pleasant.

"I hope so," I said. "I need information about adoption."

"Well, this is the place where it's done. The legal part, anyway," the woman said. "What kind of questions do you have?"

I hesitated. I could see that all the other clerks were listening. When I glanced at them, they looked away.

"I just need to know how it works," I said. "What's involved?"

"Well, it's kind of a big topic. I don't mean to be difficult . . ."

"Just the basics, then."

She put her elbows on the counter and clasped her hands. On the left hand was a small diamond and wedding band. Her blouse was cream colored and she was wearing a big multicolored pin that looked like a child might have made it in school. She had an upturned nose and was more pert than pretty. But she had a warm smile and an easy confidence that made me think I could like her a lot. She probably had nice kids.

"Have you been to an agency?" the woman asked.

"No, I haven't," I said. "I've only been here."

She smiled, as if she thought that sweet.

"Well, let's see. In Maine—and the rules differ from state to state—there are three kinds of adoptions, basically. There's what we call a private placement. That means the parent, usually the mother, just picks somebody. Usually a relative or a friend or somebody like that."

"So they just walk in and sign something and that's it?"

"Pretty much. But that's for, like when a very young girl has a child and say, her older sister wants to raise it. Or her mother, even. We've had that."

"I imagine you've seen all kinds of things," I said.

"Oh, yeah. It takes all kinds and we see 'em all. So anyway, then there's the independent placement. A lawyer or a doctor or maybe a minister handles the adoption for the natural parent."

"Just to help out?"

"More or less. A girl in the church has a baby. She wants to give it up so the minister finds somebody to adopt it. Saves the mother from having to do it herself. We don't see that all that much."

"What do you see?"

"Agencies, a lot of the time. You know, where the mother goes and has all the couples to choose from and they go through the whole selection thing."

"That's where you have couples who wait five years and all that?"

"Right."

"Well, what about these other people. What did you call it?"

"Independent or private," she said.

"Yeah. How do they rate? They don't wait five years for the kid in the next pew to have a baby."

The woman smiled.

"No. They just know somebody."

"And these other people wait for years and years?"

"And sometimes they never get a baby at all."

"Just never get picked?"

"Right. You know those ads you see in the paper. The ones where the loving couple wants to give your child a good home and all that?"

"Yeah."

She gave me that gentle smile again.

"That's what that's all about. People just putting their name out there. Hoping they'll get lucky."

"Must be tough odds," I said.

"Very. There are many more parents than babies."

I thought for a moment. The women in the background were talking about how much they loved their microwave ovens. They could talk about ovens and type at the same time. I wondered if they ever screwed up and legally changed somebody's name to "casserole" or something.

"Do they do it in the parents' home county?" I asked. "I mean the natural parents."

"That's customary. The judge can make an exception but it would be unusual."

"Do you get a lot of them here?" I said.

"Oh, I don't know. It's a steady stream. Not hundreds or anything."

"Enough so you remember the names of the people."

"I might but it's all confidential. You don't have to worry about anything ever leaving this office."

She smiled reassuringly. I smiled back and felt a twinge of regret at what I was about to do.

"You know," the nice woman said, "you and your wife can go to an agency and get lots of information. We just handle the legal part. I can give you some documents . . ."

She handed me some forms which I glanced at. One said,

AFFIDAVIT OF MOTHER OF ILLEGITIMATE CHILD. Another said, WAIVER OF NOTICE OF ADOPTION BY FATHER. A third said, SURRENDER AND RELEASE OF CHILD FOR ADOPTION.

"This is it?" I said.

"Well, the judge has to approve it."

I looked at the papers some more. Thought for a moment, then looked the nice woman in the eye, watched her expression.

"I know a woman who gave up a baby for adoption," I said. "Her name was Missy Hewett."

There wasn't even a flicker of recognition.

"As I said, all of this is confidential," the woman said.

I decided to try one more time.

"Missy Hewett. Seventeen, eighteen. Gave up a little girl. Newborn infant."

The woman looked at me blankly. Behind her, the clerks had stopped talking and were staring, instead.

"She's dead," I said. "She was killed this week in Portland."

The nice woman frowned, as if she'd just read about a plane crash in some foreign country.

"That's too bad," she said.

"Yeah," I said. "She was a nice girl."

And if she'd gone through normal channels for her adoption, it hadn't been here.

The nice woman wasn't quite as helpful after that. She stood silently and waited as I looked the documents over. The other women were quiet, too. I shuffled the papers. The silence in the room was building.

"So this is all you have to do?" I asked.

"That's right," the nice woman said, a few degrees cooler.

"But before you get to this point, everything is all set up? Having the child to adopt and all that?"

"Right."

"And the judge reviews all this stuff and approves the adoption?"

"If everything is in order," the woman said.

"And that's it?"

"More or less."

"What if things don't work out?"

"In what way?"

"What if the natural father shows up later? Or the mother—the natural mother, birth mother, or whatever—changes her mind?"

The woman thought for a moment. I got the impression she was considering whether to go to the trouble of answering any more questions for a guy who wasn't what he had seemed and was playing some sort of game. I could have told her it wasn't a game but she wouldn't have believed me.

"Once the adoption is approved, even once the natural parents sign those documents you have there, it's hard to undo an adoption," the woman said, slowly and begrudgingly. The women behind her were giving me the evil eye.

"You have to go to court and fight it out?"

"Unless you've left some sort of cushion of time before the papers are filed or something."

"That done often?"

"Not really."

I thought for a second but couldn't think of any other questions. The nice woman stood and stared at me. I smiled. She didn't.

"Thanks," I said.

"You're welcome."

She started to turn away and then turned back.

"You never told me your name," she said.

"Oh, sorry. It's Jack McMorrow."

"What are you? A private detective?"

"No," I said. "Not exactly."

She interrupted before I could explain further.

"Well, let me ask you something, Mr. McMorrow," the nice woman said. "You don't even have a wife, do you?"

"No," I said. "Hard to believe, isn't it?"

"Stranger things have happened," she said, as she turned away. "I'm sure."

So Missy Hewett hadn't had her adoption approved in Belfast, the county seat. If she had, if the court clerk had even known her only on paper, there would have been some reaction, a flinch or a flicker. The nice woman hadn't even blinked. She had never heard of Missy Hewett.

Then where had she had the adoption approved? Was there an agency involved? If not, how had Missy hooked up with a private party to place her baby? Church? I didn't get the impression that she went to church, though I could have been wrong. Just somebody she knew? No, there was a piece missing here. Who had Missy Hewett's baby?

I thought about it as I drove home, winding the truck through back roads northwest toward Prosperity. The chill drizzle had changed to a steady rain and I turned the heat on in the truck. Even with the foliage nearing its peak, it was a dreary day. The farmhouses along the way seemed shabby, the trailers with their broken-down cars even more forlorn. It was one of those days when all existence seemed grim and shabby, where there seemed to be little joy, little beauty, just people struggling to make some sort of life on the edge of these unforgiving hills. I could feel my mood sinking, feel the ultimate hopelessness of Missy's life seeping into mine. Down, down I went, headed for an afternoon I knew I'd spend staring out at the rain and mulling over Missy, this mess of a story I'd signed on for, and the growing predicament that was my solitary life.

No such luck.

There were two unmarked police cars in the driveway when I pulled up. One was Poole's brown Chevy. The other was dark blue, also a Chevy, with the telltale antenna on the back trunk lid. I stopped on the edge of the road in front of the house and turned off the motor. Two cops got out of the blue car. It was Poole and Parker, from state police.

They stood by the police car in the rain and looked serious and somber.

"Mr. McMorrow," Poole said, as I approached.

Parker just nodded.

"Boys," I said. "How 'bout a cup of coffee?"

They followed me inside. I took off my brown hunting jacket and hung it on the hook. They stood near the door as I filled the kettle and put it on the stove.

"Come on in," I said. "No need to stand over there."

They moved to the big table but still stood. I decided to stand, too. We all stood there for a minute, like shy boys at the eighth-grade dance. Finally I broke the ice.

"So what's up?" I said.

Poole was standing there with his hands in his pockets. He glanced at me, then looked to Parker. The kettle started to hiss like a snake and I went over and gave it a jiggle. Parker waited until I came back and then he looked me right in the eyes.

"It's Missy Hewett, Mr. McMorrow," he said. "We got the results of the postmortem."

Parker watched me and Poole did, too. They were doing to me what I'd just done to the nice woman at the court: watching for a reaction.

"She wasn't killed in an accident," Parker said evenly. "She died of asphyxiation."

"She suffocated?" I asked.

"No. Well, I guess so. She suffocated because somebody strangled her."

"Deliberately."

"Right," Parker said, the faintest edge coming into his voice. "Deliberately. Somebody murdered the kid."

"Hmmm," I said.

They looked at me. I looked at them. Poole the Scout leader, Parker the big ex-jock.

"That's too bad. Really too bad."

"Yeah, it is," Parker said.

"She didn't deserve that."

"Probably not."

The kettle was rattling.

"You still want coffee?"

"Sure," Parker said, giving the change in his pocket a jingle. "We got time."

I went to the counter and pulled three mugs out of the jumble of dishes next to the sink. A spoon fell out of the jumble onto the floor and I picked it up and put it back in the sink. I found three other spoons and put them on the table with instant coffee and the sugar. The milk I had to get from the refrigerator.

They stood. I poured.

When we'd taken our positions again, now with mugs in hand, I again had to initiate the conversation. These guys would be hell at a cocktail party.

"So what do you think happened, or can't you tell me?"

"We don't know," Parker said.

"But you're the only one we know had any contact with her in the day or so leading up to her being killed," Poole put in. "So we want to make sure we have all possible information from you. Anything you can tell us. From when you first met her 'til, what was it, a phone call?"

As he spoke, his expression earnest, I could feel Parker watching me closely. I felt like a sick person surrounded by doctors. One prodding, one watching. Every few minutes, they change places. And I didn't want to be their patient.

"Yeah," I said, caution creeping into my voice. "The last time was the phone call. She called me. Here."

"And she wanted to talk to you, about what?" Parker said. "Getting her baby back?"

"That's right."

"Tell us about that again. Even better, let's go back to when you first met Missy. Where was that?"

"In her apartment. In Portland. And I'm glad to talk about it. Really. But—and I'm not sure how to say this—but am I a suspect or something?"

"Oh, no. We're not anywhere near suspects. Just not

there yet at all," Poole said. "We've got a homicide and we're just trying to gather all the information we can so we can figure out where to go from here."

"But I'm not off the list."

"We're not gonna bullshit you," Parker said. "You're not on the list but that's because there isn't one."

"But I'm not off it, either."

"You got it."

But in the next couple of hours, I began to feel more ruled in than ruled out, and it was a strange feeling, indeed.

Poole diligently took notes. He was left-handed and he held his arm crooked around like left-handed people sometimes do when they write. Parker did most of the talking, first standing and then with all three of us sitting at the table, like chums getting together to do homework on a rainy day. He wasn't hostile, just very thorough. The guy would have made a good reporter, if reporters carried guns.

His was on his left side, in a shoulder holster under his armpit. When Parker moved, I could see the brown leather of the belt. Every once in a while he reached in and jiggled it, as if it were uncomfortable and he really would have liked to take it off and toss it on the table.

So he jiggled. Poole scrawled. I talked, feeling like something out of a movie. I started with the phone call from Slocum at the magazine. I hit Janice Genest and the girls and crazy Kenny and Missy's drunken mother. Roxanne and Tracy Crown and the kid from the mobile home park, or whatever it was. I even told them about the lady at the junkyard. Tried to get back to Kenny, a psycho if there ever was one. But in the end, the script had the cops interested in three things: how I got on to Missy Hewett, what we talked about when we met, what the hell I did for a living.

"So you went all the way to Portland to find this girl you'd never met, so you could interview her for this article?" Parker asked.

"Right."

"For a magazine in Massachusetts?"

"Yup."

"And you stood in the hallway until you could convince her to take the chain off the door and let you in."

"Yup."

"You must be a very persuasive fellow."

"Not really. Not any more than anybody else who does this job."

"Which is."

"Out-of-work reporter. Doing freelance stuff to pay the bills."

"For a reporter, you lead sort of an exciting life, don't you think?" Parker said, adjusting his gun.

"I don't know about that. Kind of dull really. Back in the city, they think I'm nuts living out here in the boonies in a houseful of bats."

Parker frowned in distaste.

"Place has bats?" he said. Both he and Poole paused and looked up at the ceiling.

"Just a few. They keep the bugs down."

"Give me the creeps," Parker said.

"I don't know," Poole put in. "I think they're kind of interesting. You ever fish a stream at around sundown and the bats are swooping over the water picking up bugs? It's sorta neat."

He caught himself and looked sheepish for showing a human side to a state police detective.

"I don't know," Parker said, getting back on track. "Maybe those buddies of yours from the city are right. You got bats in your belfry, right?"

He grinned and I grinned back. Always laugh when the guy telling the joke can lock you up.

"So Missy Hewett told you she wanted her baby back?"

"Right."

"How'd she put it?"

"About like that. 'I'm thinking of telling them I want my baby back.'"

"Them?"

"Yeah. Not him or her. Them. Like there was more than one."

"She didn't say who?" Parker said.

"Nope."

"Or where or anything?"

"That was about it. She said she was calling from a pay phone and somebody else was waiting to use it."

"And you never heard from her again."

"Nope."

"Did you like her?"

The question took me by surprise. Poole and Parker caught my reaction.

"Did I like her? Yeah. She was a tough kid and she was working hard to make herself a life. Nobody was helping her, either. She was just doing it on her own. Whatever it took to make it."

"Even giving her kid away?"

"Don't judge her for that," I said, getting a little irritated with this big jock cop. "It wasn't easy for her. She thought she was doing the best thing for the baby. Giving it a better life."

"That's what she said?"

"Yup. She said the baby was with a nice couple, that she'd have a good life. Something like that. There wasn't anything selfish about it."

"Didn't say where? Give you any indication?"

"Nope. None."

"Didn't say anything about the dad?"

"Didn't think much of him. I didn't get the impression they were very close."

"Close enough, right?" Parker said.

"Whatever."

"Did you have any interest in getting close to her like that?"

Poole looked up.

"Go to hell," I said.

"I gotta ask."

"And I have to tell you you're out of line."

Parker shrugged.

"Hey, somebody offed this kid you thought was so great. I can ruffle a few feathers and maybe find out who did it, or I can go through the motions and collect my check. Which would you want?"

I looked at the big son of a bitch and realized he was right.

"Consider mine ruffled," I said. "And go to it."

Parker gave me a long look, then a smile.

"Oh, I'm gonna do that, Mr. McMorrow," he said. "You don't have to worry about that."

Twenty-one ▮

It was a funny feeling, being a suspect in a murder. It was like all my life I'd tried to do the right thing, or at least something close to it, and it was all for nothing. Like the character I thought I had, the person I thought I was, didn't exist in the eyes of these cops. It was like nobody knew me in this place, or if they did, they didn't know that I wasn't capable of strangling an eighteen-year-old girl and dumping her beside the road.

God almighty. Was this what I had come to?

It didn't hit me until Poole and Parker left. Tough guy Parker had told me to keep my eye out for those bats. Poole, a quiet, thoughtful guy whom I really liked, had just nodded and walked out the door. Did he think I could do this, too?

I sat there at the table for a long time. The rain kept up

and it was quiet and eventually the light began to fade as the afternoon slowly slid away. The phone didn't ring. Not a single car went by. I had never felt so alone.

Other people had something in which to root themselves. A wife or husband to shore them up. A mother or father to give them an encouraging word. Kids to call them mom or dad and reaffirm their relationship to the rest of the world. Somebody to say, "Yeah, you are who you think you are. You're not what they're making you out to be. So don't let the bastards get you down."

What did I have?

I had a good career gone astray. A liver that probably was half shot, if I dared to check. I lived alone in a tiny town where I was, for the most part, a foreigner. I had no family and had cut myself off from the people I'd considered my friends. In Prosperity, I had Claire. In Colorado, I had Roxanne, who had loved me but I'd driven her away. I was doing a story that had turned into a tragedy, and in the back of my mind, I wondered if a little girl hadn't died because of me. That was the thought I wanted to keep buried but as I sat there, letting the dark wash around me like an incoming tide, the image of Missy Hewett, determined little Missy Hewett, kept coming to the surface like a body covered by shifting sands. What had I done?

The sound woke me, still in the chair. It was a clink, like metal hitting a rock. I sat up and wiped the bit of drool from the corner of my mouth. Listened for the sound again. It was absolutely dark in the room, absolutely still. I was facing the back window but could see nothing outside. I stared. Then turned. Noticed a glow from the front of the house.

Fire.

I lurched out of the chair and over to the door. Jerked the latch hard and bolted out into the dark and into the dooryard. On the far side of the truck, on the side of the cab, flames were stabbing up past the driver's window. I ran around the front of the truck and pulled up short. The flames were coming from the side of the cab, where something long and black was burning. And they were licking upward from the open hole where the gas cap had been. They were licking up from the filler pipe to the gas tank.

"Oh, Jesus," I said.

I ran back toward the house, not sure what I was looking for. A shovel to throw dirt on it? A bucket to fill with water? The hose? But that was out back. Or should I be taking cover, getting out of the way in case—

As I paused, paralyzed, by the door, a low whooshing sound came from behind me. I turned and held my hand in front of my face as a mushroom of flame engulfed the cab. The whoosh turned to a sort of roar, like the sound a jet makes before it takes off, and the fire jumped twenty feet in the air. I watched it, felt the heat and then there was a muffled boom and the flames jumped, then receded, leaving the form of the cab silhouetted like bones in a funeral pyre.

"Damn," I said. "And I just filled it up."

The college girls down the road called the fire department, then stood with me in their parkas and flannel nightgowns as my truck burned to a crisp.

"Bet you didn't think you'd be invited to a weenie roast," I said to the pretty girl standing next to me. She gave me a wide-eyed look that was full of, not sympathy, but suspicion.

"Who would want to blow up your truck?" she said.

"I don't think they blew it up. I think they lit it on fire."

"Why would they do that?" she asked, her eyes reflecting the flames.

"I don't know," I said. "Maybe I've been running with the wrong crowd."

It was a joke, or at least as close to a joke as you can make when you're watching your truck burn up, but the girl didn't get it. She gave me a quick sidelong glance and then moved away toward her two roommates. They stood together, in their jackets and bare legs and L.L. Bean boots, and then she whispered something to one of them and that one whispered back. I stood watching the fire, and in a minute or two, they turned and walked into the darkness and left me alone.

"Hey," I said. "Just 'cause I didn't have marshmallows."

Maybe I was becoming paranoid—I had every right to be—but the implication seemed clear. I was some sort of suspicious character. I knew people who blew up people's cars. I had offended someone to the point that he had blown up mine. I was not someone with whom respectable law-abiding college students would associate.

Unless, of course, you couldn't make bail.

It was a different feeling, being an undesirable and it didn't end when the college girls went back to their beds. I was alone no more than a minute or two when the first four-wheel-drive pickup came banging down the road, the red fire-department dash light flashing. The guy pulled up fifty feet from the house, got out, and left the motor running, the way fire department guys like to do. He was big, maybe late twenties, wearing a Red Sox hat and big rubber boots.

"Hi," I said.

"Tank blow yet?" he said.

"To hell and back."

"Was it running?"

"What? The truck?"

"Yeah," he said.

"Nope. Just sitting there."

"And it just caught fire?"

"No," I said. "Somebody torched it."

He gave me that sideways look, as the college girl had. Sizing me up. I got that look a lot in the next hour or so, as more pickups arrived and then a pumper from the volunteer fire department rumbled up, its red lights flashing all the way down the road. Five or six guys got the hoses uncoiled, fired up the pump motor, and gave my truck a blast of water that snuffed the flames with barely a hiss. It was like kicking dirt on a smoldering campfire by that point, but it was the thought that counted.

And they were thinking I was dirty.

Everybody stood around at three in the morning and looked at the blackened shell that was my sole means of transportation, assuming Claire wouldn't let me take his John Deere to town. There was some spitting and cursing and picking at the bones and then a man sidled up to me and said he was the assistant fire chief. He apologized for the fact that the chief wasn't able to come.

"Got a daughter in the hospital," he said.

"No problem," I said. "It was nice of all you guys to come out in the middle of the night like this."

"No problem," the assistant chief said.

He was forty-five, maybe, in shape and good looking in a lean sort of way. A hundred bucks said he was a high school basketball star and married a cheerleader. A hundred more said their girls were cheerleaders, too. Married to volunteer firemen.

It was all very small-town, very endearing, and it left me wishing I truly was one of the boys. I wasn't.

I told the assistant fire chief the truck had been set afire. One look at the wreck told him it wasn't an insurance job. He looked puzzled for a second, then his eyes narrowed.

"So why do you think would anybody want to burn your truck up?" he said slowly.

"Good question."

"Long story, huh?"

"Could be," I said.

We stood there as the fire guys loaded their hose back on the truck. A couple of pickups revved and spun gravel as they turned and headed back down the road into the darkness. They beeped farewell to each other and waved.

"Lived up here long?" the assistant chief said.

"No. A few months."

"You from nearby?"

"Androscoggin. Western part of the state. Before that, New York."

"What part?"

"New York City," I said.

"Got a son stationed in Plattsburgh. Can't wait to get out."

"Don't blame him."

He looked away.

"Live down there long?"

"Yeah. Until I came up here," I said.

"What do you do here?"

"I'm a writer."

He looked skeptical.

"What do you write?"

"Magazine stories."

He looked skeptical about that, too.

"You like it here?"

"Yeah."

"But you found some trouble."

"Or it found me."

It was a fine distinction to make and I didn't expect them to make it.

In fact, I figured they'd tag me as one of two things. Either somebody who couldn't keep it in his pants and was scooping somebody's wife, or somebody who ran on the other side of the law. In most cases, there's a reason you know people who burn people's cars. And it isn't because you're a Boy Scout.

So the firemen went about their business and wondered about the nature of mine. Nobody said anything to me but they all looked up when Poole drove up in his unmarked cruiser. I wondered if he confirmed or confounded their suspicions.

Poole got out, dressed in the same outfit—jeans, khaki jacket, plaid shirt, tan work boots—he'd worn every other time we'd met. Maybe it was sewn together. He put it on in one piece and his wife zipped it up the back.

He skirted the truck hulk and came up beside me.

"You couldn't sleep either?" I said.

Poole smiled, barely.

"It's the caffeine," I said. "You cops drink too much coffee, too late at night. And you should watch what you eat."

Again the smile.

"So what's your excuse?" Poole asked, still staring at the blackened truck.

"I've got a lot on my mind."

"Bats in your belfry?"

"They're out," I said. "But should be home soon."

"So what'd you see?"

"Didn't see anything. Not a person, I mean. I heard a clang, not real loud. A minute or two later I saw flames. Came out and saw something hanging out of the filler spout, burning."

"Rag?"

"Looked like it. Soaked with something, I guess. I went back to get a bucket or something and the whole thing went up."

"Kenny?" Poole asked.

"I don't know. I can't think of anybody else I've pissed off."

"Maybe Missy Hewett thought that, too."

I stopped and looked at him. He was calm and inscrutable as ever, watching the truck like he was watching a dry fly flick across the surface of some pond.

"You think these things are connected?" I said.

"I don't know, Mr. McMorrow. All I know is, for a newspaper writer or whatever you are now, you sure lead an exciting life."

"Not by choice."

"I'm not so sure," Poole said quietly. "These aren't what you'd call random crimes."

"A kid who takes a dislike to me and decides to harass me? I didn't ask for that."

"Nope."

"A girl who gets killed in the city eighty miles away. I talked to her once in my life."

"But she wanted to talk some more."

"So? That's what I do. I ask people to talk to me."

"And they end up dead."

"Not they. She. One girl. And you don't know that had anything to do with me."

"No, we don't, Mr. McMorrow," Poole said, looking at me for the first time. "No, we don't."

The "yet" was very much implied.

Poole stuck around fifteen more minutes and talked to the assistant chief. They talked in Poole's cruiser while I stood up by the wreck and felt my ears burn. As I was standing there watching them talk about me, a figure appeared behind me from out of the darkness.

"You never turn your back on the night," a voice said.

"Who said that?" I asked. "Dylan Thomas?"

"Claire Varney. And I think maybe you ought to start to listen to him."

"Why would I want to listen to that old coot?"

"Because it beats getting shot in the back."

"Now that's what I call being damned by faint praise."

Claire came up and stood beside me. He looked at the truck.

"I don't think it'll take a safety sticker," he said.

"How 'bout an unsafety sticker?"

"We ought to stick one of those on you."

We watched as Poole and the assistant fire chief got out of the cruiser and came back to my truck. They poked around the door next to the gas filler and Poole scraped something into a white envelope.

"Aren't you gonna dust it for fingerprints?" I said.

Poole looked over at me. His smile was so faint I could have imagined it. Claire watched, the old general holding his tongue. He said nothing as they poked and scraped. We both stood there as the pumper truck started up and eased off down the road. The pickups went all at once, like a departing pack of wolves. Finally Poole waved over, said "Be in touch," and walked to his car. Only when his taillights had faded into the darkness did Claire speak.

"I'm going to ask you something, Jack," he said. His voice was quiet and serious. Almost grave.

"What's that?"

He hesitated and I looked over at him. His jaw was clenched, his face muscular, his hair full of silver glints. For a moment, I felt I could picture him in Vietnam, in the jungle, in the dark.

"Jack, are you into something that I don't know about?"

I answered deliberately, knowing full well what he meant. Was I a drug dealer? Was there a side of me that he didn't know? Was there some other reason why somebody would blow out my windows and burn my truck?

"No," I said. "This is me. This is all there is."

Claire nodded.

"Glad to hear it. And I apologize for feeling I had to ask."

"Apology accepted."

"I won't ask again," Claire said. "What I will ask is for you to come down to my place in the morning. Mary'll make us breakfast and then we'll head out back. You can't just sit here and take this anymore."

"Nope," I said.

"There comes a time," Claire said. And he nodded and turned and walked off down the road. I stood alone in the dark and watched him disappear.

Twenty-two

In the bright light of a sunny morning, the truck was like something from a bad dream, a blackened souvenir of a nightmare. I walked around it, eyed the charred seat springs, the tires burned right off the rims. Hell, I wouldn't haul it off. I'd just take a picture of it and send it to Millie Tint. She could have it for her gallery.

Leaving the art world behind, I headed down the road to Claire's. The grass was damp, the trunks of the trees were dark and wet, and the leaves, orange and yellow and red, were like something hung out to dry. As I walked, a band of chickadees tumbled along in the brush beside me. A nuthatch gave a nasal "ank" and spilled down the trunk of an old broken maple, one that wore crimson like a dowager in an old ball gown.

For a moment, and only a moment, I forgot everything that had happened and saw only the pastoral dirt road, the timeless beauty of autumn in New England. Just call me Robert Frost.

But even the stillness of the morning and the palette of the woods couldn't keep everything away. By the time I hit Claire's barn, persistent little Missy Hewett had elbowed her way back into my mind, demanding my attention. I'm trying, I thought. I'm trying.

I went up the brick walk to the back porch, knocked once, and went into the kitchen. Mary, at the stove, turned over her shoulder and smiled.

"Mornin', Jack," she said. "What did we do for excitement around here before you moved here?"

"Sorry about that. You wake up last night?"

"I wouldn't have if it hadn't been for Claire, rattling around in the dark looking for his boots. Fun waking up to the sound of an old man cursing."

"What's that, woman?" Claire said, coming into the

kitchen from the shed. "God almighty, I'm barely old enough to be your husband."

"Too old," Mary said, turning a thick slice of French toast. "I'm gonna trade you in for—what do they call them? Oh, I saw it at the supermarket the other day. One of those checkout magazines. Oh, a boy toy. That's what they called it. Some movie star with this kid half her age, probably came to clean the pool."

"Well, forget the pool then, if that's what happens," Claire said.

"Were we putting one in, dear?"

"Yeah, I was gonna skim the lily pads off the farm pond. Get you one of those floating chairs with the holders for your drinks. Just keep your feet up 'cause of the leeches."

"And I say you never do anything for me."

"Take it all back, Mare. Take it all back."

I smiled. Claire went to the counter and grabbed three mugs from their hooks under the cabinet. He poured three cups of coffee from the electric coffee maker, handed me one black and motioned toward the table.

"Woman," he said. "You've got a couple of very hungry men here."

"Well," Mary said, sliding toast on to a platter, "when I've finished making myself breakfast, they can see if there's any corn flakes in the cupboard."

Corn flakes weren't on the menu. Mary served us French toast made with homemade bread, sprinkled with nutmeg and doused with real maple syrup from the Varney sugarbush. There were fried Varney potatoes, jam and toast, a bowl of sliced apples and oranges, and more coffee.

I ate like a starving man. Claire did the same and Mary dabbed at fruit and coffee.

Nobody said much. Mary said their daughter, Susan, in North Carolina had called the day before and said it was eighty-five degrees in Charlotte. Susan didn't like this because she was pregnant, her first, and she was in the early stage where you feel tired and sick. Mary said she remembered it well, feeling miserable before their girls were born. Two summer babies, she said.

Babies, babies everywhere, I thought.

I thought of Missy, wondered when her baby was born. Did she feel sick? I made a mental note to go back to her mother. But could I go see her, now that I was considered some sort of suspect?

"You're thinking of that girl, aren't you?" Claire said, bringing me back.

"Yeah," I said. "Kind of hard not to."

"That's your trouble. You sit around and think too much. Your brain's pickled in its own juice. Let's go out back."

I carried my plate to the counter and Claire did the same. I thanked Mary and she got up and started clearing the table, while Claire grabbed a stack of paper plates from the shelf, a staple gun from the drawer, and went into the den off the kitchen. It was a nice room, white walls and dark green trim and a wall-to-ceiling bookshelf full of books. Claire went to the closet next to the bookshelf, opened the door, and leaned in. When he came out, he was holding two rifles, two plastic ear protectors.

He handed me one of each.

We went back through the kitchen to the backyard. Claire carried his rifle comfortably in the crook of his arm. I carried mine at arm's length, like a live bomb.

I followed Claire out past the vegetable garden and into the back field. Across the field, on the edge of the woods, a piece of weathered plywood was nailed to two cedar posts. Attached to the center of the plywood was what appeared to be a trash-can lid.

"This thing loaded?" I said, keeping the barrel of the rifle pointed at the ground.

"Why you asking me?"

"Because you gave it to me."

"You never take anybody's word on whether a gun is loaded. You check yourself."

He put his rifle down on the ground, then reached for mine. I handed it over gladly and he slid the lever up and the bolt back.

"This is a Remington. Model 700. Bolt action. Thirty-ought six. A very popular deer rifle. Very accurate."

I nodded.

"This is the chamber."

He held the rifle so I could see the shiny silver opening where the bolt had slid out.

"Holds five rounds. Four in the magazine, one in the chamber, ready to fire. Look in there. See that spring-loaded piece? That forces the cartridges up. See how it's empty? And there's nothing in the barrel? That's how you know the gun isn't loaded. It's the only way you know."

"Right," I said.

"This is the safety."

He thumbed a small inconspicuous lever at the top of the gun.

"Back is safety on. Forward is safety off."

"That's it?"

"Yeah," Claire said. "That simple."

"Seems like it should be painted orange or something."

He continued.

"You don't check the safety by pulling the trigger. I know a kid who did that. Safety back, press trigger. Safety back, press trigger. Except he got the sequence off one time and the gun fired. Almost blew his friend's leg off. A lesson I never forgot."

"Were you the friend?"

"No. And my buddy never forgot it, either. Your finger doesn't even go near the trigger until you're ready to shoot. You ready?"

"I'm ready."

I slid the bolt back and forth. Squeezed the trigger and pulled the bolt back and forward again. The trigger barely required any pressure. Just touch and barely squeeze.

Click.

I aimed the rifle at the trash-can lid, which Claire said was about sixty yards away. The metal sight wavered with the end of the barrel.

"You don't try to hold it still," Claire said. "You try to time it so you fire as the sight crosses the target. We'll try a scope in a minute. I just want you to know what to expect so you don't ram that scope into your eye."

He took a cardboard box out of his jacket pocket, opened it, and handed me a cartridge. It was about two and a half inches long, copper with a pointed silver tip. I held it gingerly and placed it in the chamber. It dropped in and lay flat. I slid the bolt forward and down.

"That's it?"

"You're ready to shoot, Bones."

I put the stock of the rifle to my right shoulder. Claire told me not to squeeze it tightly, but to keep it loose, so all the kick wouldn't be absorbed by my shoulder. I pushed the safety forward and aimed at the can. Held my breath and squeezed.

Bam!

The barrel kicked up and back and the sound echoed across the field like a cannon shot. I couldn't tell if I hit the can lid or the plywood or even the trees behind them.

"Did I hit it?"

"Hard to say," Claire said. "Try again."

I fired five rounds without a scope. Then we walked across the field and checked the lid. I'd hit it three times, leaving raw metal holes three-eighths of an inch in diameter. One shot buried itself in the ground below the lid. Another tore through the plywood.

God, I thought. What would this do to a man?

Claire stapled a plate to the plywood with the staple gun and we walked back to where the rifles were on the ground. I picked mine up and Claire pulled a scope out of his jacket pocket and slid it in place for me. It was a Redfield four-power with a crosshair sight that drifted slowly across the plate. I fired four rounds from a crouch and hit the plate three times, just right of center.

"Missed my calling," I said. "Should have been a sniper."

"Scope's kind of useless in Maine," Claire said. "Most of the time you're in the woods, shooting twenty or thirty yards, max."

"But if it's a trophy paper plate you're after, it's just the ticket, right?"

"We'll get you that one. You can hang it on the wall of your den."

"Right beside the tin cans," I said.

We shot for a half-hour more. Claire showed me his gun, a seven-by-fifty-seven Mauser. Its cartridges were slightly narrower than the Remington's and a little shorter. I asked Claire why he was shooting such a sissy gun.

"Oh, this gun's an old friend," Claire said. "It just feels right. Got the right fit."

"And this rifle here is supposed to be my new buddy?"

"You seem to hit it off just fine. You aren't a half-bad shot, either."

"For a liberal."

"Right. For a worthless yellow-bellied pinko you're pretty good."

"Enough. I'm getting all choked up."

I slid the bolt back on the Remington and made sure it was empty. Let the barrel point down at the ground. Picked it back up. I just couldn't find a natural way to hold the thing. Anybody with a half grain of perception would take one look at me and see a city slicker with a big gun.

"Hey," I said, as Claire slid a cartridge into the Mauser's chamber. "What's this all about anyway? First shotguns and firebombs? Then they come at me with paper plates?"

Claire lowered his rifle and looked at me.

"I can't shoot anybody," I said.

"I'm not saying you should. Anything but."

"Then what's this all about?"

Claire smiled. Pushed the safety down on the Mauser. It looked natural in his arms.

"Deer hunting," he said.

"Give me a break."

He stepped in front of me. Raised the rifle to his shoulder, paused for a three-count and fired. The Mauser roared, the muzzle blast rippling the grass in front of him for twenty feet. He slid the bolt back and the empty shell flipped out onto the ground. I bent and picked it up and handed it to him.

"Well," I said.

"Jack, I don't think you quite know what you've gotten yourself in for, here. This guy isn't letting air out of your tires or throwing toilet paper around your yard. He blew the window out of your house, missed you by a couple of feet. Blew up your truck. And that's just for starters."

"So he's a little playful."

I grinned.

"Jack, I know his type. This Kenny guy. He's a psychopath. Crazy. I've had them under my command, I know them. With kids like this, things have a way of escalating out of control."

"I thought you didn't like that word."

"I don't," Claire said. "And I don't like what's going on here. This guy could kill you in a second. Wouldn't have to plan it. It'd just happen. Run you off the road. Burn your house down with you in it. Next time he shoots out a window, you're walking by on the way to the fridge."

"So what's this deer rifle supposed to do for me?"

"It's a deterrent."

"You mean like arms talks? Hey, I've never been to Geneva."

"It's what he understands. Right now he knows you're in there with nothing. What do you have? Your little reporter's hands."

"What do you mean little?"

"You know what I mean. To him you're just some wimp. All that typing and stuff."

"How 'bout I just rent a backhoe and drive it around the yard."

Claire stopped. He looked at me the way he probably once looked at a corporal.

"Jack, this isn't a joke, my friend. You got this girl who got killed. This guy blowing stuff up. It's time to stop laughing. You're a good friend and I'm telling you. I've seen these kamikaze characters at work. It's time to get serious."

Standing there in his field, with the blue sky and the golden treeline, we were suddenly somber.

"You're serious, aren't you?" I said.

"Some things you know about. This is something I know about."

"Okay. What do I do? Let him know I can shoot the eye out of a paper plate at sixty yards?"

"You get another truck. You buy a gun rack. You drive around town with that thirty odd-six in the rack."

"With a straight face?"

"Yup. Let him and his buddies know it's there. And when you're home, keep the gun within reach. You don't have to keep it loaded but don't lock it in the cellar, either."

"Why? So I can keep the paper plates at bay?"

"Better than being down there a sittin' duck."

"I'm not a sitting duck," I said. "I've got you to protect me."

"Like I said. Keep it handy."

We turned toward the house, Claire with his Mauser, me with my Remington Model 700 security blanket. When we were almost to the house, I stopped and slid the bolt back one more time. The rifle was empty.

By the back door, I stopped.

"Claire," I said. "I've got one question about all this."

He waited.

"Now is it safety on when the safety is back? Or is it safety off?"

Claire looked at me, hard.

"Just kidding," I said.

"I hope I'm wrong," he said. "But I've got this funny feeling the time for kidding's over."

I did buy a truck. It was an old red four-wheel-drive Toyota with a rusting bed and 128,000 miles on the odometer. It was eight hundred bucks. And it had a gun rack.

Claire drove me to look at it in Waterville, a little mill city about twenty miles away. The kid who was selling it said he needed the money to pay court fines. I thought that was as good a reason as any. Claire didn't say anything to the kid, just leaned over the open hood and listened to the motor. Then we drove it up and down the street, with Claire shifting it in and out of four-wheel-high and four-wheel-low. He said it sounded fine, that he liked Toyota four-wheel-drives because you couldn't kill them. I liked the gun rack because it symbolized my newfound machismo. All the way back to Prosperity it seemed that women turned their heads and watched me pass. Roxanne would melt in my arms. Maybe I'd let her watch me shoot.

I liked driving the thing, even found myself smiling as I slipped it into overdrive and listened to the big tires whine on the pavement. But the smile had barely set when everything else flooded back and wiped my face clean. Missy. Kenny. A couple of cops who wanted to nail me. I couldn't allow myself the indulgence of a joyride.

At the general store in the town of Albion, I stopped and bought a *Waterville Sentinel*. The obituaries were on the back page of the first section. Sitting in the truck by the gas pumps, I scanned down the names and didn't see Missy's. I went down the page again and there it was: "Melissa Jean Hewett, 18, of Prosperity died unexpectedly in Portland."

Somewhere at the Waterville newspaper, there was a master of understatement.

The obituary said Melissa was the daughter of Joyce Hewett. There was no mention of her father. Take that, you no good son of a bitch. The obit did list four surviving sisters with four different last names, which I supposed meant they were all married or had different fathers or both. They all lived within fifteen miles of Prosperity. Visiting hours were at the Littlefield Funeral Home in Belfast from four to six.

After reading it twice, it struck me.

Her baby had been omitted, too.

Twenty-three

It was quarter to five. I drove the last ten miles in less than ten minutes, then bounced the little truck down the dump road and slid it into the dooryard. Trotting inside, I grabbed an apple from the bowl on the table, then went up to the loft to pick out something suitable to wear to the wake of a young girl who'd been murdered. I picked a gray tweed jacket, blue shirt, dark blue Levi's corduroys, and L.L. Bean moccasins. The family might think I was one of her professors. I wondered if Missy's mom would even remember that we'd met.

The funeral home was in one of the big sea captains' mansions that lined Belfast's streets, keeping oil dealers and housepainters in business. I drove past the place once and glanced at my watch. It was quarter to four. I turned around in the driveway of a stately gray Victorian ark, where a small blonde girl, three or four years old, watched me from the yard. She had been jumping into a magnificently huge pile of multicolored leaves. I waved and she stared.

Reluctantly, I drove back. The Littlefield Funeral Home was a big Greek Revival place with the gable end facing the street and the entrance on the side. There were two pickups parked out front and, as I pulled in behind them, a car came to a stop directly behind me. I looked in the rearview mirror and saw an older woman getting out of a small red car. She was in the passenger seat and another woman, younger, was driving. The younger woman held the door open and two teenagers got out of the backseat. One was a girl wearing a short skirt and boots. The other was a boy wearing jeans and a black leather jacket.

I was not underdressed.

When they had let themselves in, I got out of the truck and followed, feeling a little queasy. It was the same feeling I'd gotten every time I'd had to go to a funeral as a reporter, elbowing my way into the inner sanctum of some family's grief. This time, I didn't even have that license to hide behind.

The door was big and heavy and opened inward with a quiet whoosh. I walked into a corridor with white painted trim, dim lights and that funeral-home carpet that's thick and spongy as sphagnum moss. Two sets of curtained French doors led off the corridor. I walked to the first doors and looked into an empty room, small with five or six rows of straight-backed wooden chairs with upholstered seats. Taking a deep breath, I walked to the next door and peered in at an identical room with the same five or six rows of chairs. This time, a dozen or so faces peered back.

Because—and only because—there was no turning back, I walked in and took a seat at the rear. The teenage boy and girl turned in their seats and stared at me. A couple of guys did the same. They were big and bearded, in their late twenties maybe, wearing plaid flannel shirts. They stared at me and I stared back and then they turned around to face the open casket where Missy Hewett lay still.

She looked like Sleeping Beauty, bathed in some sort of rosy funeral-parlor light, her cheeks rouged and her skin very white, as if she were an actor wearing stage makeup. Her hands were crossed on her chest, her fingers interlocked. They had painted her nails a pale translucent pink. Her dress was dark blue like a nun's and looked borrowed.

There was organ music playing softly from hidden speakers so that the whole thing had the air of a phony séance during which we would be expected to ask the deceased a question. I had a few questions but Missy Hewett wouldn't be able to answer them now.

One of the guys coughed, breaking the silence. As if a precedent had been set, everybody else started fidgeting and clearing their throats. From the front row came a sob. A woman with long dark hair put her arm around Missy's mother. The music droned on.

It was one of those formless rituals, like kneeling at an altar to pray. How do you know when you're done? How much is enough and how much is too little?

But one by one, they went up to a small kneeler in front of the casket, where there were a few flowers, not an abundance. When Missy's mother went, the dark-haired woman went with her, holding her by the shoulder. I wondered how many times Joyce Hewett's children had held their mother up over the years, but for a different reason.

After twenty minutes or so, the wake seemed to be winding down. A pallid expressionless undertaker in the standard black suit padded silently in and whispered something to one of the sisters. She nodded and he stepped to the front of the room and picked up a thick black prayer book.

"Dear God," the funeral home man began, "may the soul of Melissa Jean be buoyed by our heartfelt love. As she lived her life on this Earth, may she live her life in Paradise. And may all of us who knew her cherish her memory forever. Amen."

"Amen."

Everyone sat there until the undertaker left. Then they

turned to each other before rising stiffly. The mother and three other women went to the casket and said good-bye. The men turned toward me again and stared.

They left the room one by one and because I was in the rear, I left last. Before I left, I paused and took a long look at Missy. It was only her stillness that made her look dead, that and the serenity that had come over her. In life, she had never known that luxury.

When I walked out into the corridor, they had gone. I pulled the big door open and stepped outside. Cars were starting. Headlights were flicking on. I took a step toward the sidewalk and slowed. The two bearded guys and the women from the car were waiting by the curb. They looked up and kept looking, their faces hard and grim. They were waiting for me.

There was no time for preparation, mental or physical. It was about thirty feet to the curb and the committee. Ten or fifteen steps. I walked them in a straight line and stopped. The men stared, their deepset dark eyes locked onto mine. I stared back. This went on for what seemed like three or four days. Finally, one of the guys, the shorter of the two at about my height, nodded. I nodded back. One of the women—stocky and busty, pretty face, cigarette in her right hand, hand at her right hip—formed what could have been called a half-smile.

By a dreamy-eyed optimist.

"Hi," I said.

That brought nods and abbreviated guttural sounds that sounded like "heh."

The women looked at the shorter guy. I looked at the women. The two bigger guys looked at me.

"Jimmy, you do the talking," the busty woman said.

The shorter guy nodded.

"You the reporter?" he said.

"Yeah," I said.

"The one who came to see Joyce?"

"If you mean Missy's mother, then I'm the one."

"Right. And you talked to Missy?"

"That's right," I said.

"About her baby, right?"

"Yeah," I said again.

"How'd you come to do that?"

I hesitated. Looked into the faces of my sidewalk dissertation committee. Wondered what the penalty was for failure.

"I write stories for magazines," I said slowly, keeping eye contact with the shorter guy, noticing a long thin scar on his left temple. "They wanted me to do a story on teenage girls who have babies. What it does to their lives. I went to the high school and a couple girls gave me Missy's name. They told me she was in college. I was in Portland anyway so I looked her up."

"Did she want to talk to you?"

"After I explained. Not at first. I mean, she didn't know me from Adam."

"At her apartment?" the shorter guy asked.

"Yeah."

"How long did you stay?"

"I don't know. Not long. Twenty minutes maybe."

I glanced at the others. They looked at me unwaveringly. The ladies and gentlemen of the jury.

"What did she say?"

"Well, she said she put the baby up for adoption because she thought it would have a better life. She said she didn't think much of the father, didn't even think of him as a father. She didn't say who it was. She didn't come right out and say this but it seemed like it was a tough thing for her to do. And to live with after."

"And that was it?"

"Yeah. I said I'd like to talk to her again. She seemed to think that might be okay. A few days later, she called me back and said she wanted to get her baby back."

"Then what?"

"Then the next morning they found her. Found her . . ."

"Dead," the shorter guy said.

The word just sat out there. Mean and sad and sordid. They looked at me right through it.

"What did you think of her?" the busty woman said suddenly.

"What did I think of her?"

"Yeah," the shorter guy said.

"I liked her. I thought she was a tough kid. A lot of determination. Guts. She was gutsy."

"What did you think of what she did?" the woman said.

"What, with the baby? I don't know. I guess I just think it was hard on her. But she did it for the right reasons. She wasn't thinking of herself."

"You kill her?"

It was the other guy, the bigger, with the longer beard.

I looked at him.

"No," I said. "I didn't kill her."

"Why should we believe you?"

His tone was demanding, as if I should have a good answer.

"I can't make you. I just know I didn't kill her. I met her once. Talked to her maybe twenty minutes, total."

"Did you want to screw her?" the bigger guy asked.

"No," I said. "She was a little kid."

There was a pause. The women looked at the men. The men looked at the women. The busty woman sucked hard on her cigarette and dropped it glowing onto the sidewalk. The street was dark and deserted and quiet. The lights in the windows of the big old houses seemed far away.

"I think we should do it," the busty woman said, breaking the silence.

"Yeah," the shorter guy said, turning to me.

The others nodded in agreement. I steeled myself for the execution of their sentence, figured I'd try to make it back into the funeral home. At least go down swinging. I tensed as the shorter guy reached into his pocket and dug out . . .

A piece of paper.

"This is Sue's phone bill," he said, motioning to the busty woman. "That's her. There's numbers on there that Missy called. She stayed with Sue at their trailer for a while before the baby. 'Cause Sue's her sister. Nine years older. I'm her brother-in-law. Jolene's my wife. Before it was born Missy moved to Portland. I got the numbers all marked."

He held the bill out. It was three pages. I took it but it was too dark to read. The shorter guy pulled out a cigarette lighter and held it out so I could see.

"They're Portland. A couple to Providence, Rhode Island. I think it's three to Falmouth. A whole bunch to the same number in Portland."

"You try to call 'em?" I asked.

"Nope," Sue said.

"Why not?"

"We ain't detectives. Or what is it—investigative reporters?"

"Show them to the cops?"

Sue looked at Jimmy. The others looked at him, too.

"I don't talk to cops," he said. "Let's just leave it at that. Last time I tried to talk to cops I got three years in Windham. Correctional Center. Now I'm on goddamn probation. Can't even have a friggin' beer. That's what you get when you talk to cops."

Sue cut him off.

"So we're giving them to you. You can do whatever it is you do with 'em. Find out who they are or whatever. Maybe it'll have something to do with who killed her."

I looked at the bill, then folded it once and put it in the inside pocket of my jacket.

"You people know the cops have talked to me about all this?" I said. "I get the feeling they think I might be a suspect. I just want you to know that."

"Well, they're wrong again," Jimmy said. " 'Cause you can tell what a man is by looking him in the eye. I ain't been wrong yet."

"Nope," Sue said. "Maybe this'll help Missy and keep your ass out of jail."

"We'll hope so," I said.

Jimmy nodded.

"You better do more than hope, mister," he said. " 'Cause I been there and they'd eat you up."

I drove back slowly in the dark, partly because the truck just had an old plate stuck on it and wasn't registered, and partly to think. Once I got home, I'd feel a need to do something. Driving, I was relegated to contemplation of my situation.

Which sucked. To slip into the vernacular of the time.

I didn't want to go to prison. I didn't want to be a suspect in Missy's murder. I didn't want to be a murder victim. I didn't want to shoot someone with Claire's big rifle. I'd seen what it had done to plywood. I didn't want to see what it would do to flesh and bone. I did want to talk to somebody. About all of this.

By the time I hit Montville, on Route 3, I'd decided to call Roxanne. She was flying to Boston the next night. If I saw her on Friday or Saturday that would be too late. I needed to start on this soon. Tomorrow morning. Early.

I took the phone bill out of my pocket, unfolded it, and held it down under the pale green light of the dashboard. It was too dark so I groped for the switch for the dome light. I found it alongside the light and switched it on and off several times. The light flickered once and went out. I jerked it back and forth some more, reaching over my right shoulder with my left hand. The truck veered to the left and forced an oncoming car to swerve into the breakdown lane and blast the horn.

Kenny wouldn't have to kill me. I'd kill myself. I put the phone bill back on the seat and drove.

When I got home it was a little after seven. The hulk was waiting in the drive and the ashes and smoke smell still was in the air. I walked through it, went inside, and grabbed a can of beer from the fridge and a bowl of cold pasta with tomato sauce. Half the beer went down in two gulps. The pasta followed in lumps until the gnawing pain in my belly was smothered. One pain down. Several to go.

I took another beer out of the refrigerator, which left only two, and went to the table. The two beers went to the left of the phone. The phone bill went to the right. I spread out the three pages and looked over the calls Jimmy and Sue had marked.

There were four calls to Providence, to two different numbers, lasting from six to thirty seconds. Nineteen calls to Portland proper. Three different numbers but one number was called only twice. The calls to that number lasted from three to five minutes.

The second number was called five times. Times ranged from fifteen seconds to thirty-five minutes. The three calls in the middle range were from two to four minutes.

It was the third number that Missy had spent some time with. A dozen calls had been made but they were almost all long. One was an hour and twenty-five minutes and all but two were over a half-hour. Most were placed in evening hours, but the long call had been made a minute after ten, at night.

I couldn't envision my grim-faced little Missy waxing on that long with anyone. But if Jimmy and Sue were to be believed, she had.

In the movies, detectives who needed to trace a number always had a source at the phone company whom they'd call. I'd always wondered why the detectives didn't just call the number and say "Who's this?" If there was a reason why this direct approach didn't work, I figured I'd find out.

I finished my first beer, opened the second, then got up and went to get a pen and notebook. When I came back, I sipped the second beer and, pen in hand, dialed the phone.

This was the number Missy had called twice. I finished

dialing it, waited as the round thing rolled back around, and
waited.

It rang once. Twice. Three times. Then a click and the
hiss of a taped message.

"Hello. You have reached the office of the registrar, University of Southern Maine. The office is closed now. Office
hours are from eight-thirty A.M. to five P.M., Monday
through Friday, and Saturday from nine until noon. Thank
you."

So that's it, I thought. She was killed because she was
short on credit hours.

I looked at the second number and dialed again. Waited.
One ring. Two. Three. Four.

"This is the office of Wheaton, Hinckley, Prine and Mc-
Salley, attorneys. The office is closed right now. If you
know the number of the extension you want, and you are at
a touch-tone phone . . ."

A lawyer. A Portland lawyer. A Portland adoption
lawyer? What other reason would Missy Hewett have to
contact an attorney?

The Falmouth number was next. I dialed and waited. It
rang twice and a woman answered.

"Hello."

"Hello, is Dean there?"

"I'm sorry?"

"Dean. Is this the right number?"

"No, you have the wrong number."

"Oh, I'm very sorry," I said. "Didn't mean to—"

Click.

The voice had been young middle age. Fortyish, maybe.
Cool and assured. Like somebody with money. Great. I
could just keep asking for Dean until she broke down and
told me who she was and how she knew Missy Hewett.

I sat there in the quiet and looked at my pad, which was
more or less blank. A lawyer and a rich woman. I wrote
that much on my pad and decided it looked pretty meager.

Picked up the phone again and dialed the first Providence number to try to fill things out.

One ring, with different tone. Another and another. Then a click and a hiss.

"Hello," a young man's voice said. "This is the Department of Classics, Brown University. The office is closed but at the tone, you may leave a message."

It beeped and I hung up. Brown University? Could Southern Maine have been Missy's second choice? Did she know a professor?

I scrawled a question mark and picked up the phone again. Call to Rhode Island number two. It rang twice, a woman's voice answered and, ready for a recording, I almost forgot to answer.

"Hello. I said hello," she said.

She sounded exasperated or annoyed.

"Hi," I said. "This is Scott Fitzgerald with the Providence Home Improvement Company. How are you this evening?"

I waited.

"I'm quite fine, thank you. And—"

"Good," I interrupted. "I'd like to tell you about some of the services we're offering this season, including our pre-winter button-up special. Does your home have aluminum combination storm windows, ma'am, or does it have the newer insulated models?"

"Listen," she said.

"Well, with either type of window, an imperfect fit can cost you hundreds of dollars in unnecessary heating costs."

"Now you listen," the woman said. "I know you're just trying to earn a living. I understand that. But I really don't think I need anything you're selling."

"I'm not selling anything. Providence Home Improvement offers services for the homeowner that can result in sizable savings down the road. We like to think of it as an investment opportun—"

"Listen, you jerk," the woman said, her voice shrill and

loud. "Do you know how I spent the last hour? I spent the last hour trying to get a very colicky baby to go to sleep."

"Oh, I'm very sorry. I really am. I have four children and I know what that's like. I mean, I really do. I'm sorry. I apologize. A new baby, I . . . I know where you're coming from. How old is your baby?"

"She's four months, but that's really none of your business. But you people always call at the worst time, imposing on me and my family when I couldn't care less about whatever crap it is you're trying to peddle."

"Ma'am, we don't peddle crap."

"Don't tell me what you do or don't do. What you do is wake a baby who was just about asleep. Thank you very much."

Thank you very much, I thought to myself after she hung up. And my best to your four-month-old baby girl.

Twenty-four

My mind churned all night and no amount of bedtime beer could have numbed it. I heard the clock in the hall chime two o'clock. And three. And four. At two, I was on my back, staring up at the blackness where the bats, contemplating the bat bliss of hibernation, only occasionally rustled. At three, I was making mental lists of everything that had happened. I made mental lists of everything I knew. I made mental lists of everyone even remotely involved. The idea was to impose order on the chaos that was now everywhere around me, the chaos that was my life, that, no exaggeration, could cost me my life, or at least a big chunk of it.

At four I concluded I couldn't do it.

There was no clue in what I knew that could tell me why Missy had been killed. There was no clue as to why this Kenny kid had taken such a passionate dislike to me. There was no logical pattern. But stretched out there in my underwear in the dark, it occurred to me that maybe the pattern wasn't in what I knew but in what I didn't know.

I didn't know where Missy's baby was, though I suspected she was keeping her mommy up in Providence. I didn't know what adoption procedure she'd used, though I did know she hadn't gone through channels in her home county. I didn't know why I didn't know, why the whole thing seemed to be such a well-kept secret, at least from her family. But she had to confide in someone, didn't she? She had to have had help finding this lawyer in Portland, having the baby, just going through the process. If not these sisters or her mother, then who?

When I woke up at seven o'clock, after a fitful couple of hours' sleep, the question miraculously still was preserved. If not them, who?

I got up and eased myself stiffly down the loft stairs. After a shower and a bagel with peanut butter, I eased myself back up the stairs and got dressed in jeans, chamois shirt, and boots. Grabbing another bagel on the way out the door, I went out and climbed in the new truck. The old one sat in the driveway like a dead body, the skeleton of a self-immolated monk, a casualty of battle that could not be dragged away because the war still raged.

It was a coloring-book kind of day—blue sky, white clouds, orange and yellow trees—as if the artist only had four colors and wasn't allowed to blend. The air was cool and brisk and seemed to carry an extra dose of oxygen that wired me like no drug you could buy in lower Manhattan. I drove the little truck with what seemed to me to be aplomb, buoyed by what little plan I had come up with for the day. All action is better than inaction, I thought. Or as an old editor at the *Times* used to put it, motivating her metro reporters, "Get your ass out of this building and hit the streets."

So I was hitting the closest thing to streets that you could find in Waldo County, Maine. I stopped at the post office and checked my box but it was empty. I held the door for an old woman coming into the post office and she said, "Thank you, dear." From there, I drove out of town to the north, stopping at the general store on Knox Ridge to buy gas and a coffee.

"So how's Jimmy?" the woman at the cash register asked the guy in front of me. I'd been coming there for months but she didn't ask, "How's Jack?" Another thirty years, I'd be in like flint.

The coffee was still hot when I pulled into the parking lot at Waldo Regional High. I circled once like a dog going to sleep and picked a space directly across from the front door. A small sign said, "Reserved for faculty." Professor Jack McMorrow, at your service.

There in the parking lot, I sat and drank the coffee, and thus fortified, went in the front door, easing my way through the between-classes rush like a New Yorker leaving the subway. Remembering my original directions, I took "like a left" and "like a right" and soon was standing at attention in front of the guidance department secretary, who asked if I had an appointment.

I lied and said yes. With Janice Genest.

She came back and said Miss Genest was with a student. I said I'd wait and went to a plaid easy chair in the corner to make good on my promise. I looked at college catalogues and the secretary looked at me. When I got tired of her staring, I held up a pamphlet on sexually transmitted diseases and said "Yuck" out loud. She found something else to do.

In ten minutes, Genest's door opened and she stepped out. When she saw me she stopped, turned, and went back inside. I got up and went to the door and looked in to see her sitting at her desk, hair pulled back, a finely knit cotton sweater tied by the arms around her neck. It looked like a serial killer had dissolved in mid-strangle.

"Got a minute?" I said.

"And not much more," Genest said, picking up a folder.

"The secretary said you were with a student so I waited."

"Considerate of you."

"But I guess she was confused because there's no student in here."

"Apparently not."

"Unless he or she went out the back door."

"There isn't one," Genest said.

"Apparently," I said.

I smiled. She still hadn't looked up. I took a step in and sat in the green vinyl easy chair beside the door. Genest kept working.

"I didn't see you at Missy Hewett's wake," I said.

"That's because I wasn't there."

"I thought you were pretty good friends."

"We were and that's why I wasn't there. Unlike people who might have known Missy only superficially, I was too upset to see her. That way."

"I can see that," I said. "You were pretty close, weren't you?"

"For a counselor-student relationship, yes," Genest said, putting her file folder down.

"I'm sorry."

"About what?"

"About what happened," I said. "To her. What happened to her."

"Bullshit," Genest said suddenly. "Christ, don't give me that. You're just as glad 'cause now you'll get a juicier story. Am I right? Isn't the death of Missy Hewett a lot more sexy than the life of Missy Hewett? Come on, you can admit it. Missy being murdered was your lucky break."

"The cops don't think so."

"No?"

"No. They've got this idea that maybe I did it."

"Did you?"

"Nope."

The secretary came in and put a folder on Genest's desk. I gave the secretary a big smile.

"She's not with a student anymore," I said.

The secretary glared at me and turned and went back to her desk.

"Makes your day to catch somebody in a lie, doesn't it?" Genest said.

"I spent ten years trying to catch people in lies," I said. "After that long, it just wasn't fun anymore."

"So what do you do now?"

"I try to catch people telling the truth."

"Caught any lately?" Genest asked.

"Yeah. I have, actually. It isn't so hard, if you know where to look."

She gave me a long look.

"Must be nice to be so cocksure of everything."

"It's a façade," I said. "Compensation for raging insecurity."

"Somehow I find that hard to believe."

"You'd be amazed."

"That I don't doubt," Genest said.

I half expected her to announce that she had a class or a crisis or whatever it was that took her out of her office and into the field. But she didn't and instead rested her chin in her hands and appeared ready to talk until I got tired of standing. This was where all those years of leaning against bars paid off.

"I'm serious about the cops," I said.

"That they think you might be the one?"

"Yeah."

"Well, I suppose they have to start somewhere."

"That doesn't bother you?" I asked.

"Will you be insulted if I say no?"

"No," I said. "I'd be insulted if you said yes."

"Well, no, it doesn't bother me. And to be honest, Mr. McMorrow, a detective came and talked to me. Kind of a quiet guy. Poole or Houle or something like that. Not very coplike."

"Most of them aren't," I said. "Except on television."

"Yeah, well, he wanted to know if you really came here looking for information about teen pregnancy and all that, and I said, yeah, you did. He seemed disappointed."

"He's the one who tries to catch people in lies."

"I'm not saying he's given up trying with you," Genest said.

"Of course not. It's not like one character reference is gonna clear me."

"I didn't say anything about character. I just said that in this one particular case, you seemed to have accurately portrayed at least the basic facts of our brief acquaintance."

"Thanks," I said.

She almost smiled and I jumped in before her mood could swing.

"But I've got another question. If you don't mind."

Her eyes narrowed, as if maybe she minded after all.

"It's about Missy, of course. I just wondered if you could tell me more about her baby. How she came to give it up. I mean, what she did after she decided that. And how she decided. The whole process, I guess."

"I can't talk about that," Genest said, leaning back in her chair. "Students' records, what they say to me, what I say to them, that's confidential."

"But she's dead."

"Doesn't matter."

"Matters to me. I could go away for a very long time."

"Promises, promises," she said.

"Come on."

Genest pondered. Ran her fingers across her forehead and through her thick dark hair. I noticed her makeup, which was subtle but nicely done. Her nails were carefully manicured. Hers was a calculated casualness.

"Shut the door," she said grudgingly. "You ask some hypothetical questions. Maybe I'll be able to help you. Maybe I won't."

I sighed inwardly. How many times had I played this game over the years and never liked it?

"Okay. A student gets pregnant. Would she tell you? Are you on that good terms with these kids?"

"Some of them. A lot of them."

"That's good."

"Sometimes."

"So let's say this student isn't sure what to do. Have the baby? Abortion? Keep it? Give it up? What would you say?"

"This isn't family planning," Genest said.

"But you have to say something. Give some guidance, right?"

"I try."

"So what would you say?"

She gave a short annoyed sigh. She was attractive when she was irritated, I thought. I decided not to tell her.

"It just depends. On the student and the situation."

"This is the hypothetical student."

"I know. Okay, I might tell them about the options. Where to go if they choose one. There's a family planning clinic in Belfast where they can get advice. I mean specific advice. There's an adoption agency in Waterville. A good one. But you know they aren't usually coming to me all rational and calm and considering their options."

"Why not?"

"God, men are so . . . They're kids. They're upset. Petrified. Bowled over by this thing that's happened to them. They can't talk to their parents a lot of the time. I'm just this shoulder to cry on. I mean, God, they're going to have a baby. And they are babies. Unless they do something to change it, I mean."

"Are they all upset?" I asked. "Don't some just take it in stride?"

"Some do. Unfortunately. Those are the ones who never expected to finish high school anyway. Who just fall into this because it's the path of least resistance. It's what they know, you know? It's easy and familiar."

"And keeps the cycle going and all that."

"And going and going and going. One wasted life begets another. It's a goddamn tragedy, really. But it's women's lives, so nobody cares much. Not in this society. Don't kid yourself. American women are still held down. It may not be as blatant as it was fifty years ago, but it's very much there. It's insidious now."

I looked at her, surprised. There was a well of anger in there and it was full.

"I suppose not," I said. "But what about kids who don't want to do that? Who might want to go the adoption route. What can you tell them?"

Genest reached to the bookshelf to her right and pulled out a booklet. It was green and thin. She tossed it across the desk.

"I give them this. It's all about adoption. The laws. Some advice on the emotional side of the whole thing. Where they can go around here. More people to talk to. Counselors who do this kind of thing."

"And this hypothetical kid. Where might she have gone?"

"I don't know. Some kids come to me for support. Then once they're all shored up, they go off and do it without me. It's just as well. By that time, I can't be propping them up. I mean, God. It's a big decision and they have to be able to stand up themselves."

"But, hypothetically, don't they keep checking in?"

Out in the hall, a bell rang. Immediately, a low rumble could be heard, like something that would precede a volcanic interruption.

"You have to go?"

"In a minute."

"Just a couple more," I said. "If this person didn't tell anyone, what might the reason be for that?"

"This hypothetical person?"

"Right."

"Shame. Not as much for getting pregnant as for giving up the baby. Fear that family members might not approve. Some parents, I mean parents of my kids, don't want to let go of that grandchild."

"Can't really blame them."

"Yeah, but they should be able to see past that. If that's what the girl wants to do, I mean, then it's time to support her. But for this hypothetical kid, there might be another reason to do it sub rosa, so to speak."

"And what might that reason be?"

"She might be afraid of the dad," Genest said.

"What? That he might want to keep the baby?"

"Hypothetically. And he might want to stop her from going through with an adoption. It's a power thing. Men like to be in control. Almost all men, even if they don't know it. God, my father used to . . . Anyway, the girl is just property to these kids. You know. A car. A truck. A snowmobile. A girlfriend."

"And a baby."

"By extension. And this is a girl taking control of her life. I mean, some of these guys just freak. It threatens their very dominating, bullying existence. They can't handle it."

There was real anger in her voice.

"And if they're threatened they might lash out?"

"Hypothetically they might."

"So the mother might choose to go elsewhere. Get out of reach."

"Sometimes it's the prudent thing to do. The whole thing is hard enough without having some jerk telling you what you should do with your life. Where does he get off? No pun intended. All he did was cajole or bully some young girl into taking her pants off. In my book, that earns you nothing. Nothing."

Genest said it with conviction. Or was it hatred?

"You have a very romantic view of love," I said.

"God almighty, McMorrow. It's called being realistic. Romance isn't the part of these kids' lives that I have to deal with. I deal with the aftermath."

"And it isn't pretty?"

"Never. Never, never, never."

I looked at her curiously. Outside the rumble was getting louder. Genest got up from her seat, apparently to throw herself into the maelstrom. We walked out into the office. The secretary, sitting at a computer terminal, looked at us suspiciously. A sullen-looking boy in big basketball shoes and dungaree jacket looked up from a table of catalogues he wasn't reading. Genest and I stood at the edge of the hall, on the edge of the roaring torrent of adolescents. I saw kids. She probably saw something very different.

"So a girl might go to Portland to escape a violent teen-age daddy?" I said, standing beside her.

"Hypothetically," Genest said. "Remember that. I don't want to get caught in some libel or slander thing. We're not talking about Missy Hewett."

"No, but you don't have to worry about her," I said.

"Why's that?" Genest asked, looking straight ahead.

"Because you can't libel the dead."

"It isn't the dead I'm worried about," she said, and then stepped into the stream of boots and backpacks and jostling, shouting bodies and, like someone falling into the River Lethe, was swept away.

Twenty-five

So maybe it was the daddy. But who was the daddy? Did he brag to somebody about bagging Missy Hewett? In this incestuous world of small-town kids, how could she, and he, manage to keep their liaison such a secret? And if it was such a secret, why would he kill her when she was going to put a lid on it forever? Or did he kill her because she wanted to take the lid back off?

I sat there for a minute in the Toyota until a car, a new Volvo sedan, pulled up and the guy driving glared at me. I figured it was the principal or somebody so I sat some more. He came around a second time and glared again. The third time, he stopped his car and walked over. He was fifty and chubby and his bad suit was too small. I rolled down my window.

"Sir, this is faculty parking," the guy said.

"Why's that?" I asked.

"Because the sign is right there."

Ah, yes. A literalist.

"No," I said. "I mean, why is this particular area reserved for teachers?"

"Because we need parking convenient to the school."

"And the kids don't?"

"Sir," he said, puffing himself up so his chin went from double to triple, "I'm going to have to ask you to move this vehicle."

"What do they do? Pay you extra to be campus security?"

"That's none of your concern."

He stood there, arms folded, full of cheap pin-striped importance. I sighed and started the truck.

"You're right," I said. "I'm very sorry."

"Rules are rules," he said, conciliatory.

I put the truck in gear and pulled forward so I was right next to him.

"Besides," I said, "I'm taking up your time. And something tells me you've got a very important appointment."

"Well, I do have—" he said.

"With a jelly doughnut," I said. "Have a good day."

It had felt good, but only for a moment, and by the time I was a mile down the road, I felt like a cheap bully, one of Janice Genest's stereotypical domineering insecure men.

"Whadayya mean, bully?" I said aloud to myself as I drove, easing the little truck up to speed. "I oughta kick your ass."

I drove through the hayfields, past the dairy farms, where manure-spattered equipment was parked haphazardly around manure-spattered barnyards. This time of year, the last of the corn was being cut for silage and I drove alongside a field where a corn chopper was working beside a big red farm truck. Above the truck, the ground corn was pumping from a chute in a continuous stream. A tanned arm, thick and heavy, hung from the cab of the truck. It was a big arm, a man's arm, and as I drove, it made me wonder what experience had so soured Genest on men. Was she married? Had she been married? Had the creep played around? Was her father a brute and her mother battered? Did she know who the father of Missy's baby was? If so, was it fear or ethics that kept her from telling me? What was her problem?

"Damn," I said. Was that Kenny's truck ahead of me?

The tailgate was blue and when the truck leaned into a curve, I could see the blue doors. I shook myself awake, shifted down to fourth and sped up. The black-and-blue Ford was doing about fifty, rumbling along with a sort of quiet arrogance, patrolling its turf like a troop carrier cruising the narrow streets of some potentially rebellious slum.

I pulled close and saw that it was, in fact, Kenny and, unless a girl was stretched out on the seat with her head in his lap, he was alone. Him and me. Me and him. The road climbed a ridge and the heaving hills of Waldo County rose to the west, yellow and orange and the burnished color of oaks mixed with the permanent spruce green. I pictured our two trucks from high in the air, his black and mine red, following the black ribbon like those cars you see in the movies, tracing the winding Pacific Coast Highway. I wasn't sure where this scene was headed until Kenny suddenly looked in his rearview and waved. I gave him the finger. He slammed on the truck's brakes and pulled off onto the gravel shoulder, sliding the truck to a stop in a billow of dust. I did the same.

"Whadayya mean, bully?" I said to myself again. "I oughta kick your ass."

Kenny popped out of his cab and slammed the door behind him. I did the same and we walked toward each other, stopping about five feet apart, midway between our respective bumpers. He was about my height, maybe a little shorter. Densely built with thin legs and knotty arms and shoulders, the build you see in guys who like to lift motors but never ran track.

"Hey, man," Kenny said, tugging on his hat. It said "Built Ford Tough."

He grinned. I smiled.

"Long time no see," Kenny said.

"I don't know about that. I think I've been seeing you a lot. You just don't stop to say hello."

"Well, you know how it is. Places to go. People to see."

"Windows to shoot out," I said. "Trucks to burn."

"Don't know why I'd want to do that. Hey, where'd you get this little pussy truck? Feels like you're driving a little toy, don't it?"

"It's fine. Nice to be able to pass a gas station once in a while."

"Frig that. A man's gotta have something under him with some balls, you know?"

"Would you care to rephrase that?" I said.

"Huh? Oh, I get you. Goddamn, if you aren't good with words. Mister Article Writer, right? You're good at twisting little words around, right?"

I didn't say anything.

"Hey, I remember when you first come to the pit. With the girls. Are they babes or what? I mean, man, you get your piece yet or what? Hey, I bet they'd even do you, Mister Article Writer. I thought that was something girls did, you know? All that typing and secretary stuff. That pussy stuff."

"So what is it you do?"

"Go to school," he said, grinning and spitting on the gravel. "Can't you tell? I'm on a field trip."

"What's the class? Backshooting 101?"

Kenny's grin dissolved. I held mine tautly.

"You got something to say, Mister Article Writer?"

"Yeah," I said. "I'm gonna say only a coward shoots windows out and runs. Only a coward burns a man's truck and runs. Only a coward runs away and hides like a little baby."

"You calling me a coward?"

"You tell me."

"No, you tell me," Kenny said.

"Okay. I'll tell you. I'll tell you you're no good. A backshooting little wimp. You ought to have your name on your back because you're always running away. You don't have the balls to do what I'm doing right now, which is to tell you right to your face that you're a worthless piece of garbage. And you owe me for one window and one Chevy truck."

I waited. Kenny kept his eyes on mine but his expression wavered. Enraged but then a flicker of amusement. Disdain but then anger again. As if nobody had told him quite how to play this part.

"And dumb as a stump, too," I said.

So anger it was, eyes narrowed to slits, rocking ever so slightly on the balls of his feet, big hands hanging and ready. For the first time, I noticed he had a clasp knife in a leather case on his right hip. Too late to back out now.

We stood there like disarmed gunfighters, too close to look away, too far apart to swing. A car approached from behind me and slowed as the old couple in the front seat stared, then turned away as the old man sped up.

"So what's your problem?" I asked.

"I don't got one," Kenny said, the grin trickling back on to his face. "But man, you sure do. Little candy-ass pussy."

"You say that to all the guys."

"Talking's over, man."

"And just when you were getting a command of the language."

"Write about this, you little pussy."

"Where should I send the bill for my truck and the window?"

"Send it—"

He was on me in two quick steps, quick as a wrestler. I threw up my arms and he shoved me back with his left hand and followed up with a burst of quick rights, close compact punches that hit my forearms, grazed the top of my head. I set myself and drove back against him low until my head was against his belly and my arms locked around him. I spun and threw him off me. His hat flew off but he didn't go down and, instead, he came back at me again, like we were tied with elastic cord.

There was the same shove but when he grunted and pushed, I pulled him close with my left arm and drove my right fist into his face. I got nose and lip and then we spun again and Kenny fell on his back and rolled and popped back up. There was blood on his chin and he wiped it with his hand and grinned.

He was on me again, no punches this time, locking his arms around my neck as I hit him with short punches to the neck and chin and winced at the pain in my wrist and knuckles. Kenny's leg intertwined with mine and he tripped me and we went down in a thrashing pile in the gravel. The

side of my head was pressed against the ground and a sharp
stone and I felt a sudden surge of claustrophobia and, with
it, the strength to throw him off. On my back, I brought my
elbow down blindly, as hard as I could, and caught him
under the chin. The elbow got windpipe, too, and Kenny
gasped and gagged for a moment, long enough for me to
flip over on top of him and raise my fist.

So what did I do now? Just drive his head into the
ground? Grab a big rock and crush his skull? End the fight
and do five years for aggravated assault? Grab a bigger
rock and do fifteen for manslaughter?

I hesitated and Kenny's hand went down and there was a
snap as the sheath opened and the knife came out. Before
he could open it, I grabbed his right arm with both hands.
He didn't let go and I could see his fingers trying to work
the blade open, could see the blade slide out, then slip back
into the slot. Then it came out a third of the way and stayed
there, so as he kicked my legs and punched the side of my
head with his free hand, I bent down and bit his forearm
hard just above the wrist, tasting salt and feeling hair in my
mouth and then the odd sensation of my teeth breaking the
skin and sinking right into him.

"Aaaaah," Kenny yelled and his grip loosened and, lifting my head from his arm, I scuffed at the knife and it skidded five feet away. He punched me some more, a flurry
against my head, in my eyes, a hard numbing shot to my
ear. I backhanded him across the face with my right and,
still on all fours, jumped up until one knee was on his right
arm and the other across his neck. I pressed with all my
weight and he thrashed his legs to try to flip me off but
couldn't and the next thrash was weaker and then he was
gasping, an awful rasping sound that almost made me get
off.

But not quite.

A car approached and passed but I didn't look up. I took
a little of the weight off his neck but not all of it and his
face turned red and he still gasped for air. The blood from

my face dripped on to his right bicep, still pinned by my left knee. It dripped once, twice, three times until I turned to look at him and the drip moved to his chest. Once. Twice. Three times. I took a little more weight off and watched him take a real breath.

It was an odd situation, kneeling there in the gravel on the side of the road. I was on top of him, in a position that, blood and all, was strangely intimate. Physically, it was the closest I'd been to anyone in years, with the exception of sex, and I wanted to back off, get away, but couldn't. Not yet.

"You're a dead man," Kenny gasped.

I pressed my knee down on his neck.

"You could be, easier than you know," I said.

I waited and then let up.

"What's it all about?" I demanded. "What the hell's this all about?"

"You tell me."

I pressed down, let up.

"What's it all about? What the hell are you doing to me? Why are you doing this stuff to me?"

Kenny stared up and managed a grin.

"I ain't done nothin'," he rasped.

I pressed. The grin left. Kenny's face hardened. I let up.

"Now talk."

Kenny wheezed.

"You came to me, man. You came in and looked at us, mister hot shit writer. What are we, some kind of friggin' test case? Monkeys at the zoo, right? Come here from New York or some goddamn place, gonna come in here and put us in some magazine for these rich bitches to friggin' gawk at when they're sitting on the can."

"I didn't come here. I live here."

"Yeah, right," Kenny said hoarsely, staring up at me with undisguised, unvarnished hatred. "Until you get bored, man. Until we're used up and you need somebody else. I friggin' hate you bastards. Go back to friggin' New Jersey where you belong."

"I'm not writing about you."

"You're writing about my people."

"Your people? Who are your people?"

"All these kids. The kids at the pit."

"I'm not writing about kids at the pit. I'm writing about girls with babies."

"I know those girls."

"You know the girls in the pickup."

"This is Prosperity, Maine, man. Thorndike. Searsmont. Us kids all know each other. We stick together."

"And you shoot out people's windows. Burn people's trucks."

Kenny shrugged, as well as he could under the circumstances. The blood on his face was coagulating.

"Why don't you admit it? You picked me out as some kind of target."

Kenny looked up and, for a moment, didn't say anything.

"I didn't pick you out," he said slowly, his voice drained of its cockiness. "You picked me."

As I thought about this, kneeling on his neck, the knife in the dirt, there was the sound of a car approaching, slowing, then stopping. I looked up and saw a familiar dark brown Chevy. The door opened and feet in boots stepped out.

"Bargain," Poole said. "Two birds. One stone."

Poole considered calling a rescue unit but decided, instead, to give each of us a couple of envelopes of pre-moistened paper towels from the dusty first-aid kit in his trunk. I dabbed at my nose and mouth and a scrape that ran from just in front of my left ear all the way to my left eye, which already was puffing out. Kenny looked better but as he stood there, picking the dried blood out of his nose, rubbing the bite on his arm, he kept swallowing hard and grimacing, like a kid with a very sore throat.

Mess with me, I'll bruise your trachea.

Standing there by the side of the road, I felt a little silly. A farm truck came by, pulling a big John Deere tractor on a flatbed trailer, and the tanned farm boys in the cab stared at my face. I stared back, the first hardened public enemy to have once had his byline in *The New York Times*.

If the crew on the metro desk could only see me now. But then everybody had said freelancing was a rough business.

Poole waited by his car as we prettied ourselves up. After a minute, a Waldo County patrol car pulled up and he went over and spoke to the deputy behind the wheel. The deputy, a young kid, listened for a minute, then saluted and drove away. As he passed, the deputy stared at my face, too.

I was beginning to get a complex.

"You boys feeling better now?" Poole said, grinning.

"Peachy," I said. "But I think my friend here is suffering some emotional trauma."

Kenny gave me a hard stare and said nothing.

"Well, they say these things should be gotten out in the open," Poole said. "Maybe we should talk about this. Who wants to start?"

Neither of us jumped in.

"Okay. How 'bout we drive into Belfast and get to work on a disorderly charge. I could use the overtime and I'm sure you boys didn't have anything planned. If I hadn't come along, you'd probably still be scrapping in the dirt here. Kind of reminded me of my boys at home. They're always tackling each other over some nonsense or other."

He grinned.

"They're eight and ten. So what's your excuse?"

Still no comment. A couple of tough nuts, we were.

"Kind of out of your line of expertise, isn't it, Mr. Mc-Morrow? I mean, *New York Times*. That's pretty big-time journalism, isn't it? I mean, I don't know much about it but I never pictured these big-time reporters wrestling around in the gutter. And is that a bite mark on Kenny's arm?

Seems like one of you should get a tetanus shot but I'm not sure which one. What do you think, Ken-Bob? Been a while since you got in one of these face-to-face go-around. I figured you liked to work behind the scenes, where your pretty face doesn't get all beat up, you know what I'm saying? I think you do."

I looked at Kenny. He looked at Poole. I balled up my wipe and put it in my pocket.

"So what'll it be, boys?" Poole said. "You want to go for a ride?"

I shrugged, not sure how to handle this new Poole. This one was less earnest Boy Scout leader, more wise-ass tough cop. I wondered if this was the side he usually reserved for the Kenny types, if I no longer merited the polite treatment.

"I don't," I said.

"So start talking."

"I don't know. I guess we just agreed to disagree."

"About what?"

"I don't know. His extracurricular activities. My journalistic ethics. Sort of highbrow stuff."

"I can see that," Poole said. "And by the way, you missed some blood in your left highbrow."

"Not bad," I said.

"Thanks. I kind of liked it."

The police radio in Poole's car crackled. Kenny looked restless.

"Can I go?" he said, fingering the brim of his Ford hat.

"You haven't contributed to the discussion," Poole said.

"Got nothing to say."

"I've got an afternoon to kill."

He looked at me.

"Excuse the pun."

Jesus, I thought. A reminder. For Jack McMorrow, murder suspect.

"So kill it with him, 'cause I didn't do nothin'," Kenny said. "The guy comes up on my bumper, gives me the finger. I pull over and get out and he friggin' starts going on about his house and his truck and I don't know what he's talking about and then he really starts going on about me, calling me this and that and I tell him, lighten up, man, you know, get out of my face and he friggin' takes a swing at me and tries to choke me. I want to file a complaint."

"And I'm trying not to laugh," Poole said. "And the only reason I'm not laughing is I'm sick of your games."

He looked toward me.

"And yours too, Mr. McMorrow. I don't know what this is all about—coke or girls or what—but it's all gonna come out. And when it does, somebody's gonna go down for this piddly stuff. The burnt truck. Shooting up the house. And somebody's gonna go down for killing Missy Hewett."

"One would hope so," I said.

"I'm not done, sir. Let me give you some advice. Both of you. Like I said, I don't know what's going on here. But the longer you bullshit me, the deeper you get. And the deeper you get, the more you lie, the more the judge is gonna want to put you away. And we're talking a long time. None of this chickenshit five-all-but-three-suspended stuff. You hear me, Kenny? No nice little probation chitchat this time. This is heavy duty. So if you want to save yourself some serious trouble, now's the time to start talking. Get out of here. Go think about it, but not too long 'cause it's gonna be too late."

We looked at him and then walked to our trucks like a couple of chastised kids. Poole opened his car door and got in. Kenny's big Ford started with a roar and spun gravel as it lurched on to the pavement and headed down the road. I pulled the Toyota up next to Poole's car and unrolled the window.

He did the same.

"Question," I said. "Which one is the real you? This one or Mister Rogers?"

"That's for you to figure out," Poole said. "But don't guess wrong."

"Rats. I thought it was more like an essay question. You know. No wrong answer."

"Nope," Poole said. "Screw this one up and you're out of here."

And he smiled. The son of a bitch.

Twenty-six

"How are things going? Oh, good. Busy but good."

It was Roxanne on the phone, from her motel room in Cambridge. When she'd called, I'd been picking the dried blood out of my nose and my ear. It was one of those daily hygienic activities required for good grooming. Kind of like flossing your teeth.

"You still want to see me?" she said.

"More than you know."

"Maybe I should just come up there, when this conference is over. I could come Sunday morning. Save you the trip."

"No, I'd like to see you there. I mean, I need to see you there. Get out of here for a while."

Roxanne paused.

"Is something wrong?"

"No. It'd just be fun to do the city thing. You know. The restaurants. The theater. The racy movie channel in the motel room."

"In your room, you mean."

"Oh, sure. Wait, you didn't think I meant that we, I mean the two of us, would be in the same—"

"Bed? No way. We have to take this slow. The first night you can sleep on the floor."

"And the second night I'll move to the chair."

"And I'll unbutton the top button on my flannels. If things go well," Roxanne said. "Which brings me back to my original question. How are things going there?"

"And my original answer. Good."

"You're a lousy liar, Jack McMorrow."

"Some people don't think so."

"Anything you want to talk about?"

I sighed silently.

"Oh, I don't know. It can wait until I get there. I guess."

"Long story?"

"You might say so."

"Why do I have this funny déjà vu feeling?" Roxanne asked.

"I don't know. Because all motel rooms look the same?"

Neither of us spoke for a moment. I wanted to, wanted to spill the whole thing. Tell her I was picking blood off my face, that I looked like I'd just taken a 12-count and been declared a TKO. That I needed a deer rifle for protection. That the cops thought there was a distinct possibility that I'd murdered someone.

"Jack?"

"Roxanne?"

"Jack, the last time I talked to you, you were talking about babies. What's going on?"

"Well, you know how one thing leads to another."

"Like what?"

"Well, like the cops up here think maybe I'm dealing coke."

"What?"

"Either that or a murderer."

"Jack!"

"Then again, it could be both."

"My God!"

"And on top of all that, I've got a deadline coming up. When it rains, it pours, you know?"

"Jack, cut the crap and start talking."

I did. Laid it all out there, starting with Missy alive, covering Missy dead. I told Roxanne about Poole and the state police and how I came to be the proud owner of a red Toyota pickup. I almost didn't tell her about Claire and his rifle, knowing how much she hated guns, but then I figured I might as well be honest and open if we were going to try to make this thing work, which still remained to be seen.

"How do you manage this?" Roxanne asked, when my story had wound down.

"Oh, I don't know. I try to prioritize things. You know, make a lot of lists. And when I get one thing done, I check it off. Otherwise, it can get kind of overwhelming."

"Jack, come on. How do you manage to have everything get so, I don't know, so completely messed up? Why can't anything be simple? You talk to your people, write your story, cash the check. Isn't that the way it's supposed to work?"

"It's sort of what I was counting on."

"And now all this. A suspect in a murder. My God. Are they serious?"

"They try to be. After all, they are policemen. Although I must say, this guy Poole, the detective, he did drop a half-decent pun this morning. Something about having time to kill. Get it? Time to kill? You know, murder?"

I waited.

"I guess you had to be there," I said.

"Speaking of which, do you still want to see me?"

"Yeah, I do. More than ever. I need to see you."

"Should I come there?"

"The cops would like that. I'm a good-looking guy, but you'd sure liven up their surveillance. Wear something slinky. Provocative but subtle."

"Are they really watching you?"

"I'm not sure. I imagine they take a peek every once in a while, just to make sure I haven't taken off."

"How 'bout to Boston?"

"I'd like that. When are you available?"

"This thing lasts three days. Everybody leaves Sunday morning. But it's pretty much over by Saturday at five. I don't plan on hanging around the hospitality suite."

"Somebody in your class is going to be disappointed."

"That's why they fill the bathtub with beer."

"They do? Well, how 'bout I go to the hospitality suite. You stay in the room and watch bad movies."

"So I'll see you Saturday?" Roxanne said.

"I'll be there by five. The Hyatt in Cambridge, right?"

"Yup."

"Okay. That gives me a couple of days to straighten things out here. You know, vacuum the living room, put the dishes away, catch the real murderer . . ."

"Jack, take care of yourself. I mean it."

"Oh, I'll be fine," I said, fingering the scrape on the side of my head. "I'm gonna stay home today and clean my gun. Now, is the safety on when you pull the little thing back? Or is it on when you push the little thing forward?"

"I mean it," Roxanne said.

"I know."

"You know I need to see you, too," she said.

"Just look for the guy with the deer rifle. If there's more than one of us in the lobby, I'll be the guy with the Remington."

"Jack, please."

"But I won't wear the cartridge belt," I said. "Just for you."

I'd always said I worked better up against a deadline and now I had one, of sorts. I had to be in Cambridge by five on Saturday. I had to be in one piece, mentally and physically.

Still standing there by the phone, I could feel myself regrouping. It was what Roxanne did to me, among other things. She was rational and concrete and analytical. When I was with her, I focused more clearly and applied myself to the job at hand. Of course, when I was with her, she tended to become the job at hand, a phenomenon attributable to the fact that she was very pretty and very sexy and loved to make love.

Without her, I tended to let things lapse, to let myself be knocked around by events. In past months, it had become my natural state, this bemused inertia, especially if the refrigerator was full of beer. And Roxanne snapped me out of it. I didn't exactly run out and get my doctorate in biochemistry but I would pick up the beer cans. Maybe I'd even make the bed.

I slumped into the nearest chair, ran my hand thoughtfully over my cuts and bruises, and, with Roxanne's clear sweet voice still ringing in my ears, surveyed the room and my situation.

Since she'd left for Colorado, I hadn't gotten a lot done, at least not the sort of thing you could hold in your hand. I'd watched a lot of birds. Gotten much better at spring and fall warblers, though I had a long way to go. I'd spent a lot of time alone in the woods, which was good for the soul and after my last job, my soul had needed some mending. Death and deceit, violence and betrayal, do not tend to bolster your faith in humanity or even your belief in yourself. When your friends kill your friends, you lose something that isn't easy to get back.

So I'd set myself adrift, really. Camped out in this house. Protected myself with anonymity and obscurity. You couldn't hurt me if you couldn't find me. In Prosperity, Maine, this hideaway in a forgotten county, I lived under my own name with an assumed life. It was a retreat in more ways than one, a sabbatical that found me either in the woods, prowling the ridges and bogs alone, or plunked in a chair with a good book on my lap and a beer in my hand. And a pile of empties beside me.

It had taken a long while to come out of it. To talk to Claire. To see the goodness in people again. And just when I'd started to regain a little of my faith, I'd slid back into the predicament that now faced me. I'd really liked Missy Hewett. I'd liked her courage and her hardness and the little-girl naiveté that fueled her faith in herself and belief that sheer hard work really did get you someplace. And then somebody had gone and killed her. Desecrated her, really.

And sitting there in the chair, looking out on the brush and the woods and the bright blue morning, I figured I could do either of two things. I could just let myself slide way back down into my hole, maybe all the way down to a jail cell. Or I could take a little of Missy's spirit for myself. Maybe some of Roxanne's, too. And Claire's. And even something from the people at the *Times*, with their belief that they and their paper were the best in the world.

I could fight back, put a new twist on the old saying. I don't get sad. I get even.

Besides. It was too early for a beer.

I went upstairs and grabbed a couple of shirts, two pairs of boxer shorts, my razor and toothbrush. I stuffed all of it in a very weathered L.L. Bean duffel and went back down the loft stairs. Inside the back door, I stopped. Went back up to the loft and got another pair of boxers, the plaid preppy ones Roxanne had always liked.

And from the back of my sock drawer, where they'd been gathering dust, my last two condoms.

I left a note on Claire's kitchen table saying I'd be gone for a couple of days and I'd put his rifle in my kitchen closet and the bullets in my sock drawer. That done, it was down the dump road and out to Route 137. I drove the five miles to Albion, where I stopped at the general store and bought orange juice and a *Boston Globe*. From there, I headed south to China, where I picked up Route 202 and continued south, past the glimmering basin of China Lake with its fringe of fall foliage. In twenty minutes, I was in Augusta, where I drove past the gold-domed State House and noted, for the hundredth time, that it seemed too big and grand for the mini-malls that surrounded it. At the end of a long fast-food strip, I caught the interstate and quickly brought the little truck up to seventy. After an hour on the spruce-lined strip of highway, Portland broke into view.

It was a miniature city, with a couple of bank towers, a short tired Main Street that had been pummeled by a suburban mall, and a chi-chi restored waterfront that you could walk through in fifteen minutes. Portland had a little of everything. A little waterfront facing a bay full of little islands. The little university that Missy had attended. A little bit of old money, a little more of new. Little housing projects that, compared to New York's endless ghetto canyons, seemed like Plymouth Plantation. Portland even had certified genuine junkies, but only enough of them to fill a school bus, maybe. The hardcore hookers you could gather up in an airport limo. It was a civilized city where nothing had gotten out of hand, where the graffiti was restrained and the pay phones still had phone books.

I pulled up to the first phone booth I saw, on Congress Street, the main drag downtown. There was a convenient space in front of a parking hydrant so I slipped in and parked the truck. If anybody said anything, I'd break out my doughnut line.

But nobody said a word. The phone was outside a pleasant little coffee shop and the smell of brewing hazelnut filled the air. I got out my notebook and looked up the name of the law firm, the number of which had been on Missy's phone bill. Wheaton, Hinckley, Prine and McSalley. I looked in the Yellow Pages under lawyers and found their listing. The firm was medium-sized for Portland, with maybe twenty-five partners and associates, the names of whom were listed in that grave lawyerly way that somehow made them seem like twenty-five pallbearers listed in an obituary. Their grave lawyerly offices were at One Portland Center, which I presumed to be some sort of snooty office tower.

And I'd forgotten to bring a tie.

I put a piece of paper in the phone book to mark my page and went into the coffee shop and bought a large tea with two bags and a splash of milk. The tea was very hot and I came back out and set it on the stainless steel shelf of the phone booth, next to some nasty words that had been etched into the metal with some kind of blade. At some point, this booth had been occupied by a very angry person. I trusted this troubled soul had been able to find appropriate therapeutic services.

As city-type people strode by on the sidewalk—women in suits and pumps, men carrying the ubiquitous *Times* and briefcases, a homeless guy with laceless shoes and a dark-green trash bag slung Santa-style over his shoulder—I went to work. I unfolded Missy's telephone bill and put it on the shelf beside the phone book. Then, one by one, I looked up the home telephone numbers for each of the lawyers listed for Wheaton, Hinckley.

Most of them lived in one of the monied towns on the coast north or south of the city. Three of the partners lived in Cape Elizabeth, including one on Shore Road, a meandering lane that for years had been an enclave for old money. If Mr. Prine was on the ocean side, where the stately houses staked out their views of beautiful Casco Bay, the firm was pulling in some bucks.

There were others in Falmouth-Foreside, a couple in Cumberland, one in Freeport. Two had chosen the urban gentry life of big old Victorians on the Western Promenade, and a couple lived in towns a few miles inland. They probably got their ocean fix from owning very big boats.

Of the twenty-five lawyers on the Wheaton, Hinckley list, twenty-one had their home numbers in the book, a wonderfully egalitarian gesture. None of those twenty-one numbers matched the Falmouth number on Missy's bill.

I stood by the booth and sipped my tea. As I sipped, the homeless guy came back by, pausing to grope in a trash basket by the curb. A very pretty young woman in business clothes and heels started to give him a wide berth, then saw me. My rugged good looks. My battered face. She hesitated then swung back toward the homeless guy.

She knew a suspicious character when she saw one.

This didn't bode well for a warm reception in the Waspy confines of Falmouth but, for lack of an alternative, I pressed on.

What I had was four names with no home listings. Two were pretty high on the list of asterisked partners and I couldn't picture Missy Hewett having any direct dealings with the real fat cats. Two were associates: one was David T. Putnam, in the middle tier; the other a woman, Catherine G. C. Scarpetti, at the bottom of the Wheaton, Hinckley pecking order. When I'd called from Prosperity, just fishing, it had been a woman who had answered. I picked up the phone and dialed the operator and the Falmouth number.

A truck heaved by as the number rang and I covered the receiver. Four rings and a young woman answered, younger than the woman who'd answered before. I asked for Ms. Scarpetti. In the practiced manner of an experienced baby-sitter or au pair, the young woman said, no, there was no one at that number by that name.

"I'm sorry," I said. "I'm looking at the wrong name on this document. I meant to ask for Mr. Putnam. Of Wheaton, Hinckley."

"Mr. Putnam isn't available," the young woman said. "May I take a message?"

Standing there on the sidewalk outside the coffee shop, I pumped my fist in victory.

"No, I'm going to be out of the office," I said. "It would be easier for me to call back later."

"Gotcha," I said to myself, startling the homeless guy. He looked up and I said, "Sorry." I would have explained but it was a long story.

But now that I had Mr. Putnam, what would I do with him? And did I really have him when I didn't know where he was? And until I had him in front of me, I couldn't begin to answer the more pertinent questions: what was his business with Missy? Was he her adoption lawyer? Who would she have gone to if she had wanted to take her baby back?

David T. Putnam, we had some talking to do.

I was gathering up my notes and tea when a Portland police cruiser pulled up beside my truck, still in front of the hydrant. A power window hummed down and the cop in the passenger seat, a young guy who looked like he was on a career-day outing for high school, said, "Hey."

"Hi there, officer," I said. "Be right out of your way. Just had to make an emergency phone call and—"

"Negatory, pal," the kid said. "Move that piece of junk or it'll be out of here on a hook."

Oh, my, I thought. The proverbial bad apple. Only the fact that I was on official business—and the truck still was unregistered—kept me from dressing down the young brownshirt.

"Yessir," I said, tossing my notebook through the window onto the passenger seat. "But didn't you like it better when cops were cops and there was none of this public relations stuff?"

He scowled. I smiled and slammed the door shut.

"You have a good day now, you hear?"

They followed me back down Congress Street and stayed behind me when I took a right and headed for the waterfront. I expected the blue lights to come on but when I took a right at the next light, the cruiser went straight and left me to my business.

I swung back on Congress and drove north three blocks and pulled into a parking space in front of a bookstore. The truck was half on a crosswalk but then rehabilitation was a slow process.

I got out and walked up the street to a small plaza where there were pigeons and a guy actually selling soft pretzels from a cart. A couple of crack addicts and you'd have a real big-city tableau.

It was only a matter of time.

One Portland Center was at the far end of the little plaza. It was a tan, tube-shaped twenty-story tower with dark windows that made it look like it was wearing sunglasses and had something to hide. I stopped outside the revolving entrance doors and looked at the directory in the brass and glass case. Wheaton, Hinckley was on the seventh floor. I tucked my chamois shirt in my jeans and ran a hand across my hair and my unshaven chin. If I'd known the place was so nice, I would have worn my good boots.

The atrium was small but clean, with some mauve marble and captive trees and one of those trickling fountains, the sound of which always made me think some appliance had sprung a leak. A guy came out of the elevators as I approached them. He was silver-haired and well-suited, in the original sense of the phrase, and he looked at me like I was the plumber's assistant and should have known the service entrance was out back. I decided to toss out some legal terminology to let him know I couldn't solder a pipe if my life depended on it.

"De facto rigor mortis," I mumbled to myself.

He fought back the urge to invite me to lunch at his club.

The elevator was done in fake marble and mirrors, which allowed me to survey my face—probably not a good thing for my self-confidence. I looked like somebody who'd had a night out with the boys. In jail. Now he was nursing a hangover, a hundred-dollar bond and trying to remember where he'd left his car.

I'd just have to rely on my natural charm.

The elevator was very fast and in no time at all the doors swished open and, like somebody stepping out of a time machine, I stepped into the Wheaton, Hinckley lobby. There was classical music playing very softly and the floor was carpeted in cream with oriental rugs over it. On the walls were prints of sporting scenes. Retrievers with ducks in their mouths. Guys with shotguns, standing in skiffs. It was the kind of art rich guys put in their offices because their wives won't let them have it at home.

But if Wheaton, Hinckley had second-class art, it had a first-class view. I walked to a window beside an empty reception desk and looked out. The view was to the east: Casco Bay and the islands, which floated on the shimmering blue-green water like lily pads. A ferry was plugging along halfway between the mainland and Peaks Island and its wake was a long white line, like the shiny trail of a garden slug. It was beautiful and mesmerizing and I knew that if I worked here, I'd never get anything done.

"May I help you?"

A woman, fiftyish and handsome in a dark gray suit, had appeared behind the desk. She must have been the receptionist but she did not look like she was going to be receptive. In fact, she looked like she probably had one hand on the alarm button and the other on her purse.

"Oh, hi," I said. "I was just admiring your view. Beautiful."

She nodded warily.

"I'm looking for Dave Putnam."

I said it familiarly, like we were old fraternity brothers. When we met, we'd do the Delta Kappa Gamma handshake.

"Do you have an appointment with Mr. Putnam?" the receptionist said.

"No, I was just passing through town and I thought I'd take a chance. If he was just sitting looking out at the view, I'd pop in and say hello."

"Are you a personal friend of Mr. Putnam's?"

As opposed to an impersonal friend, I thought.

"No, not really. We just have a mutual acquaintance and a mutual interest."

"And your name is?"

"McMorrow. Jack McMorrow."

"And would Mr. Putnam know what this is regarding?"

I thought for a split second and decided to try to smoke him out.

"A woman named Missy Hewett," I said.

The woman took out a piece of paper and wrote a few words. If Missy's name meant anything to her, she hadn't shown it. After she finished writing, she stood up.

Here's your hat, Mr. McMorrow. What's your hurry?

"Mr. Putnam is out of the office today, Mr. McMorrow. I'll give him your message."

"Could I give you my phone number?"

"Would you like Mr. Putnam to contact you?"

No, I thought. I want him to write it on the wall of the men's room at the bus station.

"Yes, I would. I'll be out of town until Monday but I'll be available from then on. I'd appreciate if he could call. I think he'll find we have a matter of mutual interest."

The woman took the number, writing it down as if it were a dirty word. I gave her my warmest smile, turned toward the elevator and stopped.

"Is Mr. Putnam in court today?"

She gave a haughty little snort, as if I had come to her house for dinner and used the wrong fork.

"Oh, no," the woman said. "Mr. Putnam is not a litigator."

"What is his specialty?"

"Mr. Putnam is with our corporate services department."

Corporate services? What did that have to do with makin' babies?

Twenty-seven

Corporate law? What did that have to do with Missy Hewett? Did she know the guy from somewhere? The calls started before she came to Portland, so how did she connect to him from Prosperity? Did she call him to see if he could refer her to somebody else? If so, why call him several times? Did he put her off? The length of the calls said no, so did he advise her unofficially? Did he major in corporate law in school but minor in adoptions? Who was this guy?

Whatever the connection had been, Putnam would very soon know that I had made the connection, too. I decided to try him at home before the message got to him. Judging from Ms. Cool Reception, I still had time.

Falmouth was just north of the city, up Route 1 and over a bridge. It was suburbia with a monied edge, the kind of place where up-and-coming lawyers would live, inching their way closer and closer to the water as they climbed the ladder at the firm. It was a pleasant, affluent town and it gave me the willies.

I drove up Route 1, the main drag, and passed Kmart and strip malls and a tennis club. Between the malls were car dealerships where they sold fancy foreign cars that cost far more than my house. At one lot, a gray Rolls was parked out front, the pot of gold at the end of somebody's rainbow.

Not mine.

As I drove past in the old Toyota, I wondered: did people live in places like Prosperity, Maine, because they didn't want to own a Rolls? Or did they not own a Rolls because they lived in places like Prosperity? I thought of people like Claire and decided the choice to live in a place like Prosperity came first. If you'd never want a Rolls, you came to Prosperity. If you dreamed of that sort of thing, and all the other trappings of material success, you left. Then again, there were people like Missy who had left looking for something else altogether and hadn't had a chance to find it. But somewhere along the way, she had found David Putnam. Or David Putnam had found her.

And now I wanted to locate the fellow, which in a town this size couldn't be too hard. I didn't have an address and Putnam wasn't in the phone book but any reporter could solve that one. Blindfolded.

I drove north until the malls started to thin out, turned around and came back. At a service station, one that looked locally owned, I stopped and went into the waiting area where they kept the maps and plastic coffee mugs and machines that dispensed fossilized gumballs. There was nobody behind the counter so I went into the garage and found a young kid holding a shoplight and peering up underneath a car. I asked him where the town office was and he gave me directions: two miles south, left at the Pizza Hut. I asked him if he knew David Putnam and he said, no.

"How you like your Toyota?" the kid asked.

"Fine," I said.

"Tough little trucks," he said.

So I drove my tough little truck two miles south and took a left at Pizza Hut. Sure enough, the Falmouth town office was on the right, a neat brick building with two cars out front. I gave myself a last look in the rearview mirror, just to make sure the scabs were all in the right place, and went in.

It was one big room with a counter to separate the employees from the public. Seeing as this was the place that sent out the local tax bills, this probably was a good idea. An older woman with short silver hair got up from a desk and approached me and I smiled to let her know that I was not there to complain. She smiled back.

"Hi," I said. "I have a problem and I'm hoping you can help me."

"Well, I'll certainly try," she said.

"I have an old friend who I think still lives in town here. I'm on my way up north to go hunting and I thought I'd stop and surprise him. Name's Dave Putnam. I can't remember his address and he's not in the book."

I smiled again. The woman had been looking at my cuts and my black eye but she caught herself and smiled back.

"Putnam. Putnam," she mused, then turned. "Jane? Putnam. David. Mill Creek Road?"

"Back to Route 88. First right after the little bridge.

House is second on the left," another silver-haired woman said without lifting her eyes from her computer screen. "Big colonial with a big garage. Three-car."

"Oh, does she know the Putnams?" I asked.

"No," the first silver-haired woman said. "Just the names and the tax bills."

I thanked her as her gaze moved again to my damaged face.

"Bear," I said. "That's why they say you gotta kill 'em with the first shot."

Mill Creek Road led from Route 88, a meandering coastal road, down toward the bay. The biggest houses were on the water. Putnam's was at the other end.

It was a dark red colonial, set back from the road with a two-story garage off to the right and a big addition to the left. The driveway wound through lawn crowded with bushy twenty-foot pines. I paused for a moment at the entrance, then drove in, parking in the driveway next to a bright red Audi, an older one. Next to the garage was a very big sailboat propped up on those stilt-looking things and wrapped in a blue tarp. It was a very, very big sailboat, the kind that consumes money standing still. The tarp was sprinkled with pine needles. Next to the boat was a basketball hoop. Leaning against the posts of the hoop was a neon-green motorcycle with big knobby tires.

The Putnams had kids. And they spent money.

I turned off the motor and listened. A chickadee peeped but that was about it. I got out of the truck and walked slowly past the Audi and toward the back door. The chickadees were swooping to and from a wooden feeder, full of sunflower seeds, that was on a post by the back door. The ground by the feeder was littered with hulls.

Instant nature.

I stood for a moment at the door and listened. From inside the house I could hear music but only faintly, mostly the thump of the bass. I pushed the doorbell, which was cracked. In case it didn't work, I pushed it again. I wasn't born yesterday.

Nothing happened so I waited. I pushed one more time and waited some more and then the music got louder, as if somebody had opened the door to an inner room where the music was playing. There were footsteps and then a rattle and I readied myself for David Putnam or the missus.

And got the miss.

She was blonde and small, maybe fifteen, with dark brown eyes made even darker by eye shadow, and sallow skin made more so by ruby red lipstick. Her sweatshirt said "Harvard" in big letters and she was chewing gum.

"Yes?" she asked.

"Hi, is your dad home?"

The girl looked at me warily, but not warily enough.

"He isn't home."

"How 'bout your mom?"

"She isn't home, either."

"Don't you know you shouldn't say that to strangers?"

"Why not?"

"Because . . . never mind. So will they be home soon?"

"Doubt it."

She said it with an air of defiance and resignation.

"Okay," I said. "Will they be home late?"

"Maybe. You never know with them."

"Whether they're going to come home?"

"Whether. When. If. That's not true. They usually come home but I don't wait up."

I was puzzled.

"Well, where do they go?"

"My dad goes down to his boat. He goes down in the morning before work. He stops on the way home. Sometimes he has dinner there, 'cause it's a yacht club and they have a restaurant. Sometimes he stays and talks to the guys there."

"What do they talk about?"

"Boats."

"If he goes down to his boat, what's that thing under the tarp, Noah's ark?"

"That's his old one. His new one's better."

"I'm glad," I said. "Where's your mom? Down on the poop deck?"

"Are you kidding? She hates boats. She says they're boring. She goes to plays and stuff. She's going to one tonight. She's totally into the theater. She was on the stage before my parents got married."

"Then she stopped?"

"To have my brother. Then me. He's in boarding school but I wouldn't go. Now my mom just goes to her plays and parties with the theater crowd. Those people are always good for a party. They come here and drink and talk like la-de-da this, la-de-da that. Last week a whole bunch of 'em came and stayed till like midnight and this one guy tried to hit on me. I was like, 'Give me a break. You're old enough to be my father.' "

She paused to take a breath.

"So are you a friend of my dad's?"

I thought for a moment about just what I wanted David Putnam to hear from his daughter when he straggled home. While I thought, the daughter leaned against the door frame and eyed me curiously. From inside the house, the music pulsed like the beating of a giant, racing heart.

"We're not friends," I said. "We just have a mutual acquaintance. I needed to talk to him."

"What's your name?"

"Jack McMorrow."

"I'm Mariel. Are you a lawyer, too?"

"Oh, no."

"Are you a detective? Did you get beat up arresting some criminal?"

"Beat up?"

"Your face."

"Oh, that," I said. "No, I walked into a door."

"Yeah, right," she said. "So you're not a detective?"

"Nope."

"So what are you?"

"I'm a reporter."

"For what paper?"

"No paper. For myself."

She looked skeptical.

"So what do you do with your stories?"

"I sell them to magazines."

"Oh, I get it. Free-lance. So what are you working on now?"

"This and that."

She grinned.

"Oh, come on. You can tell me. I won't blow your, what do you call it, your scoop?"

I smiled back. She was beginning to grow on me. There was something appealing about her brashness and independence, this latchkey kid in mom's makeup.

"I'm doing a story about girls your age. Maybe a little older. Girls who have babies."

Her grin seemed to falter. I went with a hunch.

"Yeah, you might've heard of one of them. She was killed a few days ago, right in Portland. Maybe you saw it in the paper? Her name was Missy Hewett."

Her grin vanished and her skin went gray, leaving the garish blood-red lipstick the only color on her face.

"She was killed?" the girl said, in a hoarse whisper.

"Did you know her?"

She looked like she might collapse so I took her by the shoulder and led her inside. We were in a hallway with carpeted stairs leading up. I sat her on the bottom step and squatted beside her.

"You didn't know she was dead?"

She moved her head side to side.

"How did you know her?"

She sat for a long time and didn't say anything. I wasn't sure she'd heard the question. I didn't want to ask it again.

"We talked," she said, finally. "She called and, you

know me, I'll talk to anybody. She wanted to talk to my dad but a lot of the time he isn't home, so I'd talk to her instead. She was a nice kid."

I waited. I didn't want to spook her.

"She said she was living with her sister because her mother was a drunk or something. I could relate to that. She said she'd get in trouble if there were a lot of calls on the bill, so a couple of times I called her. I kind of thought we could be friends, you know?"

Two young girls, with loneliness in common.

"What did she talk about?"

"Nothing much, at first. Then we kind of hit it off, I guess, and she told me about how she was gonna have this baby but she didn't want to just sit home on welfare and she wouldn't raise a child in her mom's house. No way. So she was gonna have the baby adopted."

She paused. Licked her lips.

"That bothered her. I mean, it was still her kid and everything. She cried on the phone."

"What did she want with your dad?"

"He was helping her with the adoption stuff."

"Is he an adoption lawyer?"

"No, he's into corporate something. I don't know much about it. But when he first started out, he worked with a firm that did a lot of adoption kind of stuff. So he still knows how it all works."

"How did Missy come to call him?"

"I don't know. She never said."

"Did he call her back?"

"Yeah, but not as fast as she wanted."

"Why did she call him at home?"

"I don't know," she said. "I never asked her."

Sitting there on the step, David Putnam's daughter seemed to have shrunk. She sat very still and I could hear her breath going in and out in a listless wheeze. The door was still open and the chickadees were calling and peeping outside.

"How was she killed?"

I hesitated.

"They thought she'd been hit by a car," I said. "But she was dead before that. Somebody suffocated her."

"Why would they do that?"

"I don't know."

She didn't say anything. I waited.

"When did you talk to her last?" I asked.

"It was funny. We talked in the summertime. She told me how she was gonna move to Portland to go to school. We made these plans to get together, 'cause we'd never really met, you know? Not face to face, I mean. So in the summer we talked and then I didn't hear from her for a long time. I called one time and some guy said she'd moved to Portland and he didn't have the number. So I figured she'd call me and last week she finally did."

"What'd she say?"

"I don't know. My father talked to her. He was home. For once."

Twenty-eight█

The bartender at Three Dollar Dewey's was a young guy with several earrings. He brought me a pint of Samuel Smith's Nut Brown Ale, which was the color of mahogany. I stared at the glass a bit before I tried a sip. The ale was good and the pub was quiet, in that lull between lunch and the late-afternoon crush. It was just what I needed: a place to think.

I needed to think about David Putnam and his daughter, to take that step back. My first reaction had been to want to call Poole and his state police buddy from the first phone booth I found on Route 1. I wanted to tell them I knew who Missy was dealing with about the baby. And I knew who she most likely called when she decided she wanted her baby back.

If Putnam hadn't killed her, I'd bet he could point a finger at the person who had.

I felt an urgency, a need to grab the guy before he could take off or get himself an attorney or even to get the messages that some guy named Jack McMorrow had come to talk about Missy Hewett. I wanted Poole to be waiting when he got home that night. I wanted Poole to be waiting with an arrest warrant.

It was the feeling you had when you came back to the newsroom with a big one. You marched on to the floor, maybe even into the news meeting, because you knew the story would turn the news budget upside down. Early on at the *Times*, I'd done exactly that a couple of times, knocking on the door and actually calling the deputy metro editor out of the room. The first time it had been warranted: a kid killed in a drive-by had been ID'd as the son of an alderman. It made him, his death, and the story more important. The second time, the editor had walked me back to my desk and told me that the newspaper required more than information from me. It required perspective and when I rushed into the newsroom with my heart still pounding, I didn't have that.

"Sit there for a minute," he'd said. "Sit there for ten minutes if that's what it takes to put your information in context."

So I sat. The music was jazz with a funky edge and the bartender was reading some sort of hip music magazine. He looked a lot like the guy on the cover, except the guy on the cover had a ring in his nose. I sipped my beer and he read and was quiet. The only other people in the place were a man and a woman who were hunched over the other end of the bench, holding hands and staring into each other's eyes as if they were doing some kind of mutual hypnosis. The Sam Smith's went down slowly. The perspective came slowly, too.

When the pint was finished, I had a better grip on what I knew. I probably had come up with Missy's adoption advisor, if not her connection. I didn't know how she had found him, but if he didn't advertise his expertise in this part of the law, it must have been word of mouth. But whose?

I didn't know what stake David Putnam would have had in her adoption going smoothly. I didn't know if he had just steered Missy in the right direction. If that were the case, she might have come back to him for advice about how to undo what she'd done. What had he told her? Had he told anyone else? Had Putnam gone to the cops?

Undoubtedly, Missy's murder had been reported in the *Portland Press Herald*. Portland was a safe-enough city that the killing of a college girl was very big news. It must have been page one, maybe above the fold, at least the first day. Putnam must have read the stories. How could he have not come forward?

I needed to know, but would Poole tell me? Maybe all I could hope for was to tell him face to face and watch his reaction. And hope I read it right.

And now Putnam knew I knew, assuming he communicated with his daughter at all. He knew my name and what I did. He had my phone number, which meant he knew where to reach me. If he called, what would he say? If he didn't call, what did that mean?

Sitting there at the long bench, I unbuttoned my shirt pocket and took out Missy's phone bill and unfolded it. There on the list were the calls to Putnam's office. Then the calls to the office stopped and were replaced by the calls to Putnam's house, as if he had said, "Listen. You really shouldn't be calling me here. Why don't you call me at home."

Those calls had been placed in May and early June, before the baby was due. After mid-June, the calls to Putnam had stopped. The last week of August, there were the calls to Rhode Island.

Missy getting cold feet? Missy calling to hear the sound of her baby crying?

The guy with the earrings looked up from his magazine, saw that my pint was nearly empty, and drifted over.

"Another one?" he said, already reaching for my glass.

"No, thanks," I said. "I'm driving."

"Back to work?"

"Yeah. In Rhode Island."

"What do you do there?"

"That's a good question," I said.

I put a five on the table and left.

I figured I needed a plan, so as I drove I tried to come up with one. By the time I got to the ramp for the interstate, I had it all figured out: I'd go to Brown University and see what happened.

It wasn't much but I had three hours to refine it.

The drive was a straight shot, one hundred eighty miles in the southbound lane. Highlights of the trip included the Kennebunk Burger King, not far from the summer house of former President George Bush. I got tea and French fries from the drive-through window and asked the girl behind the sliding glass if the president ate there.

"Which president?" she said.

From there it was twenty miles of straight-shot highway with spruce walls on each side. The tea kept me going until things opened up near the New Hampshire border and then the highway rose to cross the bridge between Kittery, Maine, and Portsmouth, New Hampshire. The bridge arched high over the Piscataqua River and I slowed to take in the view—the river meandering inland, the flare of autumn foliage, the town of Portsmouth, all steeples and roofs, arranged in a colonial jumble—but a tractor-trailer nearly rear-ended my truck. They should have a special lane for drivers with a highly refined sense of aesthetics.

The blast from the air horn kept me awake through New Hampshire, where the highway widened and people drove faster. I was approaching the cities, where everything was imbued with a false sense of urgency. Putt-putting along in the little truck, with cars and trucks passing me like a rock in a stream, I felt like Thoreau returning to the city from a long weekend at Walden Pond.

For the rest of the trip, the feeling grew. North of Boston, I followed the narrow two-lane chute past liquor stores, video palaces, and nightclubs where women danced in G-strings. By the time I hit the city, winding along Route 3 between the high-rise downtown offices, I felt like a trapper back from the frontier. I'd been away from the city for less than two years and already I felt like an alien.

Jack McMorrow of New York City or Jack McMorrow of Prosperity, Maine? Would the real Jack McMorrow please stand up? I was pretty sure I knew which one he was. More sure by the minute.

Unlike New York, Boston didn't go on forever. Downtown Boston suddenly vanished and I was on the wide-open highway again, staring into the backyards of people who, for some absolutely inexplicable reason, had chosen to buy new homes with a breathtaking view of the breakdown lane. Their kids probably sold lemonade over the fence to stranded travelers.

The highway left the Boston suburbs behind, and for ten or fifteen minutes I was in the country again, with woods and farms that had been overlooked in the rush to turn every available acre into a shopping mall. There was a sign that said Providence, fifteen miles, and then there were a few houses, then a few more houses, and then expanses of old brick factories and a sprawling railroad yard, separated from the highway by a wire fence. When the Providence skyline swung into view, it all came rushing back.

I'd worked here for nine months, doing the police beat for the *Providence Journal*. This had been during my newspaper-hopping days when I was young and ambitious and rootless and could pack up and move in an hour. Some things changed. Some things didn't.

I swung off of one interstate and on to another, crossing the industrial river at the head of Narragansett Bay and heading for the city's East Side and Brown University. Brown sprawled across a plateau overlooking the downtown, which had been built on what once was marshland along the Providence River. But that was a long time ago, an irrelevant piece of trivia to the Vietnamese, Cambodians, Dominicans, and others who flocked to Providence now, two centuries after Roger Williams had come to get a break from those dreary Puritans. The immigrants who walked the streets now just wanted a break from dreary and hopeless poverty. In places like Providence, sometimes they got lucky. Sometimes they didn't.

My job had been to cover the unlucky ones. Mostly they were shot and stabbed. Sometimes they were dead. Half of them died before they could even learn to speak English. Some of the dead, lying in pools of blood in the gutter outside some neighborhood bar, were just kids.

I didn't sleep well in Providence. I dreamed of their dark eyes, staring but unseeing. Their mothers, kneeling in the blood, shrieking in their grief.

But where I was going they slept fine, protected by the invisible wall of the old money and new power of the Ivy League. It was an empire, this university overlooking the rest of the city. The campus was old and stately and beautiful, surviving wars and economic collapses. It went on for block after block and it seemed odd that somewhere in one of these buildings was somebody who had talked to Missy Hewett. Odder still was the idea that somewhere not far from here, but very far from Waldo County, Maine, was Missy Hewett's child.

I drove up Wickendon, through Fox Point, which used to be a Portuguese neighborhood but had been gradually taken over by students, who had the distinct advantage of being willing to pay exorbitant rents. Fox Point gave way to the

Brown campus, with old brick dorms shaded by elms, new research buildings towering above it all. I circled a couple of times, then parked by a big quadrangle bounded by granite pillars and big iron gates.

Kids were coming and going, carrying backpacks, riding bicycles. It was after four-thirty and everyone seemed in a hurry. Medical school awaited. Law school beckoned. I got out of the truck and stretched my legs.

My plan was to find the classics department, which Missy had called once. Once I found it, I would decide what to do next. It wasn't much of a plan but that was my little secret.

I walked across the quadrangle toward one of the brick buildings, feeling conspicuously empty-handed. I should have grabbed the Toyota owner's manual, just to have a book to carry, but it was too late so I just stuck my hands in my pockets and walked. It was getting dark and cold and late and I was afraid that the classics people would have locked up for the weekend. Or didn't classics people cut out early?

My first thought had been that there might be one of those campus maps, the ones behind glass cases with the little arrow that says, "You are here." But this was Brown University. Apparently it was assumed that if you were here, you knew where here was.

So I couldn't find a map, and was reduced to what I did best: ferreting information out of strangers. A dubious skill, when you thought about it. I tried not to.

The first person I approached was a young woman dressed all in black, as if in mourning for having to attend one of the best universities in the country. I smiled pleasantly and tried not to look too much like a molester. She didn't smile back but she didn't run, either.

I asked if she could direct me to the office of the classics department.

"Oh," she said, thinking. "I know I've seen it. I'm biochem."

No wonder she was in mourning, I thought. She's trying to find a cure for cancer.

But she couldn't locate the classics department, nor could the next kid I asked, a long-haired guy in ripped jeans and black Converse high-tops who looked like he should be playing guitar in a bar band downtown. He said he was in med school. I felt old.

But time was running out and I was getting desperate. If the office was closed and tomorrow was Saturday, my trip would be wasted, though it would still be tax-deductible. And chances would be a little greater that I'd be filing my return from prison.

Finally, I stopped an older professorial-looking man, who was walking with an older professorial-looking woman. The man turned and pointed to the other end of the quadrangle and told me to cut between the buildings and the door would be in the second building on the left. Which I did. And it was.

The door was open and the lights were on. There was a bulletin board in the hallway where opportunities were posted for classics majors, mostly in other classics departments. Harvard. Dartmouth. Berkeley. The world of academia, a private club. It was too late for me to get in, unless I used the service entrance.

I kept walking and passed an open door. Inside, a computer printer was squawking and a man was talking on the phone. He didn't look up.

All of the other doors on the floor were closed. I went the length of the hallway, examining each one. They were faculty offices, some singles, some doubles. I pushed aside the notes from students and copied the name of each professor, including the one on the phone. Then I found the stairwell and went up.

The second floor resembled the first, but only two of the doors had names. I wrote those in my notebook and went up one more flight. When I came out of the stairwell, I startled an older woman pushing a vacuum cleaner.

"May I help you?" she said sternly.

I glanced at my list.

"Classics?"

"French," she said. "Classics is downstairs. But you can leave the packages on the first floor."

"Oh, merci," I said. "Je suis très fatigué."

"You think you're tired? You ought to try cleaning this entire building every week."

I wondered if the janitor on the first floor spoke Greek.

Twenty-nine

A couple of blocks east was Thayer Street, an avenue with shops and cafés. I parked the truck on the street and walked until I found a quiet-looking place that had tables set up on an enclosed porch. The door to the porch was right on the sidewalk and I went in and waited for somebody to seat me. The waitress, another young woman dressed all in black, took me to a table by the window. I wondered if they'd all gone to the same wake.

The waitress left and came back and I asked what brands of beer they served. She recited for a minute or two and I ordered an Oat Sheaf Stout, from England. And a phone book. From Providence.

I had eight names. The phone number I'd brought from home. B.Y.O.C. Bring your own clue.

After the waitress had delivered and gone, I sipped the stout and flipped through the book. Most of the members of the classics department lived right in the city. Four out of the first five lived on the East Side, and probably bicycled to work wearing berets. The sixth number matched mine, the one on Missy's phone bill. Just like that.

I wondered if Philip Marlowe was hiring.

His name was Francis X. Flanagan, a name that seemed odd for a classics guy. But then maybe he started with James Joyce and worked his way back to the source. Then again, with a name like that he simply could have been educated by Jesuits. Jesuits took their classics seriously.

Flanagan lived on Benefit Street, number four-thirty-nine, which was bicycling distance, too. I didn't know if he wore a beret. I did know he had a wife because I'd tried to sell her windows. And awakened her baby.

I closed the phone book, drank my stout slowly, and tried to figure out what I would say to the Flanagans. Tell them I knew the mother of their child. That she was a nice kid but she was dead. Maybe they'd be glad to hear it. Maybe they already knew.

It was another blind alley, an unmarked door to pound on. I didn't know if I'd step into an elevator shaft or be invited in for tea. When it came down to it, I didn't know that it was Missy's baby. I wouldn't know until I asked.

The stout went down too quickly. I left money on the phone book and, leaving the waitress to her grief, went back to the truck.

Benefit was maybe a half mile away, running along the edge of what was called College Hill. The houses were close together, eighteenth and nineteenth century, graceful and imposing and very expensive. The nicer ones required family money. Four-thirty-nine was one of those.

It was a brick row-house sort of thing, except double wide with an arched brick wall in the center, leading to a private courtyard. The front door was Georgian and stately, painted a dark red, with simple windows along each side and a graceful fan up above. I pulled up across the street in front of a no-parking sign and shut off the motor.

The lights were on upstairs and down and there was a new Volvo station wagon parked in the courtyard. I sat and watched and a figure passed one of the upstairs windows. It passed again and I could see that it was a woman. If she started to get undressed, I was out of there.

I looked at myself in the rearview mirror and saw that I still looked like an escapee from a Siberian labor camp. My eye was half-closed and the skin around it was yellowing. There was stubble growing up around my cuts and scrapes like brush around a clear-cut forest. Maybe I wouldn't have to say anything to the Flanagans. Maybe they'd just beg for mercy.

The woman appeared at the window again and this time I could see she was holding a baby. I took a deep breath, got out of the truck, and walked to the door.

Beside the door was a knob. I pulled it and some sort of antique bell jangled inside the house like something on an ice cream truck. I waited. There were steps. The brass lamps beside the big red door flashed on like headlights. The door swung open.

It was a man, in jeans and a sweater. He was maybe forty, tall and bearded and lean like a runner. I took one look at him and knew he'd been warned. His face was too taut, his expression too stern, and in his eyes there was no curiosity about why a ratty-looking stranger was standing on his front step.

He knew.

"Mr. Flanagan?" I said.

"Yes," he said, his voice hard and flat.

"I'm Jack McMorrow. I'm a writer and I'm from Maine and—this sounds sort of crazy, I know—but I need to talk to you."

"About what?" Flanagan asked.

He wasn't puzzled. Wasn't wondering what the hell this guy wanted. Wasn't ready to call the cops.

I played along. He did, too.

"It's about your baby. I know this sounds strange and please don't get the wrong idea. But I just need to talk to you about her. There's no problem. Really. And I don't want to make any trouble for your family. I just need some information. For my own sake. Really. I'm not a crank. I'm really not."

He stood there and stared and said nothing. I could hear classical music playing inside the house. A car went by. I waited.

"You've got a minute," Flanagan said. "The clock's ticking."

"I think I knew the mother—the biological mother, I mean—of your baby. Her name was Missy Hewett and I met her researching a magazine story on teen-age mothers. This is all just in the last couple weeks. So Missy—she was a student at the University of Maine—she was killed this week. They thought she'd been hit by a car in Portland but it turned out she was dead before that. Suffocated."

For the first time I thought I got a reaction.

"And Missy's phone bill shows she called this house. Twice. This would have been late August. The baby would have been a couple of months old. Roughly."

"So the police in Maine are investigating this woman's death?" Flanagan said suddenly.

"Yes."

"Then why aren't they asking these questions?"

"They may be soon."

"Why are you involved? Are you doing an article about this woman's murder, if that's what it is?"

"I don't know," I said. "Right now I'm just trying to piece things together."

"For what purpose?"

"I'm not sure."

"If it's some sort of extortion then I'll tell you right now, you won't get a cent."

"I don't want any money," I said. "I just want to know what happened."

"Well, just so you understand," Flanagan said, suddenly pointing his finger at me, his voice louder, more tremulous, "I don't know anything about this woman. But I do know that I won't let anybody hurt our baby or my family. I won't let you."

"I don't want to hurt your family. I told you that."

"I won't let you. You understand that? I will do whatever it takes to protect this family. I will—"

He paused and turned and looked up the stairs. There were footsteps and then a long print skirt came into view coming down. Then a blouse, then a very beautiful red-haired woman.

"Honey, what is it?" she said.

"Nothing. There's someone here. A Mr. McMorrow. He's—"

"He's here? My God, the son of a bitch."

She took four steps toward me and pointed her finger in my face, too.

"Who do you think you are? Who the hell do you think you are? Coming into this house and questioning us. Well, I'll tell you right now, you are not going to take our little girl away from us."

"I have no intention of doing that."

"Then why are you here? How did you find us?"

I didn't say anything.

"No, I want an answer. How did you find this house? How dare you come and stand on our doorstep and ask us about our family? How dare you? Now, how did you find us?"

"Missy Hewett called you."

"And that was enough for you, you son of a bitch, you creep, coming in here. He told us we might be hearing from you. Fran, how much does he want?"

"I don't want anything," I said.

"Write him a check and—"

"Mrs. Flanagan," I said, louder. "I don't want anything. Nothing. I came here because I need to know more about Missy Hewett and the adoption. That's all. All I want to know is why Missy called."

"What business is that of yours?" the woman said.

"I was working with her. For a story about teen-age mothers and how they live. Right in the middle of that, somebody killed her. I need to know why. I need to know if it was related to what I was working on. And if she was calling you—"

"I fail to see how—" Flanagan began.

"That has nothing to do with us," his wife said, her cheeks rouged with anger. "Or our daughter. And I'll tell you. That little girl is our life. She's more than our life. She is . . . She's everything. I don't know about this girl. If what you say is true, I'm sorry for her. But let me tell you right now. If you try to do anything to take that little girl away from me, I'll stop you."

"Courtney!" Flanagan blurted.

"I don't care, Fran. We waited so long. She's ours. She's our baby. Do you have children?"

"No," I said.

"Then you can't understand, can you? You can't know what we're talking about."

"I think I understand."

"No, you don't. You can't. Until you have children, you have no idea. If you did, you wouldn't be here trying to destroy our lives. How can you live with yourself? Do you enjoy hurting people? Hurting innocent children?"

"I'm not—"

There was crying from deeper inside the house, first faint, then louder. I heard the tap of footsteps, then a door opened and the crying was right there and then a young woman appeared, younger than Missy, with a baby in her arms. The cries came in deep, heaving gasps.

"I'm sorry, Mrs. Flanagan," the girl said, her accent very Irish. "I just can't get her to settle."

Courtney Flanagan, who had just threatened to kill me, swept the baby from the girl's arms in a smooth, instinctive motion. The girl stood there, awaiting orders, I supposed. Courtney Flanagan seemed to have forgotten her as she rocked the little dark-haired baby, Missy's baby, on her shoulder.

The crying subsided into tiny sobs, like faint hiccups.

"Sorry, Mrs. Flanagan," the Irish girl said again.

"It's okay, Megan," said Fran Flanagan, who, like me, had become a mere spectator to this display of the power of a mother's love. "You can go back upstairs."

When the girl had gone, Courtney Flanagan looked at me. Her eyes were pale blue and they were filled with tears. The hiccups were fainter.

"Nobody hurts her," she said, her voice breaking. "Nobody takes her. I meant what I said."

She turned and went up the stairs in a swish of skirt. Fran Flanagan and I were left alone, and there was a strange silence, almost like a vacuum, in which we both stood. And then it was over.

"If you come here again, I'll call the police," Flanagan said. "If you contact me or my wife in any other way, I'll take legal action. You will not threaten this family."

And he swung the big door shut.

Thirty

I left because I didn't want to get roused by the Providence cops, but I didn't go far: down two blocks and over one, where I parked in the shadows under an old maple tree and shut off the motor.

And sat there feeling a little sick.

Whatever else was going on here, the feeling the Flanagans had for their baby was real. I could see it in Fran Flanagan's eyes. I could feel it emanating from his wife's body, like a sound wave. They were living for that kid. And they would kill for that kid.

But had they already?

Courtney Flanagan, with her fashion-magazine looks and very old money, would claw my heart out and eat it if it meant keeping Missy's baby. Had she done that to Missy? Had the Flanagans heard that this little girl from Maine was going to burst the bubble of their new family? Had they decided the little girl had to go?

But Courtney Flanagan had most clearly and succinctly threatened to kill me. Would somebody who had committed murder, and thus far gotten away with it, threaten to kill somebody else? It didn't make sense, but then, the Flanagans weren't operating sensibly when it came to the baby. They were very much afraid. And fear made people do strange things.

What if Missy had called them and tried to back out on the adoption? What if she'd asked for a meeting and the Flanagans had been unable to persuade her to let things stand? What if they'd offered her money? What if they'd offered her more money?

What if she'd said no?

So how could it have come off? A meeting. Things get heated. Missy wants the baby back and does what? Threatens to go to court? Threatens to have the baby put in a foster home until the matter is resolved? They argue and one of the Flanagans knocks Missy down and puts a pillow over her face. Holds it there until she stops moving and the problem goes away. The adoption is final.

But then, what to do with her? Stick some shorts and Nikes on her and dump her in the road. Do it in the middle of the night and by the time they find her, the Flanagans are back in the big brick house, listening to Mozart and rocking their baby to sleep.

It could have happened that way but I was having trouble picturing it. Would Courtney Flanagan venture out of her East Side fortress to confront Missy? Or would she lock

herself in her room with her precious baby girl and send
lawyers to take care of the matter? This was a woman who
had an Irish au pair on duty, probably before the baby even
arrived. Who had money and the power that goes with it.

Courtney Flanagan did not do diapers. Would she get her
hands dirty by killing an innocent woman?

No, I just couldn't see it. What I could picture was a guy
and his wife who, if they were innocent of everything except trying to protect their adopted child from me, had a
right to think I was slime. Sometimes I wondered myself,
but there was no turning back now.

I ate on Thayer Street, wolfing down a spinach calzone at a
vegetarian place next to the café where I'd had the Oat
Sheaf Stout. This time I tried an Anchor Steam Ale, from
the west coast. The ale was better than the calzone, which
contained a mysterious herb that made it taste faintly of
soap. I washed it down with the ale and ordered another
from a young woman who was dressed in skirts and shawls.
She looked like a refugee but probably had a trust fund.

And a grandfather who was spinning in his grave.

I was weary already and the ale was threatening to anchor me to the seat. I'd wait until closing and ask the young
woman to take me home to her camp. One refugee to another.

But I drank the second beer and then roused myself and
left, walking down the street in the cool night air. Kids
were out in force, lining up in front of an artsy movie theater, streaming into a neon-lit bar on the corner. It was time
for me to get out.

I found a pay phone up the block and dialed Maine directory assistance. They gave me Claire's number and I
charged the call to my home phone.

"Is there anyone there to verify the charge?" the operator
asked.

"Just the bats and they're shy with strangers," I said.

She thanked me for using AT&T.

I punched in the numbers. The phone rang and Claire answered.

"Jack," he said. "You in jail?"

"Not yet, but I'm trying."

"And you want me to have the bail money ready?"

"And a file in a cake," I said. "How's everything there?"

"Well, they're talking about a killing frost tonight."

"Cover your tomatoes."

"They're all tucked in. How 'bout you?"

"Me? I'm outside a bar in Providence, Rhode Island."

"They toss you out or did you leave peaceably?"

"Never went in. The place is filled with children."

"Life's like that," Claire said. "Time, it marches on."

I could hear Mary in the background and what sounded like music from an off-Broadway musical. *The Fantastiks.* She asked Claire if it was me and he said, yes, and she told him not to forget to tell me something.

"Well, your place has been busy," Claire said.

"Bats having company?"

"Yeah. The police, for one. Your detective buddy stopped and then he came over here. He asked if we knew your whereabouts. I said I didn't even know your shirt size."

"He liked that."

"Oh, yeah. No, he seemed like a nice enough fella. Said he just needed to check with you about something."

"Probably needs some help with a case," I said.

"Right. And if it works out, you could get on full time. Maybe they need somebody to chalk tires in Belfast."

"I can only hope. Who else came by?"

"Well, let's see. I was almost ready to start charging you for a goddamn message service. The next one was another good friend of yours. That kid in the four-wheel-drive."

"Kenny."

"Yeah. He drove by here twice, around five o'clock. Come by real slow the first time; and the second time I stood out by the road and stepped out and surprised him."

"What'd you do, shoot him?"

"Oh, no. Worse than that. I made him stop and talk to me. And weren't he a jumpy little bastard. I would've almost said that boy was wired on something, but I don't think so. Think he was just scared."

"You do that to people. What'd he say?"

"Said he was just looking for you. Said he needed to talk to you."

"Smoke a peace pipe?"

"I think he already smoked the peace pipe. No, but he said he needed to talk to you. Wasn't belligerent or anything. Seemed pretty nervous."

"That's funny. Last time I saw him, he pulled a knife on me."

"I hope you told him that wasn't a good idea."

"He's just lucky he didn't pull a paper plate."

"You got that right," Claire said. "You'd be hell at a picnic."

"Thanks to you."

"Don't thank me."

"Okay, I won't."

A motorcycle went by and I covered the receiver. When I uncovered it, a kid in a Jeep leaned on his horn.

"You in the middle of the road or what?" Claire asked.

"On some issues," I said. "So is that it for my message service or what?"

"Hell, no. I saved the best for last."

"The place burned down?"

"Nope. But this lady was looking for you."

"Story of my life."

"Good looking, too."

"You sound surprised."

"Hell, no. She wasn't a knockout or anything. She was just sort of pretty. In a wild sort of way. Dark curly hair. Lots of it. Nice smile. Sturdy little build."

"Jeez, Claire. Sounds like you gave her the full inspection."

"Just so I could report back to you. I told her I'm took. She looked disappointed but I think she'll get over it."

"Maybe not. Maybe she had her heart set on a father figure."

"Father figure?"

"Okay. Grandfather figure. She tell you her name?"

"Yeah," Claire said. "She said her name was Janeese. Or Janeesh. Something like that. Sounded foreign."

"From the high school?"

"Right. She said to tell you she stopped by. So you been doing some extra research on that baby story or what?"

Janice Genest. Stopped by. To do what? Slash my tires? Serve me with a harassment notice barring me from school grounds?

"Jack," I heard Claire's voice say. "You still there?"

"Yeah. I'm here. So what'd you tell her?"

"I told her you were away. Said you'd gone south to do some research on a story but you'd be back in a day or two."

"What'd she say?"

"Well, she gave me that big smile and said she'd be back. Nice girl. Mary thought so, too. She says it's about time you settled down with a nice girl like that."

Nice girl? I thanked Claire and hung up and stood there for a minute on the sidewalk, like somebody looking to buy drugs. Nice girl?

That wasn't the Janice Genest I knew. She'd been cold and sharp as an icicle and now she was coming on to Claire like my best friend. What had happened to change her mind? Had something sent her over to my side? Or someone?

Something had to have changed for her to seek me out. To find my house. To drive out and knock on my door. With a smile, no less.

Maybe it had just hit her all of a sudden. I was single. I was cute. I drove a pickup truck with a gun rack.

Best investment I'd ever made.

Things were a little off kilter now. In my head, I'd divided people up. On my side there was me. And Claire. Roxanne, long distance. Missy, in spirit. Missy's assorted family, maybe. My girlfriends in the truck, double maybe.

On the other side was Kenny. What had he wanted? Why was he there in broad daylight? Was the prospect of jail time softening him up, making him think maybe it was time for a truce? Or maybe he'd finally seen the error of his ways. Found Jesus. Was doing grocery runs for shut-ins. Needed me to help him with a term paper.

And Poole, too. Heck, if I'd known they were all coming, I would have been home. Would have made finger sandwiches. We could have stood around the backyard discussing Millie's sculptures. Yes, Kenny. I do think rusting iron symbolizes the decay of our industrial society.

And then there was David Putnam, whom I'd never met but was ready to hate. The Flanagans, whom I'd met only once but already hated me. Janice Genest I'd put in a neutral zone. She'd liked Missy but she didn't like me. One emotion nullified the other.

So I was having trouble fitting the smiling, warm Janice Genest into the scheme of things. But then, standing there on a sidewalk in a city full of strangers, I was having trouble maintaining any scheme at all.

I got in the truck and sat for a minute. Five minutes after that, I was at the bottom of College Hill, looking for the entrance to the interstate. In an hour, I was in Boston.

The Hyatt Regency was somewhere in Cambridge and Cambridge was somewhere west of the center of the city. I drove up Route 3 to where the highway threaded through the glittering canyons of downtown Boston. It was like a miniature New York, a movie-set city without the sprawling desolation beyond the skyline. As I drove, I stared up at the lights like a bumpkin. The city seemed strange and unreal and foreign. But then, what didn't?

I fought my way through three lanes of traffic to take Storrow Drive West. The road wound past nameless, half-dark buildings and under the highway and emerged along the Charles River and the riverfront park where runners, bundled in sweatsuits, were jogging in a slow, bounding procession, fending off the inevitable. Somewhere behind them, running just a little bit faster, was the Grim Reaper. Even in a two-hundred-dollar warm-up suit, you can run, but you can't hide.

I thought of Missy, in the road in her Nikes, and then I tried not to think of Missy, in the road in her Nikes, but it wasn't that easy. I thought of Roxanne, instead, and even that was unsettling. Would it be the same? Would it be different? Would it be over?

The Hyatt was beyond the river, past the sprawling complex of the Museum of Science, where knots of people were strung out forlornly along the sidewalk, like refugees who had come to an embassy to seek asylum. Cities were places where many strangers lived together. The country was where acquaintances went to live apart.

I didn't find the hotel so much as drive right into it. It was big and modern and glassy and to the parents who stayed there while visiting their kids at Harvard and MIT, it probably was reassuring. Like a McDonald's.

There was a drive to the front entrance and I pulled the truck up to the front door. A kid in a dark-blue uniform came out and around to the driver's door and gave the truck and me a very skeptical once-over.

"It's a loaner," I said. "The BMW is in the garage."

He looked at me harder.

"I'm a loner, too," I said, and looked at him hard right back.

I grabbed my duffel from the truck bed and handed the kid my keys.

"Keep it under a hundred," I said, and walked to the big double glass doors, through a red-carpeted hallway and into the foyer, feeling more nervous than I had in a long, long time.

The registration desk was across the lobby. The lobby was ringed by Naugahyde chairs and couches and a few of the chairs and couches were occupied. A handsome, moneyed-looking couple with two teen-age kids stood near the door, speaking a language that sounded like French but wasn't. A chunky balding guy in a gray suit sat on a couch, talking to a much younger woman who did not appear to be his daughter. He was leering. She was holding herself back. I figured he must have money or she would have kicked him in the groin and gone to play with someone her own age.

I went to the desk and stood there until somebody noticed that approximately three feet away there was a man with cuts on his face and a black eye. This took several minutes. Finally a woman wearing a navy-blue skirt and a white blouse with a gold name tag looked up. She looked like she worked on an airplane. She looked at me like I'd just fallen from the sky.

"I need to speak to a guest," I said.

"Anyone in particular, sir?" the woman said.

This was not getting off to a great start.

I told the woman I wanted to talk to Roxanne Masterson. I didn't know the room number. She went to a file and flipped plastic sheets and then came back and picked up a phone on the counter. Covering the receiver so I wouldn't pick up the number, she dialed and waited. I could feel myself tighten as we waited. Was Roxanne there?

"Your name?" the woman asked, startling me.

"McMorrow," I said. "Jack McMorrow."

"This is the front desk," the woman said into the phone. "There's a Jack McMorrow to see a Roxanne Masterson."

The woman listened, then looked disappointed, as if she had been hoping she would be told there was a warrant out for my arrest.

"She'll be right down," the woman said.

"Better luck next time," I said.

I sat in a Naugahyde chair next to the family that wasn't French. They talked and I stared straight ahead at the elevator doors. The doors were dark maroon and closed. The light over one was going up. The light over the other was coming down. Eight, seven, six. It stopped. Started again. Five, four, three. Stop. Start again. Two, one, lobby. Like a drumroll, the doors rumbled open.

She stepped out and started toward the desk, then saw me and stopped. There was a moment, just before she turned to me, when she hung in midstride, motionless and still and beautiful. Then she smiled and, for the first time since she'd left, I felt like I was home.

"Hi," Roxanne said.

"Hey, there," I said.

"You look like hell," she said.

"Cut myself shaving," I said. "But you look fabulous."

I stood and she took my left wrist in her right hand and pulled me toward her. We kissed gently but she squeezed my wrist hard. I swept my hand quickly through her long dark hair. It was pulled back loosely and my hand pulled out the comb thing and it fell to the floor. The family that wasn't French stopped talking and stared.

"So you want to have a beer?" Roxanne said.

"Gave it up for Lent."

"Lent's not for six months."

"All right then. But just this once."

"There's a bar on the top of this place. It's one of those bars that goes around and around."

"All bars go around and around," I said. "Eventually."

Roxanne smiled.

"Let's go up," she said, her dark eyes fixed on mine.

"Let's," I said, and I picked up my bag. We stood in front of the elevators, holding hands like school kids, and waited for one of the doors to open. One did and we stepped in, and two businessmen walked on behind us. They smelled of wine and their ties were loosened and one was talking about a restaurant on the West Side of some city, somewhere. While they talked, we stood side by side and waited silently as the elevator, like a rocket ship inching away from the launch pad, made its interminable climb to the fourth floor. After several eternities, the doors wheeled open and we stepped out.

Mercifully, room four-thirty-five was only a few steps away. Roxanne fumbled with the key card, got the door open, and we practically tumbled inside.

"Baby," Roxanne said.

"Don't leave me again," I whispered.

"Oh God, no," she said, kissing my face, my neck, my mouth.

"And I won't leave you," I said.

"I'd die," Roxanne said. "I'd just die."

We left a trail on the carpeted floor, from the door to the bed. Roxanne's little leather shoes, my shirt. Her wool slacks, my boots. Her blouse, my jeans. Our underwear, flung aside as we rolled on to the bed, turning over and over like we'd been swept underwater by some giant wave.

At first we were frantic, and then deliberate and intense and unrelenting. Our hands swept over each other with disbelief. Roxanne's skin was so soft and white, her body so smooth and sleek but strong. We didn't talk at all, not one word as we searched in each other's eyes for some clue, some reason for this feeling, but then gave up.

There was no reason. It just was.

So there in the dim light of the hotel room, with clatters from the hall and sirens from the street, we made love. Crouching over me, Roxanne ran her fingers through my hair, caressed my scrapes and cuts and continued on, never asking how or why. As her hips rocked slowly, she explored me with her hands like a blind person, and I did the same with her, taking her in, drinking her down, watching the miraculous way she responded to my touch.

It was a miracle, really, like nothing I'd ever experienced before her. Compared to making love with Roxanne, all the others had been players, stiffly reciting lines from bad movies, trying to feel like somebody had said they should feel. Some had been beautiful, some had been admirable. None of them had been like this.

After it ended, in an arching, convulsing, trembling embrace, we lay still for a long time. The sirens came creeping back. The walls of the room reappeared. I ran my hand over Roxanne's thigh and hip and side, brushing her nipple and causing her to jump.

"Sorry," I said.

"No, you're not."

"You're right," I said. "I'm not."

We were quiet for a minute. Roxanne suddenly leaned over and kissed me gently on the lips, then lay back down.

"Why did we leave each other?" she said.

"I don't know. Maybe we didn't want to give in."

"Maybe. Or maybe it was just a bad time."

"A bad time to fall in love?"

"I don't know. I think maybe I didn't want to always associate you with people dying."

"Why not?" I said. "You look great in black. You have lovely white skin."

She smiled.

"Speaking of lovely, what did you do to your face?"

"Why? What's wrong with it?"

"It's pretty beat up. Even for you."

"Would you believe I wasn't wearing my seat belt?"

"I didn't believe it the last time."

"What was it the last time?"

"Some bad guys knocked you around."

"Oh, yeah. Well, they got theirs, didn't they?"

"And this time?" Roxanne asked.

"There were six of them," I said. "They didn't have a chance."

"My tough guy."

"Did I ever tell you you're beautiful when you swoon?"

I took her hand, intertwined my fingers with hers. She'd grown her fingernails longer since we'd been apart.

"So what am I signing up for, Jack?"

Her voice carried a faint note of sadness.

"I don't know," I said.

"More of the same?"

I shrugged.

"I'm just a mild-mannered reporter," I said.

"Mild-mannered reporters don't get beat up."

"Sure they do. They just don't hit back."

"Oh, Jack."

"Oh, Jack, what?"

"Oh, Jack, what am I going to do with you?"

"I don't know," I said. "But what we just did was a heck of a start."

We talked into the night. Roxanne told me about the poor little rich kids she was working with in Colorado Springs, how their parents were every bit as screwed up, sometimes more, then any of the poor she'd worked with in Maine, how the work was harder, really, because families with money could put up better defenses.

"I used to call and get an irate daddy who'd threaten to kill me," Roxanne said. "Now I get an irate daddy who calls his two-hundred-dollar-an-hour lawyer."

"Same problems. More sophisticated means of denying them."

"You got it."

She said she'd made some good friends, that there were a couple that I'd like. One was an ornithologist who studied hawks and their migration. I said I'd made some good friends, too, including a couple she'd like. One was a retired Marine who had a big garden and could recite poetry.

"And his wife's a peach," I said.

It went that way for a while, nice and easy, our hips and thighs resting together under the blankets, Roxanne's head in the crook of my arm. And then she asked how things were going for me. The baby story. *New England Look.*

"So these teen mothers beat you up?"

"Postpartem repression."

"God, your humor hasn't changed."

"You were hoping?"

"I knew better. Besides, it's your way of evading difficult questions."

"Drop back and pun."

"Not bad, but that doesn't answer the question either."

"You want to know what's going on, huh."

"Yes, I do."

"Pushy, aren't you."

"Because I love you."

"Good reason."

"I think so."

So in the dark, in the hotel bed, I told Roxanne the latest about Missy and Janice Genest and the girls from the high school. I told her about Kenny and my new truck.

"A gun rack?" she said.

"Try to hold yourself back."

I told her about Poole and my new role as murder suspect. I threw in Putnam and his daughter, the Flanagans and their baby. For good measure.

"So right now I'm just poking and prodding. All I can do. Go around trying to hit a nerve. Shake somebody up so something will happen."

"And you'll be cleared."

"And the truth will come out," I said. "But you know what's funny?"

"No," Roxanne said.

"The people at the magazine want to send a photographer up."

"Tell 'em to make it a forensic photographer," she said.

"Hey, that's not bad."

"But it's not funny."

"Maybe not uproarious, but I liked it."

"You know what I mean, Jack."

"Yeah," I said. "I do."

We were quiet for a while. Roxanne shifted in my arm, which was going to sleep. I ran my hand over her belly. Outside, there was faint shouting but you couldn't tell if it was shouting in anger or in joy. This being a city, I'd take anger and give odds.

"I'm worried about you, Jack," Roxanne said.

"I'm a little worried myself."

"How do you get into these things?"

"Just have the knack, I guess."

"Could you really go to jail?"

"I doubt it."

"But it's possible."

"Hey, this is America. Anything's possible."

She thought for a moment.

"Then I'll tell you what I think," Roxanne said. "I think you're underestimating the power of having kids. Of parenthood."

"You think so?"

"Yeah. Some people will kill for money, I guess. Some people will kill over a relationship. You know. A jealous lover and all that. But anybody, and I mean anybody, will kill to protect their child."

"You would?"

"Of course. Wouldn't you?"

I considered it for a second.

"In a heartbeat," I said.

"So what do you have here? You have a mother who gave up her baby and wanted it back. Another mother who got that baby and somebody wanted to take it away."

"You think this Courtney Flanagan would kill Missy Hewett?"

"Without blinking. Or she'd have it done."

"This rich woman with the Ivy League husband?"

"Jack, rich people aren't any less capable of evil. In fact, they have more means of doing it."

"So I just look for the biggest Mercedes?"

"Wrong," Roxanne said. "*We* look for the biggest Mercedes."

"What do you mean, we?"

"I told you I was signing on."

"Not to this."

"To you. I'm not leaving you again. I decided that when I saw you downstairs. I just did. I've got two weeks' vacation and I'm going to Prosperity, Maine."

"It ain't the Ritz."

"Wherever we are is the Ritz, Jack."

"You know, I think you're right," I said, and I turned to her and kissed her lips and ran my hand over her breast.

This time she didn't jump.

Thirty-one

Our bags went in the back, my brown duffel and her Gucci leather.

"So I got a deal," she apologized, and hung her matching pocketbook on the gun rack. "So did you get a gun to go with this thing?"

"Well, it's kind of a long story."

Roxanne looked at me. I smiled.

"I can't believe it," she said. "No, I guess I can."

It was morning, a beautiful one and the sky was dense blue, even over Boston. We pulled out of the hotel lot, immediately got lost, and wandered for several blocks before Roxanne spotted the Storrow Drive sign. I cut across three lanes of traffic, daring a woman in a Porsche to hit me. She wimped out and we were off, just like we knew what we were doing.

Crossing the Tobin Bridge on the expressway north, Roxanne reached over and took my hand. We looked out over the harbor, which was busy with traffic, and then sped up and left Boston behind. I shifted with my left hand, squeezed Roxanne's with my right, and didn't let go until we hit I-95 at Danvers. And then I reached over, pulled her close, and gave her a kiss.

"Maybe we should go parking," I said.

"It's eight-thirty."

"Three hours to check out. Maybe we should go back to the hotel."

It was two hours to Portland, maybe a little more. Roxanne fell asleep near Hampton, New Hampshire, and I drove and watched her. Her legs were crossed, feminine even in jeans, and her sweater was the color of heather. She was beautiful and lovely and her expression, as she slept, was that of a trusting child. I wondered if I deserved that trust but it had been placed in me and now there was no going back. I hoped this wasn't a mistake, that I could keep her safe, that nothing would happen, that the Kennys of the world would leave her alone.

I watched her face, listened to the sound of her breath, and for the first time in a very long time, I prayed. Almost.

Ordinarily, I found the interstate from the Maine border to Portland to be straight as a ruler and dull as an assembly line, with toll booths set up, not just to collect money, but to rouse drivers from their stupor. I was as wide awake as Roxanne was soundly asleep, going over the players in my mind, trying to decide what to do next, if anything. Would Kenny and Putnam make that decision for me? Or would it be Poole?

Roxanne awoke as I pulled up to the South Portland toll. I handed the guy in the booth a dollar and change and we

swung off toward Portland. As we approached the downtown, Roxanne spoke for the first time in two hours.

"Get off here," she said.

"You have to go to the bathroom?"

"No," she said. "I want to see it."

She didn't have to say any more.

I took the Forest Avenue exit and drove west past the
fast-food and pizza. At the muffler shop, I took a left and
drove up the block. I pulled up in front of Missy's house.
Even the crisp fall day couldn't make the house any less
dreary.

"The poor girl," Roxanne said quietly. "Let's get out."

I didn't know if that was kosher, being a suspect, but
Roxanne was out of the truck and headed for the sidewalk
so I followed. She stopped and asked me which apartment
was Missy's and I pointed upstairs and she asked me where
the entrance was. I pointed to the left side and she started
up the walk.

"Wait a minute," I said. "You sure you want to—"

"Jack, I spent two years investigating the living. I'm sure
as hell not afraid of the dead."

She went in the door first. The bicycle still was chained
to the railing inside the door and the place still smelled of
cats. Roxanne went up the stairs to Missy's door but there
was police barricade tape stretched across it, stapled to the
molding. It said, "Crime scene. Do not cross."

We didn't.

At the bottom of the stairs, Roxanne stopped. Dishes
clattered inside the first-floor apartment.

"Take the truck and drive down the street," Roxanne
said.

"You're sure," I said.

"I'm sure."

"How long?"

"Fifteen minutes."

I left her and went out to the truck and drove up the
block. I started to park but saw that there were kids kicking

a soccer ball around in the yard directly across from the parking space. Like a good murder suspect, I kept going.

Fifteen minutes is a long time. I circled the campus five times, drove back out on to Forest Avenue, and took a right on to Missy's street. Roxanne was walking ahead of me, a couple of houses past Missy's. I slowed and watched her rear end for a minute, deciding she was gorgeous from all angles. When she was halfway up the block, I pulled over and she got in.

"Well," I said, driving away.

"I was from the university. I wanted to know if anybody had attempted to collect Missy Hewett's belongings."

"What'd you find out?"

"The lady downstairs has already talked to the police and likes to recite the entire interview, verbatim."

"Soap opera come to life."

"Yup. But she said nobody has been there. No family. No friends. 'Just a couple of the teachers from up to the college,' she said."

"Teachers? What would they want? Give her posthumous credit hours?"

"I don't know," Roxanne said. "But she said they went inside."

"Inside the apartment? Past the tape?"

"The tape wasn't there, the lady said. The cops put it up the next day."

"Did she say who these teachers were?"

"No. I tried to get her to tell me but she just said it was a man and a woman. A man in a suit and a woman in a skirt."

"That narrows it down."

"Yup. She said since I was from the college, why didn't I just ask them."

"Ah, what tangled webs we weave."

"All for love," Roxanne said.

"That's what they all say."

*   *   *

We had coffee in a Dunkin' Donuts on Congress Street. The place was filled with old men with nothing to do but stare at Roxanne. Then again, I really didn't have anything to do but stare at Roxanne, so I couldn't complain.

I had tea. Roxanne had black coffee.

"So what do you think?" she said, taking her first tentative sip.

"I think there are a lot of men in suits and women in skirts."

"What would they want?"

"The Flanagans might want any record of the adoption. Anything that could connect Missy to their daughter."

"But that would be in the court records," Roxanne said.

"I'm beginning to wonder if there are any."

"There has to be a record of an adoption."

"Can't you fake birth certificates?"

"I suppose. You can fake anything if you've got the money to have it done."

"The Flanagans have money."

"But why would they fake it?" she said. "Why not just adopt the child legally?"

"I don't know," I said. "Maybe they think there's a stigma attached to not having your own kid."

"That wouldn't bode well for the future, would it."

"Nothing bodes well in this thing. For anybody."

We left and went out to the truck and Roxanne's luggage was still there.

"In New York, it would have changed hands five times by now," I said.

"That why you moved to Prosperity?"

"Yeah," I said. "In Prosperity, they would have taken your suitcase for a short square deer and shot it."

We got back on the highway and headed north. Roxanne asked if I wanted her to drive and I said no, because in Maine, the only reason a man lets a woman drive is because his license is suspended.

"And then only if he's a wimp," I said.

"I love it when you talk macho."

"Kind of makes you weak in the knees, doesn't it?"

"For a minute there I thought I was just getting carsick," she said.

I drove out of the city, and as I approached the Falmouth exit, Roxanne turned to me.

"Well?" she said.

"I suppose," I said, and turned off again.

Route 1 was clogged with Saturday shoppers and I drove slowly, which was fine with me. I wanted to be ready if Putnam was home because I didn't think I'd get more than one shot. To ask him questions, that is.

I didn't think he'd recognize me unless, of course, his daughter or his secretary had mentioned that I looked like I'd been hit by a truck. But that had been yesterday. Maybe since then my eye had faded and my scrapes had started healing. Now maybe I looked like I'd only been hit by a small foreign car.

We turned off Route 1 and the house was in front of us. I pulled up in front, turned off the motor, and turned to Roxanne.

"Be careful," she said.

"He's a lawyer? What's he gonna do? Sue me?"

"Nobody sued Missy Hewett."

Nobody was raking leaves, either, probably because they still were on the trees. I crossed the lawn and saw that there was another car in the driveway, a silver Saab. I stood at the door for a moment and heard voices inside. I rang the bell. The door swung open and there was my little friend, Mariel.

"Hi, your dad home?" I said, smiling.

She hesitated.

"Um, I'm not . . . I don't . . ."

Just then, a man hurried by and looked up.

"Hi, Mister Putnam," I called out. "Glad to find you

home. Your daughter here tells me you're always on the run."

He was on the small side, good looking, with salt-and-pepper hair swept straight back. Wearing jeans and a T-shirt, he was obviously fit and even sinewy, one of those little guys who is all muscle and no fat. And he didn't smile as he approached the door.

I held out my hand.

"Jack McMorrow," I said. "Nice to meet you."

My hand hung out there like it was the arm of a scarecrow. Putnam grabbed the edge of the door and started to swing it shut, but Mariel was in the way.

"I don't do business at home," he said.

"Hey, but I don't want a will drawn up. I want to talk about Missy Hewett."

"We have nothing to say to each other."

Mariel, bless her precocious little heart, didn't budge.

"Yeah, we do," I boomed. "We have to talk about Missy Hewett. You know, Missy with the baby. The one who was trying to reach you so much that she got to be pals with Mariel here. She was the same age as your daughter and she's dead."

"I'm going to have to call the police," Putnam said.

"No need for that. I just thought we could compare notes. You see, I'm a writer. I'm doing a piece on girls who have babies and it's turned into a piece on girls who have babies and then get killed."

"Mariel, get out of the way," Putnam said.

I kept going. Mariel was wide-eyed and open-mouthed.

"So I thought I could tell you what I know and you could do the same for me. I know you called the Flanagans after I came here last time. Mariel and I had a nice talk, didn't we, honey? And I know the Flanagans have Missy's baby girl. Cute little kid, or didn't you see it? Maybe you just handled the paperwork."

Putnam started to turn away, then turned back. A woman with frosted hair came in, her arms full of folded towels.

"What's the matter?" she said.

"Hi, Mrs. Putnam," I said. "Jack McMorrow. Nice to meet you. I was just talking to your husband about the adoption business."

"Call the police," Putnam said.

"What's going on?" his wife asked.

"So what I need to know, Mister Putnam, is how you came to handle Missy's baby. And why you called the Flanagans to warn them. And what happened when Missy told you she wanted to back out on the deal."

"David, what's this all about?" Putnam's wife said. "You don't even do adoptions anymore."

"I don't know, dear. This guy has me mixed up with somebody else. I don't know what he's—"

"But I talked to her, Daddy," Mariel said. "Missy was a nice kid. She said she wanted to tell you she didn't want to give up her baby. She said—"

"Shut up, Mariel," Putnam said, staring at me. "And you get off this property right now. Or I'll have you arrested."

I grinned, hopefully maniacally.

"But Dave, that's the problem. Somebody already wants to have me arrested. For killing Missy Hewett. And I only met her once, a week before she was killed. So I need to know more about this adoption."

"Get out of here," Mrs. Putnam said, her voice rising. "You're some sort of madman. I'm calling the police."

"Fine. Maybe they'll listen to me. I've got quite a story to tell, you know. I'll tell them all about Missy and her baby and—"

Putnam lunged forward, grabbed his daughter by the shoulders, and shoved her aside.

"Ow," Mariel protested. "Dad!"

And the door slammed shut.

I stood there for a moment, gave the door a couple of loud bangs with my fist, then walked to the truck and got in. Roxanne looked at me in amazement.

"What the heck was that?" she said.

"That? That's called shaking the tree to see what'll fall out."

"What fell out?"

"Nothing. Yet."

We drove north in silence, the knobby truck tires whirring against the asphalt. Traffic was heavy until Freeport, home of L.L. Bean and the myriad stores that fed on its crumbs. At Brunswick, the cars thinned again and we drove more or less alone until we neared Augusta. Roxanne looked out the window. I rested my hand on her thigh. As we approached the Augusta exit, Roxanne turned to me.

"Why do you do this?" she said.

"Because I'm hoping you'll be overcome with lust and demand that we check into the next cheap motel we see. There's one coming right up, in case you've been holding back."

She moved my hand from her leg.

"Not that," Roxanne said. "All of this—I don't know—stuff. Getting involved with this girl. Harassing this lawyer. Getting in fights."

"I don't start 'em. I end 'em."

"Jack, I'm serious. Most people just go to work and come home. They have hobbies."

"I have you."

"You do, but that's not the point. The point is I left because all of the 'stuff' got so overwhelming. And here it is, what, almost a year later, and nothing's changed."

"Sure it has. I'm unemployed now and I have this great truck."

"Jack, you know what I mean."

"I know that you're gorgeous."

"Jack, when you worked for the *Times* did you get involved in these things? Were the other reporters getting in all these messes?"

"Just over alimony."

"Goddamn it, Jack. Give me a straight answer."

I thought for a minute. Roxanne waited. We came off the

interstate and on to Augusta's fast-food gauntlet. She wasn't distracted.

"They weren't interested in people," I began. "Not really. The other reporters, I mean. They used them like puzzle pieces. You know. I've got the grieving mother of the shooting victim. Now I need a couple of the dead kid's friends. It was like these people's lives were some sort of fill-in-the-blank test. A crossword puzzle or something. It was just, I don't know, cold or something. Calloused. They seemed to care. They could act like they cared. But they'd knock off that story about the six-year-old boy who got shot in the drive-by and it would be a great story and they'd file it and a minute later they'd be joking around."

"Like nurses in an emergency room."

"No, much worse than that. Nurses don't have time to get involved, because the next ambulance is pulling in. They have to be clinical or they can't get the job done. For reporters it's not quite the same."

Roxanne stared out the window, thinking. We passed the State House and then crossed a bridge over the Kennebec River, which was low and streaked with sandbars and looked tired and discouraged.

"Social workers are like that, though," Roxanne said. "You get involved emotionally and you burn out. You can only feel so much and then you just blow up, like an overloaded circuit or something."

"And you can't feel anything at all."

"Yes, but that doesn't answer my question about you."

"I know that."

"So are you going to answer me?"

It was my turn to think.

"The longer I was in the business, the harder it got for me to just walk away. I guess I felt like every time I did, it was a failure. A defeat or something. I wanted to put my arm around that mother. I wanted to come back the next day and shore her up. I really wanted to make things right."

"But that wasn't your job."

"But it wasn't a job to me."

"And this isn't either?"

"No way. I haven't gotten paid a cent. And the way things are going, I might not. I mean, what would I write now? A first-person from a prison cell maybe?"

"Jack, please don't talk that way."

"Okay, I won't."

"So where does that leave us? What will we do?"

"Well, they have visiting hours from nine to eleven, and one to three. No cash may be brought into the correctional facility. All foods should be packaged and unopened. Guards will—"

"Jack!"

"Sorry. Should we turn around so I can bring you back?"

"No, but that's the point. I'm staying. I'm not leaving you. I decided that even before I came to Boston. But what will I do? Play Nancy Drew for the next twenty years? I mean, what will our life be?"

We were on the outskirts of Augusta now, passing sad fallen-down farms that were sprouting convenience stores and strip malls. Somber Holsteins stood in the fields, as if they knew it soon would be over. It was quiet and Roxanne was waiting for an answer.

"When this is over, I'll just keep writing," I said. "You know, I really liked that last one. It was easy to write about flowers."

Thirty-two

Claire was shy around Roxanne.

It was early Sunday afternoon and we were standing in

the Varneys' kitchen, sipping coffee while Mary prepared omelets on the big Franklin wood-burning stove. Roxanne and I had made love long into the night, slowly and gently, and again in the morning, and Roxanne's skin was glowing like rose quartz against the dark shine of her hair. I stood across the kitchen and took her in, still unbelieving. But then, that had always been the magic of us being together. We took nothing for granted.

Claire had shaken Roxanne's hand with his big hard paw. Mary, strong and pretty and silver-haired, had given her a little hug. It was like they were us in twenty years, or so I hoped.

We stood and chatted. Mary asked me about my face and I said I fell in the woods at night, out looking for owls. Roxanne gave me an oh-come-on look but then Mary asked her how long she'd been in Boston, and how she liked Colorado, where Claire once had been stationed. He said he liked Colorado but his real love had been New Mexico, which he said was like "a porthole back in time." Roxanne smiled at him, surprised, and then Mary asked her if she'd bring over the plates and she did, holding them out to catch the omelets as Mary slid them from the pan.

The omelets had cheese, peppers, tomatoes and scallions, all from the Varneys' garden. We ate and drank coffee and talked about gardening and old houses and Millie Tint's sculpture and the fall warblers, which were coming through on their way south. Mary said she'd just heard that Susan and her husband were coming for Christmas. Susan wanted to get her traveling in before she got too pregnant. Mary said she was working on Jen but Jen's husband in the State Department didn't know if he could get away.

"And how is that story on the babies coming?" Mary asked me.

"Pretty good," I said. "It's very interesting."

"And sad, I'll bet," she said. "Those poor little girls. Life's hard enough."

"Sometimes," I said.

We ate and then sat for a long time. When the coffee was gone and the coffee-cake plate picked clean, Mary said she'd give Roxanne some needlepoint if Roxanne was interested. Roxanne said she was and they went upstairs, chatting all the way up the stairs. I handed the dishes to Claire and he put them in the dishwasher. The frying pan he scrubbed in the black slate sink.

"Your girl's a peach," Claire said, running the water.

"Thanks. I think so."

"If I were you, I wouldn't lose her again."

"I'm not planning on it."

He clanked the pan in the rack and reached for the coffeepot.

"Come up with anything down south?"

"Yeah, I guess I did."

He waited. If I was going to say more, it would be my choice.

"Yeah, I did. I found the lawyer who handled Missy Hewett's baby. He's from Portland. Missy called his house so much she got to know the guy's daughter."

"So how he'd react?"

"Went berserk. Pretended I had the wrong guy."

"Not very smooth."

"Nope. One of the worst no-comments I've ever seen."

"Guy must tend to panic under pressure."

"Surprising for a lawyer," I said. "Unless he's used to working in the back room, doing research in the law library. I can't imagine him in a courtroom."

"They have to go to court to do adoptions?"

"Just probate. And it's just filling out forms, basically. Showing the judge that the new parents aren't ax murderers. But, you know, I don't think the guy, his name is Putnam, I don't think he's an adoption lawyer. His wife said he didn't do adoptions anymore."

"Was she more cooperative?" Claire asked, giving the pot a last rinse.

"Not really. She said that just before she started screaming for somebody to call the cops."

"Didn't like your looks, I guess."

"Hard to believe, isn't it?"

Claire dried his hands on the towel and hung it on a hook
by the stove. We could hear Roxanne and Mary laughing
upstairs.

"Let's go outside," Claire said.

"I'll bring the cigars."

We went out the back door and around the shed to the barn.
It had turned cloudy overnight, and without the sun, the air
was cold and chilling. Claire opened the side door to the
barn and we went in. I flicked on the lights and watched as
he stuffed newspaper and cedar kindling into the stove.
When the pile was crackling, he closed the stove door and
opened the damper wide.

"That oughta do her," Claire said, and he went and
leaned against the workbench. I pulled up a chair.

"So this kid, your buddy with the shotgun?"

"Kenny."

"Yeah. He's in a bad way."

"One can only hope."

"No, I mean it. Something was wrong with the kid. Wasn't
he cocky?"

"Oh, yeah. With a big chip on his shoulder."

"Ready to fight the world, right?"

"And he picked me to go first."

Claire fiddled with a pile of open-end wrenches.

"Well, he was jumpy. Said he was looking for you.
Acted like he was looking over his shoulder, afraid of
something."

"That is different."

"Guy was spooked. He didn't look like somebody who'd
shoot out your windows."

"Maybe he was coked out," I said.

"Just plain scared, is my guess."

"Of what?"

Claire looked at me.

"He looked a little rough on the edges, but I wouldn't say you giving him a little whuping would change his attitude like that."

"What do you mean little? I kicked his butt," I said, grinning. "Now what about the teacher?"

"Hell, Jack, I would have said you should latch on to her, but now I know why you wouldn't. But hell, this one was pretty and said hello just as friendly."

"And she said she wanted to talk to me?"

"Yup. I figured you were scooping her when you were supposed to be working."

"Are you kidding? She gave me the chill like you wouldn't believe."

"Well, something must have changed her mind."

"She had a divine revelation as to my true worth."

"Maybe she was just playing hard to get," Claire said.

"But I wasn't trying to get her."

"Maybe that was the problem."

The door to the house banged and, through the window, I saw Roxanne and Mary come out. They paused by the flower gardens, then started toward the barn.

"What about Poole, the cop?" I said quickly.

"Nothing much to say there. Pretty easygoing. Said he needed to check with you. I said I didn't know where you were and he left."

I didn't say anything.

"I don't know, Jack," Claire said, moving away from the bench as the women approached. "But when people change character like that, something's going on. You be careful."

"I'm always careful," I said.

Claire looked at my face.

"That's what I'm afraid of," he said.

As we walked back down the road to the house, it started to rain. Roxanne hooked her arm through mine and I felt like she should have a parasol and I should be wearing a bowler. We strolled along and she asked me who lived in the college girls' house. I told her and said they were away for some sort of break. Roxanne said that was good, because she didn't want them coming over to borrow sugar.

When we came to the yard, she stopped and looked at my burned-out truck.

"It's art, don't you think?" I said.

"It's art in the Museum of Modern Art. Here it's junk."

"What a Philistine. You're lucky you're good-looking."

"And what if I wasn't?" Roxanne asked.

"I'd trade you in for a Bohemian."

She kissed me and held me close.

"Your trading days are over, Jack McMorrow."

"I'll retire gracefully," I said.

We went inside and Roxanne started poking around and picking up. I told her she didn't have to do that but she said she wanted to. She said if it was going to be her space, too, she had to organize it to fit her needs.

"You mean the bundles of newspapers have to go?"

"Unless you were planning on rereading them."

"I'm not planning on having that much time on my hands."

"Why's that?"

"Because I'm planning on having you on my hands."

"The best-laid plans?"

"I thought I was the one with the puns."

"It rubs off," Roxanne said.

She drifted around the house, climbed the stairs to the loft. I sat in a chair by the back window and watched the rain, which was now coming harder. It was half-past three and the light already was fading. I sat there and watched the field and the dark woods and thought about Kenny and Poole and Janice Genest and the Putnams, with the Flanagans bringing up the rear. I had made no progress when Roxanne came down the stairs and asked if I owned a broom.

"Just what are you implying?" I said.

"Nothing," she said, smiling.

"It's in the closet," I said. "Like brand-new."

"I'm sure."

I looked back out at the rain and the woods and then felt her stare on my back. When I turned, Roxanne was standing there with Claire's rifle, holding it at arm's length by the tip of the barrel, like it was a rotting carcass.

"What's this?" she asked.

"A rifle."

"Yours?"

"Claire's. He wants me to take up hunting. He says he'll make a man out of me yet."

"Is it loaded?"

"No. The shells are in the kitchen drawer, behind the dish towels."

"These things scare me," Roxanne said.

"Well, I don't exactly take it to bed with me."

"If you did, you'd be going to bed alone."

"Where's your sense of sexual adventure? How 'bout I dress up in a rubber suit and shoot apples off your head."

"God, he's not only turned macho, he's gone kinky."

"What a combo, huh? Let me tie you to my gun rack, baby."

"Let me catch the next bus to Boston. Baby."

Roxanne carried the gun back to the closet, still holding it by the barrel. She set it down gingerly and shut the door. If I hadn't been there, I think she would have nailed it shut.

"Ugh," she said.

Roxanne swept, which meant I couldn't sit, not without feeling guilty. I got up and put the dishes away, then tied the newspapers into bundles and put them out in the shed. When I came back in, she'd started coffee and put on music, a Torelli concerto. The only thing missing was the Sunday paper. I said I'd go and get one in Albion.

"I'll stay," Roxanne said. "I just want to put my feet up. I was going to have another cup of coffee but I'm starting to feel like I might take a nap. You wore me out last night."

"I think it's the other way around."

"We'll call it a draw," she said.

"Okay. But listen. If anybody comes, don't answer the door."

"Why not?"

"Just don't, okay?"

She looked at me.

"You're serious?"

"Yeah. Just for now. Until I figure some things out."

"Okay," Roxanne said, reluctantly. "But just for now."

I grabbed a ten-dollar bill off the counter and went out to the truck. It was blowing harder and yellow leaves were falling from the poplars and birches in swirling clouds. The truck started hard, as if the battery were down, but the motor sputtered and I drove out the dump road and then on to the pavement, taking a left and heading for Albion. Sodden cows stared from pastures along the way and I passed a family throwing firewood down a cellar bulkhead. The father waved and I waved back but I didn't know them.

In Albion, the general store was quiet. I pumped five dollars' worth of gas into the Toyota and went inside. There was one *Boston Globe* left and a few *Sunday Telegrams*. I took one of each and placed the stack on the counter at the checkout. After a minute, a young woman came and punched the cash register and took my money. When she handed me my change, she gave me a lingering smile. When it rains, it pours.

I went out to the truck, put the papers on the passenger seat, and turned the key. There was a click. Another click. A faint, brief growl. Then more clicks and nothing. The battery again.

It could have been worse, I thought. I could have been stuck somewhere between Providence and Boston. Or on the streets of Cambridge. Or in front of David Putnam's house. Hey, Dave. How 'bout giving me a boost?

I got out and went back into the store. The same woman was at the counter and I asked her if there was anybody who could give me a jump-start. She said, sure, she'd give me one, and she grabbed a slicker off a hook by the door and came outside.

She had jumper cables and a very big Chevy four-wheel-drive. If the Toyota didn't start, we could load it in the back of her truck and haul it home. But it started and I coiled her cables and handed them back to her.

"Your husband's truck?" I said.

"Mine," she said. "He's history."

On that note of conjugal bliss, I headed for home but I didn't get far.

Just outside Albion, the two-lane highway makes a long, sweeping curve. Halfway through it, revving the Toyota right to the red line, I looked up and saw a familiar Ford pickup. Then a familiar face.

Kenny's.

I put on the brakes. He locked his up, bringing the Ford to a long, skidding stop. I saw his backup lights come on and he pulled off on to a pasture entrance and turned the truck around. I sat by the side of the road and waited. With a roar, he pulled alongside and leaned over and rolled the passenger window down. I rolled mine up.

"Follow me," Kenny said, all business, no wise-ass. I looked at him, his long hair under his baseball hat.

"Come on," he said, and he put his truck in gear and took off. I thought for a second, then followed.

He drove a mile or so up the road, to just near the Prosperity line. There was a woods road on the right and he turned into it and disappeared into the trees. I followed him, down the narrow, rutted dirt path until it widened into an overgrown woodyard. Kenny had backed his truck into the brush, I did the same and shut off the truck. We both got out and met at the front of the trucks, which were still ticking as they cooled down.

"I've been looking for you," Kenny said.

"So what else is new."

"No, I mean it, man. No bullshit this time. I'm not fooling around. Maybe I'm even sorry about all that."

"And maybe not?"

"No, I am. But man, you're in deep shit. That's all I can say."

"What do you mean?"

"I mean watch your ass. I'm warning you. I mean, think of this as a warning. If I were you, I'd get the hell out of here."

"Why? Somebody gonna torch this truck, too."

"Oh, no," Kenny said, his voice urgent. "This isn't kid's stuff. This is serious business. If they knew I was talking to you, I'd be in the same boat, man. They don't screw around, I'm telling you."

"Who?"

"Can't say."

"Why?"

"Can't say that, either. I just know that you've got some people really riled up. And when they get riled up, they don't fool around."

"Not like you, you mean."

"No, man. We're talking serious shit."

"Like what? Break my legs?"

"Worse."

"Break my legs without anesthesia?"

"Don't you get it, man? You could get taken out," Kenny said.

"Who around here would do that?"

Kenny started to say something, then changed his mind. He looked away for a moment and I looked at him, his jeans tucked into his logger's boots, his hard fists, his faded jean jacket. The tough guy didn't seem so tough. He just seemed young.

"I can't say any more. But I'm not into that. I'm not into doing friggin' twenty-five years for something. No jail for this boy, I'll tell you."

"Did somebody ask you to kill me?"

"That's it. No more talking. Consider this a favor. I owed you one, maybe. Think about it, man. It's no joke."

And with that he turned and got back in his truck. The motor roared once and he was gone, his truck rumbling down the dirt track and out on to the road, where the roar faded into the distance.

I stood in the little clearing, stunned. The rain fell steadily and the woods around me suddenly seemed very dark and very deep but not lovely at all. Something cracked in the trees and I started visibly, then walked slowly to the truck door and got in, praying it would start. It ground once, twice, three times.

And caught.

Thirty-three

The door was open and the house was dark. I stepped in and stopped and listened. The refrigerator hummed. Something in the woodstove popped. The wind whistled against the back window.

"Roxanne," I said.

There was no answer.

"Roxanne," I called, louder.

Still no answer.

I walked to the bottom of the loft stairs and listened again. Still nothing. I climbed the stairs very slowly, waiting after each one. At the top, I peeked over and there she was, stretched out on the bed, her legs splayed over the edge.

And an open magazine on her chest.

I listened and could hear her breathing, softly. Relieved, I retreated and let Roxanne sleep. At least one of us could.

Back downstairs, I went over and turned off the tape deck and the amplifier. Then I went to the closet door, opened it, and took out the rifle. I checked to see that the safety was on and went to the kitchen drawer. The box of shells was there and I took out five. I pulled the lever back, and, pointing the barrel at the wall, slid four shells down into the magazine, and left one in the chamber. Then I went and put the rifle back in the closet.

Somehow, I didn't feel any safer.

I went to my chair by the window, my bird-watching chair, that now would be used for watching for something else. But what?

What was Kenny saying? That somebody was going to try to kill me? That there was a contract out on me? Some people, he'd said. Some people who were riled up. He wasn't going to do twenty-five years in jail. Twenty-five years in this state was the minimum for murder. Who wanted to murder me?

Putnam. Maybe I'd shaken him too hard. Maybe I didn't know what I was getting into. Maybe these people played rougher than I thought. What people? Putnam and who else? Maybe Missy's murder hadn't been committed in anger. Maybe it was just business. Maybe she had shaken the tree too hard, too. And ended up dead.

I listened for Roxanne to make sure she was still asleep, then went to the counter and got a phone book. I looked up the number of the Waldo County Sheriff's Department and dialed it. A woman dispatcher answered and I could hear other voices in the background.

"Could I speak with Officer Poole, please," I said.

"I'm sorry," she said. "Investigator Poole is off today. He'll be back on Tuesday. Can I take a message?"

Tuesday.

"Could you get a message to him at home?"

"I'm sorry, I can't," the dispatcher said. Another phone rang in the background.

"May I put you on hold?" she said, but she didn't wait for an answer.

I waited. Waited some more. There was a click and the loud voices and then she was back.

"Waldo County Sheriff's Department."

"Hi, this is me. The same guy who wanted Officer Poole."

"Well, sir, as I said, he won't be back until Tuesday. Can anyone else help you?"

I thought for a moment.

"No," I said. "If he calls in, could you ask him to call Jack McMorrow? He's looking for me."

"I'll do that, sir," the dispatcher said, and we both hung up.

Now what? I thought.

It was after five and Roxanne wasn't stirring. I thought about waking her but went up and took the magazine off of her and put a blanket over her instead. She was beautiful when she slept.

I went down and got a beer from the refrigerator, a Labatt's. Ordinarily, the first beer went down fast, but this one I sipped. After a couple of sips, I went to the phone again and called Claire. Mary said he'd gone up to the store in Knox to get some diesel for his tractor.

"Just puttering," she said. "You want him to call you?"

"Yes, thanks," I said.

It was after seven when the phone rang. Roxanne still was sleeping so I grabbed it after one ring.

"Hi, Claire," I said softly.

"Oh, baby," a man's voice said. "I just go all to pieces when you talk to me like that. Is that you, Jack? Or did I dial a wrong number and get phone sex?"

"Dave?"

"But you can call me Claire."

"Sorry, Slocum. I thought you were somebody else."

"I thought you were something else. Sounded like Clark Gable with a frog in his throat. I'll bet you can get sexy young telephone operators to undress with that voice. Can you teach me to do that?"

"Would you believe me if I told you Claire was a guy?"

"A guy? Hey, these days, I'd believe anything. Is he a transvestite, transsexual, or just a cute little cross-dresser?"

"None of the above. He's the ex-Marine down the road."

"Whoah, Jack. Now that is kinky."

"I won't tell him you said that. For your sake."

"Thanks. You always were a pal. Hey, Jack, sorry to bother you and your ex-Marine friends, but I just wanted to check to see if our story was still on schedule."

"Since when do you work Sundays?"

"Since I took Thursday and Friday off. But being a dedicated professional, I decided to come in and ensure my continued employment."

"Never anything to take for granted."

"Right," Slocum said. "A guy who can get canned by the *Times* can get canned anywhere. Speaking of my future employment, how's it coming?"

I thought for a second.

"Good," I said.

"Think that deadline is still realistic?"

"When was it?"

Slocum paused.

"When was it? Jack, this is not a good sign. Mark it on your calendar, my friend. Four weeks from tomorrow. On my desk. So I can pass it on to the powers that be and thereby take some of the credit."

"Some things never change."

"Well, at least I'm honest. So the story's coming along?"

"Oh, yeah."

"Those little mommies talking your ear off?"

"Bunch of chatterboxes."

"Sitting in a lot of smoke-filled trailers?"

"Got smoker's cough."

"Good," Slocum said. "Hack for me, just once. No, really, glad to hear it's progressing as planned. How 'bout the photos? Can we get this thing assigned? The guy will be coming over from New Hampshire. He's very good."

"Can I call you later in the week?"

"Okay. Fine. I really just wanted to know everything was okay. I know how these things can sound good on paper and then go all to hell when you start digging into them."

"No way," I said.

"Yes, way. Hey, I'll let you go. But, Jack?"

"What, Dave?"

"Give Claire a squeeze for me. Ex-Marine, my ass. You old dog, you."

I didn't give Claire a squeeze and I didn't talk to him that night, either. He didn't call, which meant Mary probably fell asleep in a chair before he got home. While Roxanne slept, too, I sat in the chair with the lights out and watched the woods. It was a dark night and it was like staring from the rail of a ship at sea: no shapes, just a diaphanous murky blackness. Not unlike the future.

At nine I got up and turned on the television. There was football. Dumb sitcom people laughing, their mouths yawning open like toothy caves. News from the Mideast, where children had been blown up over religion. A documentary about Australia's Great Barrier Reef. After five minutes I turned it off, got another Labatt's from the refrigerator, and went back to my chair. And sometime later fell into a troubled sleep.

In the morning, Roxanne told me she'd awakened at three and panicked when I wasn't in the bed. It had taken her a few minutes to find me, and when she had, feeling her way in the dark, she'd put her arms around me and kissed me gently on the cheek. She'd made tea and dragged a kitchen chair over and sat beside me in the night.

"We're a fine pair, aren't we?" I said at breakfast.

"Yeah," Roxanne said. "You know, we really are."

"Why did you leave me, then?"

"Because I loved you so much that it made me afraid. Why didn't you come with me?"

"Same reason," I said.

Roxanne reached across the table and took my hand.

It was another rainy, cold day and neither of us strayed very far. I kept the fire going and read the *Globe*. Roxanne read a Raymond Chandler novel she'd found on the shelf. It was *The Big Sleep*.

"Is it good?" she asked me.

"They're all good," I said.

She was wearing jeans and one of my sweaters and, curled up in the big chair by the window, she looked very beautiful, very safe, very content. I didn't want to burst that bubble, but telling her about my talk with Kenny wouldn't be just bursting it. It would be like taking the rifle from the closet and blowing it away.

But I had to tell her. I had to tell her the rifle was loaded now. I had to tell her why.

I walked over to her chair and stood there. Touched her cheek.

"I love you," she said.

"And I love you."

I hunched down by the chair. Roxanne smiled at me.

"This is nice," she said.

"Very. But I have to tell you something."

Her smile melted away.

"What is it?"

"I ran into somebody when I went to get the paper last night. Kenny. The guy who—"

"Burned your truck."

"Among other things. Except he didn't want to fight me this time. He wanted to tell me something."

I swallowed.

"He wanted to warn me that somebody was going to get me."

"Who?"

"He wouldn't say. He just said he wanted to warn me. He sort of apologized. Said he owed me one and this was his way of paying me back."

"What do you mean, 'going to get you'?"

"Well," I said.

This was very hard.

"Get me. Take me out."

"Kill you?" Roxanne asked, her voice a whisper.

I couldn't say yes. I just nodded.

She didn't say anything. I didn't say anything. She reached over and took my hand and held it tightly.

"I don't know if he's to be believed. Maybe he's fantasizing. Maybe he made the whole thing up to scare me."

"And are you?"

"Scared? I guess. A little."

"Did you call the police yet?"

"Not today. I will."

"Maybe we should go?"

"Where?" I said.

"Anywhere. Portland. Back to Boston. Come live with me in Colorado Springs. I've got a nice place. Plenty of room. You could write out there."

"Sounds great, but I don't think I can just leave right now. What if the cops thought I was running from this thing? I don't know. I don't want to give them any ideas."

"Did they say you couldn't leave town?"

"What? Like the movies?"

"Yeah."

"No," I said. "But Poole keeps coming by. If he comes by and the place is empty and I've disappeared, I'm not sure how that would look."

"We won't disappear. Call him and tell him what happened and tell him where you're going. He can't make you stay."

"No."

"Give him what you have. The stuff about the lawyer

and the phone calls and all that. Let him take over. We can go on with our lives."

"Yeah," I said, uncertainly.

"But what?"

"But this is mine. This place."

"I'd call him, Jack. Claire can watch your stuff. We could be in Boston tonight. Colorado tomorrow. Making love in peace."

I smiled.

"Yeah. That would be nice."

I took my hand from hers and started for the phone.

"Another thing," I said. "I loaded the gun."

Roxanne looked at me, dismayed.

"Pull the lever back, safety is on," I said. "Push it forward, safety is off. You want to try it?"

She just shook her head no.

I tried Poole twice. Once at eight o'clock in the morning, again an hour later. A different dispatcher told me he was off, but this time I told him it was an emergency. He asked me what the nature of the emergency was and I said it had to do with the Missy Hewett homicide, that I had information crucial to the case. He sounded like he'd heard that one before but he said he'd try to reach Poole at home.

That was the first time.

I sat and waited and then called Claire. He was out in the barn and Mary asked if I wanted her to go get him. I said I'd come down and she said that was fine.

"And, Jack?" Mary said, catching me before I hung up. "I think Roxanne is just lovely."

"Me, too," I said. "Me, too."

Roxanne was reading, with her bare feet up on the side of the chair. I put two chunks of beech in the stove and damped it down and told her I was going to Claire's for a minute, that I wanted her to come with me.

"Can't I just—" Roxanne said, pausing as I turned to the front of the house and listened.

A car had pulled up. Not Claire. Not a cop. Not the college girls' Subaru. The motor ticked for a few seconds and then shut off. A door snapped open. Thunked shut.

I went to the closet, opened the door, and took out the rifle. Roxanne swung her legs off the chair as I laid the gun on the counter. There was a shuffle outside the door then three loud knocks. I looked to Roxanne and then to the loft.

She shook her head no. I walked to the door, listened again, then opened it six inches. And there was Dave Putnam. He wasn't smiling.

"McMorrow," he said.

"Putnam," I said. "Funny. I didn't hear an ambulance go by."

He looked puzzled for a moment, then his face went hard.

"I need to talk to you," Putnam said.

"You should have called ahead. I would have warmed some brie."

"I'm not fooling around," he said.

"I'm not either."

I let the door open wider and turned back to the room. He took a step inside and then stopped. I stopped in front of the counter. To my right, six inches from my elbow, was the fixed black stare of the rifle barrel.

Putnam eyed it, then glanced at Roxanne and nodded.

"I thought maybe we could talk alone," he said.

"I'd tell her about it anyway," I said.

"Roxanne, Dave. Dave, Roxanne."

They neither spoke nor moved. I leaned against the counter. I didn't offer Putnam a chair.

He was dressed like a model in one of those outdoorsy catalogues for rich guys: tan boots, dark green twill pants, a brown canvas jacket with a leather shooting patch on the shoulder, the kind of jacket that has the pocket in the back for all the little birds blown apart by one's custom-made shotgun. The effect was supposed to be self-assured, to reek of the cockiness that comes from a false and ludicrous sense of caste. I reached for the rifle, fingered the safety and watched Putnam blanch.

Nothing like fear to blur class distinctions.

"That thing loaded?" Putnam said.

"Yeah," I said, "And you can't be too careful. Did you know most gun accidents occur in the home?"

"No, I didn't know that. I don't care for the things, really."

"Just getting the hang of it, myself. I've been trying to memorize it, you know? Which way the safety goes and all that."

Putnam eyed the barrel as if it were a snake. Then he glanced at Roxanne. She looked at him the same way he'd looked at the gun.

"So," I said. "You're a little far from the yacht club, aren't you, counselor?"

"I think we need to talk. Face to face."

"Last time we were face to face I almost ended up with a door in mine."

"You caught me at a bad time," Putnam said.

"Been one of those decades, huh?"

Putnam looked like he was going to start shouting, then choked it back, like medicine. Or maybe vomit.

"Are you always like this?" he asked.

Roxanne looked to me.

"No," I said. "Sometimes I'm asleep."

"Listen, McMorrow. I'm trying to make a good-faith effort to settle this thing. I've come all the way up here—"

"To the end of the earth," I interrupted.

"Damn close to it."

"How'd you find me?"

"You left that number with the Prosperity exchange on it. I drove here and asked a few people. A girl at some store up on a hill finally told me."

"Knox Ridge," I said.

"Whatever," Putnam said.

He was feeling better. I could tell because his natural ar-

rogance was returning, like color to his cheeks. I reached
for the gun again and a little of his cockiness drained away,
like beer from a glass. Roxanne watched him closely: a
shrink observing a patient. Through one-way glass.

"We have to talk," Putnam said, no more improv, back
on the script.

"About what? Missy Hewett's brutal murder?"

He winced, then got back in character.

"Listen, we're both reasonable people, McMorrow. I
know you're doing your job. I checked you out. The *Times*
and all that. You're a pro and I respect that. But you've got
to understand. All I did was try to help this kid. She didn't
know how to go about an adoption and I gave her some advice. She had a lot of questions and she kept coming to me
for answers. I could answer some. The legal ones. The personal ones—was this the right decision and all that—I told
her she had to make up her mind about that."

"Why you?" I said.

"Oh, word of mouth, I guess. I used to handle adoptions.
Way back when. She talked to somebody I'd done one
for—I don't remember who—and called me up. At home."

He grinned.

"She was a determined little gal, I'll tell you."

"Don't patronize her," I said. "Not in my house. Not in
my presence."

I didn't grin. His vanished. Roxanne watched, implaca-
ble.

"Listen, McMorrow. I did the adoption for Missy Hewett
and that's it. I don't know anything about her personal life.
I don't know what losers she may have gotten mixed up
with over at the college. You can believe me or not. That's
your choice. But what you're doing if you publish my name
in connection with this girl's death, in any way, shape, or
manner, is destroying my career. My practice. My family.
I'm done. Finished in this town. All because I tried to help
a confused little girl."

"So sue me," I said.

Putnam stopped. His mouth actually hung open. He had expensive teeth, which he bared.

"Listen, you son of a bitch. I don't know what you're doing or why you've picked me out, but you're gonna ruin me. Don't you understand?"

"I don't understand why somebody killed Missy Hewett."

"How much?"

"How much what?" I asked.

"How much are you going to make on this little story?"

"What makes you think it's gonna be little? Three thousand words might not sound like much to you, but you sit down and start typing, and some days, boy—"

"How much?" Putnam said.

"Getting kind of personal, aren't you?"

"Listen. I'll triple it. Four times it."

"That's quadruple. Five times is quintuple. Like those people who have all those babies."

"Goddamn it, McMorrow. I'll give you ten thousand dollars. Cash. Right now."

"For a whole career? Where's your self-esteem?"

"You bastard," Putnam snarled. "Twenty thousand. Goddamn blackmailer."

"You can't blackmail people who don't have anything to hide."

"I don't. But goddamn it, just my name in the paper with something like this will be enough. You know that, you bastard."

"I know I'm getting tired of being called names."

"Twenty-five thousand."

"And you know what else I know?" I said. "I know I'm tired of your silly little jacket. The last time I saw one of those was on *Upstairs Downstairs*. Some earl was going off to shoot pheasant."

"Twenty-five."

"And I'm tired of having you in my house."

"Twenty-five thousand."

He squeezed the words through clenched teeth.

"And I'm tired of worrying about having a loaded rifle right here and somebody like you right there."

"Are you threatening me, you son of a bitch?"

"You already used that one."

"Bastard."

"That one, too."

I took a step toward him and he backed away and reached for the door latch.

"You're making a big mistake," Putnam said.

"Story of my life," I said, smiling. "But I try to learn from them."

He backed through the door and then turned and walked toward a silver Saab, the one I'd seen in his driveway in Falmouth.

"My offer stands for twenty-four hours, McMorrow," Putnam said.

I stood in the doorway.

"So that's P-U-T-N-A-M, right?" I called.

He got in his fancy car, started the motor, and backed out. Going down the road, the car's tires spun as he slammed from gear to gear.

I stepped back inside and closed the door and stood. From her chair, Roxanne gave me a long look.

"What was that all about?" she said.

"I don't think he likes the country," I said.

"No, I mean you. You laid it on a little thick, didn't you? The hard-guy stuff. I don't think I've ever seen you like that."

"Reduce you to jelly?"

"Not really," Roxanne said. "Scared me a little, maybe."

I shrugged.

"This is a scary business."

"You didn't act scared."

"No," I said. "But he did."

"And?"

"And that's what I wanted to know. Is he a wimp? Is he scared?"

"And he is?" Roxanne said.

"Didn't you think so?"

"Yeah."

"So I had to push him a little to make sure," I said.

"And are you?"

"Pretty sure that he didn't kill her."

"But he seemed like he might know who did," Roxanne said.

"Maybe," I said.

She got up from the chair and turned toward the back window. I picked up the rifle and jacked the shells out onto the counter. They bounced like marbles, then rolled in small circles. Roxanne grimaced. I thought again and clicked the shells back into the magazine, one by one.

"This stinks," I said. "You know why?"

Roxanne turned to me. Her eyes were wide and dark, and after only a couple of days with me already had circles.

"Yeah," she said. "Because you had been thinking he did it. That he was the one."

"And?"

"And you don't have a plan B," Roxanne said.

I looked at her and smiled.

"Did I ever tell you you're beautiful when you're right?"

So the gun went back in the closet, still loaded, safety on. I thought. I looked out the back window and the front window, too. Roxanne picked up her book but I noticed that she was staring, not reading. Then, after a while, the phone rang and I answered it and a woman asked for Roxanne. I handed her the phone and listened until I could tell it was somebody at her office. I gathered that there was some sort of a problem with somebody in their care. The conversation went on for twenty minutes, maybe longer. To Roxanne's credit, she did not once use the phrase "in crisis."

When she got off the phone, I was sitting in a hard chair by the back window, looking at a book about hawks.

"So what's up?" I said, as Roxanne laid her hand on my shoulder.

"A problem. This family I was working with, in Colorado Springs. The fourteen-year-old girl tried to kill herself."

"Did she succeed?"

"No."

"Why would she do that?" I asked.

"Because she thinks her father doesn't love her."

"Does he?"

"No."

"Why not?"

"Because he's an asshole," Roxanne said.

"I hate social worker jargon."

"Sorry."

"So the kid suddenly realized this?"

"I guess she ran out of ways to fool herself," Roxanne said.

We were quiet for a moment. Roxanne's hand was still on my shoulder.

"Missy Hewett didn't have a father at all, to speak of," I said.

"That's easier, in some ways."

"And she didn't try to kill herself."

"Some kids are tougher than others," Roxanne said.

"And look where it got her," I said. "Her whole life was one big dirty trick."

Roxanne looked at me.

"Sorry," she said.

So for the rest of the day we stayed put. The rest of the night, too. Poole didn't call that day or night or the next morning, either. Putnam didn't stop by to up his offer. Nobody called from Colorado or anyplace else. Finally, around eleven o'clock in the morning, I ran out of distractions and called the Varneys. Mary answered and I asked if Claire was around. She said she thought he was in the barn and should she get him? I said, no, I'd skip up.

"If Poole calls, tell him I'll be right back," I told Roxanne. "Get his number. Tell him the whole story if you have to. If anybody comes, don't answer the door."

She nodded.

Claire's barn was fifty yards down, separated from my house by the college girls' house and some woods. I trotted past the college girls' house and eyed the windows as I passed. Could somebody get in there and wait for me? I wished they were home. At least I'd have witnesses. The woods were second-growth maple and I peered into them warily. At one point, I stopped and watched and listened.

Rain spattered the leaves. Branches creaked. A blue jay flushed. And Claire's truck pulled out of his driveway and headed off down the road the other way.

"Damn," I said, and trotted back home.

Poole hadn't called. We ate lunch silently: Roxanne had a salad with tuna, with lemon juice instead of mayonnaise. I had tuna on whole wheat with mustard.

"We'd have to clean out the refrigerator," she said.

"Why?"

"If we leave, I mean," Roxanne said.

"Oh, yeah," I said.

I'd forgotten.

After lunch I called the sheriff's department again. The same dispatcher answered. He recognized my voice and said he'd tried to get Poole but hadn't been able to reach him. I asked how he would reach him if it was an emergency, like somebody had been killed. He said they'd send a cruiser, but if he wasn't home, he wasn't home.

"Please try him again," I said.

"I'll do what I can, sir," the dispatcher said and hung up.

So I waited. I read all of the day-old *Globe*. Roxanne looked through my tapes and put on Pachelbel's Canon, then went back to her chair. She was three-quarters of the way through *The Big Sleep*.

She smiled at me.

"This is still sort of nice," she said. "Just being together. Don't you think?"

I smiled back, startled.

"Yeah," I said. "It is."

But when the phone rang a little after three, I jumped and grabbed the receiver. A woman's voice asked for Mr. Mc-Morrow.

Damn.

"You may not remember me, Mr. McMorrow," the woman said, her voice rough like a smoker's. "We met at Missy's funeral. Missy Hewett?"

"Yeah?"

"I'm Sue. Missy's sister. The one with the phone bill."

"Hi."

"Sorry to bother you, but I had this problem and I didn't know but you might be able to help, 'cause my husband, he drives a truck, and he's in California. He had to take a load to Arcata and then pick up strawberries and he won't be back until, maybe Friday, and I knew you were trying to help Missy and everything and, did you find anything from those numbers?"

"Yeah, I did," I said. "I found out quite a bit, but I'd rather not talk about it on the phone. Maybe we could meet."

"Sure, I'd like that, but today I have my youngest home, the boys are in school, but Jessica, she's a wild one and I don't think we'd get much meeting done."

"Okay."

"But that's not why I'm calling. I'm calling 'cause of my mother. You said you talked to her?"

"Joyce," I said.

Joyce. Tight jeans and vodka Joyce. Joyce of the come-on.

"Yeah, well I've been trying to call my mom since yesterday and she hasn't been home and I went over last night and her car wasn't there and I wondered if you had talked to her or anything."

"Not since the first time."

"Well, this is really strange then, you know? 'Cause she doesn't just take off like that. Even if she meets some guy, she stays around. She doesn't like, disappear."

"And there's no sign of her at all?"

"Nope. Nothing."

"Did you call the police?"

"Not yet," Sue said. "My family has this, like, thing about cops."

"I remember."

"My husband really does."

"Well, you know I'd grit my teeth and call them this time. Swallow your pride or whatever it is," I said. "I can't get into it all right now but I can tell you that if I were you, I'd have the police involved. This whole thing is getting kind of dangerous."

"Yeah, well, I don't know where she would have gone, you know? Without telling me? She would have called, even if it was to bitch me out. She's always doing that. God, when she's drunk, you can't get her off the phone. My husband just hangs up but I can't do that. She's my mother, you know? I mean, I have serious problems about just hanging up on my mother, I don't care how drunk she is."

And they say the family is a dying institution.

So again I told Sue to call the cops. She told me she'd think about it. I told her not to think about it too long. She thanked me and I said it was nothing. Which was true.

She hung up and Roxanne looked up from her book.

"Who was that?" she asked.

I was thinking.

"Missy Hewett's sister. She can't find her mother."

"And she thought she might be here?"

"She thought I might have talked to her."

"Have you talked to her before?"

"The mother?"

Roxanne nodded.

"Yeah," I said. "She got drunk and tried to drag me into bed."

"But you fended her off."

"Wasn't hard. Vodka. Could have knocked her over with a feather. Now the sister says the trailer is empty and the car is gone and no mom to be found."

I thought some more. Roxanne watched me, her book on her lap.

"Maybe some other guy wasn't as good a fender-offer as you are," she said.

"They are big shoes to fill," I said.

We sat for a while and didn't talk. Roxanne had gone back to her book when I told her I wanted to go out and get a paper. She said she didn't feel like coming, that maybe she'd walk down to Mary's and get the needlepoint. She'd left it in the kitchen. I said I'd drive her down. She could visit and I'd pick her up on the way back.

"I don't want to be a prisoner," Roxanne said.

"Rats," I said. "I was hoping I'd get to tie you up."

But I did drop her with Mary, who gave her a big smile and a little hug. Mary said she'd left the needlepoint and Roxanne said she knew that and Mary said she'd found some more that Roxanne might want to look at. I said I'd be back in a half-hour and walked back to the truck. Claire still was gone.

I drove up to the store in Knox in a cold mist that smeared the windshield with something that was more saliva than rain. At the store, I left the truck running and went in and bought a *Morning Sentinel* off the counter. Official business done, I went back to the truck, tossed the paper on the passenger seat, unopened and unread. I drove on, out the Knox Ridge Road and on to the Leonard Road. The gravel drummed on the underside of the Toyota as I drove. When I came to Joyce's trailer, I pulled up the dirt driveway and stopped by the front steps. I turned the motor off and there was silence.

Thirty-four

The front door was locked and the lights were out inside. I cupped my face with my hands and looked through the window next to the door but couldn't see much of anything. A glass on the counter. The clock running over the sink. A faint glow from a night light plugged into the kitchen stove.

I stood for a moment and listened. Heard crickets and chickadees and downy woodpeckers in the woods. The faint faraway sound of a truck motor. The even fainter rasp of a distant chainsaw. Then quiet.

Giving the front door a last pull, I walked down the steps and around to the back of the trailer. The backyard was an unknown strip of goldenrod and purple and white wild asters, the last flowers to give up in autumn. The grass was tall and there was a path broken through to the back door, which was narrow and had no steps and opened three feet above the ground. The path was recent and it stopped at the door. The door had been pried open and was bent.

I fought off a chill. Paused. Then swung the door open with the tip of my finger. Waited for a sound from inside. None came. I pulled myself up and in.

The trailer was quiet, a silent, carpeted box. I took two or three steps and stopped and listened. Took two or three more. I could smell cigarettes, old and stale. The chemical odor of an air freshener. Perfume, maybe. Could hear nothing.

I walked to the front door and looked at the knob. It was locked but the chain was off, as if Missy's mom had swung it shut as she left. Was that before somebody pried the back door open or after?

Tensing, I turned to the hallway that led to the other rooms. The clock on the VCR said 4:03. I noted the time and then realized why I'd noticed. If I found Joyce Hewett dead in the bedroom, somebody would ask.

There were three doors from the hallway and all three were closed. I walked slowly to the first one, on my left, and stopped. Listened but couldn't hear anything. Or anybody. Turned the knob very slowly until the catch released. I gave the door a push. It felt like it was made of balsa wood.

The room was half dark, the curtains drawn. They were pink and matched the bedspread, which was thrown back in a bunch in the middle of the unmade bed. There were white slippers on the floor between the bed and me. Beside the slippers was a woman's flannel nightgown. The nightgown was white and it was crumpled on the carpet like a body.

I walked to the bed and stopped. The covers were pulled down on a diagonal as if one person had slept there. Soundly. No reckless abandon.

There was a bureau against the wall and the top drawer was open. I went over and peered into it. Socks. I poked them aside. Condoms. Which had it been?

I walked back to the door and took a last look. It was like someone had gotten up late and dressed in a hurry. Kick off the slippers. Drop the nightgown. Throw on some clothes. Close the door on the way out to hide the clutter. Why? Was it habit or had Joyce Hewett been expecting company?

When I left the room, I left the door open so that the hallway wouldn't be so dark. The next door was on the right, and I twisted the knob and pushed again. This time, I reached for a light switch. Found it. The bathroom.

It was small. A sink, toilet, and shower stall with sliding glass door. There was a towel on the floor in front of the shower and the glass door was open. The shower head was dripping. Slowly.

There was a toothbrush still in the sink. I felt the bristles and they were dry. Felt the towel on the floor and the soap beside the sink. They were dry, too. But the balled-up washcloth next to the soap still was damp. A forensic lab could tell how long the cloth had been drying. If necessary.

Like a kid scared of the dark, I left the bathroom light on.

I went to the next door and waited. Pushed it open and
groped for the light switch again. The light came on and re-
vealed a bedroom with cartons piled on the bed. There was
a rock-band poster tacked to one wall, all long hair and
leers. A cluster of faded Polaroids. I looked closer. Kids
clowning for the camera. Girls. I recognized only one.
Missy.

So this had been her room, before she'd left to make a
life for herself in the big city. She'd been pregnant in this
room. Maybe had gotten pregnant in this room. Had laid
awake nights in this room, trying to decide what to do with
her baby. Had laid awake and pondered, while from the living room came the murmur of the television, the clink of
ice in her mother's glass.

I turned to the bed and peered into the cartons. One was
filled with books: *The History of Western Civilization. Lev-
els of Geometry. The American Short Story.* Missy's books
from high school, their covers coated with a fine layer of
dust.

Another carton was filled with jumbled notebooks. The
covers were etched with doodles. Under the notebooks was
a sheaf of papers and reports. Missy had gotten an A-minus
on a paper called "Jay Gatsby and the American Dream." A
full A for one called "Political Estrangement in an American High School."

The stuff looked like it had been scooped up and dumped
in. Somebody didn't appreciate good scholarship. Or had
been in a hurry.

I glanced at the other cartons. Sneakers and shoes. Pencils
and pens. Cassette tapes of bands I'd never heard of. The
stuff of a teenager's life, one that ended all too soon. First
with a baby. Then at someone's hands. I looked again at the
Polaroids, her smiling face. Who would have thought . . . ?

After a last look around, I stepped out of the room and
stopped. Went back in and got down on my knees and
looked under the bed. Got up and went to the closet door
and opened it. There were three or four dresses, some dusty

shoes. I left both doors open and went back down the hall
to the kitchen.

There was one coffee cup in the sink, rinsed but not
washed. Another clean in the rack. Three cigarettes in the
ashtray on the dinette table. I opened the refrigerator: a
quart of milk, starting to sour. An aluminum tray of leftover
TV-dinner lasagna, brown and crusty. Three big tomatoes,
one sliced in half. I opened the freezer door. More TV din-
ners, four ice-cube trays, and one bottle of very cold vodka.

Half full or half empty.

I looked around one more time and then left the way I'd
come in.

It was like Joyce had left for an appointment and had
never come back. Had she met a cute guy in the waiting
room at the dentist's? Met a cute dentist? Run into an old
flame at the general store? Traded her car for a one-way
ticket to someplace warm?

Her car.

It seemed as though the cops could put out a call for her
car. If she was shacked up with some guy in the area, at
least her daughter could rest easier. Mom's safe and sound
and isn't sleeping alone. Not to worry.

I started the truck and pulled ahead in the gravel drive to
start to back up to turn around. When I did, I noticed that
there were tracks that kept going where the driveway
ended, petering out at the edge of the woods. Between the
gravel and the trees, there was a fringe of tall grass and
leafy scrub and it appeared that someone had driven
through the grass and into the woods. I eased the Toyota
into four-wheel-drive, got out and turned the dials to lock
the front hubs, and followed the tracks.

They led through a break in the trees on to the remains of
an old woods road. At some point, somebody had logged
these woods and left narrow paths like this, now overgrown. Soon they would be part of the woods again, but
this one was still passable, though without four-wheel-
drive, you'd have a hard time getting through in the spring

mud, never mind the winter snow. But autumn was dry and the ground was hard and the path was easy going. Branches slashed the cab on both sides, springing away as I passed.

I drove along in first gear for fifty yards and passed a little sinkhole pond fringed with withered cattails. The road forked at a big flaming-orange maple and I went left, following the faint indentation in the grass that the car or truck had left. It was getting darker, especially in the woods, and I turned on my headlights to better see the trail. I hoped I wasn't tracking some kids out drinking, or a bunch of hunters, or even Joyce Hewett, off to commune with nature and some hot-to-trot trucker.

"Sorry, Mrs. Hewett. Just passing through. No need to get dressed."

The truck eased along but the path began to narrow. I had begun to think that I'd be backing up to get out when the headlights reflected from something red. First one. Then two.

Taillights.

I flicked on my high beams and the two red lights glowed. Nudging the gas, I drove ahead until I was fifty feet behind them. And I could see Joyce Hewett's maroon Chevy.

It was pulled nosefirst into the brush where the road came to an end. The bushes were up around the doors and only the rear end of the car poked out. A white hose was attached to the exhaust pipe and snaked around to the rear window on the right side. I left my motor running and my lights on and got out.

I knew it was her before I'd walked ten feet. Her blonde hair showed plainly in my lights, her head leaning against the window of the driver's door like someone sleeping behind the wheel in a roadside rest area. Except Joyce Hewett wasn't sleeping.

The hose was from a vacuum cleaner. It was wrapped with duct tape at the exhaust pipe and the window had been rolled up to keep the other end of the hose in the car. In front of Joyce Hewett, red dashboard lights glowed weakly but the motor wasn't running.

I squeezed between the car and the brush and started to open the door, then stopped. Joyce Hewett's face was turned to the glass and her eyes were open and still, like a statue's. Her skin was a pale white and her lips and tongue were blue. Her blonde hair looked unreal, like yellow yarn glued to the head of a doll, the kind with the eyes that swing shut if the doll is laid down, stay open when it's held up.

Swallowing, I took a breath and tried the door.

It was jammed with grass at the bottom and opened stiffly. When it did, the dome light went on dimly and whiskey smell billowed out, rancid and hard. Joyce Hewett started to fall toward me and I grabbed her shoulder and pushed her back upright. Her eyes stayed open, fixed on nothing as if she were lost in thought. She was wearing jeans and a black sweater with red flowers knitted in it and sneakers. The sneakers were white. Her ankles were bare.

I touched her behind the jawbone to find a pulse but her skin was cool and lifeless. Beside her on the seat was a bottle of Schenley whiskey, a fifth. It was empty and the metal cap to the bottle was also on the seat, near the passenger door. The car reeked of booze, as if she had opened the bottle and sprayed it, like champagne in a winning locker room. A locker room with a hose attached.

I looked around the car. The nozzle of the hose was pointed at Joyce Hewett's head from behind, like a gun. There was nothing on the backseat, nothing other than the whiskey bottle in the front.

Whiskey.

Why would Joyce Hewett choose "brown liquor" to die with? Why not her precious chilled vodka? Why would she choose what she had called a man's drink for her last cocktail? Unless she hadn't done the choosing.

She stared at me, no help. I looked her over quickly for marks but none showed. Her hands weren't tied and the keys still were in the ignition. I looked at the dashboard and noticed the gas gauge was below empty. Looking up toward the top of the dash, I saw something that looked like words. I leaned in over Joyce Hewett's lap and looked again.

she

It was written in the dust on the top of the dashboard. The letters were scrawled sloppily, probably by a finger. I picked up Joyce Hewett's right hand and turned the palm toward me and held it up toward the light.

The tip of the index finger was a dirty dark gray. I put her hand down and took a swipe at the dash, away from the writing.

Our fingers matched.

I felt a chill and suddenly was aware of the darkening woods all around me. My truck still was idling and I fought back the urge to run to it and get the hell out. Instead, I eased myself up and out of the car and let the door fall shut. I walked to the truck, backed it up, and drove back down the path, very fast.

she

Who was she and what did she do? Did she kill Joyce Hewett? Did she kill Missy? Did she kill both of them? Was she the one who wanted to kill me?

she

I passed Joyce Hewett's trailer and rattled down the road to the paved highway. At the highway, I squealed the truck around the corner to the right and drove on fast until I saw a house. It was another trailer and there was a pickup outside. I skidded to a stop in their dooryard and a dog started barking somewhere out back. Leaving the truck running, I ran to the front door and banged.

Nobody answered so I yanked the door open and went in. The place smelled of cat urine and cigarettes but there was a light on over the kitchen sink and a phone on the wall. I dialed and a man answered, "Emergency 911."

I told him there was a woman dead in a car. I told him

where it was. He asked me my name and I told him and he asked what number I was calling from and I looked at the phone but couldn't read it and had to say I didn't know.

"You said the woman is deceased?" the dispatcher asked.

"Yes."

"Tell me what you saw."

"It's Joyce Hewett and she's in her car in the woods behind her trailer on the Leonard Road, about a mile in from two-twenty, on the right. And there's a hose from the exhaust to the window. She's dead and she's got whiskey all over her. And she wrote on the dashboard before she died. She said 'she,' so I don't think she killed herself. And she didn't drink brown liquor."

He asked me my name again and where I was calling from. I told him my name and said I was calling from a trailer on Route 220 near the Leonard Road and he told me to drive back to the scene and stay in my truck on the highway with my flashers on and wait for the trooper. I said I would but when I got back out to the truck something told me to go to the other way, instead.

she

I drove home as fast as the truck would go, skidding around the corner onto the dump road. My house was dark so I kept going to Claire's and drove onto the grass by the back door. Mary's surprised face appeared in the doorway.

"Jack, what's the matter?"

"Is Roxanne still here?"

"No, she went home a little while ago. To make some supper."

"Oh, no," I said.

"Jack, you okay? You wait, I'll get Claire."

I wheeled back down the road and pulled up hard beside my burnt truck. The house still was dark so I left the headlights on but turned off the motor.

It was quiet. I pushed the back door open slowly and listened. Nothing. I took three steps inside and listened again.

Still nothing. I reached behind me for the light switch and flicked it. The lights came on. I froze.

There was a piece of typing paper in the center of the dining room table. I walked toward it, read it without picking it up. It was Roxanne's handwriting:

Jack. Went out back for a little walk. Join me. Love, Roxanne.

A little walk? In the woods in the dark?

I went to the closet and took out the rifle. Opened the chamber and jacked in a shell. Put the safety on and went back out.

I went out the side door, the way I'd come in, instead of using the big glass door to the backyard. It was very quiet and growing darker and there were stars but no moon as yet. I walked around the shed, staying in the shadows close to the building until I got to the backyard. I looked out at the edge of the woods and it looked black. With the rifle in front of me, barrel pointed slightly down, I crossed the high grass and started down the path.

How far would Roxanne go? Not far, if she were alone. If she were alone, she wouldn't go at all.

Slowly, my eyes adjusted to the darkness of the woods. The path was grassy at first, skirting its way between the poplars and small maples. Then it turned hard, littered with fallen leaves that crackled with each step. I moved to the edge of the path and listened.

I heard a bird flutter, settling onto its roost for the night. I heard the distant whine of a truck, out on the highway. I heard a rustle nearby but a light one, like a mouse or a vole moving through the leaves. I waited a minute more and continued on.

It was hard not to make a racket, moving out here at night. I tried picking my feet straight up but that didn't help, so I moved to the edge of the path where the leaves were more damp and didn't crackle when I walked. If I kept my feet low and slid them along the ground, I sounded like one elephant walking through the woods, not a herd.

After fifty feet, I stopped and listened. Fifty feet after that I was in the bigger trees now, beeches and maples, and somewhere above me I heard what I at first thought was an owl, but then realized was a mourning dove.

I walked on.

How far would she go? How far would she—or they— think I would follow? I had decided to turn back when I heard it.

"Shhhsh."

It came from behind me. A human sound. No mistaking it. Someone telling someone else to be quiet.

I froze. Slipped the safety off on the rifle. Should I move toward it? Could they see me better than I could see them?

Dropping to a crouch, I peered into the trees. I could make out the trunks, the branches, but little else. There was no movement. No sound. Then the dove again. I waited longer, holding my breath as I listened.

"Shhhsh."

It was louder this time. Unmistakable. I waited a full minute, then eased my way back down the path, bent low, pausing between each step. I had a sudden urge to call out, "Roxanne," but didn't. Instead, I continued toward the point where I'd heard the sound. One step. Another step. Still another.

"Bones," the voice whispered. "Don't shoot."

"Claire?" I said softly.

"Jack. To your right."

He moved onto the path like an apparition. His clothes were blurred in the dark. I saw a glint from his hair. Another from the gun at his side.

"It's Roxanne," I said. "She wouldn't have left. Not out here."

"I saw the note," Claire said.

"Something's wrong. I don't even know if she came this way."

"Yeah, she did. Her and somebody else."

"You saw them?"

"Their tracks," Claire said.

I looked at the blackness at my feet.

"I'll take the point," he said, and moved past me, shotgun resting under his arm.

We walked slowly, Claire in front, me five feet behind him. Every twenty steps or so, we stopped and listened. I heard rustles on the ground. Creaks from the branches above us. My own breathing. I couldn't hear Claire's.

I thought maybe we should call to her. She could yell something. We'd know where she was. She'd know we were coming. I was going to say this to Claire but he just kept walking. And listening for a sound from the black woods that wasn't the wind or the trees or the birds.

A woman screamed.

Claire broke into a silent trot, shotgun in both hands. I was right behind him. He pulled up and held his hand out behind him to slow me, too. This time it was a cry, a wail, a sob.

It wasn't Roxanne.

We almost ran into them. They were standing on the edge of the path, where it passed under a big pine. Roxanne's face was white in the darkness. Janice Genest's face was white, too. She was crying and her cheeks were wet with tears.

Thirty-five

"Roxanne," I said.

"She's got a gun," Roxanne said. "It's in her right hand."

Her voice was gentle, almost sympathetic. She looked at Genest and Genest looked at us. Her eyes were bright and her hair was wild. I stood beside Claire, five feet from Roxanne, ten from Genest. The barrels of our guns were pointed at the ground.

"What's going on?" I said.

"What's going on?" Genest repeated. "Oh, my God, I don't know what's going on. Oh, my God."

I looked at Roxanne. She looked back at me, then at Janice.

"Why don't you put that gun down, miss," Claire said softly. "We don't want anybody to get hurt."

"Hurt," Genest blurted. "Why shouldn't somebody get hurt? Everybody gets hurt. Everybody I know gets hurt. The whole world gets hurt, doesn't it? Everybody I know is hurt. I hurt them. Oh, my God. Oh, my God. Oh, my God."

She put the gun to her temple.

"No," Roxanne said. "Please, no."

"Janice, don't do that," I said.

Claire watched, motionless. Genest lowered the gun to her side.

"What do you care, McMorrow?" she said. "You could write about me, then. Can't libel the dead. It's what you said, right?"

She laughed. A girlish, unnatural chortle.

"Can't libel the dead. I like that. So you can't libel me. I'm dead. I am."

Genest paused. She wasn't looking at any of us. She wasn't looking at the woods, either.

"Oh, Jesus help me," Genest said. "It was all okay, you

know. Missy was in school. Her baby was okay, too. You
saw that house, McMorrow. The kid'll end up a doctor or
something. And there's more where they came from. She
was saved. Missy was, too. They paid cash, so the next one
was saved, too."

"Saved from what?" I said.

"Saved from what? From this goddamn society that
strangles women at birth. Saved from this goddamn country
that's like the Chinese. In some village, drowning the baby
girls. We just do it slower. Like Missy's mother. Screwing
and drinking to try to forget what she could have been."

"Like what?" I said, trying to keep her talking.

"Goddamn, McMorrow. Are you thick or what? Fulfilled
herself. Become something more than a damn receptacle
for some man's bodily fluids."

"She had Missy, didn't she?"

"Had Missy," Genest said. "Like a cat having kittens in
the barn. So they can have more kittens. All in the name of
love."

She laughed again.

"I work twelve hours a day to try to hammer home to
these girls that they can be more than an accessory to some
drunken football player. They don't have to give themselves to the first muscle-bound idiot who comes along,
grabs them, and tosses them onto the seat of some pickup
truck. It's their lives, for God's sake. They only get one."

"And you helped them," Roxanne said, her voice soft
and soothing. "You helped them."

"I tried, didn't I? We found a way to give the baby a life.
Give these girls a life, not pack it in at seventeen. Close the
book. At fifteen, the next sixty years are nothing. Post-
script. Really, we made two lives where there were none.
And we ended up with enough money to save the next
one."

"How much did the Flanagans pay?" I asked her.

"Thirty thousand," Genest said, gun still at her side.
"They didn't have to wait ten years for a healthy white

baby. Isn't that a disgrace? This color thing? But we split the money three ways. Missy got a start on college. If it hadn't been for that money, she never would have gone to college at all. Putnam, that coward, got his cut for arranging the papers. Birth certificate and everything. The new mom left for six months and came back with her own baby. Not somebody else's. Not adopted."

"So that's the catch? That it wouldn't be adopted?"

"Hey, it was what they wanted. I guess they didn't want the kid to go looking for her birth mother or something. And they were willing to pay. The money was used to fund the next case."

"And Missy screwed it up."

"Somebody got to her. One of her pea-brained relatives. The daddy. I don't know. Kenny was in pretty deep."

"The dad?"

Janice grinned.

"Mister Tough Guy. And you know why he wouldn't talk? Because he was afraid everybody would know Missy had just gone and given away his baby. His property."

She said it in a deep, mocking voice.

"Would have blown his macho cover. What a fool."

"So you told him I was gonna blow it for him."

"Right. I was hoping you'd just leave, McMorrow. But no, you had to be a tough guy, too. God, men are such idiots."

"So what happened to Missy?" I asked.

Roxanne glared at me.

"Missy was a great kid. I loved her. She was the second girl in the pipeline, the underground railroad out. The first one was Tracy. She's supposed to go to school in Florida. Missy was next and, oh, she was so bright. She wanted to be a nurse but I'll bet you she would have ended up in medical school. Just a smart, tough kid."

"Who wanted her baby back," I said.

Janice looked right at me but her eyes were strange and faraway.

"They got to her. The whole male-dominated, barefoot-and-pregnant guilt thing."

"What about the other father? Of the baby, I mean. Jimmy something? The one who just vanished?"

Janice smiled.

"He didn't vanish," she said. "He went to live with his father in San Diego."

"Courtesy of you?"

"One one-way ticket. It was the least I could do to get the guy out of the way. That one worked great. It was all set."

"What was?"

"Everything. The baby was fine. Just like Missy's."

"So let's go. It'll be okay," Roxanne said.

"No, it won't," Janice said, her face still shining from her tears. "It won't be okay. It's over. Can you believe that I killed Missy? I didn't mean to, but she was going to go to the police or something. We were there and I said no, but she said she was going right then, and I grabbed her and held her and she kept trying to get past me and I said no and then I pushed her down. I was on top of her, and I held a pillow over her head and then she was dead. It was just . . . so quick. I didn't think it could happen so quick."

"And her mother."

"Her mother wanted money. Her mother was a drunk and a slut. She found some papers of Missy's and she wanted money for them. I couldn't let the whole thing be destroyed by her, could I? Because she'd always want more. I mean, I was right. It was right. It was. It was right, and oh, God, it's gone so wrong. You asking all these questions, McMorrow. And Putnam, he was up here. He told me. He was gonna sell the whole thing out, wasn't he? He threatened to go to the police. About me. And then Missy and her mother and all I wanted to do was help. I really did. I wanted to help."

"You did want to help," Roxanne said, and took a step toward her.

Genest put the gun to her temple, a flit of a movement.

Roxanne called out, "No," and Claire's shotgun roared and blew off Genest's left foot.

Thirty-six

Claire had fired the shotgun from the hip. It was loaded with buckshot. Genest had screamed as she was falling, and then she had lain there on her back, breathing in rapid, shallow breaths and looking up at all of us like she'd never seen us before. Claire had put his belt around her ankle for a tourniquet.

He carried her back to the house, his big arms wrapped around her shoulders and legs like a lifeguard's. I carried the guns. We ran all the way down the trail to the house. Roxanne stayed alongside Genest, talking to her to try to keep her from going into shock. When we reached the house, Claire laid Genest on the floor next to the woodstove in the kitchen. Mary put blankets over her and Claire had put a pillow under her legs to raise her feet. Except one was more or less gone.

The cruiser beat the rescue truck to the house by five minutes. The cops, county deputies, questioned us and took the guns. And then, as the paramedics worked feverishly on Genest on the kitchen floor, Claire stood over them and watched quietly.

"You okay?" I said, sidling up to him.

"Oh, yeah," Claire said. "How 'bout you?"

"I don't know yet."

"She'll make it okay," he said.

"Foot's gone."

"Yup."

"You seem pretty calm about it."

Claire gave a little shrug.

"From the list of options, this was the best one. You have to remember that. Consider everything in context."

I looked at him.

"Like in war. You'd get out of a firefight with two men lost. Three. People would expect you to just crack up over it but they'd forget that, given the crappy situation you were in, losing nobody wasn't an option. The other choice was losing twenty. Thirty."

I thought about that as I watched. What war had done to make Claire what he was. What something in Genest's life had done to mold her.

The paramedics had her lower leg wrapped in bandages, an IV in her arm. Her eyes were open but she was staring blankly, in a state that was something other than consciousness.

"A foot is better than a head?" I murmured to Claire.

"And much better than losing her and Roxanne. Those were the choices."

"I know that," I said. "It's just hard."

"Yup," Claire said. "Life's hard sometimes."

"And this is one of those times."

"Yeah, it is," he said.

For a couple of days I stayed home with Roxanne, drinking tea and talking to Poole and a bunch of other cops. Roxanne came and sat at the table with the cops, too. They were shy with her, except for one detective who was a woman. She and Roxanne talked a lot about other things and it helped.

I told the story so many times that after a while I began to wonder if any of it was true. It was like I'd read it somewhere, seen it on television. It came in snatches, vivid but disconnected and unreal.

Genest had simply knocked at my door. The police had found her car pulled into the brush near the main road, a half mile away. They figured she'd come through the woods. Nobody had seen her come or go.

She had been friendly, smiling. Genest had said she was an acquaintance of mine, that we'd met as I was doing the baby story and she had some more information. Roxanne had liked her and had invited her in for coffee while she waited for me to get back. When Roxanne turned her back to fill the kettle, the gun had come out. The plan, Genest had told police, had been to kill both of us. Then, on the path in the woods, Roxanne had reached out and put her arm around Genest's shoulders. She had told Genest she understood and the whole thing had come tumbling down. But I feared it would be a long time before Roxanne trusted her instincts again.

"I underestimated everything," I told Poole. "I never thought it could end up like that. I never thought we could be killed."

"People kill for reasons you wouldn't believe," he said, his hand wrapped around a mug of coffee. "It just seems like a good idea at the time."

"But killing us to save some baby who hasn't even been conceived?"

"That's one of the more sensible reasons I've heard," Poole said.

"Why didn't I see it coming then?"

"If everybody saw it coming, people like me would be out of work," he said.

"Don't thank me," I said.

Putnam and the Flanagans were in trouble but no one could say how much. I asked Poole if the Flanagans would lose Missy's baby and he said he didn't know. Poole said he figured Kenny would be charged, too, but it looked like he didn't know much. Kenny told the cops he thought Missy had been killed by some college kids. Neither her death nor the fate of his baby daughter concerned him as much as the prospect of going to jail.

Poole said it would be tough to tag Putnam for the murder, but he would be an accessory, get a conspiracy charge for the cover-up. The baby stuff alone would get him disbarred. He was finished and I hadn't written a word.

Genest had been in surgery a lot, as doctors tried to fix her leg as best they could. Poole said her lawyer would try to get her off on an insanity plea but it was a long shot, that she'd probably go from her hospital room to a cell.

"But she's insane in some way," I said.

"They all are," Poole said. "It's just a question of degree."

The police stopped coming after three days. The reporters stopped calling and the television crews went on to the next tragedy. I asked Roxanne if she wanted to go back to Colorado but she said no. I asked her if she wanted to go to an inn on the coast and hide out and she said no to that, too.

"I want to do it here," she said.

"Do what?" I said.

"Just love you," she said. "I feel like it's all we have left and I don't want to lose it."

So that's what we did.

We spent the days very quietly. Both of us read books and neither of us went near a newspaper. We read all of my Hemingway and Fitzgerald. Roxanne tried a John D. McDonald novel but it had a murder in it, of course, and she had to put it down. I picked it up and read five pages and did the same. That afternoon I called Dave Slocum and apologized. The deal was off.

For three days, we slept wrapped around each other, like people sleeping on a windy mountain ledge who do not want to be swept off. On the fourth day, in the morning, we made love almost solemnly but with a conviction I'd never felt before. It was like we were possessed. Roxanne said we'd just fallen deeply and irrevocably in love.

"Isn't that redundant?" I said, as we lay there in the bed.

"No," she said. "Not at all."

We were quiet for a moment.

"You know what the saddest thing is?" I said, as Roxanne nestled in the crook of my arm.

"That Missy never felt this. That she never had any of this. And she was a good person. She tried so hard. Didn't give up, you know? She was sort of small and vulnerable but then she had these dreams that she wouldn't let go of. And she did it all alone, the stuff with her baby. Can you imagine what courage that took?"

"To give her up or try to get her back?"

"Either, I guess. It was this huge sacrifice, either way. And then she's gone. This little kid. There really is no justice."

"There is," Roxanne said. "It's just sporadic."

"And based entirely on luck."

"But you knew that, didn't you?"

"No," I said. "I guess I only suspected it."

That night we had dinner with the Varneys because they were leaving the next day to go see their daughter, Susan, the one in North Carolina. Their other daughter, Jennifer, was driving down from Maryland. Mary chatted about this, trying to keep things going, but Claire was quiet. We ate turkey and vegetables and pie and then Claire and I cleared the table. In the kitchen, he started in with his Wilfred Owen poem.

"What passing bells for these who die as cattle? . . ."

I gave his shoulder a squeeze. He gave me a wistful, sad smile.

Later, I walked home in the cool darkness with Roxanne. We climbed the ladder and got undressed and lay together under the blankets and were still.

"After all this, would you like to have a baby someday, Jack?" Roxanne asked, in a whisper.

"As long as it's with you, I wouldn't rule it out," I said.
"Because I don't want to grow old all alone," she said.
"What makes you think we're alone?"
Somewhere above us a bat fluttered in the dark.